Sis hanne - TWINS
KAT OLIVER

(38) _ Family law
AIDEN + MOLLY
Immie
laugh

Therapist
Graham
Cousin DANI - mom CLAUD A
Faiba - w chair - asst Russell
Bro
Trevor - + Teru

M + J Sean
18 mo EVAN
Sis d andic   Amber

PRETENDING TO DANCE

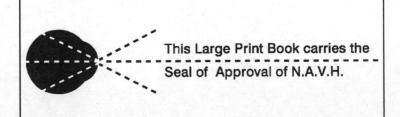

This Large Print Book carries the
Seal of Approval of N.A.V.H.

PRETENDING TO DANCE

DIANE CHAMBERLAIN

THORNDIKE PRESS

A part of Gale, Cengage Learning

GALE
CENGAGE Learning·

Farmington Hills, Mich • San Francisco • New York • Waterville, Maine
Meriden, Conn • Mason, Ohio • Chicago

GALE
CENGAGE Learning·

LIBRARY OF CONGRESS CATALOGING-IN-PUBLICATION DATA

Chamberlain, Diane, 1950-
    Pretending to dance / Diane Chamberlain. — Large print edition.
        pages cm. — (Thorndike Press large print core)
    ISBN 978-1-4104-8040-8 (hardback) — ISBN 1-4104-8040-2 (hardcover)
    1. Family secrets—Fiction. 2. Adoption—Fiction. 3. Large type books. 4. Domestic fiction. I. Title.
PS3553.H2485P74 2015b
813'.54—dc23   2015030579

Published in 2015 by arrangement with St. Martin's Press, LLC

Printed in the United States of America
1 2 3 4 5 6 7 19 18 17 16 15

For my sister, Joann Lopresti Scanlon,
my inspiration and dearest friend

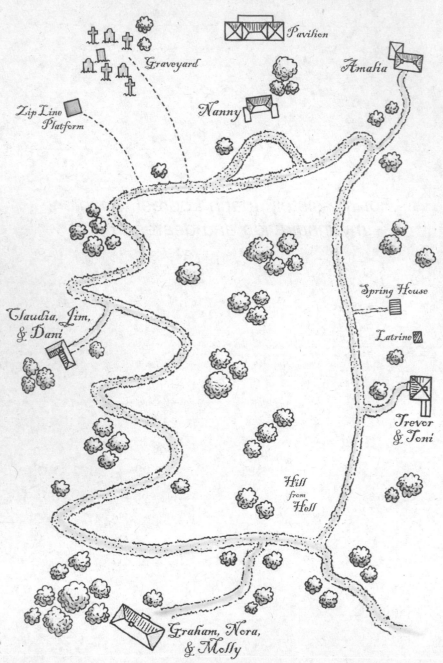

Pavilion

Graveyard

Amalia

Zip Line
Platform

Nanny

Spring House

Latrine

Claudia, Jim,
& Dani

Trevor
& Toni

Hill
from
Hell

Graham, Nora,
& Molly

RHYS DAVIES

1
SAN DIEGO

2014

I'm a good liar.

I take comfort in that fact as Aidan and I sit next to each other on our leather sectional, so close together that our thighs touch. I wonder if that's too close. Patti, the social worker sitting on the other wing of our sectional, writes something in her notes, and with every scribble of her pen, I worry her words will cost us our baby. I imagine she's writing *The couple appears to be co-dependent to an unhealthy degree.* As if picking up on my nervousness, Aidan takes my hand, squeezing it against his warm palm. How can he be so calm?

"You're both thirty-eight, is that right?" Patti asks.

We nod in unison.

Patti isn't at all what I expected. In my mind I've dubbed her "Perky Patti." I'd expected someone dour, older, judgmental.

7

She's a licensed social worker, but she can't be any older than twenty-five. Her blond hair is in a ponytail, her blue eyes are huge, and her eyelashes look like something out of an advertisement in *Vogue*. She has a quick smile and bubbly enthusiasm. Yet, still, Perky Patti holds our future in her hands, and despite her youth and bubbly charm, she intimidates me.

Patti looks up from her notes. "How did you meet?" she asks.

"At a law conference," I say. "In 2003."

"It was love at first sight for me," Aidan says. I know he means it. He's told me often enough. *It was your freckles,* he'd say, touching his finger to the bridge of my nose. Right now, I feel the warmth of his gaze on me.

"We hit it off right away." I smile at Aidan, remembering the first time I saw him. The workshop was on immigration law, which would later become Aidan's specialization. He'd come in late, backpack slung over one shoulder, bicycle helmet dangling from his hand, blond hair jutting up in all directions. His gray T-shirt was damp with sweat and he was out of breath. Our workshop leader, a humorless woman with a stiff-looking black bob, glared at him but he gave her that endearing smile of his, his big brown

8

eyes apologetic behind his glasses. His smile said, *I know I'm late and I'm sorry, but I'll make you happy that I'm in your workshop.* I watched her melt, her features softening as she nodded toward an empty chair in the center of the room. I'd been a wounded soul back then. I'd sworn off men a couple of years earlier after a soul-searing broken engagement to my longtime boyfriend Jordan, but I knew in that moment that I wanted to get to know this particular man, Aidan James, and I introduced myself to him during the break. I was smitten. Aidan was playful, sexy, and brainy, an irresistible combination. Eleven years later, I still can't resist him.

"You're in immigration law, is that right?" Patti looks at Aidan.

"Yes. I'm teaching at the University of San Diego right now."

"And you're family law?" She looks at me and I nod.

"How long did you date before you got married?" she asks.

"About a year," Aidan says. It had only been eight months, but I knew he thought a year sounded better.

"Did you try to have children right away?"

"No," I say. "We wanted to focus on our careers first. We never realized we'd have a problem when we finally started trying."

"And why are you unable to have children of your own?"

"Well, initially it was just that we couldn't get pregnant," Aidan says. "We tried for two years before going to a specialist."

I remember those years all too well. I'd cry every time I'd get my period. Every single time.

"When I finally did get pregnant," I say, "I lost the baby at twenty weeks and had to have a hysterectomy." The words sound dry as they leave my mouth, no hint of the agony behind them. Our lost daughter, Sara. Our lost dreams.

"I'm sorry," Patti says.

"It was a nightmare," Adam adds.

"How did you cope?"

"We talked a lot," I say. Aidan still holds my hand, and I tighten my grip on him. "We talked with a counselor a few times, too, but mostly to each other."

"That's the way we always cope," Aidan says. "We don't keep things bottled up around here, and we're good listeners. It's easy when you love each other."

I think he's laying it on a little thick, but I know he believes he's telling the truth. We congratulate ourselves often for the way we communicate in our marriage and, usually, we do a good job of it. Right now, though, with my lies between us, I squirm at his words.

"Do you have some anger over losing your baby?" Patti directs her question to me.

I think back to a year ago. The emergency surgery. The end of any chance to have another child. I don't remember anger. "I think I was too devastated to be angry," I say.

"We regrouped," Aidan says. "When we were finally able to think straight, we knew we still wanted . . . still want . . . a family, and we began researching open adoption." He makes it sound like the decision to pursue adoption was easy. I guess for him it was.

"Why *open* adoption?" Patti asks.

"Because we don't want any secrets from our child," I say with a little too much force, but I feel passionately about this. I know all about secrets and the damage they do to a child. "We don't want him — or her — to wonder about his birth parents or why he was placed for adoption." I sound so strong and firm. Inside, my stomach turns itself into a knot. Aidan and I are not in total agreement over what our open adoption will look like.

"Are you willing to give the birth parents

11

updates on your child? Share pictures? Perhaps even allow your child to have a relationship with them, if that's what the birth parents would like?"

"Absolutely," Aidan says and I nod. Now is not the time to talk about my reservations. Although I already feel love for the nameless, faceless people who would entrust their child to us, I'm not sure to what degree I want them in our lives.

Patti shifts on the sectional and gives a little tug on her ponytail. "How would you describe your lifestyle?" she asks in a sudden change of topic, and I have to give my head a shake to clear it of the image of those selfless birth parents. "How will a child fit into your lives?" she adds.

"Well, right now we're both working full-time," Aidan says, "but Molly can easily go to half-time."

"And I can take six weeks off if we get a baby."

"When." Aidan squeezes my hand. "Be an optimist."

I smile at him. To be honest, I wouldn't mind quitting my job altogether. I'm tired of divorce after divorce after divorce. The longer I practice law, the more I dislike it. But that is for another conversation.

"We're pretty active," I tell Patti. "We hike

and camp and bike. We spend a lot of time at the beach in the summer. We both surf."

"It'd be fun to share all that with a kid," Aidan says. I imagine I feel excitement in his hand where it presses against mine.

Patti turns a page in her notebook. "Tell me about your families," she says. "How were you raised? How do they feel about your decision to adopt?"

Here is where this interview falls apart, I think. *Here is where my lies begin.* I'm relieved when Aidan goes first.

"My family's totally on board," he says. "I grew up right here in San Diego. Dad is also a lawyer."

"Lawyers coming out of the woodwork around here." Patti smiles.

"Well, Mom is a retired teacher and my sister, Laurie, is a chef," Aidan says. "They're already buying things for the baby." His family sounds perfect. They *are* perfect. I love them — his brilliant father, his gentle mother, his creative, nurturing sister and her little twin boys. Over the years, they've become my family, too.

"How would you describe your parents' parenting style?" Patti asks Aidan.

"Laid-back," Aidan says, and even his body seems to relax as the words leave his mouth. "They provided good values and then encouraged Laurie and me to make our own decisions. We both turned out fine."

"How did they handle discipline?"

"Took away privileges, for the most part," Aidan says. "No corporal punishment. I would never spank a child."

"How about discipline in your family, Molly?" Patti asks, and I think, *Oh thank God,* because she skipped right over the "tell me about your family" question.

"Everything was talked to death." I smile. "My father was a therapist, so if I did something wrong, I had to talk it out." There were times I would have preferred a spanking.

"Did your mother work outside the home as well?" Patti asks.

"She was a pharmacist," I say. She might *still* be a pharmacist, for all I know. Nora would be in her mid to late sixties now.

"Are your parents local, too?" Patti asks.

"No. They died," I say, the first real lie out of my mouth during this interview. I have the feeling it won't be the last.

"Oh, I'm sorry," Patti says. "How about brothers and sisters?"

"No siblings," I say, happy to be able to tell the truth. "And I grew up in North Carolina, so I don't get to see my extended family often." As in, never. The only person

I have any contact with is my cousin Dani, and that's minimal. Next to me, I feel Aidan stiffen ever so slightly. He knows we're in dangerous territory. He doesn't know exactly how dangerous.

"Well, let's talk about health for a moment," Patti says. "How old were your parents when they passed away, Molly? And what from?"

I hesitate. "Why does this matter?" I try to keep my voice friendly. "I mean, if we had our own children, no one would ask us —"

"Honey," Aidan interrupts me. "It matters because —"

"Well, it sounds like your parents died fairly young," Patti interrupts, but her voice is gentle. "That doesn't rule you out as a candidate for adoption, but if they had inheritable diseases, that's something the birth parents should know."

I let go of Aidan's hand and flatten my damp palms on my skirt. "My father had multiple sclerosis," I say. "And my mother had breast cancer." I wish I'd never told Aidan that particular lie. It might be a problem for us now. "I'm fine, though," I add quickly. "I've been tested for the . . ." I hesitate. What was the name of that gene? If my mother'd actually had breast cancer, the

15

acronym would probably roll off my tongue with ease.

"BRCA," Patti supplies.

"Right." I smile. "I'm fine."

"Neither of us has any chronic problems," Aidan says.

"How do you feel about vaccinations?"

"Bring 'em on," Aidan says, and I nod.

"It's hard for me to understand not protecting your child if you can," I say, happy to be off the questions about my family.

The rest of the interview goes smoothly, at least from my perspective. When Patti finally shuts her notebook, she announces that she'd like to see the rest of the house and our yard. Aidan and I had spent the morning dusting and vacuuming, so we're ready for her. We show her the room that will become the nursery. The walls are a sterile white and the hardwood floors are bare, but there is a beautiful mahogany crib against one wall. Aidan's parents gave it to us when I was pregnant with Sara. The only other furniture in the room is a small white bookshelf that I'd stocked with my favorite children's books. Aidan and I had done nothing else to the room to prepare for our daughter, and I'm glad. I never go in there. It hurts too much to see that crib and

16

remember the joy I felt as I searched for those books. But now with Patti at my side, I dare to feel hope and I can imagine the room painted a soft yellow. I picture a rocker in the corner. A changing table near the window. My arms tingle with an uneasy anticipation.

We walk outside after showing her the bedrooms. We live in a white two-story Spanish-style house in Kensington, one of the older parts of San Diego, and in the bright sunlight our well-maintained neighborhood sparkles. Our yard is small, but it has two orange trees, a lemon tree, and a small swing set — another premature gift from Aidan's parents. Exploring our little yard, Patti says the word *awesome* at least five times. Aidan and I smile at each other. This is going to happen, I think. We are going to be approved as potential adoptive parents. Some birth parents will select us to raise their child. The thought both excites and terrifies me.

Patti waves as she gets into her car in the driveway. Aidan puts his arm around me and we smile as we watch her drive away. "I think we passed with flying colors," Aidan says. He squeezes my shoulder and plants a kiss on my cheek.

"I think we did," I agree. I pull a big gulp

of oxygen into my lungs and feel as though I've been holding my breath all afternoon. I turn to him and circle my arms around his neck. "Let's work on our portfolio this weekend, okay?" I ask. We've been afraid to take that step, afraid to pull together the necessary photographs and information about ourselves in case we somehow failed the home study.

"Let's." He kisses me on the lips and one of our neighbors honks his horn as he drives by. We laugh, and Aidan kisses me again.

I remember how I'd wondered if our daughter would have his brown eyes or my blue. His brawny athletic build or my long, slender arms and legs. His easygoing nature or my occasional moodiness. Now our child will have none of those things — at least not from us — and I tell myself it doesn't matter. Aidan and I have too much love for just two people. Sometimes I feel as though we're bursting with it. At the same time, I pray I'll be able to extend that love to a baby I didn't carry. Didn't give birth to. What is wrong with me that I have so many doubts?

That night, Aidan falls asleep first and I lie next to him, thinking about the interview with Patti. There was nothing there to come back to haunt me, I assure myself. Patti's not going to search for my mother's obituary. We are safe.

The lies I told Aidan when we were first dating — my dead mother and her breast cancer, my cold relatives — had been accepted without question and set aside. He knew I meant it when I said I'd laid the past to rest the day I left North Carolina at eighteen. We never revisited those lies. There'd been no need to, until today. I hope the interview with Patti will be the end of it. I want to move on. We need to create our own healthy, happy, sane, and loving family.

I think about our "open communication" Aidan had described to Patti. Our honest relationship. At times I feel guilty for keeping so much about my past from him, but I'm honestly not sure he would want to know. I try to imagine telling him: *My mother murdered my father.* I'd said those words once and they had cost me. I will never say them out loud again.

2
MORRISON RIDGE SWANNANOA, NORTH CAROLINA

Summer 1990

Daddy sat across from me in his wheelchair at the small table in the springhouse, a beam of sunlight resting on his thick dark hair.

"Check it out," he said, nodding toward the window, and I turned to see a dragonfly on the inside of the glass. Centered in one of the wavy panes, it looked as though it had been painted there with a fine-tipped brush.

I got up for a closer look. "A common green darner," I said, although I wasn't certain. "There was one in my bedroom last night, too," I added, sitting down again. "I think it might have been a dragonhunter."

Daddy looked amused. "You just like the sound of that name," he said.

"True. It was pretty, whatever it was." I'd forgotten a lot of what I'd learned last summer when I was thirteen and so into insects I thought I'd grow up to be an entomologist. This was the summer nothing felt quite right. One minute I wanted to ride my bike at top speed up and down Morrison Ridge's hilly dirt roads. The next minute I was shaving my legs and tweezing my eyebrows. Even nature seemed confused this summer in the mountains where we lived outside Swannanoa, North Carolina. The laurel was trying to bloom again, even though it was July, and the dragonflies were everywhere. I was careful when I touched the porch railing or the handle of my bicycle, not wanting to squash one of them.

I picked up a chocolate chip cookie from the plate in front of me and held it across the table to him, aiming for his mouth.

"How many calories?" he asked before taking a bite.

"I don't know," I said. "And besides, you're skinny."

"That's because I count calories," he said, chewing the bite he'd taken. "I'm heavy enough for Russell to lift as it is." My father was tall, or at least he'd been tall back when he could stand up, and he had a lanky build that I'd inherited along with his light blue eyes. I doubted he'd ever been overweight.

"So, what are you reading?" he asked once he'd swallowed the last bite of the cookie. I followed his gaze to the thin brown

21

bedspread of one of the two twin beds where I'd tossed the book I was currently reading.

"It's called *Flowers in the Attic,*" I said.

"Ah, yes." He smiled. "V. C. Andrews. The Dollanganger family, right?"

My father always seemed to know something about everything. It could get annoying. "You've read it?" I asked.

"No, but so many of the kids I work with have read it that I feel like I have," he said. "The siblings are trapped in the attic, right? A metaphor for being trapped in adolescence?"

"You really know how to ruin a good story," I said.

"It's a gift." He smiled modestly. "So, are you enjoying the book?"

"I *was*. Not so sure now that I have to think about the metaphor and all that."

"Sorry, darling."

I hoped he wouldn't call me "darling" in front of Stacy when she came over later that afternoon. I didn't know Stacy very well, but she was the only one of my friends around for the summer, so when my mother suggested I invite someone to sleep over, I thought of her. She loved the New Kids on the Block and she promised to bring her *Teen Beat* and *Sassy* magazines, so we'd have plenty to talk about.

As if reading my mind, Daddy nodded toward one of the three New Kids on the Block posters I'd taped to the fieldstone walls. I'd moved them from my bedroom to the springhouse for the summer. "Play me some of their music," he said.

I stood up and walked over to the cassette player, which was on the floor under the sink. There were not many places to put things in the small cramped springhouse. *Step by Step* was already loaded in the player. I hit the power switch and music filled the little building. The springhouse had electricity provided by a generator along with a microwave and running water diverted from the nearby spring. Daddy and Uncle Trevor had fixed the place up for me when I was six years old. Daddy must have still been able to walk a bit then, but I could barely remember him without the wheelchair. I'd gone through summers of tea parties in the tiny stone building and I'd spent the night out here a few times with one of my parents sleeping in the second twin bed. Then I spent a couple of recent summers fascinated with the insect and plant life that filled Morrison Ridge's thick green woods. My microscope still sat on the ledge beneath one of the springhouse's two windows, but I hadn't touched it yet this summer and probably wouldn't. Now I was into dancing and music and fantasizing about the boys who made it. Oh, and Johnny Depp. I'd lie awake at night, trying to come up with a way to meet him. In that fantasy I wore contacts instead of glasses and somehow miraculously had great hair instead of my shoulder-length flyaway brown frizz. And I had actual breasts. Right now, I barely filled out the AA cups on my bra. We would fall in love and get married and have a family. I wasn't sure how I was going to make that happen, but it was my favorite thing to think about.

"It's warm in here, don't you think?" Daddy said. He couldn't stand being hot — it made him feel very weak — and he was right about the heat. Despite the fact that we lived in the mountains and the stone walls of the springhouse were twelve inches thick, it *was* toasty in here today. "Why don't you open the windows?" he said.

"They're stuck."

He looked at the window closest to the sink as though he could open it with his eyes. "Shall I tell you how to unstick them?"

"Okay." I stood up and crossed the small space until I was in front of the window. I stood there bouncing a little in time with

24

the music, waiting for him to tell me what to do. I was always dancing these days, even while I brushed my teeth.

"Now, right where the lower pane meets the upper pane, pound your fist." Daddy didn't lift his hands to demonstrate the way someone else might. Two years ago he might have been able to lift them, at least a little. Now his hands rested uselessly on the arms of his wheelchair. His right hand curled up on itself in a way that I knew irritated him.

"Here?" I pointed to a spot on the window frame.

"That's right. Give it a good whack on both sides."

It took a couple of tries, but the window finally gave way and I raised it. I could hear the rippling sound of the nearby spring, but as soon as I walked to the window on the other side of the springhouse, the sound was overwhelmed by the New Kids singing "Tonight." I used the same technique to open the second window, and a forest-scented breeze slipped across the room.

Daddy smiled as I sat down again. My mother said his smile was "infectious," and she was right. I smiled back at him.

"Much better," he said. "Even when I was a kid, those windows would stick."

I held his lemonade glass close to his lips

and he took a sip through the straw. "I love thinking about how the spring ran though this little house back then," I said. I'd seen old pictures of the building. A gutter filled with springwater ran along one interior wall and, in the old days, my Morrison Ridge ancestors would keep their milk and cheese and other perishable food cool in the water.

"Well, my father changed that early on when he added the windows. Your uncle Trevor and I helped him, or as much help as we could give him. We were really small. Once it dried out in here, we had sleepovers nearly every weekend in the summer."

"You and Uncle Trevor?"

"And your aunt Claudia and our friends — with one of our parents, of course — until we got old enough that the boys didn't want to hang out with the girls and vice versa. Later Trevor and I would stay out here alone. There were no beds in here then, but we'd sleep in our sleeping bags. We'd build a fire outside — we had no microwave, of course. No electricity, for that matter." He looked into the distance, seeing something in his memory that I couldn't see. "It was great fun," he said. Then he glanced at the wall above one of the twin beds, to the left of the Johnny Depp posters. "So, what do you keep in the secret rock these days?" he asked. When they were boys, he and Uncle Trevor had chipped one of the stones from the wall to create a small hollow, covering it over with a lightweight plaster cast of a stone. You'd never know the hollow was there unless someone told you. I kept some shells and two small shark teeth in there from one of our trips to the beach, along with a pack of cigarettes my cousin Dani had left on our porch the year before. I didn't know why I was holding on to them. They'd seemed like something exciting to hide at the time. Now they seemed stupid. I also had a blue glass bird my mother had given me for my fifth birthday in the secret rock, along with a corsage — all dried out, now — that Daddy'd given me before my cousin Samantha's wedding. And I kept my amethyst palm stone up there. Daddy had given the stone to me when I was five and afraid to get on the school bus. He'd presented it to me in a velvet-lined jewelry box and I didn't take it out of my pocket for a full year. He told me the story of the stone, how the amethyst had been found on Morrison Ridge land in 1850 when they broke ground for the main house where my grandmother now lived. How it had been carved and smoothed into the palm stone with a gentle indentation for the thumb, then passed down through the generations. How his own father had given it to him, and how it helped him when he was afraid as a child. He'd never believed that the amethyst had actually been found on our land, but he'd treasured the stone anyway and he seemed to believe in its calming powers.

Now he sent away to a New Age shop for palm stones — sometimes he called them "worry stones" — to give the kids he worked with in his private practice.

"The palm stone is there," I said.

"Why up there?" he asked. "You used to carry it around with you."

"Not in years, Daddy," I said. "I don't need it anymore. I still love it, though," I assured him, and I did. "But seriously. What am I afraid of?"

"Not much," he admitted. "You're a pretty brave kid."

"At least I don't have any booze in the secret rock, like you and Uncle Trevor used to hide in there."

He laughed. "I'm glad to hear it," he said. "What time is your friend . . . Stacy Bateman is it? What time is she arriving?"

"Five," I said. He'd given me an idea with his talk of sleepovers. "Could Stacy and I sleep out here tonight?" It would be so cool to stay in the springhouse, away from my parents and Russell.

"Hmm, I don't know," he said. "Awfully far from the house. From *any* of the houses."

"Yeah, but you just said that you and Uncle —"

"We were older. Besides, now that I remember the sort of things we did out here, I don't think I want you sleeping out here unsupervised." He laughed.

"Like what?" I asked. "What did you do?"

"None of your business." He winked at me.

"Well, we won't do anything terrible," I promised. "Just listen to music and talk."

"You know how spooky it gets out here at night," he said.

"Oh, please let us!"

He looked thoughtful, then nodded. "We'll check with Mom, but she'll probably say it will be all right. Can you help me with a bit of writing before Stacy arrives?"

"Sure," I said, eager to please him now that he'd given me permission to spend the night in the springhouse. And besides, I loved typing and not just because he paid me and I would soon have enough money for the purple Doc Martens I was dying to buy. It was because I felt proud of him when

I typed for him. Sometimes I typed his case notes, and I liked seeing the progress his patients made. Daddy would label the notes by number instead of name in case I knew one of his patients, since he sometimes saw kids who went to my school. But most of all, I loved typing his books for him. They were about Pretend Therapy. He had a more technical name for the approach he used with his patients, but that's what he called it when talking to laypeople. "In a nutshell," he would say when anyone asked him about it, "if you pretend you're the sort of person you want to be, you will gradually become that person." I saw the approach work with his patients as I typed his notes week to week. So far, he'd written two books about Pretend Therapy, one for other therapists and one for kids. Now he was almost finished with one for adults and I knew he was anxious to be done with it. Soon he'd be going on a book tour set up by a publicist he hired to promote the book for kids, and I'd be going with him, since, he said, I'd been his guinea pig as he developed the techniques he used with children and teens. And of course Russell would go with us. Daddy couldn't go anywhere without his aide, but that was okay. In the three years Russell had lived with us, I'd grown to appreciate him. Maybe even love him like part of the family. He made my father's life bearable.

I stood up and turned off the cassette player. "We should go now if I'm going to type," I said. I only had a couple of hours before Stacy was due to arrive.

"All right," he said. "My walkie-talkie's on my belt. Give Russell a shout."

"I can push you home," I said, reaching for the push handles of his chair and turning him around.

"You think you can manage the Hill from Hell?"

"You scared?" I teased him. The main road through Morrison Ridge was a two-mile-long loop. The side of the loop farthest from the springhouse was made up of a series of hairpin turns that eased the descent a bit. But the segment of the road closest to us was a long, mostly gentle slope until it abruptly seemed to drop off the face of the earth. It was the greatest sledding hill ever, but that was about all it was good for. I took the Hill from Hell too fast on my bike one time and ended up with a broken arm.

"Yes, I'm scared," Daddy admitted. "I don't need any broken bones on top of everything else."

"Pretend you're not afraid, Daddy," I

31

teased him again.

"You can be a real twit sometimes, you know that?" he said, but he was laughing quietly. I felt the vibrations in the handles of his chair.

I pushed him down the path that ran from the springhouse to the loop road. The path was nearly hidden, littered with leaves and other debris, but I knew exactly where it ran between the trees. I had to stop a few times to pull vines from the spokes of the wheels, but soon we reached the loop road and I turned left onto it. The dirt road, cradled in a canopy of green, was just wide enough for two cars to carefully pass one another. That was a rare occurrence — two cars passing one another. Only eleven people lived on Morrison Ridge's hundred acres these days, since my two older cousins, Samantha and her brother Cal, had moved to Colorado the year before, much to my grandmother's distress. Nanny thought that anyone born on Morrison Ridge should also die on Morrison Ridge. I tended to agree with her. I couldn't imagine living anyplace else.

Our five homes were well spread out, invisible to one another. The zigzagging roads connected us all. Love did, too, for the most part anyway, because all of us were related in one way or another. But there was also anger. I couldn't deny it. As I walked Daddy past the turnoff to Uncle Trevor and Aunt Toni's house, I felt some of that anger bubble up inside me.

Daddy looked down the lane in the direction of their house, which was well hidden behind the trees. I thought he was thinking about his latest argument with Uncle Trevor, who was toying with the idea of developing part of his twenty-five acres of Morrison Ridge. He was trying to talk my father and Aunt Claudia into selling him part of their twenty-five-acre parcels so he could go into the development business in a bigger way.

But that wasn't what Daddy was thinking about at all.

"There's Amalia," he said, and I saw Amalia walk around the bend in the lane from Uncle Trevor's house.

I would have recognized Amalia from a mile away. She had the lithe body of a dancer and I envied the graceful way she moved. Even dressed in shorts and a T-shirt, as she was now, she seemed to float more than walk. I set the locks on the wheelchair and ran to meet her on the lane. She was carrying her basket of cleaning supplies and she set it down to wrap me in a hug. Her long wavy brown hair brushed over my bare arms. Her hair always smelled like honeysuckle to me.

"When's my next dance lesson?" I asked as we started walking up the lane toward my father. He was smiling at us. I knew he loved seeing us together. Amalia held the basket in one hand, her other arm warm around my shoulders.

"Wednesday?" she suggested.

"Afternoon?"

"Perfect," she said.

Spending more time with Amalia was one of the highlights of the summer. I felt so free with her. No rules. No chores. She didn't even have certain steps I was supposed to follow during our dance lessons. Amalia was all about total freedom.

We reached my father. "Where's Russell?" Amalia asked.

"Molly's pushing me home," Daddy said.

"Don't lose him on the hill," Amalia warned me, but I knew she wasn't serious. She was not a worrier. At least, she'd never let me see her worry. "Maybe I should help going down the hill?" she suggested.

Daddy shook his head. "Then you'd have an uphill climb all the way home," he said. Amalia lived in the old slave quarters near my grandmother's house at the very peak of Morrison Ridge. The slave quarters had been expanded and modernized, the two tiny buildings connected into one large open expanse of wood and glass. Amalia had turned the remodeled cabin into something pretty and inviting, but there were those at Morrison Ridge who believed the slave quarters was a fitting place for her to live. My father wasn't one of them, however.

"Well, if you're sure you're okay," Amalia said, and I wasn't certain which of us she was talking to.

"We're fine," Daddy said. "It sounds like Molly's enjoying her dance lessons this summer."

"She's a natural." Amalia touched my arm. "Focused and unafraid."

It seemed like such an odd word for her to use to describe my dancing: *unafraid.* But I loved it. I thought I knew what she meant. When we started moving around her house, I felt like I was a million miles away from everyone and everything.

"Molly has a friend coming to visit tonight," Daddy said. "They're going to stay in the springhouse."

"As long as Mom says it's okay," I added. He seemed to have forgotten that hurdle.

"Yes," he said. "As long as Nora says it's okay."

"An adventure!" Amalia's green eyes lit

up and I nodded, but she wasn't looking at me. Her gaze was on my father and I had the disoriented feeling I sometimes got around them. Was it my imagination or could the two of them communicate without words?

Amalia picked up her basket again and put it over her forearm. I spotted a bottle of white vinegar poking out from beneath a dust cloth. Dani told me that after Amalia cleaned their house, it stank of vinegar for days. Amalia cleaned every house on Morrison Ridge. Except ours.

"We'd better get going," Daddy said. "I'd like to get the hill behind us."

"Bye, Amalia," I said.

"See you Wednesday, baby." She waved her free hand in my direction and I unlocked Daddy's chair and began pushing him down the road.

"So what will you and Stacy do in the springhouse tonight?" he asked.

We were passing one of the wooden benches my grandfather had built at the side of the road. I guessed there'd been a view of the mountains from that bench long ago, but now the trees blocked everything. "Listen to music," I said. "Talk."

"And giggle," Daddy said. "I like hearing you giggle with your friends."

"I don't giggle," I said, irked. He still talked to me like I was ten years old sometimes.

"No?" he said. "Could have fooled me."

"Here's the hill," I said. I turned around so we'd be going down backward and tightened my grip on the handles. I'd seen Russell take him down the hill a dozen times. He made it look simple. "Are you ready?"

"As I'll ever be," he said.

If he'd been capable of bracing himself — tightening his muscles, girding for the ride — I was sure he would have done it, but he could do little except hope for the best.

I started walking backward, holding tight, digging my tennis shoes into the dirt road. My father and the chair were frighteningly heavy, far heavier than I'd anticipated, and the muscles in my arms trembled. This had been a mistake, I knew as we picked up speed. My heartbeat raced in my ears. When we reached the bottom of the hill, I was close to tears and glad he was facing away from me so he couldn't see my face.

"Ta-da!" I said, as if it had been nothing.

"Brava!" he said, then added with a chuckle, "Let's not ever do that again."

"All right," I agreed. Impulsively I leaned forward and wrapped my arms around him.

For a moment, I simply held him tight. I didn't ever want to lose him.

3

Russell's eyes nearly popped out of his head when I wheeled Daddy into the house.

"You carried him down the hill?" he asked as I pushed Daddy through the front door into the living room. I knew he didn't mean that I literally carried him. Russell had a few turns of phrase that were all his own.

"Of course," I said, like it had been nothing.

"Next time, we'll call you," Daddy said to Russell.

"Damn straight you will." Russell gave me a scolding look, or at least he tried to, but he had these big cocker spaniel eyes the same chocolate brown as his skin, and I'd never seen him able to pull off a convincing angry expression. Anyway, I knew he wasn't mad. Just worried. He loved my father. He did everything for him. Lifted him out of bed in the morning, bathed him, emptied his urine bag, changed his catheter, dressed him, brushed his teeth. I guessed when someone depended on you as much as my father depended on Russell, you either started loving that person or you ended up hating him. I didn't see how there could be an in-between.

"Let's say hi to Mom," Daddy said. "Then we can type."

"You got him?" Russell asked me, and I nodded. Russell headed down the hall toward his room, which was right next to my parents' room. He was always close by in case Daddy needed him.

I pushed Daddy past the broad living room windows that overlooked the mountains in the distance. Uncle Trevor helped my grandfather build our house when my parents got engaged. In my opinion, it was the nicest of the Morrison Ridge houses, with its sky-blue exterior and dozens of windows that overlooked the tree-covered peaks and valleys that stretched on and on forever. It was hypnotizing, that view. When I was younger, I'd sometimes sit on the window seat in the dining room and imagine what it would be like to be an eagle soaring from our house to those mountains. That was before the New Kids on the Block and Johnny Depp entered the scene and my fantasies switched to something a bit more provocative.

Mom was in the kitchen, chopping onions on a wooden chopping board. She still had on her white pharmacy coat with the embroidered *Nora Arnette, PharmD.* above the pocket. She was also wearing her harried look. That "I've been on my feet all day and now I have to make dinner for my family and a guest and I don't even have time to take my white coat off" look. My mother always had too much on her mind. If there weren't a zillion things to do, she would make up stuff that needed doing. It was impossible for her to relax. She was very pretty, but her prettiness had a fragile quality to it, especially when she was tired or rushing to get something done, the way she seemed to be now. She had the sort of blond hair that was so fair, no one would notice when it eventually turned gray. It was shoulder length and she almost always wore it in a small ponytail at the nape of her neck. Her eyes were the palest blue; her skin a nearly translucent white, but she had full lips that were so deeply colored she never bothered with lipstick. I knew this because I'd pawed through her makeup bag more than once, trying out the eyeliner and mascara and blush, disappointed that there was nothing to spice up my own pale lips.

"Does your friend eat everything, do you know?" Mom asked me once I'd pushed Daddy into the room.

I shrugged. "No clue," I said. "What are we having?"

She crossed the room and bent over to give my father a kiss on the lips, holding the knife well out of the way. "Enchiladas," she said, heading back to the chopping board.

"Awesome." I flopped onto one of the kitchen chairs. "Stacy and I are going to sleep in the springhouse tonight." I looked at my father, who gave a barely perceptible nod in my mother's direction. "If it's okay with you," I added quickly.

She looked over at me, the knife in her hand hovering above an onion. "Oh, Molly, I don't think so," she said. "It's too far from the house. It's too isolated and do you have any idea how dark it will be out there in the middle of the night?"

"The springhouse has lights," I pointed out.

"Remember the time you tried to camp out? And that was just in our back —"

She stopped mid-sentence and I knew my father had given her some kind of warning look to shut her up.

"I was only twelve then," I said. "And I was alone. I'll have Stacy with me this time and it'll be fine. Daddy's okay with it."

My mother turned to my father, her hand on her hip. "You're going to make me be the bad guy?" She sounded annoyed.

"Well, you don't *have* to be the bad guy," Daddy said calmly.

She frowned, two little lines forming between her eyebrows. "You think the two of them sleeping out there is a good idea?"

"Maybe not a *stupendous* idea, but I don't see a problem with it." He was teasing her and I could tell by the color in her cheeks that she was very close to shifting from annoyance to anger.

"Don't make light of this, Graham," Mom said, leaning one hip against the black granite countertop. "It's not just Molly we have to think about. We don't even know this other girl."

"She's really nice," I said, as though I knew Stacy better than I did . . . and as though her niceness had anything to do with us sleeping in the springhouse.

My mother didn't seem to hear me. "Maybe we should talk to her parents about it," she said, giving in a bit. "Get their permission?"

"You don't have to make such a major production out of it, Mom," I said.

"Molly," Dad said, "when Stacy's parents

43

drop her off, let Mom or me talk to them before they leave, all right?"

"Okay," I said, getting up. "You ready for me to type?"

"I think Mom and I might need to perform an opera first," he said.

"Oh no." My mother groaned. "I don't have time for an opera. We don't need one. I'm not really mad. I'm over it."

"It's more important than your onions," he said.

"*Graham*. Dinner will be late."

"Do we care?" He looked at me where I stood in the doorway, and I obediently shook my head.

"I'll be in your office," I said. I walked out the door to the hallway, but instead of going to my father's office, I stood against the wall, waiting. Listening.

"So what shall we sing about?" Daddy asked my mother.

She gave a resigned sigh. "I don't care. You pick."

"Hm," he said. "The dishwasher?"

"Whatever," Mom said.

"Ohhh!" my father sang in a booming operatic voice. "The dishwasher! The dish-waaaasher!"

"The diiiiishwasher!" Mom sang, and then she laughed, and pretty soon they were both singing their two-word nonsensical opera at the top of their lungs, their voices rising and falling with an air of great drama.

Russell stepped out of his room and looked at me. "Did they have a fight?" he whispered.

I shook my head. "A minor disagreement." I smiled.

He plugged his ears with his fingers, but he was grinning as he walked back into his room. I didn't budge. I liked listening. I thought I could actually feel my parents' spirits lifting as I stood there in the hallway, smiling to myself. My father could change the mood of a room, I thought. He could ease sorrow, erase fear, diffuse anger. There were times, and this was one of them, when I thought he was a magician.

4
SAN DIEGO

"What do you think of this one?" Aidan asks. "It's one of my favorites." He turns his laptop so that I can see the photograph. In the picture, we're sitting on a beach in Hawaii, Diamond Head in the background, and we look tanned and fit and very, very happy. But the picture won't work for our portfolio.

"You're forgetting the rules," I say. "No sunglasses. No bathing suits."

"Hmm. I forgot." He straightens the computer on his lap again. We're sitting side by side on our sectional going through hundreds of photographs, trying to find the right combination for our portfolio. Besides the "no sunglasses and no bathing suits" rules, we've been admonished not to show any booze in our pictures. And no baseball caps. What is that about? I have no idea, but Aidan and I have turned into rule followers. We need to maximize our chances at being selected by a birth mother.

We'd finally completed all the paperwork for the adoption agency two weeks before. They now had copies of our marriage license, our birth certificates, our medical records, our tax returns, and the reference letters written by our friends and employers. We passed our criminal background checks and our physicals. I'd worried about the medical records. Somewhere, sometime, I'm sure I filled out a medical questionnaire that asked if a parent had ever had cancer, and I'm sure I would have said *no.* How closely would the agency study those records? Would they compare that answer to the tale I told Patti about my mother's putative breast cancer? I could drive myself crazy worrying about details like that.

Three weeks have passed since our last visit from Patti and we are only now getting down to business on the portfolio, which will culminate in the writing of a "Dear Expecting Mother" letter we are both dreading. It's simply been too nerve-racking to work on the portfolio before we knew we had approval from the agency. But the letter arrived yesterday: *Congratulations! You've been approved to adopt a child through Hope Springs Adoption Agency. You now join Hope Springs' ninety-two other waiting families.* I was deflated by that number. A birth mother has ninety-two other potential placements for her baby. At thirty-eight, are we the oldest? How will that young woman view Aidan's receding hairline? The laugh lines around my eyes? What expectant mother will consider a couple the age of her own parents to raise her child?

I look at the photograph on my laptop screen. In it, I'm plucking a lemon from the tree in our backyard. Perfect, I think, until I remember the "no sunglasses" rule. Of course I'm wearing them. You live in San Diego, you wear sunglasses. Maybe we'll have to stick to indoor pictures.

"How can we make our portfolio stand out from the others?" I ask Aidan.

"I think we should make it cute," he says.

"Cute?" I laugh. "How exactly do we do that?"

"We should look at how teen magazines do their layouts and mimic them," he says, and I can tell he's been seriously thinking about this. "Maybe some cutesier graphics. A collage of photographs, some on an angle. Vibrant colors, maybe."

I turn my head to study him, smiling. He is adorable. Mr. Sunshine. "I don't know," I say. "I think we should go with something more serious and heartfelt. I don't want to

48

come across as frivolous."

"We'll find a balance," he reassures me. He turns his computer to face me again. "What about this one with the twins?" he asks.

In the photograph, Aidan and I are on a carousel, each of us standing next to a horse as we hold on to his sister Laurie's two-year-old twin boys, Kai and Oliver. The agency told us we should be sure to include pictures of us with children, and this one is perfect.

"Definitely, yes!" I say.

"Except . . ." Aidan points to the sunglasses on my face in the photograph.

"Screw the sunglasses," I say. "That's a great picture."

Aidan marked the picture to be included in the portfolio. "As long as we're now following the 'screw the sunglasses' rule," he said, "I think we should put in a bunch of action shots of us. You know, canoeing and skiing and those hiking pictures we have from last fall."

"But maybe they'll make us look too . . . hedonistic, or too adventurous to be able to fit a baby into our lives. I think we should show us in our house so she can see where her baby will grow up."

"Well, how about some of each?" Aidan suggests.

"I think we need more of us with the twins," I say.

Aidan nods. "Laurie says she has a bunch. She's going to bring them to Mom and Dad's on Sunday."

He clicks to another page on his laptop, this one full of dozens of small images. I know what they are. Pictures from his childhood. Zoe, the social worker at the agency, said to include a few. "Show the happy families you grew up in," she suggested. Aidan loves the idea, and now I watch him sort through the old pictures. He is so family oriented. Not only did he scan family photographs into his computer, he organized them by year. What other man would do something like that? He treasures his history. I watch him smile as he clicks through the pictures, and I feel a powerful sadness wash over me.

I have no old family photographs. I'd taken a handful with me when I left home at eighteen, but I threw them away one day when my anger got the better of me.

I wish old memories could be as easily discarded.

5
MORRISON RIDGE

"Oh sure, that's fine," Stacy's mother said to Mom through the open window of her silver van. Stacy was already out of the van and standing next to me, her stuffed backpack slung over her shoulder.

"All right then," Mom said. "I just thought I should run it by you before we —"

"I've got to scoot!" Stacy's mother said, the van already rolling. "You girls have fun!" she called through the window.

I had the distinct impression that Stacy's mother was more relaxed about things than my mother was. We watched her drive away, then Mom turned to Stacy.

"I'm Nora," she said, holding out her hand. When I was younger, my friends were supposed to call her "Miss Nora" and my father "Mr. Graham," but that changed about a year or so ago. My mother grew up in Pennsylvania and she never really embraced that "Miss So and So" culture of

North Carolina, so now everyone was on a first-name basis. I still wasn't quite used to it.

"I'm Stacy." Stacy laughed at the formality as she shook my mother's hand. She looked different to me than she did at school, although I couldn't have said what it was exactly. There was still that unbelievably shiny straight black hair that she wore to her shoulders, her thick bangs almost long enough to touch her eyelashes. Her eyes were nearly black and her lashes thick. She had a body the boys at school couldn't take their eyes off of, and right now her pink tank top and white shorts seemed to show it all off. Even though I was wearing almost the same outfit — my top was blue instead of pink — I felt . . . not ugly exactly, but really plain and skinny and flat-chested and bespectacled. My hair was an out-of-control mess compared to hers, and I hated the freckles splattered across my nose. I did have one thing going for me, though: those distinctive blue eyes that ran in the Arnette family. The light irises were rimmed in navy blue, almost black. On me, those eyes were practically hidden behind my glasses, but at least I had them. Standing next to Stacy, though, I felt skinny and plain and suddenly wished I hadn't invited her over, which I knew was really small of me. She couldn't help how she looked any more than I could.

"Do you like enchiladas?" Mom asked her as we walked into the house.

"I love Mexican food!" Stacy said.

"Excellent," Mom said. "You girls can make the salad while I finish up the rice."

I felt awkward with Stacy as we chopped the tomatoes and tore the lettuce. Conversation would have been easy with my other friends, but I didn't know Stacy well enough to know what to talk about . . . unless we started talking about the New Kids on the Block, and I didn't want to get into that with my mother right there, so we were quiet.

Mom took the enchiladas from the oven and set the pan on a couple of trivets. "Russell!" she called over her shoulder. "Dinner's ready!"

We carried everything into the dining room and Stacy and I were already seated when Russell pushed my father into the room and up to the table. Stacy's face registered surprise at the sight of Daddy in a wheelchair. "You must be Stacy." Daddy smiled at her and she quickly recovered her composure.

"Yes." She smiled her pretty smile.

"I'm Graham," he said. "And this is Russell." Daddy and Russell were dressed like twins tonight, both wearing black T-shirts and jeans.

Russell looked across the table at me from behind my father's wheelchair. "I'm going to a friend's for dinner tonight," he said. "You want to do the honors, Molly?"

"Sure," I said, pushing back my chair and getting to my feet. Usually Mom or I fed Daddy dinner, while Russell often took care of breakfast and lunch. Dinner was family time, my mother said, and that was fine with me. I'd mastered feeding myself and my father at the same time. I walked around the table and sat down next to him, turning my chair so that I was half facing him, half facing the table. Stacy was across from us and Mom took the seat at the head of the table. I felt Stacy's eyes on Daddy and me as I tucked his napkin into his collar.

"So, how long have you two known each other?" Daddy asked.

Stacy and I looked at each other. "Just, like, two years," she said. "My family moved here two years ago from Washington, D.C."

"Big change," Mom said as she lifted a couple of enchiladas onto a plate and handed it to Stacy.

"*Huge* change." Stacy took the plate from

54

her. "Like another planet. But I like it. The kids are nice." She smiled at me and I felt bad for wishing I hadn't invited her.

"Brothers and sisters?" Daddy asked.

"Two sisters and a brother," she said. "All older."

"Ah," Daddy said. "Do they spoil you?"

"Are you kidding?" She laughed. "They torment me!"

Mom handed me Daddy's plate, and I used the side of my fork to cut a bite for him.

"How do they do that?" he asked, before taking the bite of enchilada from the fork.

"Like, they'd tease me *relentlessly* and try to get me in trouble for things they'd do. They're incorrigible."

"What's the very worst thing they've ever done to you?" Daddy asked once he'd swallowed. He was good at questioning people, especially kids. Too good. It was his job. It could sound like an interrogation, though I had to admit, Stacy didn't seem to mind. She talked about the time her brother told a boy she liked that she had lice, while I shoveled food into Daddy's mouth more quickly to try to shut him up.

"My father's a therapist," I explained to Stacy when she'd finished her lice story.

"And sometimes he forgets he's not at

work," Mom added, but she was smiling at my father. It was her "I love you" smile. Now that she had dinner on the table and they'd sung their little opera, she was more relaxed.

"Oh," Stacy said. "It's okay."

"How about your parents?" Daddy asked. "What sort of work do they do?"

"Well, my father does something with computers," she said. "He still lives in D.C., actually. They're divorced. That was the whole reason we moved. My family's, like, totally dysfunctional."

"Most are." Daddy gave her a sympathetic smile.

Stacy poked at her enchilada with her fork. "My sisters and brother all stayed with him, but I wanted to be with my mother, so I came down here with her."

"What's it been like for you?" Daddy asked. "The divorce?"

"Intense," Stacy said. "Like, our lives turned upside down overnight. He's not being great about child support for me and all that stuff. Plus I never see him. And my mother's working in her brother's office. That's why we moved here. Because her brother lives in Black Mountain and can help us out." She continued poking at her enchilada, eyes downcast. "It's really kind

56

of a mess," she said.

Now I was definitely glad I'd invited her. In thirty minutes, she'd gone from being an exceptionally beautiful princess type to a girl who really needed a friend.

"I'm sorry you're going through all that," Daddy said.

"After dinner, why don't you show Stacy around Morrison Ridge?" Mom suggested.

"I'm planning on it," I said. "Can she borrow your bike?"

"Sure," Mom said, and she sent her "I love you" smile down the table to me, and I felt lucky to have the family I did.

6

After we cleaned up the kitchen, I got my mother's bike from the garage and we started pedaling up the loop road for our tour of Morrison Ridge. When we reached the Hill from Hell, we got off our bikes to walk them up.

"It's impossible to ride a bike up this hill," I said. Then I told her about the time I flew down it and broke my arm.

We were halfway to the top and breathing hard when she asked, "What's wrong with your father?"

"He has multiple sclerosis," I said.

"Can he move at all?"

"Well, you could see he has no problem *talking*," I said, and she laughed. "But no. He can move his head and neck, but that's about all. Most people don't get that disabled, but he just keeps getting worse."

"Wow," she said. "He's really nice. It's sad he's . . . like that."

I shrugged. "He still does everything he wants," I said, though I knew that wasn't the truth. It was just that he wasn't a complainer. "He's a 'glass is half full' kind of person."

We were both quiet for a minute. A couple of dragonflies darted across the road in front of us, and a bird tweeted from somewhere in the forest to our left. I could hear both of us breathing hard as we climbed the hill.

"Must be weird living with a shrink," Stacy said after a while. "Like, he knows what you're thinking all the time."

"He's a psychologist, not a psychic," I said.

"Still. You know what I mean." She stopped to scratch her knee, then started pushing the bike again. "How can he do his job when he's, you know, so handicapped?"

"He can listen and talk and think. That's all he needs to be able to do."

We were both too winded to talk by the time we reached the top of the hill, but we climbed on our bikes and began riding up the road. After a while, I pointed down the lane where my father and I had bumped into Amalia a few hours earlier. "So," I said, "that little lane goes to my aunt Toni and uncle Trevor's house."

"You can't even see a house out there," Stacy said, peering into the trees to our right. "I'm not used to all these woods."

I thought the forest was a wonderland and hoped she could appreciate it. I couldn't tell by the tone of her voice.

We rode a short distance farther and I pointed to the almost invisible path leading into the woods on our right. "Down that path is the springhouse where we'll spend the night," I said.

"Way out here?" She sounded shocked. "Wow. It's so cool your parents will let us do that. My mother probably thought it was, like, in your backyard."

"Would she still have said yes if she knew where it was?"

"Oh yeah. She doesn't care what I do."

I didn't know if I was imagining the bitter edge to her words or not and decided to change the subject. "I have a cassette player there," I said.

"Oh cool! I brought a bunch of tapes, but I was afraid you might have a CD player."

"I'm saving up for one, but I don't have it yet," I said. "We probably have all the same tapes, anyhow."

"Do you have *Step by Step*?"

"Of course! I got it the first day it came out." We'd come to a short rise in the road and I had to stand up on the pedals to climb it. "I wish so much we could go to one of their concerts this summer," I said, once we'd gotten over the hill.

"The Magic Summer Tour," Stacy said dreamily. "They're not even coming close to us, though, and my mother could never afford a ticket for me." She suddenly let out a groan. "Does this road only go *uphill*?" she asked.

I laughed. My thighs were burning and I'm sure hers were, too. "Only a little while longer," I said. Even though it was not yet seven o'clock, it was already starting to get a little dusky on the ridge because of all the trees. We'd make the rest of the loop through Morrison Ridge and then get our things and head to the springhouse before it was too dark to find our way.

"The old slave quarters is down that road," I said, pointing off to the right again, this time to a much narrower lane that looked like a tunnel, it was nestled so tightly among the trees.

"Slave quarters!" Stacy said. "God, I'll never get used to living in the South."

"Washington D.C. is the South," I pointed out.

"Not hardly."

"Well, anyway, that was long ago." I felt a

little defensive about Morrison Ridge all of a sudden. "Now this woman lives there — Amalia. She's a dancer and an artist. She paints and does stained glass and gives me dance lessons."

"Like . . . ballet or what?"

"Interpretive dance," I said. "That's where you just move however the music makes you feel." We pedaled around a curve and the evening sunlight suddenly turned the road golden as the trees gave way to a clearing. "This house coming up on the right is the main house," I said. "My grandmother lives here." I stopped my bike and Stacy pulled up alongside me. "It's one of the only old brick houses in these mountains," I said, feeling like a tour guide. "It's been here a hundred and forty years. The land's been in our family all that time."

"So your family owned the slaves?" She was really stuck on that.

"Well, a hundred and forty years ago, yes, but only a few," I said, as though owning five slaves instead of fifty made it better somehow. I thought of Russell and wondered how he felt when someone talked about the slave quarters. Maybe we should start calling it something else.

Unlike the four other houses on Morrison Ridge that were each tucked into the trees,

Nanny's stood on a circular driveway surrounding the only real lawn in all of the Ridge. With its red brick and white pillars, it had a refined look about it, while the rest of our houses definitely belonged in the mountains. The front door to the house opened and Nanny stepped onto the porch, waving her hand high above her head. "Hello, Molly!" she called. She trotted down the steps in her denim jumper and pale blue tennis shoes, her gray hair in her usual short, swingy bob. "You have a friend with you?" She walked down the driveway toward us. She had a quick step. Even though she'd recently turned seventy, there was nothing old about Nanny. My mother said she was "spry."

"This is my friend Stacy," I said when Nanny had nearly reached us. "And this is my grandmother, Nanny. I mean Miss Bess." Nanny was Southern born and bred and she was appalled that my friends now called my parents by their first names.

"Hi, Stacy," Nanny said. "You'll be joining us for our big midsummer party on the twenty-eighth, I hope?"

"Um . . ." Stacy looked at me.

"I didn't tell her about it yet, Nanny," I said. My grandmother was absolutely fixated on Morrison Ridge's annual midsummer party. She'd been planning it all year.

Nanny pointed toward the house, but I knew she was really pointing far *behind* the house to the pavilion where the party would be held. "There'll be fireworks!" she said. "Music! Dancing!" She clapped her hands together. "Plenty to eat! You have to join us."

Stacy looked at me and I smiled.

"Seriously," I said. "You should come."

Nanny reached out and slapped me on the arm, and I looked at her, startled.

"A skeeter," she said, laughing. "Didn't mean to scare you."

I suddenly felt them on my bare legs. The minute you stopped moving, they attacked. "We'd better get back on our bikes," I said. "Bye, Nanny," I called as we started to ride away. "Love you!"

"Don't forget the party!" she called after us.

We rode a little ways, both of us relieved to be on a level road for a change.

"I think it's so cool, how your family has its own neighborhood," Stacy said after a while.

"It is," I agreed. We were nearing one of my favorite spots in all of Morrison Ridge, and I stopped pedaling and straddled my bike.

"Look up there," I said, pointing to our right.

She squinted into the dusky light. "I just see trees," she said.

"Can you see the wire up there?" I asked. "It's a zip line."

"A zip line? You mean, the kind you ride?"

"Exactly." I pointed again. "Move over here and you can see the tower. The line goes from up here all the way down to a spot near my house."

"I see it now. It's so high! It looks like it goes right through the treetops."

"It actually runs above them," I said. "For a while, anyway."

"Awesome!" she said. "Can we ride it?"

"Well, not tonight," I said. "It's kind of a major production. The harnesses are down at the bottom right now and they have to be brought up here, but maybe we can do it someday soon, if you want."

"Definitely!"

We started riding our bikes again. I pointed to the right. "That's the family graveyard," I said.

"What? You're kidding."

"Too late to explore it tonight," I said. "Maybe tomorrow."

"Pass," Stacy said. "That would freak me out."

I liked the graveyard myself. It was small — the Morrison and Arnette families had never been large — and during the day, I liked reading the headstones and imagining the lives of my ancestors. I'd only been there once at night, though, and definitely not alone. On Halloween when I was eight years old, my cousin Cal dragged Dani and me there to try to terrify us. It worked. Everyone in our family — every single person who died after 1850 and their spouses, and in some cases, their children — was in that "hallowed earth," as Nanny called it. There were three babies, one who was born and died on the same day. And there were several slaves buried there. Although their graves had smaller headstones and were tucked into a corner of the graveyard, they were still inside the low iron fence, as though they'd been part of the family. When I walked among those headstones and markers, I was filled with a sense of pride and curiosity. I wanted to know everything about my ancestors. I picked Nanny's brain from time to time to see what she remembered, but I had the feeling she was making a lot of it up. Like most families, we were quickly losing our yesterdays.

We were getting close to my aunt Claudia and uncle Jim's house when I spotted Dani at the end of their driveway. She looked like a zombie walking out of the woods.

"Oh my God." Stacy slowed her bike. "Who the hell is that?"

"It's my cousin," I said, slowing down myself. I wasn't sure I wanted to talk to Dani. "She looks like she just walked out of the graveyard herself, doesn't she?" I said quietly. "I think she's just getting the mail." Sure enough, Dani glanced in our direction, then opened the mailbox on the post next to the street. As usual, she had her Goth thing going on. In spite of the heat, she was dressed in black jeans and a sleeveless black turtleneck. Her hair, which used to be the same brown as my own, had been jet black for years now. It was chin length and looked like it had been cut with a dull knife. She had the same unusual blue eyes that ran in our family but hers were outlined in smudged black pencil that made her look like she needed a good night's sleep. Her lips were always a sort of reddish-black color, and she wore a lip ring decorated with a small, red-eyed snake.

She took a few envelopes from the mailbox, then shut it and stood there waiting for us, so we really had no choice but to stop.

I pressed my brakes. "Hi, Dani," I said, coming to a stop. Stacy straddled her bike next to me.

"Who's this?" Dani asked, her smudged eyes on Stacy.

"My friend Stacy. She's staying overnight." I wouldn't tell her about our plan to sleep in the springhouse. I knew Danielle. She'd get some of her weird friends together and try to scare us in the middle of the night. Dani was seventeen and she'd been a thorn in my side my entire life. Two years ago, Aunt Claudia and Uncle Jim pulled her out of the local high school and shipped her off to Virginia Dare boarding school in High Point. I'd been happy to see her go. Of course, she was home now for the summer. I didn't feel like I really knew her any longer, but that was okay with me. "I gave Stacy a tour of Morrison Ridge and now we're headed home," I said, for something to say.

"Radical hair," Dani said to Stacy. I could see how Stacy's thick, straight shimmery black hair would appeal to Dani. Still, I was surprised that she said something nice to one of my friends. She'd never liked me any more than I liked her.

"Thanks," Stacy said.

"Come on," I said, starting to pedal again. "See you, Dani."

"Wow," Stacy said when we were out of earshot. "She's intense."

"She's weird, is what she is," I said. "And she's my only cousin left in Morrison Ridge."

"So you have all this family living here but you two are the only kids?"

"Right."

Stacy sighed. "Sounds like paradise to me," she said, and I once again had the sense that my life was at least a little bit better than hers.

7
SAN DIEGO

"How long do they predict the wait to be?" Aidan's mother asks from the sofa in the James's living room. She still holds a photograph album on her lap, although we're finished looking through it.

"The average wait is fourteen months," Aidan says. Our nephew Oliver is on his lap, doing his best to unbuckle the strap of Aidan's watch.

"That's a long time." Aidan's father sounds disappointed.

"But worth it if you have a baby at the end of it," Laurie says. Her gaze is on her son in Aidan's lap and I can tell she's debating whether or not to stop him from playing with the watch. I know Aidan could care less.

We've had dinner and sorted through about a hundred photographs, looking for — and finding — good ones of Aidan and myself with Kai and Oliver that we can use in the portfolio. Now we're relaxing over coffee and chatter in the living room. Kai is on my lap and I bend over to kiss the top of his head. I'm not sure if the boys gravitate to us or we gravitate to them, but Aidan and I always seem to end up holding them. I don't look forward to the day the little boys no longer want to cuddle. By then, though, with any luck, we will have our own child to hold.

Kai is nearly asleep. I love the heavy weight of him in my lap. His head rests against my breast and he still has a baby scent about him that I'm drinking in. There were moments early on when I could barely look at Kai and Oliver, much less hold them. They were born three months after I lost Sara and I had to fake much of my enthusiasm for the first few months of their lives. During that terrible time, it seemed every one of my friends was having a baby. Every magazine facing me in the grocery store checkout line had a cover article about pregnancy. And everywhere I went, women were pushing strollers or rubbing their hands over their swollen bellies. For a long time, I was filled with resentment and envy and anger. When it came to Laurie, though, I did my best to mask it. She was my sister-in-law and one of my favorite people in the world. She didn't deserve my wrath, and with a husband who traveled constantly for his job, she needed Aidan's and my help more than our grief and anger. Every time I saw her with those babies, though, I felt physically ill. Then, suddenly, something shifted in me and I couldn't get enough of the twins. It was as though my hormones snapped back into balance and I was able to love again. I grew to adore those little boys and now I can't wait to give them a cousin.

"Is there any" — my mother-in-law hesitates, then chuckles — "quality control?" she asks.

"Well, there wouldn't be much quality control if it was our natural child," Aidan says with a smirk.

"They gave us a form to fill out, Mom," I say. I'd never had a problem calling Aidan's mother "Mom." Calling his father "Dad" had been more of a struggle. Only one man in my life had earned that title. "The form asks very specifically what sort of child we'd accept. Would we take a biracial child or a child with a cleft palate, for example, or with cerebral palsy or whose mother was an addict. You get the idea." The form had been both overwhelming and sobering. It made us look at ourselves and our biases. And our limitations. Our fantasy was of a healthy beautiful Caucasian child. The form woke us up: reality could be much different. We spent days talking about the options. Aidan pointed out that, most likely, I would be the person giving the greatest physical care to our child and I needed to think our choice through carefully. We could handle a deformity, we thought. Could we handle cerebral palsy? We decided we could not, and yet something kept us from putting that in writing on the form. That night I had a dream about my father. He was in his wheelchair perched on a cliff and the look on his face was more forlorn than I'd ever seen it. I would have happily taken care of him for the rest of his life. I wish I'd had that chance. I know a grown man and a child are hardly the same thing, but nevertheless, when I woke up, I knew what I wanted to do with the form. Over breakfast that morning, I told Aidan I thought we could handle anything. "I agree," he said, as though he'd only been waiting for me to come to the same conclusion. We signed the form and sent it in. And now we wait.

"So is it like on one of those dating sites where they match you up, only this time it's with a woman who's having a baby?" his mother asks.

"Sort of," I say. "They make an initial match by sending the girl — the young woman — several portfolios of families that the agency thinks will be a good fit for her. Then she picks one or more to get in touch with. And then she decides."

"You'll meet in person at that point?" Laurie asks.

"Hard to say," Aidan says, rescuing his now loose watch from Oliver's grasp. "Contact can take a lot of different forms," he says. "It might be e-mail first or a phone call and then an in-person meeting. We'll have to wait and see."

"Nerve-racking," says his mother. "Will you let us know every step of the way?"

I smile. When I was pregnant, she called me nearly every day to ask how I was feeling, what did the doctor say, did I need any help. When Aidan called to tell her I'd lost the baby, I could hear her sobbing through the phone even though I was on the other side of the room, sobbing myself.

"You know we'll love that baby just as much as we love Kai and Oliver," Aidan's father said. "You'll never have to worry about that."

I hadn't been worried about it, but I'm touched by his desire to reassure us. There are moments I need to reassure myself that

I will feel the same way.

"Thank you, Dad," I say. "I know you will."

"Any baby that lands with you two will be the luckiest child on earth," his mother says, and now my eyes fill.

When I'm with Aidan's family, I want a baby with all my heart and soul and body. I feel certain I'll be a good mother. Maybe even a great mother. Life is so normal in this house, the house Aidan and Laurie grew up in. In this house with this family, I feel none of the ambivalence that dogs me late at night when I can't fall asleep.

I press my lips to the silky hair on Kai's head. He is sound asleep now. He and Oliver are not biologically mine and yet I couldn't love them any more than I do. I am sure I'll feel the same way about our child.

When we get home, Aidan and I sit in our office to check e-mail. We have two large identical desks that face each other and he begins typing at a rapid clip while I pull my mail up on my screen. There is only one message and it's from DanielleK422. My cousin Dani. I stare at the link without moving my cursor over it. I haven't spoken to Dani in several years, although I received

75

the usual card from her at Christmas. It had been a photograph of Dani and her husband, Sean, their two dogs, and their eighteen-year-old son, Evan, whom they'd somehow roped into posing with them. Evan's hair hung down to his shoulders and he sported a barbed-wire tattoo around his neck. Dani, who looked like a straitlaced woman approaching middle age in the photograph, is getting the same run for her money that she gave her own parents. I feel for her. At least her eye makeup washed off.

Although Aidan and I also send out picture cards at Christmas, I never send one to my cousin. I'm afraid she'll share it with my relatives, and the less they know about my life, the better. I usually get a birthday card from Nora. Although Nora doesn't have my address, she sends the card to Dani, who sends it on to me. Letters always accompany those cards, but I haven't read a single one. Straight into the trash. I've never relented. I haven't seen or spoken with anyone from Morrison Ridge other than Dani since I was eighteen.

I click on the message.

Hi Molly. Thought I should let you know Amalia broke her leg and has to have a bunch of surgeries to repair it. Mom doesn't know how she did it — you know they don't talk. She just knows Amalia is going to be in the hospital for a while afterward and then go into rehab. Thought you might want to know. Xoxo Dani.

"You're frowning," Aidan says from his side of our double desks. "Is there something from Hope Springs?"

I shake my head and try to smile. "No," I say. I'm staring at the e-mail. Staring without seeing. I can't remember Dani ever mentioning Amalia in an e-mail to me before. "Just an e-mail from my cousin Dani about a family friend who broke her leg."

"Someone you were close to?" he asks.

I hesitate before shaking my head again. I imagine the scent of honeysuckle in the room. "No," I say. "It's no big deal." I lift my fingers to the keyboard and type.

Thanks for letting me know, Dani.

I don't sign it. No little *X*s or *O*s. Nothing that happened at Morrison Ridge was Dani's responsibility, and yet the chill I feel for my family extends easily to her.

"I love you, babe," Aidan says, out of the blue from across the sea of our desks.

I smile at him. "Love you, too," I say, and

I return my attention to my computer screen, although I don't really see it.

Aidan is the last person I want to hide things from. Once a friend asked us what our secret is, since our marriage seems so strong, and we both answered, almost at the same moment, "Honesty." When that word left my mouth, I didn't feel hypocritical. I believe Aidan and I do have an honest relationship. I told him my relatives were caustic and crazy and I needed to cut ties with them to have a healthy future. That was the truth. Yes, I embellished as needed: my mother was dead, for example. But most of my dishonesty is due simply to omission. Sometimes he jokes about my family, calling them "inbred Southern mountain people." I never bother to correct him. What does it matter?

He knows I'd loved my father, though. And he knows that once my father was gone I'd found living at Morrison Ridge intolerable. That had certainly been the truth.

I used to wish I could tell Aidan everything, but I've moved past that now. It's too dangerous. I trust him more than I trust anyone I know, and yet, I am a lawyer. I've seen too many good marriages go sour, and when they do, all bets are off. Confidences shared over the years become fair game. I

78

will never tell him what happened on Morrison Ridge. I will never tell him why I left my family. It no longer has any bearing on my life. At least, that's what I tell myself. But this e-mail from Dani coupled with the prospect of adoption leaves me shaken. I suddenly feel as though I'm walking a tightrope and gravity is nipping at my heels.

Most days I think I'm over it. I've moved way beyond my adolescence and replaced the pain and anger with my degrees, my career, my volunteer work, my fabulous friends, my loving husband. But it doesn't take much to bring it back to me. It might take an article in the newspaper about someone with MS, or something on the news about North Carolina. Or, I see now, a short e-mail from Dani. *Yes,* I think as I stare blindly at my screen. That's enough to bring it all back.

8
MORRISON RIDGE

Two flights of steps bordered either side of the Hill from Hell. I didn't know who constructed them or when, but it was sometime before I was born. Maybe even before Daddy was born. In one stretch, the steps were made of large semiflat stones. In another, wood. In a third, slate. All of them were in terrible disrepair, but it was still easier to climb them than to try to walk up the dirt road itself, especially since Stacy and I were weighed down with our backpacks, slices of pie in Tupperware containers, bottles of Pepsi, and a bunch of cassette tapes. We stopped halfway up to catch our breath. I really didn't need to, but I could tell Stacy was not used to trudging up hills.

By the time we reached the turnoff to the springhouse, it was getting seriously dark and the buzz of the cicadas was so loud we could hardly hear each other speak.

"How do you know we're on the path?" she asked after we'd been walking for a few minutes. "Everything looks the same out here."

"We're fine," I said. "Trust me." If it had been daylight, we'd be able to see the fieldstone walls of the springhouse by now, but all I could see ahead of us was the muted greenish gray of the trees.

"Maybe this isn't such a great idea," Stacy said with a nervous laugh. "We're like a million miles from everything."

"We'll be fine." I pointed ahead of us. "See? There it is. Wait till you see inside. It's really cool."

"It *is* cute," she said, when we were close enough to really see the building. "So tiny."

The door squeaked as I pulled it open and Stacy followed me into the dark interior. She let out an excited yelp when I turned on the floor lamp and my little home away from home popped into view.

"Look at the posters!" she said, turning in a circle to take them in. "I had to get rid of mine when we moved down here." She knelt on one of the twin beds to get closer to the New Kids on the Block posters, and I could tell she was drooling over Joey McIntyre. "Oh my God, look at his eyes!" She reached out to touch Joey's cheek. Then she suddenly seemed to notice the rest of the room — the sink and microwave and little dresser. She climbed off the bed and held her arms out at her sides. "I *love* this," she said. "Oh my God, you're so lucky, Molly!" I saw the wistfulness in her face and felt guilty that I took everything I had for granted.

"Here's the cassette player," I said, pointing beneath the sink. I bent over to push the power button and *Step by Step* started up again. I'd never get tired of that tape. Stacy started nodding her head to the music as she looked at the rest of my posters.

"You really are stuck on Johnny Depp, aren't you," she said, pointing to the posters of him above the other bed.

"Do you watch *21 Jump Street*?" I asked.

"Of course." She sat down on the edge of the bed. "But he's way too old for you. He's, like, twenty-six. You could never get him."

I leaned against the sink, arms folded. "Well, do you seriously think you could get Joey McIntyre?" I asked.

"He's only seventeen. Better chance of getting him than Johnny Depp."

"It's only a fantasy, anyhow," I said.

Stacy looked toward the window. "Those bugs are so loud you practically can't hear the music," she said.

"They're cicadas." I'd left the windows

open from when Daddy and I had been in the springhouse earlier. "Help me close the windows before the mosquitoes find us, okay?" She tugged one of the unscreened windows shut while I shut the other, and the hum of the cicadas turned to a soft, distant buzz.

"Who are these people?" Stacy picked up a framed photograph from the top of the dresser. I barely noticed the photograph these days. The picture of a man, a woman, and their three teenagers had been part of my life for as long as I could remember.

"Nanny and my grandpa Arnette, who died before I was born." I stood next to Stacy and pointed to my grandparents. "And their kids. That's my aunt and uncle and father."

"Oh my God, *that's* your father? He was so hot!"

I looked at the picture, trying to see it through her eyes. No doubt about it. My father had been good-looking. Dark hair, strong chin, white teeth in a killer smile, and those riveting blue eyes. How had I never noticed before?

I pointed to the teenaged girl. "This is my aunt Claudia. Dani's mother. And the other boy is my uncle Trevor."

"Your father got the looks," Stacy said,

summing up the family as she set the frame back on the dresser. Then she flopped down on the bed beneath the Johnny Depp posters. It was technically my bed, but I'd let her have it for tonight. "Would you do it with him?" she asked, looking at one of the posters. "Johnny Depp?"

I sat down on the other bed. "Of course," I said. I had not yet figured out exactly how "doing it" was accomplished, but I didn't want to look like a complete moron. "Would you do it with Joey?"

"Oh, hell yes! In a heartbeat." She looked over at me. "We should practice French kissing with each other for when we get to do it for real."

"Um." I laughed. "I don't think so."

"Have you kissed anybody?"

"No," I said, embarrassed. "Have you?"

"Bryan Watkins," she said. "I'm kind of going with him. But we only Frenched once and I'm not sure I did it right."

I was shocked. Bryan Watkins was in high school. "He's a junior, isn't he?" I asked.

"Going into his senior year, actually." She sounded so sophisticated all of a sudden. Even her voice sounded different, like a woman in a commercial for an expensive car. "Do you know him?" she asked. "He reminds me of Joey." She pointed across the room at the New Kids poster. "A little bit, anyway."

What did she mean, she was kind of going with him? I suddenly realized that Stacy and I were worlds apart in more ways than I'd guessed. "How did you even meet him?" I asked.

"He lives in my neighborhood."

"So . . . you're actually going out with him?"

"No one knows." She rolled onto her side, facing me, her arm beneath her head. "I sneak out to be with him."

I wanted to ask her what exactly she did with him, but it sounded way too nosy. Maybe she'd tell me eventually. She didn't seem at all shy about telling me her deep dark secrets. She seemed so much older than me all of a sudden. I knew my birthday was actually a month before hers, but I was still fantasizing about Johnny Depp while she was sneaking out and doing who-knew-what with flesh-and-blood boys three years older than us.

"My sister's boyfriend goes down on her, which I think is totally disgusting," she said, out of the blue. "Can you imagine?"

No, I couldn't imagine it because I had no idea what she was talking about. "What does that mean?" I asked.

She wrinkled her nose. "He *eats* her," she said.

"What are you *talking* about?" I heard frustration in my voice. It was like she was speaking some language I didn't understand.

"He licks her . . . between her legs."

"What?" The image forming in my mind was revolting. "Why would he . . . that's sick!"

"I know. But it makes her come."

"Come . . . where?"

She gave me a quizzical look, as though I'd asked an unbelievably stupid question. "Molly." She sounded like a tired old schoolteacher. "Don't you at least know what *coming* means?"

I shook my head.

"You really missed out by not having any older brothers and sisters." She sat up and leaned against the stone wall. "Coming's this amazing feeling," she said. "It's not like anything else. It's totally intense. And it happens when you have sex, though you can do it to yourself, too. Make yourself come. I never have, but my sister says she does it all the time."

I laughed nervously. This was the strangest conversation I'd ever had in my life.

"Have you read *Forever*?" Stacy asked.

86

"The Judy Blume book?"

I shook my head.

"You really should. You'll learn everything. It's so awesome. I can loan you my copy."

"Okay," I said. I'd known I had a few things to learn, but I had no idea how much.

We both went really quiet for a few minutes. "Where Do I Go from Here" came on the cassette player, and Stacy flopped onto her back again. "Ah, Joey," she said, staring at the ceiling. She sang along softly with the song.

I lay down myself, and the moment my head hit the pillow, a memory came to me. A year ago — maybe two — I'd walked into my parents' room one evening. I should have knocked, but I'd been in a hurry and didn't stop to think. The light in the room was very dim, but I could make out Daddy lying naked on his back in the bed. My mother seemed to be sitting on his face, her knees on either side of his head. She leaned forward, one hand grasping the headboard, the other holding her breast. She was moving her hips and moaning. Her blond hair was out of its ponytail, loose and crazy around her head. I'd stood utterly frozen in the doorway, paralyzed by shock. Was she trying to suffocate him? Kill him in some weird, perverted way? And yet . . . I knew that wasn't it. I'd backed out of the room, shaken and a little sick, and I'd stayed outside their closed door until I finally heard my father's voice and knew he was still alive. Not only alive, but laughing with her. Now I wondered. Daddy couldn't touch her with his hands. Was his mouth the only way he could make her feel good? The only way he could make her come?

"Don't tell your parents about me seeing Bryan." Stacy's voice brought me back to the springhouse.

I made a face at the ceiling. "Like I talk to them about that kind of thing," I said. I sat up and shook out my arms as though shaking off our conversation. "Let's put on another tape."

"Can you see without your glasses?" Stacy said as we ate the last mouthfuls of peach pie from our Tupperware containers.

"I can see close up," I said. "Not very well at a distance."

"You have such amazing eyes. Can I make them up?"

"I don't have any makeup here." And all I had in my room at home was blush and lip gloss.

"I have a ton in my backpack," she said. "Let me do you. I'm really good at doing eyes. I have a supersteady hand."

"Okay," I said, wishing the light was better in the springhouse. Plus, the only mirror was a small frameless one attached to the wall above the sink.

We washed the Tupperware and then sat facing each other on the bed beneath the Johnny Depp posters. Stacy had pulled the floor lamp close to us and adjusted the shade. My eyeglass frames were large, a pale pink plastic I'd hoped would blend into my face and not be very noticeable, but I wasn't fooling anyone. The glasses were probably the first thing people noticed about my face. Daddy said I could get contacts when I was sixteen, which was several lifetimes away. I took my glasses off now and offered Stacy my face.

"Hmm," she said, studying me. "I can't decide if I should cover your freckles with foundation or not. They're kind of cute. Some boys really go for cute, you know?"

"Cover them over," I said. I was curious to see myself without freckles for the first time in my life.

"Okay." She'd taken an overstuffed makeup case from her backpack and when she opened it, bottles and tubes and compacts spilled out onto the brown bedspread. I'd never seen so much makeup.

89

Even my mother had only a fraction of Stacy's bounty.

"Wow," I said.

Stacy picked up a bottle and began shaking it. "I love this foundation," she said. "It covers zits and everything."

I studied her perfect skin. "Do you have it on now?" I asked.

"No. I only use it when I see Bryan or when I break out." She opened the top. "It smells good, too." She held it under my nose. "Sniff."

I did. "Nice," I said, although I really didn't smell much of anything other than the peaches on her breath.

"Let me dot this on. Close your eyes."

I felt her fingertips smooth the liquid over my nose and cheeks.

"Oh, this is cool!" she said. "Wait till you see. This covers your freckles totally." She finished with the foundation and I opened my eyes to see her pick up a small case of purple eye shadow from the bed. "I stole this," she said, opening the case. She smoothed a foam-tipped applicator across the purple powder.

"From one of your sisters?" I asked.

"Close your eyes," she said.

I shut my eyes and she began brushing the eye shadow over my lids.

"Not from my sisters, though some of this stuff is theirs. Or *was* theirs, anyhow." She giggled. "No, I got this from a drugstore near my house."

I opened my eyes. "You shoplifted it?"

"Close," she commanded, and I shut my eyes again waiting for her to answer.

"Yes," she said. "I don't do it a lot but this stuff is so expensive and it's so easy just to slip in your pocket. You've never stolen anything from a store?"

"No," I said. I didn't have the guts to steal something. I'd get caught for sure.

"I can teach you how," she said. "Open."

I opened my eyes and looked into her face, and I saw a beautiful girl who looked so much older than me. I wasn't sure if I envied her or feared her.

It took her half an hour to make me up, but I looked absolutely amazing by the time she was finished. I had to get close to the mirror to see her handiwork, and I finally took the mirror off the wall so I could stare at myself while I sat on the bed. "I don't even look like myself," I said.

"You look at least sixteen," Stacy said as she loaded her bottles and pencils back into her makeup bag.

I thought she was right. I loved how I

looked without freckles. And without glasses. Too bad the real me came with both.

She zipped her makeup bag closed. "I have to pee," she said, getting to her feet. "Where's the bathroom in this place?"

"Oh, it's a latrine," I said. "It's outside. I have to go too, so I'll show —"

"We have to go *outside* to use the bathroom?" Her eyes were open so wide that her lashes lifted her bangs.

"It's not too far."

"If I'd known that, I would've said we should stay in your house."

"Put on your sandals," I said, tying my tennis shoes. I slipped on my glasses. I hadn't used the latrine in a few weeks and I remembered how overgrown the path was even then. By now, it would be impossible to find without my glasses, especially in the dark.

I grabbed a roll of toilet paper from the bottom drawer of the dresser, picked up the two flashlights from the counter and handed one of them to her. "Come on," I said. "Just follow me."

We stepped outside and the sound of the cicadas fell over us like a blanket of noise. I pointed my flashlight at the ground and could just make out the vine-covered path. Another week and it would be indiscernible from the forest floor. "Come on," I said.

"Oh God." The path was too narrow for us to walk next to each other, but she had a death grip on my arm from behind me. "Are there snakes out here?" she asked.

"Not at night," I said.

"That is not reassuring!"

One of Morrison Ridge's barred owls picked that moment to start its eerie howling and Stacy let out a scream and stopped walking completely, her fingernails digging into my bicep. "What *is* that?" she asked.

"Just an owl," I said.

She seemed frozen in place. "I thought owls just said 'who, who'?"

"They say all kinds of things." I pointed the beam of my flashlight ahead of us. "Come on." I moved forward and was relieved when she came along with me. I hoped the owl was the worst of what we'd hear. There were nights when, between the howling and screeching and soul-piercing animal screams, I was certain something was being killed in our woods. That's all Stacy needed tonight.

After a minute or two, I spotted the wooden side of the latrine through the trees. "It's just a little ways," I said.

She followed me, sputtering against the cobwebs and bugs and complaining about the lack of a path, and we finally reached the latrine. It was ancient, the wooden door warped so that it wouldn't close all the way, and one of the boards hung off the roof by a nail. I had no idea when it had been built. I carefully opened the door. There was no terrible smell like you might expect, since it was so rarely used. I shined my flashlight on the wooden plank with the hole in its center.

"Oh no," Stacy said. "No way. Oh, this is the worst thing ever. What am I supposed to do with that?"

"You just sit on the board and go," I said. "Want me to go first?"

"First and last. I'll hold it, thanks."

I went inside and did my business and came out again. "It's no big deal," I said. "Go on. You don't want to have to hold it all night."

I could hear her teeth chattering and knew she was genuinely scared.

"Pretend you use this latrine all the time," I said.

"What are you talking about?"

"Just pretend. I'm serious. You use it every day of your life. It's no big deal. As a matter of fact, you're really, really glad it's here for you to use."

"You're crazy."

"Try it," I said. "You *love* this latrine. You

94

love it as much as you love Joey McIntyre."

She laughed. "Now you're seriously sick."

I had to laugh myself. At least her teeth were no longer chattering. "Please," I said. "Just try it. Just pretend you love it. Say it. That you love it."

"I love it," she said.

"Excellent!"

"I love this fucking latrine!" she shouted, and she pulled open the door and went inside. I was so shocked that she said the f-word that I hardly realized she was actually inside, sitting above that wooden hole, peeing.

"I need toilet paper!" she shouted.

I cracked the door open and handed it to her.

In another minute she was outside again, shuddering.

"You did it!" I said.

"And I hope I never have to do it again."

We walked back to the springhouse. She was much calmer than she had been on our way to the latrine. I told her about Daddy's Pretend Therapy as we walked.

"That's crazy," she said.

"Tell me it didn't just work for you."

"Well, I don't *really* love it!"

"You love that it was here for you when you needed it."

"He's written actual books about pretend-ing?"

"He doesn't call it Pretend Therapy when he's talking to other psychologists. He calls it Cognitive Behavioral Self-intervention. CBSI. But really, it's all about the power of pretending."

"That's crazy," she said again.

I thought about the two therapists Daddy shared his Asheville office with. One of them, Peter, also thought my father was crazy. Daddy didn't think much of Peter's approach to therapy, either. "Peter still thinks Freud hung the moon," he'd complain, "but we love each other, anyway." The other therapist in Daddy's office, Janet, worshiped my father . . . at least according to my mother. Janet had come to Daddy as an intern, wanting to learn more about CBSI, and she'd stayed on with him and Peter in the office they shared after she got her license. I knew Janet and Peter — and Peter's wife, Helen — pretty well. All three of them were really nice.

"And you help him write his books?" Stacy was asking.

"No, I type for him. He tells me what he wants to say and I type it."

"Wow," she said. "That's so cool."

We were back at the springhouse. *Step by*

96

Step was playing on the cassette player for the fourth or fifth time and we lay down on our beds. Suddenly, Stacy bolted upright, her eyes enormous, as she pointed to the floor by my bed. "Someone's under there!" she mouthed. "We have to get out!" She'd put her flashlight next to her on the bed. Now she grabbed it and ran for the door.

"No one's there!" I jumped up and ran after her. She'd already pushed the door open. Once I was outside with her, she shut the door and stood against it, pressing her body against the door so whoever she thought was inside wouldn't be able to get to us.

"Seriously!" she said. "Someone was under your bed!"

"That's insane," I said. "No one would even *fit* under those beds. They're too close to the floor."

The owl picked that moment to start its eerie howling again and Stacy yelped.

"I want to go back to your house, Molly!" she said. "Please! Really. I'm scared. And don't tell me to pretend! Someone is *in* there. They must have come in while we were at that stupid latrine."

She was being ridiculous, but I could tell I wasn't going to win this time. "Your backpack is still in there," I said.

"We can get it tomorrow. I'm not going in there again."

"I'll get it." I started to reach behind her for the doorknob, but she grabbed my arm.

"No! Don't leave me out here alone."

"All right." I gave in. I pictured our long walk home in the dark, down the winding loop road, then inching our way down the Hill from Hell. But it looked like I had no choice.

Stacy hung on to my arm as we made our way along the path in the dark. She kept turning to look behind us and I nearly tripped over her feet a couple of times. I was relieved when we finally made it to the loop road. Almost immediately, though, I stopped walking. The beam of my flashlight had landed on something shiny on the road ahead of us.

"What's that?" I whispered.

"Where?" Stacy held my arm so tightly it hurt.

I took a step closer and knew exactly what I was looking at: the spokes on my father's wheelchair. The chair was parked next to the bench my grandfather had built. My father sat on the bench, sound asleep, but he was not alone. Amalia sat sleeping next to him, her head on his shoulder, her hand wrapped around his where it rested on his thigh.

Stacy caught her breath. "That's not your mother," she whispered.

I nodded. "It's Amalia," I said quietly. "And look. They're sitting here to watch over us. To be sure we're safe." I smiled to myself, touched that my father and Amalia had done this. "And we *are* safe," I added, "so let's go back, okay? They're right here if we need them. I absolutely swear to you, there's no one in the springhouse."

"But . . ." She looked perplexed that I wasn't finding the scene in front of us the least bit upsetting. That I seemed to actually find it a comfort. And I did. "She's not your mother," Stacy said again, "and she's sitting with him like —"

"It's okay," I said. And I turned back toward the springhouse, glad when I heard her begin to follow me.

She grabbed my arm. "But that's not your mother!" she said again. "Aren't you even a little bit upset?"

I stopped walking and looked at her. "Actually," I said, "that *is* my mother."

9

Back at the springhouse, Stacy stood outside the open door while I showed her that it would be impossible for anyone to hide beneath our beds. I lifted the dusty bed skirt on one of the beds and shined my flashlight on the wooden platform that was no more than two inches from the floor.

"I could have sworn I saw fingers coming out from under your bed," she said sheepishly as she inched her way back into the building.

We sat on the beds, our backs resting against the cool stone walls, and I told her about Amalia.

"She's my birth mother," I said. "She lives in the slave —" I caught myself. "She lives in this cool cabin between here and Nanny's house. She's the one I told you about who gives me dance lessons."

"So . . . you're adopted?"

"Well, only partly. My father's my real . . .

my birth father." I wasn't sure if that was the right term when talking about a man. "But my mother — the one you met. Nora. She adopted me. So I guess I'm half adopted."

"This is mind-blowing," Stacy said.

"Not really. Not to me. I mean, this is just my life." I shrugged. *No big deal.* "Amalia's lived here all my life and I've always known she was my birth mother, so it's never been a big deep dark secret or anything."

"But . . . I mean . . . she was, like, all over your dad!"

"She wasn't all over him," I said, annoyed.

"She was leaning on him and holding his hand. On his thigh!"

"They're friends," I said, although I had to admit, I'd never seen my father and Amalia that close before. Would it bother Mom, I wondered, seeing them like that? I wasn't going to let Stacy know I suddenly had any doubts. "You're making a big deal out of nothing," I said.

Stacy leaned her head back against the wall and studied the beamed ceiling. "So, was your father married to your mother when he screwed Amalia?" she asked.

"What? No! Of course not!" Had he been? How did it happen? I suddenly realized there were pieces of the story I didn't know.

101

Questions I'd never thought to ask.

"My father had an affair," Stacy said quietly. "That's why he and my mom split up. It was disgusting, picturing him doing it with this other woman. She was, like, practically my sister's age."

I tried to imagine my father kissing Amalia. Lying in a bed with her, back when he was healthy. Having sex with her. I felt sick. I didn't want to think about it.

"I don't want to talk about this anymore," I said. "Did you bring your magazines with you?"

She looked at me hard for a moment and then gave in. Reaching for her backpack, she pulled out a stack of *Teen Beat* and *Sassy* magazines. She brought them over to my bed and we sat side by side, turning the pages, studying photos of the boys in the bands — those cute, safe-looking guys who I could imagine kissing but little more than that — and I tried hard to erase the new thoughts and images that were suddenly fighting for space inside my head.

Stacy slept to the muffled hum of the cicadas, but I was awake for most of the night, my mind blazing. At some point, I thought, either during the night or early in the morning, Russell would drive the van up the hill and take my father home. Would he see Amalia or would she leave before he arrived? I didn't think she would leave him alone. It wasn't easy for Daddy to sit upright like that without support. He could easily topple over. Did Russell know she was with my father? Did *Mom* know? The fact that *I* knew was disturbing enough and I wasn't sure what to make of it. Was it possible that Daddy *had* cheated on my mother with Amalia? *Amalia is your birth mother. Nora adopted you.* I'd known that from the time I was small. I realized now there had to be far more to the story, and I was going to have to find out what it was.

10
SAN DIEGO

How could a letter be so hard to write?

Our "Dear Expecting Mother" letter is the last thing we have to do to make our application one hundred percent complete. Until we do it, there is no chance of that call telling us we've been matched. I am the one slowing us down and I've run out of excuses.

We sit on the deck, Aidan's laptop on his knees as we try to compose the letter that will create our family. The screen is bothering him in the sunlight and he keeps taking off his sunglasses, then putting them back on. But he doesn't complain. He's focused on our task.

"We should try for a playful tone," he says. "Lighthearted."

"I think we should be factual," I say. "Talk about our work and the problems we had trying to have a baby and what our lifestyle is like and what we can offer a child, et cetera."

"Boring," he says. "Picture some fifteen-year-old girl trying to slog her way through a letter like that. It needs to be catchy."

I stare at our yard. From where I sit, I have a clear view of the little swing set my father-in-law built for us, but I'm not really seeing it. Instead, I'm imagining a scared teenaged girl searching uncertainly through a stack of "dear expecting mother" letters, trying to find the right person to raise her child. It's the first time I've truly let myself envision that girl. *Poor thing,* I think. Was Amalia frightened when she discovered she was pregnant with me? I wonder.

"Oh, *Aidan,*" I say. My voice is a quiet wail.

"What, babe?"

"I just feel for her," I say. "Whoever that girl — or woman — is."

His smile is sad as he leans over to take my hand. "I know," he says.

"I don't like this. I feel as though we're trying to do a sales job on her."

"We're not. We're working toward a mutually beneficial relationship."

I say nothing, still picturing that frightened young woman riffling through the pages of ninety-two letters.

"She's going to pick someone, Molly," he says. "It might as well be us."

"Then . . ." I say, "I know you think we need to appeal to her youth and be very contemporary, but that's not who we are. We want the letter to truly reflect us, don't we? Are we so deadly dull that no one will pick us if we're honest about ourselves?" I can hardly believe those hypocritical words just came out of my mouth.

Aidan looks at me for a long moment. "You're right," he says finally. He opens a new document on his screen. "Back to the drawing board."

We write the letter. It takes us all weekend and we barely stop to eat. It's only two pages long, single-spaced, but it's a gripping story of our struggle to have a child, our love for each other, and our passion for our work. We write about San Diego and all it can offer a child, and last but absolutely not least, we share our belief that we can provide a stable and loving home for her baby. We slip the letter in an envelope, seal it, place it in our mailbox and send it on its way, with all the hope we can muster.

11
MORRISON RIDGE

When Stacy and I got to my house the morning after our night in the springhouse, we found the kitchen packed with people. Aunt Claudia and Uncle Jim — Dani's parents — sat on one side of the big kitchen table, and Aunt Toni and Uncle Trevor sat on the other. Mom was feeding Dad at the head of the table and everyone was laughing when Stacy and I walked in the room, but there was a weird, tense undercurrent to the sound. Or maybe *I* felt weird and tense. I was afraid Stacy would say something about seeing Daddy and Amalia together. I wished I'd told her not to, but I was still busily acting like it was no big deal, so I supposed saying anything to her about it would have blown that façade.

I introduced Stacy to everyone and we sat down at the opposite end of the table from my parents, where someone — my mother, most likely — had set plates and glasses for us. I reached for the pitcher of orange juice and poured some into Stacy's glass.

"What time is your mom picking you up, Stacy?" my mother asked as she gave my father a sip from his coffee cup.

"Between nine-thirty and ten," she said.

Aunt Claudia held a basket of muffins out to Stacy and me. "Fresh baked blackberry muffins, Molly," she said.

"Cool," I said, taking the basket from her and offering the muffins to Stacy.

"Delicious with butter," Aunt Toni said, sliding the butter plate down the table toward us. Aunt Toni had very short, very dark hair with a stripe of gray that ran from her left temple back over her ear. That stripe of hair always reminded me of a skunk. She was tan and very fit and played tennis year-round.

"Aunt Claudia's a really good baker," I said to Stacy as we broke the muffins apart on our plates.

"Thank you, Molly." Aunt Claudia beamed. She was forty years old, four years younger than Daddy, but where Daddy was slim and dark-haired, Aunt Claudia had a doughy sort of build and she wore her copper-colored hair in a pixie cut that was way too short for her round face. Ever since I was a little kid, her face had reminded me of a pumpkin. She was nice, though. I could never figure out how she ended up with a bitchy daughter like Dani.

"We saw Dani yesterday while we were riding our bikes around Morrison Ridge," I said to her now.

"Oh, poor Dani's at loose ends this summer," Aunt Claudia said.

"She needs to get a job," Uncle Jim said.

Aunt Claudia ignored him. "She doesn't have many friends left in the area since she's been going to Virginia Dare," she said. "She likes it there, though. It's a tolerant school. They don't try to make a child fit some sort of mold."

Which was a good thing, I thought, because Dani was never going to fit into anybody's mold.

"I hear you girls stayed in the old springhouse last night," Aunt Toni piped in. "Hope you didn't have to go to the bathroom in the middle of the night."

"We did," Stacy said. She looked at my father. "That latrine thing was gross, and I wasn't going to use it, but your crazy daughter made me pretend that I loved it."

"Oh, she did, did she?" Daddy asked. I thought there was an amused sort of pride in his expression. "So, did pretending work?"

"Well, I did use it," Stacy admitted.

"I hated that latrine with a vengeance," Aunt Claudia said. "Remember the copperhead that lived in there that one summer?"

"Copperhead?" Stacy shuddered.

"Trevor planted that thing to scare the girls," Daddy said to Stacy. "You had nothing to fear."

"I did not plant it," Uncle Trevor said as he reached for the coffeepot on the table. "Swear on a stack of Bibles." His forearm was big and meaty and I watched the muscles and tendons move beneath his tanned skin as he poured coffee into his cup. He worked out constantly in the gym in his house, plus he was a contractor, so he was always in great shape, especially when you looked at him next to his brother — my skinny, calorie-counting father. But his face was full of wrinkles from working outside all the time. He was forty-six, two years older than my father, and he always complained that Daddy got to go to college while he had to stay home and help my grandfather with his carpentry business. It really irritated me that he could look my father in the eye — my father who could barely move a muscle — and complain that Daddy had it better than him. He drank a lot and I'd seen him drunk a few times. He scared me when he was drunk. That mixture of brawn and booze felt dangerous to me.

"What did you do all night out there?" Aunt Claudia asked Stacy and me.

We looked at each other and smiled. "Talked," Stacy said. She wasn't going to say anything about Amalia, I thought, relieved. It would have come out by now.

"Only teenaged girls could spend a whole night talking," Aunt Toni said.

"So, back to the conversation we were having, Graham," Uncle Trevor said. He was clearly not interested in Stacy and me. "I've run the numbers backward and forward, and I can tell you, we're sitting on a gold mine here. It's ridiculous to let the land rot beneath our feet."

Daddy smiled the sort of indulgent smile he gave me when I was trying his patience. "It's hardly rotting, Trev," he said. "And now's not the right time to discuss this." He nodded toward Stacy, or maybe toward both of us.

"You're always so overly dramatic, Trevor," Aunt Claudia said. "Even as a kid, you were just ridicu—"

"Forget about what I was like as a kid," Uncle Trevor snapped at his sister. "I don't know why I can't get the four of you to see logic. You have kids to get through college. Don't you want to be able to put them through without them being strapped with loans once they get out, the way we were with Samantha and Cal?"

God, this was not only boring but embarrassing. Stacy chewed her muffin, her gaze out the window toward the mountains in the distance. We'd have to make a break for it as soon as we could politely excuse ourselves.

"That's true, Graham," Aunt Claudia said to Daddy. "Danielle's not going to qualify for any big scholarships. I'm about to get laid off from the blanket factory. And Jim's beer-making enterprise isn't exactly bringing home the bacon."

"Yet," Uncle Jim said. I knew he was trying to get out of the trash-hauling business by making beer in his cellar, an enterprise my father thought was a waste of time and money.

"Right." Aunt Claudia patted Uncle Jim's hand. "Not yet, anyway."

"Are you wearing makeup, Molly?" Mom asked suddenly.

I'd forgotten. I'd brushed my teeth that morning, but hardly glanced in the little mirror above the sink. I was probably a smeared mess by now.

"I made her up," Stacy said. "Don't her eyes look awesome?"

"Very pretty." Mom nodded.

"Makes your eyes really stand out," Daddy said.

"I didn't let Danielle wear makeup until she was fifteen," Aunt Claudia said.

I knew for a fact that Dani started wearing makeup when she was twelve years old. She'd put on her black eyeliner the second she got on the school bus, then take it off again on the bus home. I'm sure she did whatever she pleased once she started going to her boarding school.

"Oh, I don't know," Daddy said. "I think, especially if you have to wear glasses, you should be allowed to wear makeup so your eyes pop."

"Maybe a little lighter on the eye shadow, at least for everyday," Mom said.

I thought of the shoplifted eye shadow and tried to imagine how it would feel to slip something in my pocket and stroll out of a store without paying.

"You did a nice job, Stacy," Daddy said. "Are you artistic?"

"Can we get back to talking about the land?" Uncle Trevor asked.

"Oh, let them have a little time with Molly and her friend, Trevor," Aunt Claudia said.

Daddy once told me Aunt Claudia had been the peacemaker in his family when they were growing up and that it took a toll on her. Ever since then, I'd noticed that she walked a fine line between everybody's wants and needs. It made my stomach hurt to think about having to do that.

"I guess I'm a little artistic," Stacy said to my father. "I like to draw, but I don't think I'm great at it or anything."

"Did Molly tell you I'm taking her with me on my book tour?" Daddy asked her.

"You are?" Aunt Claudia reached for another muffin.

"I was his guinea pig when he worked on some of the techniques," I said.

"That's so cool," Stacy said, and Uncle Trevor folded his arms across his chest with an impatient sigh.

"She'll connect with the kids in the audience in the bookstores," Daddy said. "Assuming I *have* an audience. And she'll be her usual good company." He looked down the table at me and I filled up with so much love for him. Everyone turned in my direction, and I wondered if the love was visible, like a big red cartoon heart over my head.

"I'll teach you how to do the makeup for the book tour," Stacy offered.

Daddy looked at Trevor, and I knew he

hadn't missed his brother's impatient posture. "Trevor," he said, "here's the thing. Even if Claudia and Jim and Nora and I wanted to sell off some of our land — which, I hasten to add, we don't — we can't do anything while Mom is still alive. It would kill her if we sold any of it. She'd —"

"She's only seventy years old!" Uncle Trevor was nearly shouting.

"Don't be such a hothead!" Aunt Claudia said.

"She could live another twenty years," Trevor said. "Another thirty! We could use that money *now.*"

"We need it for our retirement, Graham," Aunt Toni said. She went on about wanting to travel someday, and I caught Stacy's eye and nodded toward the living room. This was too boring for words.

We sat on the front steps, waiting for Stacy's mother. "I love your parents," she said. "They're supernice, and it's like, after a few seconds you completely forget your dad is in a wheelchair, you know?"

I nodded, barely listening to her. I was waiting for her to say something about Amalia, but it was as if she'd completely forgotten about seeing them together the night before. I was the one who couldn't get the image out of her mind.

"I seriously want to fix you up with one of Bryan's friends," she said.

"Cool," I said, though I was sure my parents would never let me go out with a seventeen-year-old. I didn't think they'd let me go out with anyone, actually.

"There's my mom!" She hopped to her feet as the silver van came around the bend in our dirt road. Stacy leaned over and hugged me. "Thank you!" she said. "I had an awesome time!"

I watched her climb into her mother's van, and as they drove away, her mom gave a little toot on her horn. Sitting there, I could still feel Stacy's arms around me. I'd never had a hugging friend before and I liked that I had one now, even if she was a very different person from me. I liked my life, with my two loving parents and one loving birth mother and my happy innocent fantasies of Johnny Depp, but I had the feeling I was going to like my life with Stacy Bateman in it even more.

12

Daddy asked me to type for him late that afternoon. I got everything set up before Russell brought him into the office. That meant I had the computer turned on and *Pretend Therapy for Grown-ups* — Daddy's working title for his book — open on the computer. Until a year ago, I also had to stick a floppy disk into the machine, but now we had a new computer and everything was on a hard drive, which was much easier, though Daddy still made me back everything up to floppy disks anyhow. I loved typing and would have done it even if Daddy didn't pay me. Mom taught me when I was ten years old and wanted to write some stories. "No daughter of mine is going to be a two-fingered typist," she'd said. I remembered her saying those words almost every time I typed, and this afternoon, I was particularly stuck on the phrase *daughter of mine.*

Daddy's office was small and compact, lined with bookcases on two walls. Daddy loved his books. The physical act of reading was no longer easy for him, though. He listened to a lot of books on tape these days, and he had a really clumsy sort of page-turning machine some guy at the university made for him, but every third page or so, the machine would get stuck and one of us would have to help out, which frustrated him no end. Daddy was determined to read, though. He wouldn't let his inability to turn the pages get in the way.

His huge desk took up half the room. The desk was actually a long, wide door that he'd kept when the old Morrison Ridge stable had been demolished. He'd had the door refinished and Uncle Trevor attached some legs to it. I knew Daddy liked giving new life to something old and meaningful from the Ridge, and I thought it was ironic that the old door was now topped with a shiny new computer and printer.

I straightened a few books that had been piled on one corner of the desk and picked up the two pens and one pencil lying loose near the computer. I hunted on the desk for the stained-glass pencil case Amalia had made for my father a few years ago. The case, with its crazy quilt pattern of blue-

and-white iridescent glass, would be hard to miss, but it was nowhere to be found, and I set the pens and pencil next to the pile of books.

"Sorry to keep you waiting," Daddy said, as Russell pushed him into the room.

"No problem," I said.

"Need anything before I take off?" Russell asked.

"Could you adjust the head support?" Daddy asked him.

"This thing's still irking you, isn't it," Russell said as he fiddled with the knob on the side of the head support. Daddy'd had the old head support replaced and he couldn't seem to get comfortable with the new one. It reminded me of a baseball mitt, the way it cradled his head. "You want me to switch this out for the old one later today?" Russell asked. "I still have it."

"Good idea," Daddy said. "This one doesn't let me move my head the way I want. I'd like to be able to move the one body part I still have some control over." He smiled at me but his voice gave away his irritation.

"I can't find your pencil case," I said to him. "Do you know where it is?"

Daddy looked at the spot on the desk where the case usually sat. *"Hm,"* he said.

"Not a clue. Do you know, Russell?"

Russell shook his head. "I'll keep my eye open for it," he said. "Do you need anything else before I go?"

"I think we're good," Daddy said, and Russell left us alone in the room.

I wiggled my fingers as though warming them up, then I rested them on the keyboard.

"Where were we?" Daddy asked. "Read me the last couple of paragraphs we worked on." I knew he was anxious to get going. He wanted to finish the book by the end of the summer.

I found the last page of the document and read the paragraphs to him. Then he began dictating and I began typing, and we were off. I made more mistakes than usual, though, because my mind was on the questions I planned to ask him once we were finished working. I wasn't sure how I was going to dive into the topic of Amalia, but he made it easy for me.

"Where's your mind today, Molly?" he asked after we'd been working for half an hour and I'd had to stop his dictating so I could correct yet another typing mistake. "It's definitely not here in this room," he said. "What's up?"

It was often a mixed blessing that he could

read me so easily. Today, though, I was glad.

I dropped my hands from the keyboard to my lap and swiveled the chair to face him. "There *is* something that's bugging me," I said.

"Talk to me," he said.

I took a deep breath. "Were you married to Amalia before Mom?" I asked. "Or were you married to Mom and you cheated on her with Amalia? Or . . . I don't know." I screwed up my face, uncomfortable with my own questions. "What really happened back then?"

He looked at me, eyebrows raised, as though he didn't quite understand what I was asking. "Well," he said finally, "I wondered when you'd ask. I'd hoped it would be later. Or perhaps never." He chuckled, then gave me one of his totally attentive looks. If he could have leaned forward, he would have. He had to make his face do all the work someone else could do with his body. "Nobody cheated on anyone, darling," he said. "Would you like to hear the story of how you came to be?"

"Yes," I said. "Absolutely."

He looked out the window toward the forest, as if gathering his thoughts. "It might not be the happiest story ever told," he said, returning his gaze to me, "but it's one for which I'll be forever grateful, because it brought you into the world."

I smiled, relaxing a bit as I folded my hands in my lap, ready to listen.

"So," he said with a nod of his head, "I was twenty-eight when I received my doctorate from UNC and came home to Morrison Ridge. I moved back into the brick house with my parents and Claudia, who was still living there at the time. Trevor was already married to Toni and they'd built their house and had Samantha and Cal. So anyway, I got a job as a psychologist at a facility called Highland Hospital in Asheville. It doesn't exist any longer, but it was a bit of an unorthodox place."

"What does that mean?"

"They had a unique approach to treating patients," he said. "They often used art or music or nature to try to heal troubled people instead of relying exclusively on medication or shock treatment or psychotherapy. I found that outside-the-box approach appealing, as you can probably imagine." He gave me a conspiratorial smile. "At any rate, here's something you don't know about me, Molly," he continued with a bit of a sigh. "I used to love to dance, just like you."

"Really?" I could barely remember him

walking, much less dancing.

"Trevor and Toni and Claudia and I would go dancing every weekend," he said. "Then we started going to the coast. Wrightsville Beach or sometimes Myrtle. Everyone there was playing beach music and doing the Carolina shag and we really got into it. We brought the dance back here to the mountains and helped start a shag group."

"Is that the group Aunt Claudia and Uncle Jim go to in Asheville?"

"Yes, Claudia actually met Jim there, and the group's still in existence, although obviously I'm no longer a part of it. And Trevor and Toni lost interest somewhere along the way."

"Is that where you met Mom?"

He shook his head. "No," he said. "Nor is it where I met Amalia." He shifted his head on the headrest and I could tell it was bothering him. "Amalia was hired by Highland Hospital to teach dance to the patients," he said. "Well, not 'hired' exactly." He looked off into space, kind of talking to himself. "Well, let's just call it 'hired,' " he said. "Easier that way. The hospital gave her room and board. She was only twenty years old and she was a wonderful dancer, as you know," he said. "There was an easygoing element to her dancing that allowed her to connect to many different types of patients. She was so uninhibited." He was someplace else in his mind, and I waited as patiently as I could. I was anxious for him to get to the part about me. "She had a very difficult childhood," he said. "Her parents weren't together and her mother was not a very good or caring mother. But that's Amalia's story to tell, not mine." He gave his head a small shake. "Anyway, I told her about the dance group and she started going there with me. It was a friendship at first but gradually turned into . . . something more. I fell in love with her, although we were very different. I was nine years older, to begin with. She had a high school education and I had a PhD. We came from very different family and economic backgrounds. My parents and Trevor and Claudia discouraged the relationship from the start. But . . . well, you know her." He smiled at me. "You know she has a sort of . . . magnetic personality."

I nodded. This was so weird, hearing him talk about a romance with someone other than my mother. My stomach felt knotted up and I pressed my hands together in my lap, but I'd asked for the story, and I didn't want him to sanitize it for me even if it made me squirm.

"I'd never known anyone like her," Daddy said. "My family seemed so rigid . . . so uptight by comparison. It was as though I'd found someone I could finally relax around."

I knew what he meant. It seemed impossible to do anything that would shake Amalia up. She rolled with whatever came her way.

"So, anyway, we had fun together and I decided our differences didn't matter. But then I began having trouble with my legs. Sometimes when I danced — or even walked — my legs felt leaden and it took extra effort to make them move. At first I thought it was my imagination. I had no idea what was wrong with me. I saw a doctor — well, several — and had too many tests to count, and eventually got the diagnosis of MS. I didn't handle that diagnosis particularly well." He smiled again, and I had the feeling he was understating what had happened.

"Were you a basket case?" I asked.

He laughed. "You could say that. And at first, Amalia was very supportive, but then she — quite suddenly — seemed to withdraw. And one day, she simply disappeared."

"Disappeared?"

He nodded. "One night, she packed up all her things in her room at Highland Hospital and left without a word to anyone. I was . . ." He looked at the ceiling. "Well, I guess the word is *devastated,*" he said, his eyes back on me. "I searched for her, but she had vanished, and I assumed the MS had scared her away. She couldn't deal with it and couldn't tell me to my face, so she simply left. It was too much for her."

I couldn't imagine the Amalia I knew behaving so cowardly. "That was cruel." I frowned.

"It did feel cruel at that moment," he agreed. "But anyway, a couple of months after she left, I met Nora," he said. "She'd been hired by the hospital as a pharmacist and we struck up a friendship. She wasn't the least bit put off by the MS. As a matter of fact, she invented ways I could deal with my ever-increasing limitations and accompanied me to doctors' appointments and came up with work-arounds so that I could still do things I wanted or needed to do."

"That is so Mom." I smiled.

"She was amazing. She was definitely a person you could count on, and I needed that. I fell in love with her, and of course my family adored her. She fit in much better with them, plus they were so relieved Amalia was gone."

"I still can't believe Amalia deserted . . . Oh!" I suddenly got it. "Was she *pregnant*?"

"You are one smart cookie," Daddy said. "She certainly was. Of course, I had no clue. You can draw your own conclusions as to why she thought she needed to leave. Maybe she didn't want to tie me down to someone my family disliked, or she was just plain scared. So your mom and I were married and then one day Amalia appeared on our doorstep with a baby — you. She was overwhelmed trying to care for you as a single parent. Your mom — Nora — was unable to have children. . . . I think you knew that?"

I nodded.

"And while I was disappointed about it, I thought maybe it was just as well, given the progression of the MS." He looked out the window toward the trees again, then back at me with a smile. "But then *you* showed up," he said, "and your appearance seemed like a miracle. It made sense for us to make you ours, and Amalia was — although she loved you very much — relieved, and she entrusted you to us. But the three of us wanted you to be able to have a relationship

127

with her, so that's why she lives at Morrison Ridge. We thought it would be best for her to be close to you, and of course that's what she wanted, so —"

"But no one really wants her here, do they?" I couldn't forget a conversation I once overheard between my two uncles about the appropriateness of Amalia living in the slave quarters, since she was their housekeeper. "Cinderella," they'd called her. "They don't like her."

"Oh, they've come to like her well enough," Daddy said. "Your grandmother has never approved of her being here, but she'll get over it one of these days."

"It's been fourteen years," I pointed out. "If she's not over it by now, I don't think she ever will be."

"Doesn't really matter, does it? You have Amalia close by and that's what counts."

"Right." I thought of my mother — Nora — and tried to imagine how I would feel, having my husband's old girlfriend living so close by. "Has it been weird for Mom?" I asked. "Having Amalia here?"

Daddy sighed. "Well, I'd be lying if I said her relationship with Amalia hasn't had its share of tension," he said. "I'm sure you've picked up on some of it from time to time. But you're the most important thing in the world to Nora, so she and Amalia tolerate each other for your sake."

I looked down at my hands. I thought about how many sentences he'd used to tell me about falling in love with Amalia. How few sentences he'd allotted to my mother.

"What's running through your head, Moll?" he asked.

I looked up at him. "Are you still . . . are you in love with her?" I asked. "Amalia?"

He smiled. "I love her and always will, but 'in love'?" He shook his head. "No. 'In love' belongs to your mother, who's pretty extraordinary, wouldn't you say?"

"Yes." I wished I felt totally relieved by his answer, but I still couldn't get the image of Amalia's head on his shoulder out of my mind. "Daddy," I said, my eyes locked onto his, "I saw you and Amalia on the bench last night. You were both asleep. She was holding your hand."

He lost his smile. "I'm sorry," he said. "Was that upsetting?"

"Confusing."

"Are you wondering if Mom knows Amalia was there with me?"

I nodded.

"She knows. We have no secrets."

"Doesn't she get jealous?"

"I guess you'd have to ask her how she

129

feels, darling. I can't speak for her."

I gave a small nod. I could never talk to my mother like this. She was an awesome mother in about a million ways, but she was not the sort of person you could easily bare your soul to.

"Now," he said, "there's one more thing we have to talk about, and that's a family meeting coming up Wednesday night."

I frowned. "Family meeting?" I vaguely remembered a family meeting from about three years ago. It had to do with our trash pickup and mail delivery. I distinctly remembered falling asleep with my head on Daddy's lap.

"You don't have to be there," he said, as if reading my mind. "Nanny's not coming, either, so she suggested you go over to her house and the two of you can watch a movie. How's that sound?"

"Is this about Uncle Trevor's idea for the land?" I asked.

"Yes, darling, as well as a few other issues," he said. "It'll be boring, that much I can guarantee. You'll be better off with Nanny."

"Okay with me," I said.

"Great." He looked at the computer screen. "Let's give up on the book for today," he said. "How about you save it —

and back it up — and then push me to the kitchen? Save Russell a trip."

"Sure." I backed up the work I'd done and then turned his chair around. I was pushing him into the hallway when the phone rang. Someone picked it up, and in a moment Mom's voice called from the kitchen.

"Molly!" she called. "Stacy for you."

"Okay!" I called back. "I'll be there in a minute." I continued pushing my father toward the kitchen, wondering if I could ever adequately explain my family to Stacy. There was no need to go into the whole "Amalia on the bench with my dad" thing with her again, since she seemed to have forgotten about it . . . which was good, I decided, because no matter how easily my father had handled my questions, deep down I wasn't completely sure of his answers.

13
SAN DIEGO

Aidan and I join sixteen other people in a large room at the Hope Springs Adoption Agency. We sit in a circle on folding metal chairs and as we wait for the arrival of Zoe, who will lead the group, everyone talks in hushed whispers as if we're in church. I don't really want to be here. I'm afraid it's going to be one of those soul-baring groups where I end up crying my eyes out over the baby I lost.

I feel an air of desperation in the room and wonder how much Aidan and I are contributing to it. I glance furtively around the circle. There are a few people who are older than us and several who are younger. We are comfortably in the middle, agewise, I think, and that's reassuring.

Although I feel as though I know Zoe after talking to her more than a dozen times on the phone during the application process, Aidan and I have never met her in person.

From her voice and her gently supportive, almost maternal, attitude, I would guess her to be a matronly fifty-year-old. I picture her with dark hair streaked by strands of gray, so I'm surprised when a beautiful red-haired woman walks into the room in stiletto heels and introduces herself as Zoe. Aidan and I exchange a look.

"*Not* what I imagined," Aidan whispers to me.

"This can't be 'our' Zoe," I whisper back, but as soon as the woman opens her mouth, I recognize her comforting voice.

"It may take some time," she says, turning to take us all in, "but every one of you in this room is going to find your baby."

A man begins to applaud and several people join him. Aidan and I share a nervous glance. He has his arm across the back of my chair and he gives my shoulder an encouraging squeeze.

Zoe asks all of us to introduce ourselves and tell a little about our "story." I learn quickly that we are quite a mix of waiting parents. In addition to several straight couples waiting for their first child, there are two lesbian couples, one gay couple, and two single women, and there are two couples trying to adopt for the second time. One of them already has three adopted children and is coming back for a fourth. I feel bitter about them. I can't help it. *Let the rest of us have a turn,* I want to say. I'm fairly certain I'm not the only person in the room with that sentiment. The stories of infertility are heartbreaking to hear. The failed IVF attempts. The multiple miscarriages. One of the lesbian couples talks about the nightmare of being chosen by a birth mother only to have the young woman change her mind a week after the baby had been placed with them. Everyone in the room visibly shudders as the women speak about the agony they went through after bonding with the baby they'd quickly come to think of as theirs. I feel tears growing closer and closer to the surface as I listen to everyone's story and I make the decision I won't tell them about the baby I lost. I can't get through it. I will simply talk about our infertility and my hysterectomy. But when it is our turn, Aidan blurts out, "We lost our daughter when Molly was twenty weeks pregnant," and there it is, out in the open before I can stop it. Murmurs of sympathy ripple through the group. Tears well up in my eyes and my voice is stuck in my throat. I try to smile a grateful smile and don't even attempt to speak. I let Aidan do the talking for both of us.

"I came from a very loving, happy family," he says, "and I want to recreate that. Molly's parents both passed away when she was young and she has no siblings and I know she wants the opportunity to create a real family of her own."

I'm relieved when Aidan is done talking and Zoe takes over again. Balancing on her stilettos in the middle of the room, she gives us information most of us already know. She describes the legalities surrounding our relationship with the — so far phantom — birth parents. She tells us the agency will provide counseling for the birth mothers, and goes over the cost of medical care and other potential expenses we'll be expected to cover. She talks for about twenty minutes, then suddenly shifts gears.

"So," she says, "I'd like each of you who is here with a partner to tell us why your partner will make a good parent. Those of you here alone, of course, will tell us about yourselves."

She looks directly at us, and I know we're expected to go first. I'm embarrassed by my inability to speak during our last attempt at sharing, so I dive right in. I talk about Aidan's easygoing nature and how he'd love a son or daughter to share his passion for sports and adventure. "He's the sort of person you can count on," I say. "He has strong values and puts them into action, which is why he practices immigration law. He'll make a wonderful role model for a child."

I turn to Aidan and he smiles at me. "Thanks, babe," he says. Then he looks around the circle.

"Molly is the most generous person I know," he says. "She's one of those people who sees what other people need even before they know they need it. I first realized this about her when we were dating. Of course she was very attentive to my needs back then." He offers a mildly prurient smile to the group. "But it was the way she treated other people that I really noticed," he continues. "The way she'd look out for the needs of the underdog or help her friends who were in trouble. She offers pro bono legal services at the women's shelter downtown. She arranged one of those meal trains for my sister after my sister gave birth to twins, even though it was only a few months after Molly had lost our own baby. I don't know how she did it; I couldn't have."

My throat tightens again. I don't know how I did it, either.

"She takes extraordinary care of the

people she loves," Aidan says. "She'll make a phenomenal mother."

He turns to the woman on his right to let her know he is finished and it's her turn. She begins to speak, but I don't hear her. I'm overwhelmed by Aidan's description of me. Am I really the generous, caring person he described? I want to be. Maybe I truly am. I'm so hung up on my dishonesty these days that I've lost track of anything good about myself.

"Now, you know when we talk about open adoption that there are many different levels of openness," Zoe says after everyone in our circle has had the chance to speak. "There's no right or wrong," she says, "only that degree of openness you and the birth parents settle on in your 'contact agreement.' I thought it would be fun, though, to invite a family here today that epitomizes openness in adoption." Smiling, she nods toward the door behind me and I turn to see two women, a man, and a little girl. They move toward us and Aidan gets up to make room for them to walk into the center of our circle, where Zoe and another man are setting up three chairs.

The man and women sit down and one of the women offers a stuffed kitten to the little girl, who cannot be much more than a year old. Zoe introduces them to us. They are an adoptive couple in their late thirties with their little girl and the child's twenty-year-old birth mother. They begin to tell us about their relationship.

"Gracie lived with us the last month of her pregnancy," the adoptive mother says. "Things were rough for her at home and we'd already come to love her, so it just made sense."

"I live with my boyfriend now, though," Gracie says.

"We still have dinner together a couple of Sunday nights during the month," the adoptive father adds.

"And we just hang out sometimes during the week," Gracie says. The little girl taps the kitten on Gracie's knee and Gracie lifts the child onto her lap. I wish I could steal a glance at Aidan.

I am not the only person in the room who appears stunned by the relationship in front of us. Is this what we want? Is this what *I* want? To share my child to this degree? I decide right then that I can't handle it. I'm afraid of it. I'm afraid of losing my child's affections to his or her birth mother. *There.* I let the thought in. I feel weak for having it, but it's the truth. I am not that generous person Aidan described. Secretly, I wonder if those old-fashioned closed adoptions still exist and, if so, can we find one.

"How about that family!" Aidan says as soon as we get in the car. "Was that fantastic or what?"

"I thought it was a little much," I say. "I mean, that couple didn't just adopt a *baby*. For all intents and purposes, they adopted the baby's mother as well."

"Well, that's an exaggeration, but can you imagine how great it is for that little girl to have a relationship with her birth mom like that? It's too bad the birth father couldn't have been equally as involved." The birth father, it had turned out, had been "unknown."

"Do you really want an adoption that's that open?" I ask.

He nods. "Absolutely," he says, then he turns to frown at me. "I thought you did, too. You said there should be no deep dark secrets."

He doesn't understand. I have never told him enough about myself to *let* him understand.

"Well, like Zoe says," I say, "there are different degrees of openness." I press my hands together in my lap. "I don't want deep dark secrets," I say, "but I don't want the birth mother to move in with us, either."

"She was only with them for a short time," Aidan says. "You're really blowing their situation out of proportion."

"You're the father," I say. "You can't see it from my perspective."

"You mean . . . are you talking about competition? That's ridiculous."

"Is it?"

"Yes. That little girl knows who her mother is. But she loves them both, and more importantly, she's loved *by* them both. You've said that yourself, babe. How great open adoption is because the child knows he or she is loved by so many people."

Had I really said that? These days, I seem to say one thing when I mean another. I'm a mess. I turn my face away from Aidan and look into the darkness outside the car window. I think of my father. If he were here right now, he would root out my true feelings in ten seconds flat. He'd know I'm afraid of losing the child I haven't even met yet.

14
MORRISON RIDGE

If someone was plunked down on Morrison Ridge and asked to pick which of the five houses had once been the slave quarters, they might pick Amalia's last. Well, that wasn't quite the truth. Nanny's big brick house was clearly the main building, but Amalia's small house was so modern and cool, no one would guess it had ever housed Morrison Ridge's slaves. Amalia's half acre was technically part of Nanny's twenty-five. I don't know how Daddy did it, but he'd talked Nanny into letting Amalia live there. I expected she would live there for all time.

I heard music as soon as I turned my bike off the loop road and onto the narrow lane that led to her house, although I had to ride another ten yards or so before I could make out what it was: Phil Collins singing, "I Can Feel It Coming in the Air Tonight." I loved dancing to that one, and I pedaled faster.

Amalia's house seemed to pop out of the

141

woods. One minute it wasn't there, and the next it was. Only one story, it seemed to hug the earth with wood and glass.

I hopped off my bike and leaned it against one of the trees in her yard. Through the wall of windows, I could see that she was already dancing in the long living room. She was a shadowy figure blending in with the reflection of the trees in the glass. I ran inside, and when she spotted me, she smiled and held out her hand. I took it and we moved slowly across the wide wood plank floor to the final haunting refrain of the song. She had on a black spandex camisole and a loose lavender chiffon skirt that fell below her knees and was split up the middle to give her the freedom to kick her legs high. She had a bunch of those skirts in all different colors. The skirt floated in the air when she turned and her long hair swung around her shoulders. When Amalia spun in circles, everything spun with her.

By contrast, I was in my cutoff denim shorts and pink tank top, my hair up in a ponytail. I kicked off my sandals so we were both barefoot.

The room was perfect for dancing, the only furniture two huge round Papasan chairs at one end and a disorganized pile of floor pillows against the windows. The tops of the windows were filled with the abstract stained-glass designs she loved to make and the colors seemed to sway around us as we moved. I watched, mesmerized, as my arms turned blue, then gold, then red. I loved dancing so much. At school, my friends and I were into the Electric Slide and the Running Man, but I really liked the freedom of Amalia's interpretive dance, moving however the music made me feel. How I felt today, though, was undeniably different than how I'd felt the last time I danced with her. I knew things about Amalia now that I hadn't known then.

The song ended and Amalia put on some Gregorian chants. We always warmed up to that quiet, eerie, echoey music, doing our slow stretches on her smooth wooden floor. She'd give instructions, although she called them "suggestions," since she really wanted me to do what felt right to me rather than be precise or rigid in my steps. "Put your weight on your front leg," she'd say. "Slide it to the side. Imagine a string attached to your breastbone, gently pulling you forward." When I was younger, I was impatient through the stretches, anxious to get to the dancing. But then she taught me to pay attention to my breath and to how every little movement felt in my body and how I felt inside as I moved. She slowed me down. She centered me. Today, though, as I sat on the floor across from her, leaning forward, reaching for my toes, I couldn't stop thinking about how different Amalia was from my mother. Everything Amalia did was slow and gentle and thoughtfully done. Everything my mother did was quick and precise and efficient. How had my father fallen in love with two such different women?

Ever since my talk with Daddy on Sunday, I'd been consumed by the oddness of our living situation. Something that had seemed so perfectly normal to me all my life now seemed bizarre, and, in a way I couldn't explain even to myself, dangerous. *We have no secrets*, Daddy had said about him and my mother. I wanted that to be the truth, and yet . . . would my mother truly have thought nothing of Amalia's head resting on his shoulder? Why couldn't I get that image out of my mind?

I looked across the room to where Amalia was spread-eagled on the floor, her chiffon skirt hiked up high on her white thighs, her upper body stretching forward, arms nearly flat on the floor, and that long thick brown hair fanned out in front of her. I saw her in a new way, now. I pictured her teaching

144

dancing at that "unorthodox" hospital. I imagined her falling in love with my father and the lovemaking that had created me. What must it have been like for Daddy when she suddenly disappeared? And what must it have been like for Mom when Amalia turned up on our doorstep with my father's baby?

Suddenly I had to speak.

"Daddy told me about meeting you and everything," I said.

She lifted her head in surprise, then raised her upper body slowly from the floor. "So long ago," she said dismissively. "Are you warmed up enough? Do you want to start fast or slow?"

All right, I thought. *I guess we're not talking about her and Daddy.*

"Slow," I said.

Colors from the stained glass passed over her body as she walked to the CD player. I stayed on the floor, waiting to hear what music she'd put on. The theme song from *Chariots of Fire.* I stood up and shut my eyes, swaying a little, waiting to see what feelings would come to me that I could express through dance, but nothing came. I started moving anyway, hoping the motion would inspire me, and although Amalia was

145

dancing herself, I was aware of her eyes on me.

"Molly," she said after a while. "Are you thinking too much today, baby? Try *feeling* instead."

How did she know? I wondered. How could she tell simply by the way I was moving that I was caught up in my thoughts?

"Here," she said, taking a few steps to the cabinet beneath the CD player. She opened it and pulled out a plastic bag. I knew what was in it. Rolls of crepe paper. They would help.

"Oh good," I said. I held out my hand and she reached into the bag and pulled out a roll of red crepe paper, handing it to me. I tore off a strip and handed the roll back to her. She took a strip for herself and we continued dancing, letting the crepe paper streamers wind and unwind around us. Letting them float through the air.

"Could I use some of that crepe paper to decorate Daddy's wheelchair for the midsummer party?" I asked, when the music had stopped.

"Oh sure." She motioned toward the bag where it rested on the floor as she headed back to the CD player. "You can take the whole bag."

"Do you want to help me decorate it?" I asked.

"I don't think so," she said as she sorted through the CDs on the bookshelf above the player. Then she suddenly stilled her hands and looked over at me. "You know I'm not going to the party, don't you?" she asked.

"Are you kidding?"

"I haven't been invited, and that's fine," she said. "I understand."

"What do you mean, you haven't been invited? Everyone's invited. It's automatic."

Amalia lowered her hands to her sides. "It's your grandmother, Molly," she said. "I really do understand where she's coming from. The party is for the family, and —"

"That's not true!" I said. "Lots of people outside the family are coming. My friend Stacy, for starters. Nanny invited her herself. And I know Peter and Helen are coming, and Janet, and they just work with Daddy. They don't have anything to do with the family. You're my *mother*. You have a massive connection to my family! You *are* my family."

"Baby." She smiled at me. "It's really all right."

"It's not like people got invitations in the mail or anything," I said. "Everybody knows about it. You're supposed to just show up."

Amalia bit her lip and I thought she was debating whether to tell me something or not. Finally she walked into her kitchen, and when she returned, she handed me a note. "This was on my door last week," she said.

Amalia, As you no doubt know, I'm throwing the midsummer soiree in a couple of weeks. I think it's best if you sit it out this year, dear. Nora is generous with you and shares so much with you. Let her have her family to herself this once. Yours truly, Bess Morrison Arnette

I knew anger at my grandmother was in my face when I looked up from the note.

"I'm fine with it," Amalia said quickly. "It's one night out of my life and she's right. Nora shares you with me every other day of the year."

"Well, *I'm* not fine with it." I sat down on one of the Papasan chairs, sinking into its big round pale blue cushion, my arms folded across my chest in a huff. "I can't believe she'd be such a bitch to you." I knew Nanny didn't like Amalia but she'd always hidden her feelings from me. Seeing her nastiness toward her in the note really galled me.

"Okay, then!" Amalia folded her arms across her own chest, mimicking me. "Looks like we need some angry music for you!" She turned her attention back to the shelf of CDs and rooted through them while I seethed. My grandmother was so wrong to exclude her. *Yours truly.* So wrong and so mean.

"How about this?" Amalia said as she inserted a disc into the player and in a moment Twisted Sister's "We're Not Gonna Take It" filled the room. I couldn't help myself: I laughed. She reached for my hands, pulled me to my feet, and in a moment we were stomping and jumping and punching the air.

I was out of breath by the time the song ended and Amalia put on the third movement of Rachmaninoff's second piano concerto, which was my favorite music to dance to and a complete change from Twisted Sister. She sat down in one of the Papasan chairs and folded her legs beneath her long skirt.

"Dance what you feel, Molly," she said.

I crouched down on the floor, unsure *what* I felt now. The anger was gone. I knew I could get it back in about two seconds, but

I didn't want it. Not with this beautiful music surrounding me. I thought of what Daddy had told me about Amalia showing up on our doorstep. How he'd been happy to learn I existed. How my mother had accepted me. How surrounded I felt by three people who loved me. I stood up slowly, unfurling like a flower. I let my arms fall open, encompassing the whole world, then brought them in close and I filled up with a kind of joy and peace. When I felt finished with my dance and looked at Amalia, she was smiling at me, her head tilted to the side, light from the windows flickering in her green eyes. She looked so beautiful. I smiled back at her.

"That was lovely," she said, getting to her feet. "I felt your sense of peace."

"You did?" I loved when I succeeded in expressing what I felt through the dance.

"Absolutely crystal clear," she said. "And I almost hate to ruin that mood with our finale, but really, it's our ritual. And we don't want to mess with a ritual, do we?"

"No way," I agreed, watching as she pressed a couple of buttons on the CD player. "Footloose" poured out of the speakers, bringing an instant smile to my lips. I couldn't hold still when that song came on. Neither of us could. We danced around the house, swirling and swaying, feeling joyful, and I forgot every other emotion that had come before.

But when I went out to my bike and began riding home, I thought about Nanny again. I would be with her tonight while that family meeting took place at my house. I would talk to her. I'd tell her I wanted both my mothers to come to the party. Nanny had never been any good at turning me down.

15

I was late getting out of the house that night because I was talking to Stacy on the phone.

"Bryan has this friend, Chris Turner," she said. "Bryan showed him your picture in the yearbook and Chris thinks you're really cute and wants to meet you!"

My picture in our middle-school yearbook was hideous. I'd taken my glasses off for the picture, but somehow I ended up looking cross-eyed and my smile was crooked, as though part of me thought I should wear an overjoyed expression but the rest of me wasn't so sure. If this guy really thought I was cute, there must have been something wrong with him. Still, her words excited me.

"My parents won't let me go out with a seventeen-year-old, though," I said.

"They never have to know," she said.

I felt a shiver and had that feeling I always got when I spoke to Stacy. That strange, enticed, and a little bit jealous feeling. She lived in a different sort of world than I did. A freer world. I wanted some of that freedom.

I started to speak again. "But how would we work it —"

"Molly!" my mother called up the stairs. "It's five of seven. Time to get going."

"I have to go," I said to Stacy.

"Where to?"

"My grandmother's. There's a family meeting here and I'm escaping to Nanny's instead."

"Well, I'll be plotting a way to get you and Chris together, all right?"

A thrill of excitement ran through me at the thought of actually meeting a boy who said I was cute.

"Cool," I said.

Russell was lifting my father from his wheelchair to the recliner when I walked into the living room, and I guessed that was where Daddy planned to sit for the meeting. The house smelled of my mother's chocolate walnut fudge, and my mouth watered at the aroma.

Russell tugged at the legs of my father's jeans, which had ridden up above his socks during the move from chair to recliner. "Mom has the tape for you." Daddy looked past Russell toward me. "It's just the first part of the session, but you don't want to bore Nanny out of her mind, so I'll watch the rest of it with you some other time, all right?"

"Okay," I said. I knew he wanted me to watch an actual Pretend Therapy session before I went on his book tour with him. I didn't think I needed to. After all, I'd been living with a pretend therapist my whole life.

Mom poked her head into the room from the kitchen. "Get going, Molly," she said. "Nanny's expecting you at seven and it's almost that now."

"Kiss before you go?" Daddy looked up at me where I stood next to the recliner.

"It's not like I'm going across the country," I said, surprised by the request, but I leaned over and gave him a kiss on the cheek, my arms around his neck.

"Love you, darling." He smiled at me when I straightened up.

"You, too," I said.

I heard voices in the kitchen and when I walked into the room to get the tape from my mother, Aunt Claudia and Uncle Jim and Dani stood near the back door. Aunt Claudia and Uncle Jim were talking to Mom, while Dani leaned against the wall

154

looking bored. I was surprised to see her there. I felt jealous that, at seventeen, she was considered adult enough to take part in a family meeting and, at fourteen, I was not. At the same time, I felt sorry for her that she'd have to somehow survive whatever sleep-inducing topics came up.

"I didn't think you were going to be here," Dani said to me. The beady red snake eyes in her lip ring glowed in the overhead light.

"I'm not," I said. "I'm going over to Nanny's."

"Here you go!" My mother handed me the tape.

"Can I take some of the fudge to Nanny's?" I asked.

She hesitated a moment, then gave in. "Oh sure," she said. "There's plenty."

"Here, I'll cut you some." Aunt Claudia headed for the big kitchen table where two pans of fudge sat cooling. She carried a plate of cookies which she set down next to the pans. "You can take a few of my peanut butter cookies with you, too." She smiled at me with her big round pumpkin face. "Then you'll have all the food groups covered." My mother handed her a knife and she began cutting the fudge.

"Hello!"

I turned to see Amalia walk into the

kitchen.

Mom had moved to the coffeemaker and was now scooping beans into the grinder at the top, but she looked up when Amalia walked into the room. "Hi, Amalia," she said.

"Smells lovely and chocolaty in here, Nora," Amalia said. Then she caught sight of me, a look of surprise on her face. "I didn't think you were going to be here, Molly," she said.

"I'm leaving," I said. "As soon as I get some fudge to take to Nanny's."

"Can I help with anything?" Amalia asked.

"You could put the kettle on for tea," my mother said, pouring water into the coffeemaker.

I watched the two of them, searching their faces for a hint of that tension Daddy said existed between them. They weren't exactly embracing each other like long-lost sisters, but I didn't pick up any glaring animosity. I didn't think I ever had.

Aunt Claudia put the fudge and cookies in a small white paper sack and handed it to me. "Have fun at Nanny's," she said.

"Russell will pick you up at eleven," Mom said as she pulled cups from the cabinet above the coffeemaker.

"All right," I said. "Bye!"

It was still light outside, the air balmy and fragrant, and the cicadas were starting to sing. As I walked across our wooded lot, a blue car pulled into the driveway. I didn't recognize it until it came to a stop and Daddy's office mate Janet got out of the backseat, while Peter and his wife, Helen, got out of the front. Peter and Helen could have been mistaken for any forty-something-year-old couple. They were about the same height and they wore khaki pants and T-shirts — Peter's blue and Helen's gold — and they both had hair the same shade of brown. Janet, on the other hand, stood out as she always did. She waved to me.

"Hey, Molly girl!" she called, and I walked over to the car. "Where're you off to?" she asked. Janet wore wigs and she didn't seem to care who knew it. Every time I saw her, she had different hair. Tonight she wore really curly reddish-blond hair that fell to her shoulders and looked amazing against her dark skin. She looked like Whitney Houston in that wig.

"My grandmother's," I said.

"Ah." Janet glanced at Peter.

"Bess isn't coming to the meeting?" Peter asked me, and I shook my head.

"I smell chocolate," Helen said, and I opened the bag to let her see the fudge.

157

"There's lots more inside," I said. "And Aunt Claudia brought peanut butter cookies."

Peter nodded toward the tape in my hand. "You and Bess going to watch a movie tonight?" he asked.

"Probably, but this is one of Daddy's therapy sessions."

"Ah, where he pretends to do therapy?" The look on Peter's face was more of a smirk than a smile. Helen poked him in the ribs with her elbow and Janet rolled her eyes.

"A little professional jealousy going on here," she said to me. "Don't pay him any mind."

I was fairly certain what she meant. Peter had written a book, too, but had never been able to get it published.

"I've got to go," I said. I was going to be a good twenty minutes late to Nanny's.

They waved good-bye to me, and I started walking toward the loop road, and it wasn't until I'd reached the Hill from Hell that I wondered what Janet and Peter and Helen were doing at a meeting of my family.

16
SAN DIEGO

There is a teeny-tiny crack in my marriage. It's barely perceptible right now. As a matter of fact, I'm not sure Aidan knows it's there, but I do. Two months have passed since that group meeting at Hope Springs and our discussion in the car about open adoption. In the few days following that talk, I became aware of the crack. I saw it whenever Aidan mentioned that happy family of four. If I referred to them that way, my voice the teensiest bit sarcastic, it would upset him, so I bit my own tongue, not wanting to argue with him about it. I would simply have to hope and pray we found a birth mother who didn't want that level of involvement.

The crack worries me. The last thing I want is our hope for a baby to pull us apart. We're supposed to be working together right now. More than ever, we need to be on the same team.

The call we've both been waiting for comes when I'm at work and I recognize Zoe's voice right away. "Guess what, Molly?" she says. "A birth mom is interested in you and Aidan!"

"Already?" I ask. "It's only been a couple of months."

She is quiet for a moment and I know right away my response is wrong. I have the feeling my shock came across as disappointment at being matched so soon.

"Well, she's looking at a couple of other families, too," Zoe says, "but she would really like to speak with you and Aidan. She said she fell in love with you through your profile."

She fell in love with us. Instantly, I love her back, whoever she is. "Aidan's out of town at a conference all week." I wince. I sound as though I'm throwing obstacles into the works. "But I can talk to her," I add. "I'd *love* to talk to her. When is she due?"

"Three months," she says.

"You mean she's three months along or —"

"No, she's due in three months."

Oh my God. Okay. Deep breath.

"What else can you tell me about her?" I ask.

"Well, she — her name is Sienna — she's

seventeen. The birth father — his name is Dillon — is the same age and they're no longer in a relationship and he's willing to relinquish his rights. Sienna's in a special program for pregnant girls at her school. She's in her junior year and really wants to finish. She lives with her mother and younger brother." She hesitates. "I'd like *her* to be the one to tell you more about herself," she says. "Can you talk with her tonight?"

Tonight is my night at the women's shelter, but I'm afraid to throw out one more obstacle that might make Zoe think I'm not excited or grateful. "Yes," I say. "Absolutely. I can't wait!"

"You're kidding!" Aidan says when I call him. "Already?" I can hear the smile in his voice. "It was that dynamite 'dear expecting mother' letter we wrote. We are so awesome!"

I laugh. In my mind's eye, I see the crack healing. We are going to be fine. Freak-out moments have to be normal in this situation.

"Do you want me to see if she can wait until you're back in town to talk to both of us on the phone?" I ask.

"No, no. Let's not give her the chance to

161

'fall in love' with another couple. You talk to her. You're better at that sort of thing than I am, anyhow. Two women. It's always better."

"You're selling yourself short," I say. Aidan can talk to almost anyone with ease.

"What's her name?"

"Sienna."

"Oh, great name," he says. "I like that name." He talks quickly. He's so excited. "How far along is she?"

"She's due in three months," I say.

"Holy shit!"

"I know."

"Just . . ." he says. "Don't grill her, okay?"

"Of course I won't grill her!"

"Well, sometimes your lawyer side comes out in social situations and —"

"It does?"

"Occasionally," he says. "You can be intimidating. And you don't want to intimidate her. Be nice."

"Of course." I'm getting annoyed.

"Has she been getting prenatal care?"

"I . . . well, she knows how far along she is, so I guess so."

"I think you should keep your opinions about things to yourself," he says. "I mean, like politics and . . . just little things, like what movies you like and —"

162

"Aidan," I say, "what are you talking about?"

"What if you say you love *Mad Men* and she hates *Mad Men*? It's not worth risking losing her over something silly like that."

"Sweetheart." I smile. He is wound up and I realize I'm not alone in being nervous about this whole thing. I like feeling like the calm one for a change. "I'll be fine," I say. "And I'll call you the second I get off the phone with her, all right?"

I am to call her at seven-thirty. When I get home, I pour myself a bowl of cereal for dinner but I'm too anxious to eat it. Instead, I walk down the hall and open the door to the nursery. I haven't been inside that room since showing it to Perky Patti during our home study. I turn on the light and stand in the doorway, looking at the empty crib. The longing for a baby fills me up in a way I haven't allowed in a long time. It's so strong it nearly knocks me over and I lean against the doorjamb to stay upright. *Oh my God,* I want a child! The realization is such a relief to me. I truly, truly do. Yet when I look down at the floor, I see that I have one foot inside the nursery, and the other firmly planted in the hall.

17
MORRISON RIDGE

"Molly," Nanny said when I walked into her living room, and she wrapped her arms around me as though she hadn't seen me in a year rather than a few days. She seemed to have trouble letting go of me, but she finally did. "I'm so glad you'll spend the evening with me!" She still held on to my left arm. "Come with me," she said. "I want to show you something." She took my hand in her cool one, her skin silky smooth beneath my fingers. "I was hoping you'd get here before they ran off," she said.

"Before who ran off?" I asked, setting the bag of fudge and cookies on the coffee table as I passed it.

"You'll see."

We'd reached the back door and she let go of me and raised a finger to her lips as she quietly pulled the door open. We walked across her screened porch and out into the yard. Nanny's backyard was a sea of thick grass surrounded by fat, healthy-looking rhododendrons. In the evening light, the grass was a deep rich green, and in the distance, I could see the massive pavilion where, in a couple of weeks, we'd have the midsummer party. The fireworks would be visible from where we stood.

She took my arm to stop my walking, then pointed toward the rhododendrons on our right. "There," she whispered.

Between two broad shrubs grazed a doe and three spotted fawns. I caught my breath.

"*Three* of them?" I asked.

"Triplets," she said. "I've never seen triplets before. I've heard it's a sign of a healthy herd." She sounded proud, as though she was personally responsible for the health of the dozens of deer that roamed Morrison Ridge.

"They're so cute," I said.

"I put a salt lick out for them. Don't tell your uncle Trevor. He'll bring his bow."

"I won't."

"I could watch the deer all day long," she said. Then she sighed. She seemed tired to me tonight.

I looked toward the pavilion again, picturing it crowded with happy people and tons of food and loud music, too far from any neighbors to bother them. I could imagine the scene vividly. It was crazy that Amalia would not be allowed to be part of it.

"Nanny," I said, "I'd really like Amalia to be able to come to the party."

Nanny kept her gaze on the deer, but her eyebrows lifted in what I guessed was surprise. "That's settled, Molly," she said quietly, and I knew she didn't want to disturb the deer. "Amalia understands."

"But *I* don't understand." I struggled to keep my own voice low. "I know you think Mom would be uncomfortable or something, but I'm a hundred percent sure she wouldn't have a problem with it. Amalia's over at our house right this minute," I added. "They're *fine* together," I said. "They've always been fine together."

Nanny smiled at me. "You're so young, Molly." She smoothed my hair away from my cheek. "I know it's hard for you to understand what it's really been like for your mother."

"Daddy said she's been totally okay about Amalia." That wasn't exactly what he'd said, I knew, but I continued. "Mom wanted Amalia to live here so I'd have them both," I said. "And I *love* them both."

Nanny looked at me without speaking and I took that opportunity to add, "I think I should get to have a say in who comes."

Nanny sighed again, then gnawed her lower lip. "Yes, I suppose you should," she said finally.

"Really?" I couldn't mask my surprise. I felt suddenly powerful. "She can come?"

Nanny nodded. "I'll write her a note to tell her I've reconsidered," she said. "If she wants to be there, she can come."

I turned to hug her. "Thank you!" I said, too loudly. The doe and her babies raised their heads, flicked their tails, and ran off toward the woods.

Nanny's house was an enigma. From the outside, it looked like a rich old woman's house, with its red brick and white pillars and manicured lawn. Inside, though, it looked more like a hunter's cabin. The mantel was a thick slab of wood and on the wall above it hung the head of a ten-point buck my grandfather had shot. The furniture was upholstered in plaid and brown and green, and the arms of the heavy chairs were thick and masculine. Nanny fit right into her house. Tonight, she wore jeans and a long-sleeved shirt with a button-down collar and her gray hair was in its usual swingy bob. She was simply not like any other grandmother I'd ever met.

In the kitchen, Nanny took the fudge and

167

cookies from the paper bag and placed them neatly on a heavy stoneware plate, while I poured us glasses of Pepsi. "So," she said as she pulled a few napkins from the basket on the table, "what movie do you want to watch tonight?"

"You can pick," I said, "but Daddy wants me to watch this tape of part of one of his sessions first, okay? It's really short," I said. "Then we can watch one of your movies." Nanny was a movie buff. She had a bookcase filled with tapes. She loved the really old ones like *The African Queen* — anything with Katharine Hepburn in it, actually — but we bought her new ones for every birthday or simply because we wanted to see them.

Nanny didn't seem to hear my question about the movie, and as we carried the sodas and desserts out of the kitchen, she was distracted, turning right toward the living room before she caught herself and made a left toward the den and the TV. I thought there was a weight hanging over her and wondered if she knew they were talking about Uncle Trevor's ideas for the land. Maybe that was why she didn't want to be at the meeting tonight.

"Nanny," I said when we'd set our glasses and the plate down on the coffee table in the den. There was another buck head in this room. It was smaller than the one in the living room and hung on the wall above the television. "How come you're not at the family meeting tonight?" I asked. "I think Uncle Trevor's going to try to get everyone on his side about developing the land. Maybe you should be there."

Her cheeks suddenly flushed red. "I don't know how a son of mine can be so callous about his family land," she said as she sat down on the sofa. "He was raised better than that. Can you picture our beautiful hillsides covered with paved streets of identical ticky-tacky houses, people right on top of one another? Strangers who know nothing about the Ridge and could care less?" She picked up a piece of fudge, then set it down again. "He's gotten so greedy!" She shook her head. "And his children! When Samantha and Cal picked up and moved to Colorado, it was a knife in my heart, Molly." She stared at me and I nodded, wishing I hadn't brought the subject up. "And he just let them go. It's their generation that's supposed to carry on Morrison Ridge and its traditions."

"I know," I said, more to soothe her than to agree with her.

"Danielle has a foot out the door, you can

see that, right?" Nanny said. "It's going to be up to you, I'm afraid. You need to have lots of children and keep Morrison Ridge alive."

I laughed, unable to picture what I was going to do tomorrow, much less imagine myself getting married and having a bunch of kids. Her cheeks still had red coins of color on them and I wished I could roll back time to when we were in the kitchen. I wouldn't say a word about the meeting. I still didn't understand why she wasn't there. She should be talking about her feelings to everyone at the meeting, where it could do some good, instead of to me, who couldn't do a thing about it.

"Put on your tape," she said suddenly. "I don't want to think about the ticky-tacky houses any longer." She reached for a piece of fudge, then kicked off her sandals and rested her feet against the edge of the coffee table, getting comfortable.

I stood up to put Daddy's tape in the VCR. There was a tape already in the machine and I hit the eject button. "Were you watching a movie?" I asked.

"What?" She sounded confused. "Oh, not a movie."

I pulled out the tape and looked at the handwritten label. *Graham and Nora, wed-*

ding dance. "Oh my gosh." I turned to her. "Is this from Mom and Daddy's wedding?"

"Just their first dance." Nanny suddenly stood up and took the tape from my hand. She bent over to set it on the lower shelf of the TV stand. "Go ahead and put yours in," she said.

I put Daddy's tape in the VCR and sat down at the other end of the couch from Nanny. I recognized Daddy's Asheville office on the screen. A girl sat in one of the three leather chairs, but I didn't get a good look at her because the camera swung around to face my father. The tape must have been from at least two years ago, because he was sitting in his desk chair like he used to and he was able to lift his right hand a bit as he spoke to the camera. He explained that he had the permission of his patient and her parents to allow others to view the tape, but that he would call the girl Dorianna, which was not her real name.

"He can still move his hand like that, can't he, Molly?" Nanny asked.

"Not really," I said, which sounded better than "no way." Nanny didn't say anything and I bit my lip. I should have said he could move it "a little." White lies were not all that terrible to tell.

The camera filmed the session at an angle,

171

so that we saw my father in profile but Dorianna from the front. I felt proud as I watched him talk to her. Proud and, to be honest, jealous. Dorianna — or whatever her name was — was a few years younger than me and I couldn't help but feel some envy at how he was talking to her. I was used to being the only important child in his life. I could tell he was making Dorianna feel important, too.

I quickly gathered that Dorianna's problem was a crippling shyness. I knew kids like her. They were invisible to most people, but Daddy had taught me to see them. To be nice to them. *They will surprise you with their value,* he'd said.

"Some of the most important and creative people in our history were shy," Daddy said to the girl. "Abraham Lincoln, Elvis Presley, Albert Einstein, Johnny Depp."

I laughed. "He added Johnny Depp for me," I said. I hadn't realized I'd had a thing for Johnny Depp for that long.

"Who's that?" Nanny asked.

"Tell you later."

Daddy also had lists of famous people who were dyslexic or had anger issues or were autistic like the Dustin Hoffman character in *Rain Man.* He had a list for anyone who walked in his office door.

Dorianna looked heartened by my father's list of names, but then she described how painful school was for her because of her shyness, and tears filled her eyes.

"Oh, now he made her cry," Nanny said.

"Sometimes that's a good thing," I said. "It means she's really into the session. She's engaged."

"Where'd you learn so much?"

I shrugged. "He teaches me things."

Nanny's smile was sad. *"Oh, Molly,"* she said.

"What's the matter?" I asked.

"Nothing," she said, then added, "It just breaks my heart, how he suffers."

"He does okay," I reassured her. I never heard my father complain.

We watched the rest of the tape. Daddy set up exercises with Dorianna to help her pretend away her shyness, but the screen went black before we could see the results.

"Oh no," Nanny said. "Is that the end?"

"There's a part two," I said, "and I'm sure it worked. He wouldn't have picked a case that didn't. That girl is probably homecoming queen by now."

"He can change someone that quickly?"

I nibbled a piece of fudge, slouching on the sofa, my bare feet up on the coffee table, same as Nanny's. "He wouldn't say *he*'s changing them. He'd say they're changing themselves." I took another bite of fudge. "You know Peter?" I asked.

"The other therapist he works with?"

"Right. He says Daddy's losing money because he works too fast. He says Daddy should treat the underlying cause of her shyness, which could take months or even years, but Daddy thinks the underlying cause usually doesn't matter and that most problems can be treated quickly."

"Hm." Nanny looked at the ceiling. "I've never understood his Pretend Therapy, really."

"You should read the book he wrote for kids, Nanny. It's really simple."

"Are you calling me simple?" She smiled at me and I was relieved to see that her odd mood seemed to have lifted.

"Never," I said, getting to my feet. I hit the eject button on the VCR. "So what should we watch now?" I asked.

Nanny hesitated a moment, her gaze moving to the bottom shelf of the TV stand. "Put the dance one in, Molly," she said. "The one from your parents' wedding. I want you to see it."

I was surprised. A few minutes ago, she was practically hiding it from me. I picked it up from the bottom shelf.

"I had the old film made into a VHS tape," Nanny said. "It's a little blurry and only three or four minutes long. Plus there's no sound. They didn't have sound back in those days. But it's good enough."

I put it into the machine, then went back and sat on the sofa next to her. I'd seen pictures from their wedding, of course. There was a beautiful photograph on the sideboard in our dining room. My mother in her long white wedding dress. Daddy standing behind her, his arms around her waist. Both of them smiling and looking so much younger than they did today. But those photographs didn't prepare me for what I saw when the tape started to run. It didn't prepare me to see my father dance.

They moved to music I couldn't hear. Unbelievable. I felt strangely wooden, watching them. In shock. The tape was just blurry enough that I could imagine it was not my father at all. Who was that man with the long dark hair that brushed his shoulders as he twirled my mother around? As he pulled her body tightly against his, then spun her away?

I got up from the couch and sat down on the floor in front of the television to see them better. "What's the music?" I asked.

"Oh, I don't remember," Nanny said. "A

shame there's no sound."

They looked as though they danced together every day of their lives, their steps fluid, their eyes locked on one another, their smiles so, so genuine. I'd been wrong to worry that Daddy might have loved Amalia more than my mother.

"Thank goodness he found Nora," Nanny said as we watched. "So straight and steadfast. She grounded him, and if your daddy needed anything, it was grounding." She chuckled. "He kept his strong family values when it came to choosing a wife."

Was that a dig at Amalia? I didn't know. There was so much I didn't know.

The tape ended abruptly and I turned to look at Nanny. "It's crazy how fast he got sick," I said.

"He was already sick then, when they got married," Nanny said.

"I know," I said. "He told me. But he looked so good. So healthy."

"He had that one good dance in him at the reception," she said. "I think he was so happy that day, his body forgot about being sick." She stared at the TV screen as though the tape was still playing. "Nora knew, of course, but I don't think any of us thought it would move so quickly and get so terrible. I look at that tape and weep, Molly," she said, turning her gaze to me. "His life is so hard now and he's so depressed."

Depressed? I thought of how much my father loved his work and writing his books. I thought of how much he loved *me*. "I don't think he's depressed, Nanny," I said.

"He's very good at hiding his misery," she said.

"He's *not* miserable," I argued. "Ask him. I bet he'd laugh if he could hear you talk like that."

She waved a hand through the air as if dismissing the whole conversation. "Oh, I'm just talking like a mother, I suppose," she said. "An old woman, worrying about her grown son."

"He never complains or anything," I said.

She gave me a long strange stare. "Molly, Molly, Molly," she said finally, followed by a great sigh. "I think we should watch a movie, don't you? Better than listening to me ramble. You pick out a movie or else I'll do it and you know you'll end up with Kate Hepburn again. How about Hitchcock?"

As I stood up and walked over to the bookcase filled with her movies, I was suddenly filled with sadness myself. Was my father truly miserable? Was I so wrapped up in my own life that I didn't even notice his unhappiness?

18

At eleven, Russell came to the door to pick me up. To "carry me home," as he would say. I sat up front with him in the van.

"What did you watch?" he asked when he turned onto the loop road in the darkness.

"Rear Window," I said. "Have you seen it?"

"Jimmy Stewart, right? Hitchcock?"

"Right." *Rear Window* was one of my favorite movies, yet my concentration had been off tonight. I kept picturing my parents spinning around on the dance floor. What had it been like for my father to lose the use of his body, bit by bit? I was still upset by what Nanny said about him being depressed. I felt like a cold, unfeeling girl to not even notice that he was that unhappy.

The thin crescent moon was partially hidden behind thick clouds, and Russell put on his brights and drove slowly along the dirt loop road. I could see the turnoff to Amalia's coming up on our left.

"Russell," I said, "does it bother you when we call Amalia's house 'the slave quarters'?"

I could barely see his face in the dark interior of the van, but I thought I saw the white flash of his smile. "Since you ask," he said, "yes it does. Your daddy never calls it that, you notice. Nor your mama. Nor Amalia herself."

"Where'd I learn to call it that?" I asked, perplexed, because I thought he was right. Mom and Daddy never did use those words.

"Oh, I'm not one for naming names." He chuckled.

Nanny, I thought. My aunts and uncles and cousins.

"I'm sorry," I said. "I won't call it that any longer."

"Appreciate it." He turned to face me and this time I was sure of his smile. He looked at the road again. "I came up in some so-called slave quarters," he said.

"What do you mean?"

"Log cabin outside of Hendersonville."

"That's where your family is." I'd heard him mention Hendersonville before.

"Right. There weren't a lot of slaves in western North Carolina because there wasn't all that much farming," he said, "but my great-great-great-granddaddy was one of six owned by a wealthy man in Hendersonville. They were mostly house and stable slaves, and he was the best treated." He glanced at me. "Can you guess why?"

" 'Cause he was the best at his job?"

Russell laughed. "I don't think that was it." He chuckled to himself another few seconds before speaking again. "Story has it," he said finally, "he was the son of the master."

"Son of the . . . ? Oh," I said. "Wow."

"They taught him to read and write, which was against the law, actually, but was fortunate for those of us who came along after him, since we all understood the importance of getting an education. When my great-great-great-granddaddy was freed, the master turned the slave quarters and thirty acres over to him. So we have a home place there, just like you have here, only smaller. My mama and sisters and aunties and one uncle are all there. I came up in one of the cabins." He glanced at me again. "We never called it the 'slave quarters' though," he said. "We called it home."

I tried to picture Russell growing up on a Morrison Ridge–type place all his own. "Your great-great-great-grandfather was really lucky," I said, wondering how the other slaves were treated.

"Yes, he was," Russell said, then added,

"His mama, probably not so much."

It took me a minute to understand what he meant, and I didn't know what to say when I finally figured it out. We'd come to the Hill from Hell, and Russell put the van in low gear. I waited until we reached the bottom to change the subject to the one that was weighing heavily on my mind.

"Do you think my father is happy?" I asked.

"Happy?" He sounded surprised by the question. "Why would you ask that?"

"Something Nanny said made me think about it. She said he's depressed and . . . I just never noticed that about him and I thought maybe he hides it from me or something."

Russell was quiet, his hands opening and closing on the steering wheel. I didn't like his silence. I wanted him to tell me that my father was perfectly content with his life. Instead, for the longest time, he said nothing.

I was about to ask the question again when he finally spoke. "Your daddy has a hard row to hoe, Molly," he said as he pulled into our driveway and turned off the engine. "Let's just do all we can to make his life enjoyable." Then he looked over at me. "You're the one person who brings him

181

the most happiness, Molly," he said. "Don't you forget that."

The meeting had been over for a while when Russell and I walked in the front door of the house. Everyone was gone and I could hear Daddy singing in his bedroom. He used to sing a lot, just random tunes as he wheeled around the house, but I realized it had been a long time since I'd heard him sing. He was belting out the Eagles' "Take It to the Limit." I looked at Russell who smiled at me.

"He's one of a kind," he said.

I heard Mom cleaning up in the kitchen as I headed for their bedroom. Daddy lay on the bed, his head propped up on a couple of pillows, his body still, as always. He stopped singing mid-sentence when I walked in the room.

"Hey, Moll!" he said. He nodded toward the narrow space between his body and the edge of the mattress, and I sat down — carefully. Once, a couple of years ago, I'd sat right on his urine bag, creating a giant mess for Russell to clean up. "How'd you make out at Nanny's?" he asked.

"Good," I said. "We watched the Dorianna tape and a movie." I wouldn't mention the tape of him dancing. "How'd things

182

turn out with Dorianna?" I asked.

"Brilliantly," he said. "She was a skillful pretender. Shy kids often are, since they spend so much time inside their heads to begin with. What movie did you watch?"

"Rear Window."

"Ah, great film! I've always liked that one because the Jimmy Stewart character is disabled. At least, partially. Yet his disability doesn't render him helpless."

"Right," I agreed.

"Then there's what Hitchcock is saying about marriage." Daddy raised his eyebrows. "And of course, there's the whole feminist perspective on the Grace Kelly character."

I groaned. "You have a way of picking things apart so much that you sap all the fun out of them," I said.

"Oh, I do, do I?" He laughed. "Your mom looks a bit like her, don't you think?"

"Like who? Like Grace Kelly?" I asked, incredulous, but I caught myself before I laughed. Stacy'd told me the biggest erogenous zone was the brain. Maybe that was the only place my father could have sex anymore — in his brain — and if he needed to see Grace Kelly when he looked at my mom, I wasn't going to ruin his fantasy. "A little," I agreed. I folded my hands in my lap. "So, how did the meeting go?" I asked.

"The meeting was . . . rejuvenating." He smiled. He *did* seem rejuvenated.

"How come Janet and Peter and Helen were here?" I asked.

"Oh, you know," he said. "It can be good to have an outside brain or two in the room to mediate sometimes."

"So, Uncle Trevor changed his mind about selling the land?" I asked.

"Well, Trevor is still basically being an asshole, but let's not think about that right now. Lie down here and sing with me, all right?" He nodded toward Mom's side of the bed. "Pick an Eagles song and you do the harmony."

It had been a long time since we sang together. We did it a lot when I was younger. I climbed over him and flopped down on my mother's side of the bed. " 'Lyin' Eyes,' " I said.

"All those verses!" he said. "I bet you five bucks you won't remember all the words." He'd been doing this since I was a kid — betting me I couldn't do something that he knew perfectly well I could do. It made me feel like I was about eight years old, but I wanted to please him tonight so I would go along with it.

"You're on," I said, and I started us out

184

with the first verse. We sang every verse and I waved my arms in the air each time the chorus came along. I messed up the words a few times, but so did he.

"Good job," he said when the song was over. "I'll ask Mom to give you a five tomorrow."

"Okay," I said, happily looking at the ceiling above us. He was in such a great mood that I knew Nanny was worrying about nothing. I wished she could see him right now. It would ease her mind.

"What do you think of the woman in 'Lyin' Eyes'?" Daddy asked. "She leaves her husband for her old boyfriend, but then she's still not happy."

"She's a slut," I said simply.

"Hm. A tad harsh, don't you think? What motivates her?"

I thought about the lyrics. "She's married to a man with hands as cold as ice," I said. Then I rolled onto my side and smacked him playfully on the shoulder. "You're doing it again!" I said. "Picking something apart. It's only a song. Can't you just enjoy it for what it is?"

He turned his head to look at me and his serious expression surprised me. "You're right, Molly girl," he said. "Life's too short to pick it all apart. I'll try to do better."

"Molly, what are you still doing up?" Mom said as she walked into the room carrying a stack of my father's folded T-shirts.

"We were singing," I said.

"So I heard." She pulled open the top dresser drawer and lowered the T-shirts inside it. "But you need to go to bed, now," she said. "It's after midnight."

"After all these years, Nora, I finally figured out who you remind me of," Daddy said.

She shut the dresser drawer and turned to face him "Who?" she asked.

"Grace Kelly," Daddy said.

Mom laughed. She hit his foot lightly through the blanket, then tucked a lock of her blond hair behind her ear and suddenly she *did* remind me a little of Grace Kelly. She smiled at my father and they exchanged a look that I was no part of. I shouldn't even have witnessed that look.

"I'm going to bed," I said, rolling off her side of the bed. I stood up and headed past her toward the door.

"Sleep tight," she said, and she sounded a thousand miles away from me.

"Night, darling," Daddy said, but he never moved his gaze from my mother's face.

19
SAN DIEGO

Sienna answers the phone and I'm instantly struck by the tenor of her voice when she says hello. Her voice is pitched low, reminding me of the actress Julia Stiles and making her sound older than seventeen. I think of Amalia who was twenty-one or twenty-two when she was pregnant with me. In my mind, I have a pregnant young Amalia on the phone and I feel those same twisty-turny feelings of love and anger that always accompany my thoughts about my own birth mother.

Ridiculous, I think. *She's a stranger. A seventeen-year-old stranger.*

"My husband and I are so happy you want to talk with us, Sienna," I say. "I know you're talking with a couple of other families as well, and —"

"I already talked to them," she says. "It didn't go so well."

My spirits rise a little. I'm dying to ask

why her conversations with the other families "didn't go so well" so I don't make whatever mistakes they made, but I think better of it.

"It must be nerve-racking talking to people when there's so much at stake," I say. "I know I'm a little nervous making this call myself."

She says nothing for so long, I'm afraid she's hung up. Then I realize she's crying.

"Sienna?" I prod. "Are you all right?"

"Yes," she manages to say.

"This is really hard, huh?"

"Really."

"Can you tell me about it? About how you feel?" I remember Zoe saying that we should keep things light in our initial conversations with a birth mother. Talk about things we like to do. Talk about the weather. Don't just dive into the heart of the adoption. But here we are.

She is sniffling. I bite my lip as I wait. Her voice may be deep and adult, but her crying is that of a little girl and my heart breaks for her.

"Just . . ." she begins, "just that I want to be sure I find a really perfect place for my baby. I screwed up by getting pregnant and now I owe it to her to make sure she has a good home. A perfect home."

Her. It's a girl! I can't wait to talk to Aidan. "I don't think there is any such thing as a perfect home, Sienna," I say slowly. "But there are certainly good homes and I think my husband and I can offer that to your baby. Would you like to ask any questions about us?"

"No. I mean, I got it all from your portfolio. I like how you already have a little girl so she'd have a sister. And that you have a dog. I always wanted a dog but —"

"Sienna?" I stop her, my heart sinking. "I think you might have our profile mixed up with someone else's. We don't have a little girl. Or a dog. Though we might get a dog." We'd never talked about it, but I would happily get a dog if it meant also getting a baby.

"You're kidding," she says. I hear her rustling papers on her end of the line. "What's your name again?"

"I'm Molly," I say. "My husband's Aidan."

"Oh shit. I get these all mixed up."

I shut my eyes. I'm afraid I'm going to cry as well. I feel suddenly, fiercely competitive with that couple who has the little girl and the dog. *What's best for the baby,* I remind myself. "Well, why don't we talk for a while anyway. You must have picked our profile, too, so —"

"Yeah, okay, I just found yours. I liked

189

yours, too. I liked those twin boys."

"Right! That's us. The twins are our nephews. Aren't they adorable?"

"Yeah." She's smiling now. I can hear it and I feel encouraged. "They look really happy. I think you said they live close by?"

"Just a few miles away. Your baby would get to see them all the time. They'd grow up together as cousins."

"Cool," she says.

Silence falls between us and my mind goes blank. I'm still shaken by the mix-up. I scramble for something to say.

"How are you feeling?" I ask. "Has it been an easy pregnancy?"

"I was sick a lot in the beginning but now it's just . . . I'm tired of being so fat. I just want it to be over."

"Yes, I can imagine," I say. I never got to the point of feeling fat when I was pregnant with Sara. I wish I had. "I think you're really brave," I say. "You made a hard choice to have the baby and now a hard choice to place it with a family who can give it — give her — a wonderful life."

That silence again. "My friends at school say I'm making a huge mistake," she says finally.

"Why do they say that?"

"I go to this class with girls who are

190

pregnant or who already had babies," she says. "I'm the only one who's giving her baby up."

I'm glad now for the language of open adoption. "I don't think of it as giving her up," I say. "I think of it as finding the right home for her. You'll be giving her the things you feel unable to give her yourself right now."

"Yeah, but they say I must not love her if I give her . . . if I adopt her out. But I do. I really do."

"I think you must love her a lot to make such a hard choice for her."

"Exactly."

We're both quiet and I'm not sure what to say next. I don't like this. I don't like the sense of coercion I feel in trying to pick the right words that will make her like me.

"Can you tell me about your baby's father?" I ask.

"He's an asshole," she says.

"Oh. I'm sorry. Were you together long?"

"I don't want to talk about him."

Time to shift gears, I think. "Would you like to meet in person, Sienna?" I offer. "My husband gets home from a business trip on Friday. We could meet for lunch on Saturday if that would work for you."

She hesitates. I hear the rustling of paper

again and worry she's checking her calendar. Maybe squeezing us in between meetings with other adoptive couples. That couple with the dog, for example. "That'll be good," she says.

"Oh, that's wonderful. You're in Leucadia, right? Is there a restaurant you know of where you'd like to meet?"

She names a place I've never heard of. I give her my e-mail address and our phone number. "Please e-mail me if you have any questions, and I'll give you a call Friday evening to firm up our plans for Saturday, okay?"

"Okay," she says, then adds. "I just thought of something."

"What's that?"

"Your name is Molly," she says. "That's my cat's name. I think maybe that's a sign."

My heart soars again. "I bet it is," I say, smiling. "I'll talk to you Friday."

20
MORRISON RIDGE

I spent the next morning typing for my father. I was a little slower than usual because I hadn't slept well. Even though he'd been in a good mood after the family meeting, I kept thinking of what Russell had said: *Let's just do all we can to make his life enjoyable.* I'd stared at my dark ceiling half the night, thinking of ways to do that. I'd been raised to believe I could accomplish whatever I set out to do, so it wasn't a question of *can* I make his life enjoyable but rather a question of *how* I would do it. I came up with a few good ideas, lying there. First, I'd remind him of how he always said he loved his work. His books touched many lives and he helped his patients every day. I'd point that out to him. I'd have to be subtle about it so he didn't catch on to what I was doing. Second, I'd think of ways to make this summer fun for him. I thought of asking to go to Carowinds, the theme park I

193

loved, but then I realized that was *my* kind of fun, not his. Then I hit on the idea of the zip line. He loved the zip line. It made him feel free, he said. I knew he hadn't been on it in a couple of years. I was going to change that. I was going to change a lot of things. This was the summer I'd make him happy to be alive.

"Had an idea," Daddy said now as I opened a document for the second-to-last chapter of his book. He was going to make his goal of finishing the book by summer's end. "I think your friend Stacy lives on the way to my office, right? So how about when Russell takes me to work Monday afternoon, we drop you off at her house for a few hours, if it's okay with her mother. We can pick you up on our way home."

"Cool!" I said. Stacy and I talked on the phone nearly every day but I hadn't seen her in the week since we slept in the spring-house. Our conversations had taken a strange turn, in that I'd talk about the New Kids and she'd talk about Bryan, who she now referred to as her boyfriend, and Chris, that boy she wanted to fix me up with. Every time she changed the subject to them, I felt a mixture of excitement and trepidation. It made me want to hold my old amethyst palm stone in my hand to calm myself down. I actually planned to get the stone from the secret rock in the spring-house the next time I got the chance. "I'll call her later and see if it's okay," I said.

"Great," he said, then he nodded toward the computer. "Ready for chapter eleven?" he asked.

He started dictating again and I started typing, and we worked for another half hour before he said we should quit for the day. I saved the document, then turned to him.

"You know what I really, really want to do today?" I asked.

"What's that?"

"The zip line!" I said.

"The zip line?" he asked. "Where'd that idea come from?"

"And I want you to do it, too," I said. "Seriously."

"Oh man, Molly. Do you know how much work that is for Russell?"

"He won't mind." I was pretty certain he wouldn't. "And I can help him."

"I don't think —"

"Come on," I pleaded. "You know you want to do it."

He smiled, then glanced out the window. "Pretty day for it," he admitted. "We'll see if Russell has the time. But first, there's something else I need you to do for me."

"Sure," I said.

"Start a new document."

I felt like groaning. We'd been at it for hours this morning. But I obediently opened a new document on the computer. "Ready," I said, my hands on the keyboard.

"Now right in the center, type the words *pretend to dance.*"

"What?" I laughed.

"You heard me right. *Pretend to dance.*"

I typed the sentence. "Is this for one of your clients?"

"Now print it," he said, ignoring my question.

"Whatever." I hit print and the page worked its way through the printer.

"Now get an envelope."

I reached into the desk drawer and pulled out an envelope.

"Fold the paper up and seal it inside."

I did as he asked.

"Now, what's your favorite music to dance to these days when you're at Amalia's?"

I thought about it a moment. "Rachmaninoff's second concerto," I said.

"Good Lord!" He laughed. "She has you dancing to the eastern European composers? Wrist-slitting music. Way too heavy!"

I pouted. "I think it's beautiful," I said.

He wiped the smile off his face, but it

looked like it took some effort. "You're right. It's beautiful. But we need something lighter."

"At the end of our lesson, she always puts on 'Footloose' and we just dance around. It's our tradition."

"Kenny Loggins?" he asked.

"Uh-huh." I sang a couple of lines, bopping my head to the music, and he nodded.

"Perfect," he said. "On the envelope, write *play 'Footloose.'* "

I held my hand above the envelope. "What's this for, Daddy?" I asked.

"Just write it."

I did.

"Okay, leave the envelope on the desk. Mom will take care of it."

I propped the envelope up against the printer and looked at him. "Okay?" I asked.

"Perfect," he said. "Now how about you find Russell and see if he has time to take us on the zip line?"

21

Russell was in the kitchen, counting Daddy's pills into his weekly pill container, and I waited at the kitchen table until he was finished. I knew there weren't as many pills as there used to be because Daddy'd given up on the experimental drug he'd been taking. It had only seemed to make him worse. Mom wanted to get him into another study, but he wasn't eligible because of the type of MS he had.

Russell screwed the lid on the last pill bottle and looked over at me. "What's on your mind?" he asked.

"Could you help Daddy and me ride the zip line today?"

He raised his eyebrows in surprise, but then he smiled. "That's some smart thinking, Molly," he said, pressing the top of the pill case shut. "He loves the zip line."

"Oh good!" I clapped my hands together. "You'll do it?"

"Yes, but I think we'll need some help."

"Maybe Uncle Trevor's home," I said. Having Uncle Trevor with us would sap some of the fun out of the afternoon, but he was brawny and strong and I guessed that was what we needed.

Russell shook his head. "After that meeting last night, I don't think Trevor'll be in a mood to help your father," he said. "Try Amalia. We don't need brute force. Just another pair of hands."

I called Amalia and she said she'd be happy to help. I told her we'd pick her up in about an hour. Then I got the two harnesses and the helmets out of our shed and put them in the rear of the van.

Daddy sat in his chair in the middle of the second row of seats in the van, while I sat up front with Russell. The van didn't start when Russell turned the key. It sort of made a chugging sound but didn't catch, and my heart sank. All this for nothing? On the third try, though, he got it going.

"I've got to take the van in, Graham," he said, looking at Daddy in the rearview mirror. "What's your schedule like next week? Is there a day we can do without it?"

"Tuesday," Daddy said. "Sounds like the battery." Our van was worth nearly as much as our house, Daddy always said. It had been specially built to transport him and his chair and it was usually very reliable, but it occasionally acted up. Without the van, Daddy could go nowhere, and I was afraid Russell might nix this whole adventure. What if the van got stuck by the zip line platform and we couldn't get it home?

But he put the van in gear and we took off. As we drove up the loop road, it occurred to me that I could pick up my palm stone on the way.

"Could we stop by the springhouse, please?" I asked when we were nearly to the springhouse path. "I need to get something."

"Sure," Russell said. He pulled to the side of the road near the path and kept the engine running while I hopped out of the van and ran down the leaf-and-ivy-littered path to the springhouse. Inside, I climbed onto my twin bed under Johnny Depp's watchful eyes. I pulled the fake stone away from the wall and reached into the dark space for the amethyst palm stone, slipping it into the pocket of my shorts.

Back in the van, Daddy and Russell were talking about the Asheville Tourists baseball team, but they stopped when I got in, and Russell began driving again.

"Get what you needed?" Daddy asked me,

as if he knew.

"Uh-huh." I remembered telling him my palm stone was in the secret rock. He probably thought I wanted it for the ride on the zip line. I'd let him think that. He didn't need to know I wanted it to get through those "I want to fix you up with this boy" conversations with Stacy.

Russell turned onto the narrow lane that led to Amalia's house. We bumped along the road for a little while, and when he pulled into the clearing by her house, she was waiting out front, sitting on a tree stump that someone had carved into the shape of a chair years before I was born.

She opened the side door of the van and got in, sitting down next to my father's chair, and the whole van filled with the honeysuckle scent of her hair.

"Hey, everybody," she said. She reached around the side of my seat to squeeze my shoulder.

"Hey," I said back to her as Russell started up the road again.

"How're you feeling after last night?" I heard her ask my father. Was she talking about the meeting? That was the only thing I knew of that had happened last night, but it seemed like a weird question for her to ask.

"Excellent," Daddy said. "You?"

She didn't answer right away, or maybe she'd spoken too quietly for me to hear. Then she said something that sounded like *brokenhearted* and my father said something even harder to hear. I glanced at Russell who kept his eyes on the road, pretending there was no conversation at all happening behind us. I tried to do the same.

We passed Nanny's house, then made a little turn into the woods, and the zip line platform poked up through the trees to our right. Even though it had been a year since any of us had been on the zip line, we all seemed to know the drill. Russell lowered the van's mechanical ramp and Amalia pushed the wheelchair down it to the ground. I got the harnesses and helmets from the rear of the van, while Russell headed for the cables that hung from the platform high above us.

Amalia wheeled Daddy to the foot of the platform, and I handed one of the harnesses and helmets to Russell, then headed for the platform stairs. "See you at the top, Dad!" I said.

I climbed the hundred and thirty-two steps to the platform without once stopping to catch my breath, though I'd really slowed down by the time I reached the top. I'd forgotten how beautiful it was up there. I set down the harness and gulped in the clean mountain air. Standing next to the hoist, I looked over the railing to see Russell and Amalia still struggling to fit my father's uncooperative body into the harness. I had a flash of guilt that I'd suggested the zip line at all. Maybe I was only making things worse for him. Whenever I had to move part of his body, I understood why Russell had those thick, ropy muscles in his arms. Daddy's limbs were rigid and almost impossible to bend. It was like trying to move something far heavier than its mass. I once heard Uncle Trevor say that lifting Daddy was like lifting a "deadweight," and Russell had cut him a look that could kill.

"Hello, down there!" I called, trying to make my voice cheerful, mostly for my own sake.

Amalia looked up and waved. "How's the atmosphere up there?" she called.

"Awesome!" I said.

Russell looked up at me. "He's hooked up," he said. "You ready?"

"Yup. Tell me when."

"Now," Russell said.

I started the hoist, watching as the cables lifted my father from his wheelchair. Uncle Trevor had come up with the whole hoist idea years ago, when it became impossible for Daddy to make it up the steps. Slowly, my father rose into the air and I watched his blue helmet getting closer and closer to me. The hoist groaned and clanked so noisily that, if I hadn't known the sounds were normal, I would have been worried. Russell and Amalia had disappeared from the ground below and I knew they were climbing the stairs to the platform. I hoped at least one of them made it to the top by the time Daddy was even with the gate. I'd never had to pull him onto the platform by myself and doubted I could do it. As my father rose closer, I saw the stillness of his body. His legs dangled. His arms looked rigid against his sides. It was like looking at a lifeless body and I had to turn my gaze out to the trees, my throat suddenly tight.

I heard Russell and Amalia on the stairs below, getting closer, their steps slowing down while their breathing sped up. In a moment, the hoist pulled my father even with the platform, and I stopped the machine. He dangled there, smiling at me.

"Hey, Daddy," I said, opening the hinged gate on the side of the platform.

"Hey, kiddo," he said.

"We're here, we're here!" Amalia announced as she and Russell emerged from

204

the steps onto the platform. She bent over to catch her breath, her hair nearly sweeping the wooden floor.

"Good job, Molly," Russell said. He held on to the railing, his back muscles tensing beneath his black T-shirt as he stretched to reach the crane, swinging it forward to bring Daddy onto the platform. I never would have been able to do it by myself.

In a moment, we had my father on the floor of the platform and Russell moved the carabiners from his harness to the zip line. Then Amalia and I kept Daddy sitting upright while Russell adjusted the harness so that my father was suspended a foot or so from the floor.

"All right," Russell said, straightening up. He handed me one of the walkie-talkies. "I'll go to the other end and tell you when to let him go." The zip line ended on a bed of soft pine needles. It had a braking system that slowed it way down before reaching the trees, but in my father's case, it was still important that someone be there to help him stop.

Daddy hadn't been kidding when he said how much work the zip line was for Russell, I thought. I grabbed Russell's wrist as he headed for the stairs and he looked at me expectantly.

"Thank you." I tried to say it quietly so that only he would hear, and I thought I succeeded.

He smiled at me. "It's okay, Molly," he said, just as quietly. "It's all good."

I listened as Russell started down the steps, then turned back to my father. He was suspended a couple of feet in the air above the platform, his feet against the gate that would hold him in until Russell gave the all clear. I sat down in one corner of the platform by the gate and Amalia sat in the other, both of us facing my father. After a couple of minutes, we heard the van start up far below us, and I let out my breath in relief, grateful that the fading battery seemed to have healed itself.

Amalia's gaze was on my father. "Uncomfortable?" she asked him.

"Not at all," Daddy said. "Merely anticipatory."

I felt strange being with Amalia and my father, just the three of us. I was keenly aware that I was sitting with my biological parents. If either of them felt the same strangeness, it didn't show in their faces. Amalia tipped her head back, eyes closed to catch the little bit of sun that found its way through the trees, and Daddy looked content to be hanging suspended above the platform. I held the walkie-talkie on my bare knee, staring at it as though I could hurry Russell up.

"When's the last time you rode this thing?" Daddy suddenly asked Amalia.

She lowered her head to look at him, brushing a thick strand of hair over her shoulder. "Just a few weeks ago, actually," she said.

"What?" I stared at her, wide-eyed. "I thought nobody'd used it since last year?"

"*You* haven't used it since last year," she said. "But Trevor wanted to make sure there were no new branches or anything that could whack a rider in the face, so I volunteered to try it out. Russell helped us."

Daddy laughed. "So what would you have done if there *had* been branches to whack a rider in the face?"

"I guess I might not be here to tell the tale." She smiled.

"Molly?" The walkie-talkie suddenly squawked to life with Russell's staticky voice. I scrambled to my feet and held it to my mouth. "Ready down there?" I asked.

"All set," he said through the static.

"Okay!" I said.

Amalia stood up and rested her hand on my father's shoulder. "You ready to go?" she asked.

"Bring it on," Daddy said.

I leaned over to kiss his cheek. Then I pulled the clasp that held the gate in place, and Daddy let out a *whoop* as he sailed from the platform, suspended in the air by a few twisted threads of wire. I was totally surprised when my eyes filled with tears. I felt his sudden freedom. I watched him until I lost him in the trees, and I knew that in a second or two, he'd be over the best part of the course. The earth would fall away beneath him and, for a good quarter mile, he'd soar through space, Morrison Ridge spread out below him like a leafy green paradise. I hoped it made his day. I hoped it made him want to have thousands of other days just like this one.

I handed the walkie-talkie to Amalia, then began buckling myself into my own harness. I was nearly ready when Russell spoke again.

"The eagle has landed," he said. It sounded like he was laughing, but with the static, I couldn't be sure.

"Do you want me to come down there to help get him out of the harness?" Amalia asked.

"No, we're good," Russell said. "Send Molly on down."

I was relieved by his answer. Amalia would have had a mile-long walk on the loop road to get to the end of the zip line, and while I knew the harness would feel like nothing to me in the air, it was binding and uncomfortable as I waited on the platform.

"I'm ready," I said, once I'd attached the carabiner to the line.

Amalia moved in front of the clasp on the gate. "Have fun, baby!" she said, as she pulled the clasp. The gate fell open in front of me and I sailed into the air. I'd forgotten the hum of the line, the rush of wind against my face. I laughed out loud as my feet brushed over the treetops, sending a flock of birds squawking into the sky. And when I reached the place where the earth opened up beneath me, I stretched my arms out wide and soared. It was wonderful — maybe the best trip I'd ever had on the zip line — but it couldn't compare to the sense of freedom and joy I'd already imagined through my father's eyes.

22
SAN DIEGO

Aidan calls me from the road several times a day, wanting me to repeat over and over again everything Sienna said, which in retrospect was not all that much. He's distressed when I tell him she had us mixed up with another couple. "But I straightened it out," I reassure him. "And then she talked about Kai and Oliver. She sounded really excited that her baby would have them as cousins."

"How open does she want the adoption to be?" he asks.

"We didn't talk about that yet," I say. "She wasn't very forthcoming. I think we were both nervous." I'm *still* nervous. I can't believe this is happening. "We can talk more at lunch," I say, "but I think we should just make it a 'getting to know you' lunch without delving into a lot of heavy topics. I don't want to scare her off."

"Agreed," he says.

On Friday evening, Aidan has been home from his business trip for two hours when I call Sienna to firm up our plans for lunch tomorrow. He sits on a stool at our kitchen island, watching me as I dial. On Sienna's end of the line, the phone rings and rings and rings, and Aidan and I exchange a look.

"She's not there?" he asks.

Before I can say anything, a young male voice answers. "Hello?" he says.

"May I speak with Sienna, please?" I ask. Could he be the birth father? He sounds too young. I remember she has a younger brother.

"She's not here," the boy says, but I can swear I hear Sienna's distinctive adult-sounding voice in the background.

"Can you tell me a good time to call back?" I ask.

He hesitates. "Maybe tomorrow?" He sounds uncertain. And then he hangs up without saying good-bye.

"What's going on?" Aidan asks anxiously.

I hang up slowly and look at him. "Something's not right," I say. I tell him about the conversation and hearing Sienna's voice in the background.

"Call Zoe." He gets to his feet and begins

digging in his pants pocket for his wallet and her card.

"Now?" I say. "It's after hours."

"She gave us her cell number for a reason," he says, reaching into the wallet. He hands me Zoe's card and I dial the number.

"Oh no," Zoe says, instead of hello. "I was hoping to catch you before you tried to call her tonight."

"What's going on?" I ask, but I think I know: Sienna's baby will be going to that couple with the built-in older sister and the dog.

"She's decided to keep her baby," Zoe says.

I'm astonished. "Really? She didn't sound at all ready to do that."

"What?" Aidan asks. He's hovering over me, trying to listen in on the call. I hold up a hand to quiet him.

"Well, she may not be ready," Zoe says, "but she's getting a lot of peer pressure. It happens sometimes."

"I guess it's good she realized it now rather than later," I say, but what I really want to do is cry.

"Exactly," Zoe says. "Sorry this didn't work out, but there will be more opportunities. It's still early days for you and Aidan.

Hang in there!"

I hang up the phone and look at Aidan. "She's keeping the baby," I say.

He stares at me. His brown eyes are huge behind his glasses. "What did you say to her on the phone?" he asks.

"What do you mean?" I'm taken aback by his accusatory tone. "I told you our whole conversation," I say, then add, "half a dozen times."

"Did you talk about her keeping it?" he asks. He rests one hand on the island as though holding himself up. "Do you think you influenced her?"

"Aidan! No, of course not."

"Maybe subconsciously?"

I lower myself to one of the chairs at our kitchen table and try to remember the awkward conversation with Sienna. I can't think of anything I said to encourage her to keep the baby. "Not consciously and not subconsciously," I say, feeling defensive. "And really, Aidan, whether I did or didn't say something to her is immaterial. If she wants to keep the baby, then that's the right choice for her. It doesn't depend on some magical words from me."

He shakes his head at me. Folding his arms across his chest, he looks out the window. I can see the pink of the sunset reflected in his glasses. "Molly," he says quietly, turning to face me, "you need to tell me, are you in or out?"

"What do you mean?"

"I think you've had mixed feelings about adoption from the start," he says. "I know you wanted us to have our own . . . our biological baby, but we have to face the fact that that isn't in the cards for us. I just don't think you've ever really embraced the idea of adoption."

I look up at him, incredulous. "How can you say that?" I ask, my voice rising. "I've done everything I'm supposed to do. That portfolio and the meetings and the home study and the birth mother letter. I was really excited to talk to her," I add defensively. "I was very careful what I said."

"Can you honestly tell me your heart's in this?"

"Yes."

"I just hear about other women who are excited about adopting and they're so into it, it's all they can think about. You . . . sometimes I feel like you're dragging your feet."

I feel tears very close to the surface. I hate it that Aidan's unhappy with me. But is he right? Am I into this with my whole heart?

"I don't think I'm dragging my feet," I

say, "but I *am* scared." I'm nearly whispering. It feels liberating to say those words to him. "I can't help it. I am."

Instantly, he softens. He stands up and reaches for my hand, pulling me up from the chair and into his arms. "What are you afraid of?" he asks gently, his lips against my ear, and I think, *He is the best man. He will make the most understanding father.* I wish I could pour it all out to him. But one admission would lead to another to another, and I can't go there.

"I'm not sure," I say. "Maybe that I won't love him or her as much as I would our biological child," I say.

"Oh, I don't buy that," he says with a soft chuckle. "Look how much you love Kai and Oliver."

"But they're related to you."

"You're going to be fine," he says.

"And I'm nervous about the whole open adoption thing," I admit. "I know you want a more open relationship with the birth parents than I do."

"We can work all that out," he says. "Yes, I lean more toward a fully open adoption, but there's wiggle room. Don't get hung up on that, babe. There's time to figure it out."

"Okay." I press my forehead against his shoulder. "Just . . . I didn't do anything wrong in my conversation with Sienna," I say. "Please don't accuse me of anything like that ever again."

"I'm sorry." He reaches past me to close the blind on the window next to us, shutting out our neighbors. Then he kisses me. "Sorry," he whispers again. His hands are beneath my shirt, pressing against my back, unhooking my bra. We end up in our bedroom, where we make love and it's good the way it always is, but my heart is only halfway in it. I lie in his arms afterward. My past is in my way, I think. It feels like something physical, a roadblock, holding me back, keeping me from moving forward.

I have no idea how to make it go away.

23
SWANNANOA

"Can you see the street numbers?" Russell asked as he drove the van slowly down Snapping Turtle Lane. Stacy's house was supposed to be number 28, but so far, we hadn't seen a single street number on any of the houses in the sad-looking neighborhood. The tiny houses butted up against one another, and parked cars and trucks made the narrow road even narrower. We'd been searching for ten minutes already, and if we didn't find the house soon, I'd have to go to Daddy's office with him and wait while he saw his patients.

"Does that say twenty-eight?" Daddy asked from his wheelchair in the middle row. "There. On the post by the carport?"

"Yes!" I said, relieved when I spotted the number. The eight was on its side, looking more like an infinity sign than an eight, but this had to be it.

Russell pulled the van into the driveway

of the world's ugliest house. It had probably been blue at one time, but the paint had faded to a moldy-looking gray, and in some spots, it had been completely worn away. A gutter hung at a forty-five-degree angle from the roof above the front door and part of the ceiling of the carport had completely caved in and lay in chunks on the carport floor. An upstairs window was broken, a long crack through the glass, and the screen door flapped in the breeze.

"Someone's fallen on some hard times," Daddy said from behind me.

"Maybe this isn't the right place, after all," I said. I couldn't picture Stacy, with her shiny hair and perfectly applied makeup, living in a house that looked like this one. But even before I'd finished the sentence, Stacy appeared in the doorway. She caught hold of the flapping screen door and stepped onto the small front porch, waving to us.

"Guess it's the right place after all," I said, grabbing my backpack from the floor of the van and opening the door.

"We'll pick you up after your dad's last patient," Russell said.

"About four-thirty," Daddy said. "Have fun."

"I will." I hopped out of the van and walked toward the house.

Stacy peered behind me at the van. "Is your dad with him?" she asked.

"Yeah, in the back," I said. "He's going to his office in Asheville to see a few patients and they'll pick me up at four-thirty."

"Awesome!" She grabbed my arm and pulled me into the house. "Wait till you hear my plan!"

We were in a small square living room that smelled of spaghetti sauce. Towels and clothes and VHS tapes and books were strewn on the furniture and the floor.

"Where's your mom?" I asked.

"At work!" She flung her arms joyfully out to her sides. "We have the house totally to ourselves and guess who's coming over?"

My hand slipped into my shorts pocket and wrapped around my palm stone, the movement involuntary. "Who?" I asked.

"Bryan and Chris! Chris is so hot to meet you."

I wished I'd known she had this up her sleeve. I would have tried to do something with my hair, at the very least. Without thinking, I tried to smooth it down with my free hand. "When are they coming?" I asked.

"Like, in half an hour. Let's do our makeup!"

I followed her upstairs and into a small room crammed with two twin beds, one of them unmade. Clothes and makeup seemed to be growing from every surface in the room and a sweet floral scent filled the air.

Stacy grabbed her makeup bag from the dresser. "Oh!" she said, reaching for a book that was lying on the unmade twin bed. "Here's the Judy Blume book I told you about. *Forever?* Oh my God, you are going to love it!"

She handed it to me and I looked at the cover. The girl in the center of the cover actually looked a little like an older version of me. If I didn't wear glasses, anyhow. *A moving story of the end of innocence,* it read below the picture.

"It's a really good love story," Stacy said, "plus it'll tell you everything you ever wanted to know about sex. Trust me."

"Thanks," I said, unzipping my backpack to slip the book inside. While I had the backpack open, I took off my glasses and put them in the inside pocket. No way would I meet this guy with my big pink glasses hanging on my face.

In the small bathroom, we took turns in front of the mirror to put on our makeup.

"He already saw your freckles in the picture and he thinks you're cute, so you don't need to cover them," Stacy said.

"I want to, though," I said, reaching for her magical foundation. *Be yourself,* my father always said. *You're perfect the way you are.* I could hear his voice in my head, but it wasn't helping. When I was with my parents, I *did* feel perfect. Right at that moment, though, standing next to one of the most beautiful girls in my school, I wasn't feeling it. "What can I do about my hair?" I looked at her straight, glossy hair in the mirror.

"It looks good," Stacy said. "I wish my hair had some of that lift in it."

I didn't believe her. She couldn't possibly envy my hair. I shifted my gaze from my hair back to my face. At least there was something I could do about that, I thought as I smoothed the foundation over my freckles. Then I brushed mascara on my lashes with a shaky hand, and Stacy's dark eyes met mine in the mirror. She smiled.

"Don't be nervous," she said. "We'll just listen to music and talk."

"I'm not nervous," I lied, but when I set the mascara on the ledge above the sink, my hand slipped back in my pocket to wrap around my palm stone again.

Chris was probably the best-looking boy I'd ever seen in real life, in spite of the fact that, unlike all the guys in the posters on my springhouse walls, he had blond hair. Maybe *best-looking boy* was an exaggeration, but when he walked into Stacy's living room and smiled at me like I was the only girl in the world, my insides turned to mush. It was an even stronger feeling than I had when I looked at Johnny Depp's picture. Stronger and deeper and altogether better. It was a scary feeling, too. It made me feel like I could do something really, really stupid if I didn't keep my wits about me. It made me *want* to do something really, really stupid.

Love at first sight, I told myself. *This is what it feels like.*

Bryan zoned in on Stacy like a magnet. He was tall — maybe six feet — and his hair was as dark and silky as Stacy's. It swooped over his forehead above blue eyes. He wrapped his arms around Stacy with a familiarity that made my stomach drop. Hooking his thumbs under the waistband at the back of her cutoffs, he leaned down for a kiss so deep I looked away, embarrassed. My gaze locked with Chris's, who seemed amused by the whole thing.

"Get a room," he said to them, and I smiled. They didn't seem to hear him, or else they didn't care, and Chris had to walk around them to come closer to where I stood, awkwardly, at one side of the living room.

"Do you like this song?" He motioned toward the cassette player in the corner of the room.

"What?" I said, stupidly. I hadn't even noticed that Stacy had put on a Bon Jovi tape. "Oh. Yes," I said. "A lot." Chris actually looked a little like Jon Bon Jovi, I thought. He was growing more amazing looking with each passing minute.

He walked over to the cassette player and started looking through the tapes scattered around it on the table. I didn't know whether to follow him or what, and Stacy and Bryan were in their own little world, still standing in the middle of the floor, kissing. Chris turned to wave me over and in a moment I was standing next to him, glad to have something to do other than feel out of place at the side of the room. I thought he smelled like cigarettes. I'd never liked that smell, but it was suddenly, curiously, delicious.

"How about this one?" He held a Metallica tape in front of me, and when I wrinkled my nose, he laughed. "All right," he said. "We'll stick with Bon Jovi."

We turned back to the room and I saw

that Stacy and Bryan had disappeared. "Guess they took my advice about the room," he said. I couldn't believe she would actually go into a bedroom with Bryan, but from where I stood, I could see into the kitchen and the dining room, and unless they'd gone outside, they had to be upstairs.

Chris sat down on the sofa and patted the cushion next to him. "So come tell me everything there is to know about you, Molly Arnette," he said, and I loved that he knew my last name. "You're a lot prettier in person than you are in that yearbook picture."

"Thank you." I sat down, leaving one full couch cushion worth of space between us. My mind didn't seem to be functioning properly. Tell him everything there was to know about me? I couldn't think of a single intelligent thing to say. I wasn't shy . . . or at least I'd never thought of myself as shy. But maybe I was. I heard laughter coming from upstairs. They *were* upstairs. Stacy was a whole lot braver than me.

Chris reached into his T-shirt pocket and pulled out a joint. I'd never seen one in person before, but I knew that's what it was. "You'll join me?" he asked, holding it in the air.

I shook my head. "I never have."

"Always a first time." His blond eyelashes were long and thick. *Oh God.* He was so hot.

He held the unlit joint toward me and I shook my head again. What was I so afraid of? All I knew was, I couldn't do it. "No, thank you," I said.

"No, thank you," he repeated after me with a smile. I didn't think he was mocking me, exactly. It was closer to teasing, and I smiled back at him. He lit the joint and drew in a long inhalation. The smell was new to me and I decided I liked it.

"Stacy said you live on this family compound or something," he said. "Is it, like, a religious cult?"

"What? No!" I laughed. "It's nothing like that." I explained how the land had been in our family forever, and as I spoke, I felt my equilibrium returning. It was easy for me to talk about Morrison Ridge and he was interested, or else he was faking it well.

"You seem really normal for someone who lives on a family compound," he said.

"Family *land,*" I corrected him. Hadn't he been listening to me? "We never call it a compound."

"There was this Goth chick in my class who lived on a family compound," he said. "She was whacked. I thought maybe it came

225

with the territory."

Oh no, I thought. "That's my cousin Dan-ielle," I said. "She's your age so you prob-ably —"

"Yes! That was her name."

"She's the only family member like that," I said.

"She disappeared," he said. "We figured she ended up in a loony bin or something."

"She goes to a boarding school now," I said. I suddenly felt defensive of Dani. Life must have been harder for her in school than I'd ever known. "She's really not that bad."

The joint was half gone and, almost without thinking, I moved closer to him and reached for it. With a smile, he set it between my thumb and index finger. "Inhale and hold your breath a few seconds. You want to keep it in as long as you can."

I held the joint to my lips and breathed in. I expected to cough, but I didn't, and I held my breath so long he laughed. Then I started laughing, the smoke coming out in a cloud.

"You're so cute." He took my hand and held it on his thigh. It was the best feeling, the warmth of his hand against mine. Then he laughed again. "I don't think I've ever used that word before," he said. "*Cute.*

Crazy word."

He's high, I thought, and I took another drag on the joint, wanting to feel whatever it was he was feeling. He took the joint from me and tamped it out in an ashtray on the end table. "Enough for your first time," he said. "This stuff's potent."

"I don't feel anything," I said,

"Takes a few minutes to hit," he said. "Come here." He pulled me snugly against him, and before I knew what was happening, his lips were on mine. I felt that kiss straight down to my toes. It was so much better than my fantasy of a kiss. He laid me down on the couch and I thought, *I'll stop him if he tries anything more than kissing,* but except for touching my tongue lightly with his, which I discovered I really liked, he didn't try a thing.

I wasn't sure if it was the marijuana or the kissing that made me feel light-headed — in a good way — and I was thinking, *I could do this for days,* when I heard footsteps on the stairs behind us.

"We're going to make popcorn!" Stacy's voice seemed to come from miles away. "Are you two hungry?"

Chris stopped kissing me. He sat up on the couch, looking down at me. I couldn't tell if his eyes were blue or gray. Either way,

227

they were mesmerizing and I didn't want to look away from them. "Got the munchies?" he asked me.

I *was* hungry. He stood up and pulled me to my feet and I was suddenly so dizzy I fell against him. "Whoa, girl." He laughed. "You're a lightweight. Next time, just a toke for you."

We sat at the kitchen table munching microwave popcorn and laughing, over what, I couldn't have said. Stacy's lips were red and her chin was raw-looking and I thought I'd better check my own face before Russell and my father came to pick me up. The clock on the stove said three-fifty. They'd be here at four-thirty. I felt my nerves kick back to life.

"You guys have to leave before my dad gets here," I said.

"When's that?" Chris asked.

"Four-thirty," I said.

"We'll take off at four-fifteen," Chris promised.

"Speak for yourself," Bryan said to him.

Chris looked apologetically at me. "It's his truck," he said.

"Just meet your dad out front," Stacy said. "Go out at twenty after four and watch for the van."

I was annoyed that Stacy wasn't helping me out, but I nodded, my eyes on the clock. His appointment would be ending about now, I thought. And it would take them at least twenty minutes to get here. I was safe for a little while longer . . . although they'd see Bryan's truck in the driveway. I'd have to meet them at the curb and I'd talk a lot when I got in the van. Maybe then they wouldn't notice.

When we finished the bowl of popcorn, Bryan and Chris went into the living room to change the music while Stacy and I talked quietly at the kitchen table.

"Do you like him?" she asked.

I nodded. "He's really cool," I said.

"How far did you go?" she asked.

"Just kissing," I said.

Chris suddenly walked into the kitchen. He looked at Stacy rather than at me. "Black dude here for Molly," he said, and I felt the color drain from my cheeks.

"Oh God!" I covered my face with my hands, my mind racing. I would say Chris was Stacy's brother. Or her cousin. Or something. I lowered my hands to see Chris and Stacy staring at me, waiting for me to do something. I tried to act calm as I walked into the living room. Bryan was over by the tape player, his back to the room, acting like he didn't know anything was going on. The front door was open and Russell stood on the step, unsmiling.

"Hi, Russell!" I said. My voice sounded unnaturally high as I grabbed my backpack from the chair in the corner. I wondered if he could smell the pot in the room. All I could smell was the popcorn and I hoped that scent covered up any other. "You're early," I said, heading for the door.

"Your dad had a cancellation. You ready to go?"

"Sure!" I was speaking too loud but couldn't seem to help myself. My whole body trembled as I tossed my backpack over my shoulder.

"Where are your glasses?" he asked.

"Oh." I balanced the backpack against my thigh and unzipped it with hands that suddenly seemed too big and clumsy. I pulled my glasses from the inside pocket and slipped them on. "Bye, Stacy!" I called over my shoulder and I ran ahead of Russell toward the van. Russell caught up to me when I reached the van, his hand pressing against the door so I couldn't open it.

"Those boys are way too old for you," he said.

"I don't know what you're talking about."

The lie about Chris being Stacy's brother or cousin was caught in my throat. I couldn't make it come out.

"I believe you do," he said. Even his big cocker spaniel eyes couldn't mask his worry.

"Please, Russell," I pleaded, "don't say anything."

He opened the door for me without responding and I climbed in. Even my kneecaps were shaking. I turned to look at my father. "Hi, Daddy," I said. "You got done early."

"Did you have fun?" he asked.

"Uh-huh." I faced forward again, worried the afternoon was somehow written on my face. Did my clothes smell like pot? My lips still felt hot from all the kissing and I wished I'd checked them in the mirror to see if they were as red and raw-looking as Stacy's. In the carport, Bryan's truck sat like a giant red flag waving in front of our eyes. An empty gun rack was on the back window and the cargo door bore two bumper stickers: BETTER TO BURN OUT THAN TO FADE AWAY and INSURED BY SMITH & WESSON. I was waiting for my father to ask whose truck it was. I tried to pretend it was invisible.

Russell turned the key in the ignition but nothing happened. The van didn't even make the chugging sound it had made in our driveway a few days earlier.

"Oh no." Russell frowned at the dashboard. "I never should have turned it off." He tried turning the key three more times and I started to panic.

"Maybe you should try again," I said, reaching toward the key like I might try to turn it myself. "Maybe you're not holding it right," I said.

Russell gave me a "who are you trying to kid?" look, and I dropped my hand into my lap as I sank deeper in the seat.

"I'll have to use your friend's phone," he said.

24

It was too hot for Daddy to stay in the van, so Russell lowered the platform and wheeled him around Bryan's pickup and into the shade of the carport, tucking his chair in between the chunks of carport ceiling that were on the concrete pad. While he was doing that, I ran back into Stacy's house to find the three of them sitting in the living room, sharing another joint. *Oh God.*

"Put that out!" I snapped. "My father's aide has to come in to use the phone. Our van won't start."

"What do you mean, your father's aide?" Bryan asked. "Is he royalty or something?"

"He's crippled!" Stacy grabbed the joint from Chris's fingers and stubbed it out in an ashtray on the coffee table. "You guys better leave. Go out the back —"

"No!" I said. "My father's sitting in the carport. He'll see them if they leave."

"Go upstairs, then!" Stacy carried the

ashtray into the kitchen, and the boys bolted for the stairs just as Russell knocked on the frame of the broken screen door.

I pushed the door open for him. "The phone's in the kitchen," I said. I was breathless.

Russell followed me into the kitchen. I knew he smelled the marijuana. How could he not? Maybe he wouldn't know what it was.

"Hi, Mr. . . ." Stacy said. The empty ashtray rested on the counter.

"Ellis," I said.

"Mr. Ellis." She smiled. "Sorry about the car trouble. You want the phone book?" Stacy was amazing. No shiver in her voice. No insincerity in her smile. She was an ice queen. The only giveaway that she was guilty of anything was in her red lips and raw chin.

"Yes, the phone book, please," Russell said.

Stacy was already reaching to the top of the refrigerator for the phone book and she put it on the counter in front of him.

He started turning the pages while Stacy and I exchanged looks — mine frantic, hers calming. Then suddenly Russell's fingers stopped moving on the book and he looked at Stacy. "You know," he said, "I have a set of long jumper cables. If whoever owns that red truck out there is willing to give me a jump, we'll be all set."

I froze, watching Russell's brown eyes bore into Stacy's nearly black ones. She glanced at me. "It's my brother's," she said, easy as pie. "I'll get him."

She went into the living room and we heard her on the stairs. Russell looked at me. "Her brother?" he asked. I knew he didn't believe her.

I nodded, but the motion was more in my mind than my body. I doubted he even noticed.

"I'll go stay with Daddy," I said. I headed for the living room, desperate to get away from his gaze.

"Molly," Russell said, and I turned to look at him.

He nodded toward the stairs. "That girl is trouble," he said quietly.

I didn't know what to say. I walked through the living room, then outside to the carport. Daddy smiled at me from his wheelchair. "Did Russell reach someone?" he asked.

There was an empty ice chest at the side of the carport and I dragged it next to my father's chair, kicking away a piece of the carport's ceiling to make room for it. I sat down on the lid.

"I've got to tell you something," I said quickly. "Some boys came over. One of them — Bryan — this is his truck. Stacy just told Russell he's her brother, but that's a lie. I didn't know they would be here. Honest, I —"

"Thanks for telling me," Daddy interrupted, and we heard the back door slam. "I hope Russell's jumper cables are long enough to reach," he said.

My eyes burned. Was that all he was going to say? I felt no relief, only an intensifying of my guilt.

Chris and Bryan walked through the carport and I stood up. I didn't know whether to look at them or my father or what. Bryan walked straight to his truck and popped the hood, but Chris came up to the wheelchair and held out his hand.

"Hi, sir," he said and in spite of everything that had happened in the last fifteen minutes, I practically melted into a puddle of love for him right then and there.

My father looked at him with an expression I couldn't read. "I can't shake hands," he said, "but I'm happy to meet you. I'm Graham, Molly's father. And you're . . . ?"

"Chris Turner." Chris dropped his hand to his side.

Russell had come out the front door and now walked over to the carport, van keys jingling in his hand.

"Bryan here is going to give us a jump, Doc," he said to my father. He only called Daddy "Doc" or "Doctor" when he wanted someone to show my father some respect. It always worked.

"Excellent," Daddy said.

Russell headed for the van and my father returned his attention to Chris.

"You go to Owen High, Chris?" he asked.

"Yes, sir."

"Rising senior, I'd guess?"

"Yes, sir."

"I know the counselors over there," Daddy said. "The principal and assistant principal, too. Very well. They're a great group."

Those few words had the effect of draining the color from Chris's face.

"Is that right?" he said, but it wasn't really a question.

"Uh-huh," Daddy said, and I knew the language he and Chris were speaking went a lot deeper than the words. I wondered what the counselors and principals at Owen High School would have to say about Chris that was making him squirm.

"Give me a hand here, Chris," Bryan said, and I saw the relief in Chris's face as he

237

excused himself to help Bryan and Russell with the jumper cables.

Once he'd gotten the van started, Russell turned on the air-conditioning to cool it down, then started pushing my father toward the ramp with me at his side. Chris looked awkward as he stood nearby, his hands in his pockets, and I avoided his eyes.

"Thanks for the jump," Russell said to Bryan, who gave him a wave.

"Hold on a second, Russ," Daddy said, when we were nearly to the ramp. He looked at Chris. "She's fourteen, Chris," he said. "Remember being fourteen?"

"Yes, sir."

"What did you want when you were fourteen?" Daddy asked.

"Daddy," I pleaded, embarrassed. I wanted us to get in the van and drive away, not prolong the agony of this encounter any longer.

"I know I was old enough to choose my own friends," Chris said, and Daddy shot him a look.

"Watch it, son," he said, and Chris seemed to shrink back a little.

Daddy nodded toward the ramp and Russell pushed him into the van. I looked at Chris. I wasn't sure if my expression conveyed the apology I was hoping for or not, but he smiled at me in a way that told me my father's intimidation wasn't going to put an end to whatever it was we'd started.

I couldn't remember another time when I'd felt nervous around my father. In the van on the way back to Morrison Ridge, my insides were tied in a knot and the silence was so thick it was hard to breathe. I wished he'd say something. I wished he'd yell at me and get it over with — my mother certainly would have — but that had never been his style. I stared out the side window of the passenger seat, my head turned away from Russell, my cheeks hot, wondering who was going to break the silence. I knew it wouldn't be me.

Ten minutes passed before Daddy finally spoke.

"So, Moll," he said from behind me, "if you had today to do over again, tell me what it would look like."

God. Couldn't he lecture me like a normal parent?

"I don't know," I said.

"Yes you do."

I hesitated. "I would have told Stacy not to ask those guys over," I said.

"Oh bullshit," my father said.

I stared out the passenger side window at the mountains in the distance. "I don't know what you want me to say," I said finally.

"Don't give me the answer you think I want," he said. "I really want to know how you would have liked today to be different."

I thought about it. About how sweet Chris had been to me. How he didn't try anything more than a few kisses. And how much I'd liked those kisses.

"The truth?" I asked.

"Of course."

"I wish you and Russell hadn't come early and the van hadn't broken down."

Daddy laughed. It was a big belly laugh and I smiled cautiously. I glanced at Russell whose expression never changed as he stared at the road ahead of him.

"I love your honesty, Moll," Daddy said. "Next time you go to Stacy's, though, Mom or I will talk to her mother to be sure an adult is going to be there."

"Okay," I said. I knew I was getting off easy, and with the relief came the memory of Chris lying next to me on the sofa, his lips against mine, his tongue slipping into my mouth.

I couldn't wait to see him again.

25
SAN DIEGO

Two weeks have passed since that phone call with Sienna and I must think of her a dozen times a day. Is she relieved at her decision to keep her baby? I hope it's the right choice for her. I barely know her — well, I don't know her at all, actually — and yet I'm worried about her.

"I wish I could talk to her," I tell Aidan over breakfast one morning.

He looks surprised. "You'll get us kicked off the waiting list," he says. "You know you can't try to change her mind."

"No, that's not what I want to do." I move the blueberries around in my yogurt with my spoon. My appetite has been almost nonexistent ever since Zoe told us Sienna changed her mind. "I just want to let her know we're not angry or hurt or anything like that," I say. "I don't like the idea that she might feel guilty about the way she handled things."

Aidan slices a banana onto his granola. "You're making too much out of it," he says, setting down the knife. He gives me an indulgent smile. "You had one phone call with her and she thought she was talking to a different woman for half of it," he says.

I have to smile myself. He's right. I'm going overboard.

"She's forgotten all about you," Aidan continues, "so why are you still thinking about her?" He lifts a spoonful of granola to his mouth. "There will be another baby," he says, before touching the cereal with his lips. "This one wasn't meant to be ours."

I remember that Sienna has a mother and a younger brother and a bunch of friends at school who are all in the same boat. "I hope she has a lot of support, that's all," I say.

"She's not our problem." He sips his coffee. "Let it go."

I hold up my hands in surrender. "Okay." I say. He's right. I spoke with Sienna for all of ten awkward minutes. Why am I so worried about her?

I have half an hour before I need to get to the office, so I pour my second cup of coffee and carry it to my desk to check my e-mail. I scan the list of messages until I reach *DanielleK422*. I stare at the address for a moment before clicking on it.

Amalia's back in the hospital. My mother heard about it through the grapevine. I guess she's pretty sick. It's some infection she picked up after one of those surgeries for her broken leg, and they haven't been able to get rid of it. Just passing that info along in case you're interested. xoxo Dani

I read her e-mail twice. I'm truly sorry Amalia's going through this. I try to picture her in a hospital bed as she fights to get well, but her face is blurry in my imagination. I bring up Google images on my screen and type in her name. I've done this before — searched for pictures of Amalia, and have never had any success in finding an image. Why there would be a photograph of her on the Internet, I can't imagine, and yet I can't stop myself from looking. An array of images fills my screen and I hunt through them searching for her. This time, I find her, although I have to enlarge the photo to be sure it's her. I barely recognize her. She's only about sixty years old but her hair, still long and thick, is as white as cotton. Her body is slender and she wears a flowy purple top. Her hair may be different but her sense of style hasn't changed. She's smiling, standing next to a painting on an easel, and when I click on the page, I see that her picture is from an article about a painting class she taught in Asheville.

I'm going to be late for my first appointment this morning but I don't care. I can't tear my gaze away from Amalia's face.

There have been months . . . maybe even years . . . when I haven't thought once about Amalia. What happened wasn't her fault, though I've never been able to forgive her for her response to it. I know she's tried to get in touch with me through Dani over the years, the same way Nora has, and I know that my cousin has kept my whereabouts to herself. I owe her for that. I was finished with Morrison Ridge long ago.

And yet, I stare at Amalia's picture. I touch my own face. My cheeks. My lips. I feel for some resemblance, but I know there is little. I have always been my father's daughter. Yet there's no denying that the woman on the screen is my birth mother.

I will call her.

Not now, though, I think, as I shut down my computer. I *will* call her. Just not today.

26
MORRISON RIDGE

I rode my bike into the clearing in front of Amalia's house the day after I was with Chris at Stacy's house and found her loading her basket of cleaning supplies into the back of her car. We'd moved my dance lesson to Tuesday this week — today — because she had something else she needed to do on Wednesday, but she was in her shorts and T-shirt instead of her dance clothes and she looked surprised when she saw me.

"Oh, Molly!" she said. "Oh my God, baby, I completely forgot we moved our lesson to today! It's my day to clean Claudia and Jim's house."

I straddled my bike next to the tree stump shaped like a chair. A dragonfly lit on the rim of my bike basket, wings fluttering. "Oh," I said, disappointed. I wanted time with her. Time away from my house. At home, I felt like everyone was staring at me when I walked in a room, upset with me over what had happened at Stacy's yesterday. Daddy, Russell, my mother. I felt all their eyes on me. Yet I had the feeling neither Daddy nor Russell had said anything to my mother. Surely she would have said something to me about it if they had.

I was obsessed. In the less than twenty-four hours since I'd met Chris, he'd become all I could think about. I felt the gazes of the New Kids and Johnny Depp following me around the springhouse, silently chiding me for leaving them behind. In my room the night before, I literally jumped each time the phone rang, hoping it was Chris or, at the very least, Stacy, but no one called me all evening and when I tried to reach Stacy around ten o'clock, there was no answer. I needed to talk to her to find out what had happened after I left. I worried my father's attempt to scare Chris off had worked.

"Do you want to come with me?" Amalia asked now. "It's not much fun, but we could chat while I clean."

"I could help you," I said, getting off my bike and leaning it against the tree stump.

"Hop in," she said, and I got into the passenger seat and directed the vent for the air conditioner toward my face.

"So," Amalia said as she turned onto the loop road through Morrison Ridge. "I believe I have you to thank for an invitation to the midsummer party."

"Oh good!" I said. "Did Nanny leave you a note?"

"She called," Amalia said. "Chilly, as usual, but she said she couldn't deny you anything." She turned to smile at me. "Thank you." She reached over to smooth the back of her warm fingers down my cheek. "I truly do want to be there. Morrison Ridge has been my home for a long time, too."

I felt angry. "I don't think it's fair how people treat you here," I said.

"It doesn't matter." She shrugged. "I get to be close to you and that's what counts."

"But you didn't do anything more wrong than what Daddy did," I said. She was quiet and I thought she was going to change the subject again the way she had during our dance lesson the week before, so I kept talking before she had the chance. "I never really knew about you showing up with me the way you did," I said. "I didn't know if you were married to Daddy when I was born or what."

She smiled. "You never asked, and we decided we'd wait until you did rather than

247

dump a lot of information on you before you were ready to hear it."

We drove past Nanny's house and in a moment I could see the zip line platform poking out of the trees. Our rides on the zip line seemed like months ago rather than a few days. I had to come up with another adventure that would be fun for my father. One that wasn't quite so labor intensive. I worried the whole fiasco the day before — the problems with the van and the problems with *me* — had undone any positive feelings sailing through the air might have given him.

I turned back to Amalia after we passed the zip line. "Did you ever think of keeping me?" I asked.

She hesitated. "I'm not good mother material, Molly," she said finally.

I felt a little stab in my chest. There were plenty of women who were crappy mother material, but they still mothered. Had she been thrilled she could give me away? Somehow, her forgetting about our dance lesson seemed to fit with her turning me over to my father. It must have been a relief to her to be able to do that.

I felt her glance at me. "I loved you so much," she assured me. "But I thought it was best for you to be with your father and

Nora rather than with a single mother . . . and a flaky single mother at that." She shrugged. Smiled. "Nora rose to the occasion beautifully, didn't she? She put your needs above everything else, which was what I'd hoped for. I'm sure it wasn't easy for her to share her neighborhood with her husband's former lover."

The word *lover* made me cringe. I didn't want to imagine my father as *anyone's* lover, yet lately it seemed I was being forced to think about it whether I wanted to or not.

Amalia turned onto the road leading to Aunt Claudia and Uncle Jim's house. "She's not Miss Warmth, Nora, but she's very practical, and when you came along, she embraced you as her own. You ended up with two wonderful parents, don't you think?"

I nodded. "I'm lucky I get to have all three of you," I said, but that little niggling new hurt wasn't going away any time soon.

Of the five houses on Morrison Ridge, Aunt Claudia and Uncle Jim's looked the worst. I guessed it had been pretty when it was first built. It was two stories tall and a taupe color with black trim, but it was hard to really notice the house because of the three old cars and one old pickup in the clearing around it, plus the shrubbery was a mess, growing up one side of the house, and ivy nearly blocked the front steps with long green leafy tendrils.

It had been a while since I'd been inside their house. I thought back. Dani had a big birthday party when she was thirteen and that must have been the last time. She'd still looked like a typical young girl back then, with hair the same boring brown as mine and skin bare of makeup. I would have been ten. All I remembered about that day was that Aunt Claudia told Dani to share her jewelry-making kit with me, and rather than let me play with it, Dani flushed the beads and strings down the toilet. I really couldn't stand her. Mom once told me we'd like each other as we got older but I couldn't picture that ever happening.

As soon as Amalia and I walked inside the house, I remembered the smell. I'd never smelled anything like it anywhere else. It reminded me of the aroma of baking bread, warm and yeasty.

"Jim's beer," Amalia said. "That smell is in every corner of this house."

"I think I like it," I said, trying to decide. It was a good smell, but it had a strange, sour edge to it.

"In small doses, I do, too," she said, setting her cleaning basket on the kitchen table. "At least it covers up the smell of their cigarettes. By the time I'm done cleaning this house, though, all I can think about is taking a shower and washing that smell out of my hair."

"Sh," I said, worried that someone might be home.

"Oh, they're not here." Amalia reached into the cabinet beneath the sink and pulled out a bottle of dish detergent. "Jim's out hauling trash and today is Claudia's stitching circle, or something like that, and I don't remember what Dani's doing, but something."

"Probably at the mall buying some more black clothes."

Amalia smiled. "Don't be so rough on her," she said, squeezing the detergent under running water in the sink. "Back when I showed up at Morrison Ridge with you, she had a harder time with it than anyone. With the exception of Nora, of course."

"*Dani* did? Why? She was just a little kid."

"Your father doted on her, that's why," Amalia said, holding her fingertips beneath the water as she adjusted the temperature. "She was the little princess and then you

251

came along and sucked up all his attention. Have some compassion for her."

That surprised me, although when I thought about it, my father *was* always really nice to Dani. When someone in the family made fun of her makeup or how weird she'd become, he'd defend her, saying something about her "testing her wings."

Dani's house, though, was undeniably filthy, at least judging from the kitchen and what I could see of the living room. My own house was always "picked up," as Nora would say.

"I can clean Bess's — your grandmother's — house or Trevor and Toni's house in two hours." Amalia turned off the faucet and dried her hands on a dish towel. "This house, a minimum of four. Toni straightens up before I get to their place, but Claudia . . . look at this mess. This is for me, trust me."

"What do you mean, it's for you?"

"Claudia adored Nora, so when I showed up . . . well, she was against me living at Morrison Ridge. She thought I'd be a home wrecker." She smiled. "I'd never do that to Nora." She pulled out one of the chairs at the kitchen table. "Why don't you sit here and keep me company while I work?" she asked.

"Want me to clean one of the other rooms?" I offered.

"Oh, you don't have to help, Molly. If they paid me something, that would be one thing and I could split it with you, but since they don't, I don't think you should help. You can put on the radio and dance, or just chat with me."

I sat down on the chair and rested my elbows on the table. "What do you mean, they don't pay you?" I'd always thought that cleaning houses was Amalia's job.

"Well, they don't pay me in money, anyway," she said as she pulled on yellow rubber gloves and began washing the dishes that had been left in the sink. "But I get a place to live, and that's a lot, so I'm not complaining."

"But . . . how do you buy food and clothes or other things you need?" I thought of how her long hair always had that honeysuckle scent. "How do you buy shampoo and things?"

I couldn't tell if she didn't answer right away because she was busy scrubbing a frying pan or if she was reluctant to tell me. "Your father," she said finally. "He gives me money each month. Not a lot, but enough."

"Does Mom know?" I nearly whispered the question.

"Oh, of course!" She rinsed the frying pan under the faucet. "He wouldn't do something like that behind her back."

I shook my head. "I have a really crazy family," I said with a laugh.

"Please don't use that word," she said, setting the pan in the dish drainer. "I hate it so much."

"Crazy?" I wasn't sure whether she was reacting to *crazy* or *family.*

"Yes. I hate that word." Her shoulders scrunched up. Then she turned to look at me. "Are you excited about the book tour?" she asked, in one of her abrupt changes of topic.

"Yes," I said, going along with the new subject. I remembered Amalia had taught dance at that mental hospital where Daddy'd worked. I guessed that had made her sensitive to the word *crazy.* "They've added a couple of radio interviews, too," I said. "Isn't that cool?" Daddy's publicist had called that morning to give us addresses to radio stations in Charlotte and Raleigh. The publicist seemed to have forgotten his handicap, though, and for a couple of hours everything was on hold while she verified that the studios were accessible.

"Very cool," Amalia agreed.

"But I'm nervous, too," I admitted. "I

want the tour to be really good for Daddy." The tour was another chance to show my father how appreciated he was and I wanted him to have a good time.

Amalia slipped off her gloves and rested them on the edge of the dish drainer, then smiled at me. "God, I love you," she said. "You're such a good daughter, Molly."

I looked down at my hands where they rested on the table. I didn't feel like a good daughter. There was one giant negative about the book tour and I was having trouble thinking about much else: if Chris had the guts to call me after what happened the day before, I wouldn't be around to talk to him.

Amalia picked up a sponge and began wiping down the counter. "So," she said without looking at me, "I hear there might be a guy in your life."

My chin dropped. How did she know I was thinking about him right that minute? Plus, I couldn't believe Daddy had already told her. It had been less than twenty-four hours since the whole van-breakdown episode at Stacy's. When had he had time?

"Is Daddy as furious as I think he is?" I asked.

She looked at me in surprise. "When have you ever seen him furious?"

"You know what I mean," I said.

"Concerned, perhaps," she said. That didn't sound too bad. "So, what is he like?" Amalia asked. "The new guy?"

I felt my cheeks turn red and couldn't stop a smile. "Cute," I said. "And really nice."

"Sexy?" Amalia glanced at me.

"Amalia." My cheeks were blazing hot. "I don't know! I guess so. He looks like Jon Bon Jovi. Do you know who that is?"

"Of course." She moved the toaster to clean the counter beneath it.

"But I think Daddy might have messed it up giving him the third degree. He was upset because Chris is three years older than me."

Amalia laughed. "He's a fine one to talk," she said, and I'd forgotten that he'd been *nine* years older than Amalia when they were together.

"Exactly!" I said. "He's a hypocrite!" I felt like Amalia and I were suddenly on the same team. "So," I said, "did you have a boyfriend when you were my age?"

Amalia laughed. "Oh," she said, "we're not going *there*!" She turned to face me, her face suddenly flushed. "You know what would be a huge help to me?" she asked. "You could pick up things. Bring me any dirty dishes you find and put things away as

256

much as you can so I can dust and vacuum. Okay?"

"Sure," I said, reluctantly getting to my feet, and I knew that was the end of any meaningful conversation we might have had today.

27

I sat on the glider on our front porch the following evening, reading *Forever,* the book Stacy had loaned me. What an eye opener! It made me want to be with Chris in the worst way. I wanted to kiss him again. I wanted to have the sort of intense and loving relationship with him that Katherine had with Michael in the book. The only thing I didn't like was that Michael called his penis "Ralph." I really hoped Chris didn't have a name for his, or if he did, that it wasn't that idiotic.

Tomorrow, Daddy and Russell and I were heading out of town for the book tour. That meant no hope at all of seeing or talking to Chris. Not that he was exactly getting in touch with me as it was, but at least with me being at home there was hope.

I was deep into *Forever* when I heard a car coming up our road. Because of all the trees, we always heard a car long before we could see it, and I peered through the woods, curious to know who was coming. Dani's little green car appeared after a moment, turning into our driveway.

I tensed. In spite of everything Amalia had told me about Dani being my father's princess before I came along, I disliked her even more than before now that I'd seen the mess she and her parents had left for Amalia to clean up. Dani's room had been especially disgusting, with plates of hardened food on the dresser and clothes knee-deep on the floor.

Dani parked her car near our porch steps. She got out, opened the rear door, and reached into the backseat for a stack of cookie sheets I knew Mom wanted to borrow from Aunt Claudia. She needed them to make appetizers for the midsummer party.

I stood up, tucking *Forever* upside down in the corner of the glider. I didn't want Dani to see what I was reading.

"Hi," I said, as she climbed the porch steps. "Do you need any help?"

She didn't answer, and when she'd reached the porch, she stood looking at me, holding the stack of cookie sheets in her arms like a pile of giant books. She had on sunglasses and when she moved them to the top of her head, her black-rimmed eyes came into view. "So," she said, "what's going on with you and Chris Turner?"

Wow. How did she know anything? Yet I felt a thrill that my one brief encounter with Chris had been enough to start rumors.

"I don't know what you're talking about," I said.

"Don't give me that innocent look. I know you hooked up with him."

"How can you know anything?"

"He told me. I saw him at the mall."

I hated the thought of him talking to her. *Hated* it! I tried to keep my voice calm. "What did he say?" I asked.

She shifted the cookie sheets in her arms. "Wouldn't you like to know," she said.

My cheeks burned, and I walked back to the glider and sat down. "Whatever," I said to her, as if I didn't care. To be honest, I was afraid to know what he'd said.

She sat down on one of the rockers near the glider, laying the cookie sheets flat on her lap. "Listen, Molly," she said. "Chris hooks up with everybody, so don't get hung up on him. He doesn't think you're anyone special, okay? I don't want you to get hurt."

I tried to laugh, but I thought I sounded as though I was being strangled. "Oh," I said, "for the first time in my life, you're

260

looking out for me."

"Come on," she said, her blue eyes intent on mine. "We're cousins. When it comes right down to it, we have to take care of each other, so of course I'd look out for you." She sounded so sincere, I almost believed her. "And he's bad news for you," she continued. "He'll take advantage of you because you're a baby and he knows you don't know anything."

"I can take care of myself, thank you," I said. And thanks to *Forever,* I thought, knew a whole lot more than I had hours earlier.

Dani sighed and stood up. "There's a cooler in the backseat of my car," she said. "Can you get it? Aunt Nora wants to borrow it."

I tromped down the steps, my cheeks still burning over the thought of Chris talking to her about me. Did he make fun of my kissing, or my flat chest, or how easily I got stoned, or . . . something? I lugged the cooler out of the backseat and carried it up the steps and into the house, where the smell of shit instantly stung my nostrils, and I knew Daddy'd had an accident. Danielle had set the cookie sheets on the kitchen counter and now had her hand over her mouth as though she might get sick.

"Oh my God," she said, "I've got to get

261

out of here."

She swept past me toward the living room and the front door, and I felt embarrassed for my father. This was happening more often these days, at least once a month, and it seemed to happen with no rhyme or reason that I could tell. I could hear my mother and Russell talking with him in the bedroom.

I walked back outside where Dani stood on the porch, gulping fresh air. She looked at me.

"That is so gross," she said.

"It's not his fault."

She looked toward the front door. "His life really sucks," she said.

"No it doesn't," I snapped. "You have no right to say that."

"He's so trapped," she said. "He must feel like his life is totally worthless."

My hands formed fists at my sides, I was so angry. "Worthless?" I shouted. "His life is a hundred times more" — I hunted for a word that would counter her *worthless* — "more valuable than *your* father's," I said. "*My* father helps people every single day. What does your father do? He's either hauling junk or sitting around killing himself smoking or making beer, which is so incredibly stupid and . . . plus, it stinks!"

She stared at me. "Wow, you're turning into an incredible bitch." She laughed an ugly laugh and pointed toward the house. "And you say *my* father stinks?"

I lunged for her, filled with an explosive hatred I'd never felt before. Knocking her to the floor of the porch, I straddled her and smashed my fist into her face. I felt momentarily out of my mind as I felt my knuckles connect with her cheek. She howled with pain, and that sound snapped me back to reality. What was I *doing*?

I leaped to my feet quickly, locking my hands behind my back, suddenly afraid of my anger. Dani slowly sat up, her hand on her red cheek, tears burning in her eyes. "You spoiled little bitch!" she shouted. "You don't even belong here. You and your twisted family. Aunt Nora should have just said no when your whore mother dumped you here. We all would have been better off without the two of you."

"She didn't 'dump' me," I said. "She offered me to them. Mom couldn't have children, and —"

"*Offered* you?" Dani laughed. She opened and closed her mouth, her hand on her cheek, as if testing how badly I'd hurt her. The skin over her cheekbone was already bruising. "Who told you that fairy tale?"

she asked.

I knew I had it wrong. I knew that wasn't exactly how my father had described the situation to me, but it was close enough.

"It's not a fairy tale." I rubbed the hand I'd hit her with. My knuckles had a buzzing feeling. "Amalia couldn't take good care of a baby, so she brought me to my father, and that's when —"

"You weren't a *baby*." Dani got to her feet, slowly, holding on to the arm of the rocker, and I took a step back from her. "You were two years old."

"No," I corrected her. "I was a baby."

"No, you were *two*." She dusted the seat of her black jeans with her hands. "I should know," she said. "I was five and I remember everyone saying how you could be my playmate and I'm, like, rolling my eyes because you were just *two*. Amalia's social worker dragged her here and they dumped you on Uncle Graham and poor Aunt Nora. Aunt Nora had to take you in to hold on to Uncle Graham. You probably aren't even his."

The image I'd had of Amalia standing on our doorstep, holding me — a tiny infant swaddled in a soft blanket — and presenting me to my father, began to break apart.

Dani leaned against the porch railing.

"You had sores on you," she said. "Some neighbor of Amalia's turned her in for neglect. She was crazy. You know she was a patient at that loony bin where your father worked before they hired her as a so-called dance teacher, right? Nobody wanted her to live here, but Uncle Graham insisted and he always got whatever he wanted." She looked toward the house again, where I imagined Mom and Russell were changing my father into clean clothing. I thought I saw a flash of sincere sympathy cross my cousin's face. "Now I guess he's paying for it," she said.

"I don't believe any of this," I said. I pulled open the door and stomped into the house, slamming the door behind me. The air was filled now with the citrusy scent of air freshener. I stood with my back against the door and breathed it in, doing my best to clear my head of the last miserable thirty minutes.

28

An hour later, I was once again reading on the glider when Russell pushed Daddy onto the porch. I was only *trying* to read, actually, because everything Dani had said to me was running backward and forward through my head, not leaving much room for anything else. The air on the porch still felt tainted by her ugly words.

"Here you are," Daddy said, as if he'd been searching the house for me. "Can you take a break from your book to do some typing for me? I want to jot down a few notes for tomorrow's radio interview."

"Okay," I said, closing my book and getting slowly to my feet.

"Such enthusiasm!" Daddy teased. "Would you rather do it later tonight?"

"No, now's fine." I looked at Russell. "I can push him inside," I said. I thought it was the first time I'd looked squarely at Russell since the big mess at Stacy's, and I was relieved when he smiled at me.

"Give a shout if you need me, Graham," Russell said, walking back inside the house.

I struggled a bit getting the wheelchair over the threshold into the house. I didn't have a good grip on the handles, thanks to the paperback book in my hand, but once we were inside it was smooth sailing. I felt emotional as I pushed him down the hallway. I remembered a stomach virus that came on me at school when I was nine years old. I would never forget the embarrassment of not making it to the bathroom in time. Was there anything more humiliating? And I'd only been a kid. He was a grown man who needed diapers. Who couldn't wipe his own bottom. I looked down at the top of his head where the gray strands were beginning to crowd out the black at his temples, and at his hands where they rested on the arms of his chair like curled white shells. I was so overcome with love for him that I stopped the chair in the middle of the hallway and leaned over to hug him, my cheek pressed against his temple.

"Hey," he said, his voice soft. "What's that for?"

"I love you," I said, holding on to him for so long that it must have seemed weird to him.

"What's going on, Moll?" he asked.

"Nothing," I said, getting a grip on myself, and I stood up straight and started pushing him again.

In his office, I took my usual place in front of his computer. I set my book on the desk and held my hands above the keys.

"So, what are you reading now?" he asked. I could see he was trying to check out the title, but even though Russell had replaced Daddy's headrest with his old one, he still couldn't crane his neck well enough to see the cover of the book.

"Oh, just this story," I said. "It's called *Forever.*"

"Judy Blume's *Forever*?" he asked.

I felt my cheeks go hot. Was there any book I could safely read without him knowing about it?

"Uh-huh," I said easily, as if we were talking about Nancy Drew or *Little Women.*

"Do you like it?" he asked.

"It's all right." I sounded as though *Forever* was the most boring thing I'd ever read. I risked looking at him. "You sound like you've read it or something," I said.

He made a little motion with his head that I knew was his attempt at a shrug. "Well, it's been around a long time and I work with teenagers," he said, which still didn't tell me if he'd read it. I hoped not. "Do you know it was banned in some places?"

"That's stupid," I said. I was afraid he was about to ban it right here in my house.

"I agree completely," he said. "I'm not big on banning books. So," he said, smiling, "what have you learned from reading it?"

"I'm not very far into it," I lied, then added in mock exasperation, "and we're supposed to be *working,* here, aren't we?"

"You're right," he said, letting me off the hook.

He began spouting off ideas he wanted to cover in his interviews and I typed them in a list with bullet points. Then we rearranged them into an order he liked, and I printed the list for him.

"Are we all done?" I asked, once the paper had come out of the printer. I set it on a corner of the desk where he'd be able to read it from his chair.

"Almost," he said. "But I wanted to talk to you about something."

Oh no. Chris? Stacy? Judy Blume? I braced myself. "What about?" I asked.

"Mom said she overheard you and Dani having some sort of . . . altercation earlier."

"Oh," I said. "Dani hates me."

"I doubt that."

"Yes she does."

"Well, just remember there's a fine line between love and hate," he said. He tipped his head and I felt him searching my face. "So is everything okay with you two?"

I shrugged. "It's fine," I said. "Though I sort of . . . beat her up."

His eyes flew open. "Is she all right?"

"Yes, but I bruised her cheek, I think."

"Molly! Are you kidding me?"

"She really pissed me off!"

"What about?"

I wasn't going to get into Dani's reaction to his accident, but there were plenty of other issues in our conversation that I'd love to get his reaction to. And so I poured it all out. How, according to Dani, Amalia hadn't shown up alone on our doorstep but rather with a social worker, and how I'd been two years old, not a baby, and how I'd had sores on my body, and how Amalia had been a patient at the hospital before she was a dance teacher, and — finally — how I'd actually been dumped on him and my mother rather than offered to them like a precious gift. I watched his face as I ticked off each hurtful thing Dani had told me, wishing he would shake his head *no* at each new revelation. Instead, he only nodded, not uttering a word, his face sober, frown lines between his eyebrows.

"Amalia shouldn't have been a patient," he said when I'd finished, as though that was the most earth-shattering thing in all Dani had revealed. "She was simply UU." He smiled. "She still is, wouldn't you say?"

I tried to smile myself. I knew what he meant because I often typed that acronym into his case notes. *UU: Unalterably Unique.* He'd made up that diagnosis, and he liked it far better than the ordinary psychiatric labels, which he ultimately had to come up with anyway in order to get the insurance companies to pay him. He used UU for anyone who was a little bit outside the norm.

"But as I told you before," he said, "Highland Hospital was unorthodox." He looked down at the paper I'd typed where it rested on the corner of the desk. "She was admitted there when she was just fourteen."

I gasped. "My age?"

He nodded. "I wish she would tell you this rather than me, but she doesn't like talking about it, and since you need to know at this moment, and I'm here and she's not, I guess I'm elected." He sighed. "Her mother was a call girl. Do you know what that is?"

I shook my head. I'd heard the term, but could only guess at its meaning.

"Do you know what a prostitute is?"

"Women who get paid to have sex."

He nodded. "Well, a call girl gets paid to . . . sort of be an escort, or a temporary girlfriend for a man. She might have sex with him or she might not. Anyway, that's what Amalia's mother did, and when Amalia turned thirteen, her mother tried to get her into that line of work as well."

"Eww," I said. "She had to go out with old men?"

"Well, *men,* anyway. I don't know how old they were. A lot older than she was, that's for sure. She hated it, of course. Being pawed at. Unable to just be a kid." He looked at the sheet of paper again. "But there was one man who was quite wealthy and who took her to plays and concerts and he's the one who fostered her interest in dancing and art." He lifted his eyes to mine again. "He was also very overweight and quite old, but I guess he treated her well and took her places, so she put up with it," he said.

I wanted to ask if she had to have sex with this fat old man, but I couldn't bring myself to say the words. I had the feeling he wouldn't tell me that, anyway.

"When she was fourteen, her mother was arrested for drug trafficking and prostitu-

272

tion, and Amalia was put in a foster home, where she acted so, well, UU, that she landed herself in the Highland Hospital." Daddy smiled with what looked like admiration and I smiled back, as though we shared a secret about Amalia, though I wasn't quite certain what that secret was.

"And she stayed there," he said. "The hospital became her home, and it was a lot better than any other home she'd ever had. She loved it. She danced. She painted. She learned how to play the oboe, although she claims to have forgotten how." He chuckled. "And when she was ready to leave there, they kept her on, exchanging her room and board for the dance lessons she gave. And that's when I met her."

"And so . . ." I said slowly, "she got pregnant and disappeared, and then you married Mom and Amalia showed up with a baby — me — on our doorstep, wanting to give me to you. And Mom wanted children but couldn't have any, so —"

"I don't think I went into that much detail, darling." He looked at me quizzically. "Do you feel as though I misled you?"

I nodded.

"Well, perhaps I did," he admitted. "When she left Highland, someone told her that her mother had gone to Charlotte, so Amalia went there, but was unable to track her mother down. She found a job as a maid in a hotel and shared an apartment with another girl. And then she had you and I believe she tried her best to be a mother to you, but" — he shook his head — "she'd had such terrible mothering herself, that she really didn't know how."

"I was really two when she brought me here?"

"Almost."

"Did I really have sores all over my body?"

"Oh, just prickly heat," Daddy said. "Dani is a drama queen. But you *were* malnourished. There was no denying that. And she'd leave you alone sometimes when she couldn't find anyone to babysit and needed to work. So she lost custody of you, and that's when she told the social worker about me and then they showed up here. With you."

A worrisome thought came to me. "How do you know I'm your daughter?"

"Have you looked in the mirror lately?" he asked. "I knew the second I saw you. But for Nora . . . for your mom's sake, we had a blood test run, which provided all the proof she needed."

"Dani made it sound like Mom didn't want me," I said.

274

"She was mildly freaked out at first," he admitted, "but she quickly came to adore you. Why don't you ask her about it? She could tell you what it was like for her."

"You always want me to talk to her about things that are hard to talk about," I said.

He nodded. "Yes. I do," he said. "It's important that the two of you learn to communicate better."

"We communicate fine through you."

He tilted his head to the side. "I may not always be here, Molly," he said, and the way he said it struck so much terror in me that I suddenly couldn't think straight. Abruptly, I picked up the list I'd typed and held it in front of his face.

"This is going to be so cool, Daddy!" I said, the paper shaking in my hands. I didn't want him to think about dying. I didn't want him to think about anything sad. "Will I be able to hear you on the radio when you're being interviewed? Like, could I listen to the radio in the van?"

He studied me, a bemused expression on his face, and I knew he was trying to decide if he should let me change the topic so easily.

"I'm sure we can work it out, Moll," he said finally. "One way or another, we'll work it out."

29
SAN DIEGO

"Molly?" Laurie looks at me across the table. We're meeting for lunch at the Mission Valley restaurant where she's a chef and she's polished off a vegetarian wrap while I've barely touched my salad. "Are you all right?"

I raise my eyes to her in surprise. "Why do you ask?"

"You're uncharacteristically quiet today."

She's right. Laurie has been doing most of the talking, nearly all of it about Kai and Oliver. I don't remember her going on about them to this degree, but I have the feeling she feels freer to talk to me about them now that I am — she hopes — going to be a mother myself one of these days. I know she used to be afraid that talking about the twins would bring up the pain of losing Sara for me, and it did.

"Plus," she adds when I don't respond right away, "you've lost a lot of weight. And you've barely touched your lunch." She motions toward my salad. "Does it bother you when I talk about the twins? I thought —"

"No." I smile. "It doesn't bother me at all. I love them to pieces and I love hearing about them, so talk away." I run my fingertips down the side of my water glass. "But you're right that I'm not exactly myself right now," I add. "I'm . . . preoccupied."

"With work?"

I shake my head. I've been moving the lettuce around on my plate and now I set down my fork. "That birth mother who changed her mind really shook me up," I say. "It made me realize what an iffy proposition this is."

"And yet, most of the time, it works out, right?" Laurie says, hope in her eyes. "I mean, I told you about my two friends who adopted children and everything went pretty smoothly for them."

"I know, and I'm sure it will eventually work out for us, too," I say. "It's just that I keep thinking about her. The birth mother. Sienna." This was not a lie exactly. I keep thinking about a birth mother, all right, but it's Amalia I can't seem to get out of my head. I still haven't asked Dani for her number or address.

"She really got under your skin."

"I just hope she's okay," I say. "I keep picturing her going through her everyday life . . . and I don't even know what she looks like, which makes picturing her difficult." I laugh. "She has a voice like Julia Stiles. Do you know who that is?"

"The actress?"

"Right. So in my imagination, she looks like Julia Stiles. And I picture her in her class with all her pregnant girlfriends. And I picture her feeling afraid of the future and —"

"Aidan told me you were obsessed," she says.

"Well, I'm not *obsessed,*" I say, annoyed with Aidan. "I just can't stop thinking about her." We both laugh at how that sounds. I *am* obsessed.

Laurie gives me one of her warm smiles. "I hope you get another call very soon so you can put this one to rest," she says.

I sit back in my chair, giving up on my salad entirely. "I just wish we could have done it the old-fashioned way, Laurie." I rest my hand on my flat belly. "I loved being pregnant," I say. "I wanted to experience all of it. Every part of bringing a baby into the world."

"Well," she says, "do you want to be pregnant or do you want to be a mother?"

I'm startled by her words. Then I smile. "You are wise," I say.

She makes it sound so simple. She doesn't know, because I can't tell her, that I'm afraid I'll make a poor adoptive mother. What if I'm too distant? Too cold? I can't tell her that I'm afraid to share my child with the woman who gave her life and who might steal her affection away from me. I can't tell her about Amalia, who has ruined my sleep by visiting me in dreams every night since I received that e-mail from Dani.

So when Laurie and I part after paying for the lunch I didn't touch, and she gives me a hug and tells me she loves me and that I am going to be the best mother in the world, I let her believe that. There's no one who could understand the root of all my doubts.

When I get home that evening, Aidan has candles burning on the dining room table and something in the oven. I smell ginger and garlic. He takes my briefcase from me and hands me a glass of wine. "Here's the good thing about being an expectant adoptive mom," he says, kissing me on the lips. "You can drink."

"What's this all about?" I ask.

"A chat with my sister." He sets his glass

on the counter and puts his hands on my shoulders. "I'm sorry, Molly," he says. "I don't think I've realized how stressed you've been."

I wonder what Laurie told him about our lunch. I don't know whether to be grateful to Laurie or angry with her.

"Oh, I'm all right," I say, but I can't deny that the thought of him cooking dinner and pampering me a little is appealing. "What's in the oven?"

"Salmon with a brown sugar and ginger glaze," he says. "Laurie gave me the recipe. It smells good, huh?"

"It does."

"And after dinner, I'm giving you a long massage."

"You're kidding," I say. Before we were married, massages were frequent. I don't think he's given me one — or vice versa — since before our wedding.

"You remember when we were trying to get pregnant and everyone told us to relax? That it would happen if we chilled out? And that's when you got pregnant with Sara?"

I nod.

"I think it's the same with adoption," he says. "There's nothing we can do to rush it. We've done our best with the application and the portfolio and the letter. We might as well relax and enjoy our lives while we wait."

"You're right," I say, and I make up my mind to enjoy the evening. The wine. The salmon. The massage and the lovemaking that will almost certainly follow.

And every time I picture Amalia in the hospital, I'll simply block the image from my mind.

30
Morrison Ridge

Chris called.

I went to bed at nine o'clock, anxious to finish reading *Forever,* and I'd turned the last page when the phone rang. After the way my father had intimidated Chris and all those things Dani had said about him, I didn't think he would ever call, but he did. I was glad I was the one to answer the phone and glad I was upstairs. My parents' and Russell's rooms were both downstairs, so I had the privacy to talk to him.

"When do I get to see you again?" he asked. It was the first thing out of his mouth after, "Hi. This is Chris."

"Soon, I hope." I was lying on my bed and wondered if he could hear the smile in my voice. Maybe I shouldn't sound all that available, but I couldn't help myself. I didn't want to play games with him.

"Do you ever hang out at the mall?" he asked. "We could meet up there."

I'd never been to the mall without one of my parents. It wasn't exactly around the corner from Morrison Ridge, either. How would I get there? How would I get home? I couldn't drive for another two years. "Not really," I said.

"Maybe we could meet over at Stacy's again," he said. Then he laughed. "Only you better have someone other than your father pick you up after."

"Maybe," I said, trying to think who else might drive me over there. Possibly Amalia. Maybe my mother. But my parents would never let me go there again without checking to be sure Stacy's mother was home first.

"Can you send me your picture?" he asked. "Not that dorky yearbook picture, but one that shows what you look like now?"

I thought of the pictures from my friend Genevieve's birthday party, which had been the day before school ended, so they were recent. Mom had them somewhere. There was a good one of me, although I'd been posing with Genevieve, who was really pretty. I'd have to cut her out of it.

"I can send you one," I said. "Can you send me one of you?"

"Yeah, it's not great. Junior-year photo. They're always lame, but I can send it to you. What's your address?"

We exchanged addresses, but then I remembered I'd be out of town for a few days. "I won't get your picture till next week, though," I said. "I'm going on my dad's book tour with him. We leave tomorrow and won't be back until Tuesday."

The line was quiet for a moment. "Your dad's a scary dude," he said finally.

I laughed. "He's the least scary person on earth," I said. "I'm sorry he gave you a hard time."

"Stacy told me about that disease he has," he said. "That sucks."

"He does okay."

"Can you call me while you're on that book trip thing?" he asked.

"Maybe," I said, wondering if I could call him from a pay phone. "I don't know if I'll be near a phone, though."

"I saw your crazy cousin at the mall," he said.

"Dani?" I asked innocently, like I had another cousin who hung out at the mall.

"Is she your pit bull or what?"

"What do you mean?"

"She went off on me when I told her I met you. Said if I hurt you she'd cut my dick off."

"She said *that*?"

"She's so warped," he said. "I don't plan to hurt you, by the way," he added.

I stared at my ceiling. I had to be misunderstanding him. "She was actually *defending* me?" I asked.

"She acted like your personal bodyguard," he said.

Oh my God. I wished I could take back that moment when my fist connected with Dani's cheek. I thought about what Daddy'd said: *There's a fine line between love and hate.*

"She's not my personal bodyguard," I said. "Actually, we're not very close at all."

"I don't think she's gotten that memo," he said.

We talked a while longer, mostly about people we knew in common, and I tried to only mention the older kids so I didn't remind him how young I was. It was nearly eleven when we finally got off the phone, and while I fully planned to think about him when I got under the covers and closed my eyes, it was Dani, sitting up on our porch floor, her cheek red and bruising, who filled my head.

31

I could tell my mother was worried as she helped Russell and me load our suitcases into the back of the van the following morning. Her face was paler than usual, and the skin below her eyes had a purplish cast to it. "I wish I were going with you," she said, for what had to be the fifth time.

"Somebody has to bring home the bacon," Daddy said to her. If any of us should have been worried, it should have been him. He would be away from home for four days. Away from the house where everything was so carefully set up for his needs. He'd be speaking to groups of strangers and talking on the radio. But he wore his usual calm demeanor. As a matter of fact, he seemed happy, and I thought all my recent worries about him being depressed were ridiculous. Still, I was going to do everything I could think of to make the next few days good for him.

Once his chair was locked into position behind the driver's seat and Russell was getting into the van, my mother took me by the hand and led me back into the house, all the way to the kitchen.

"Please make sure he always has water in his water bottle," she said. "Don't let him get dehydrated. And you have a copy of his medication schedule, right?"

"Right." I'd printed out two copies, one for Russell and a second for me at my mother's insistence. Mine was in my backpack.

"Keep an eye on him, Molly," she said. In the light from the kitchen window, the purplish skin beneath her eyes took on a translucent glow. She looked like a woman who could be blown away by the slightest breeze. "I'm not ready to lose him yet," she said.

She was being so overly dramatic. "It's only a little book tour," I said, wondering if I should be more worried than I was. I'd tossed my palm stone into my backpack almost as an afterthought. Maybe I didn't have a good understanding of what a book tour entailed. How could it lead to losing him? "And he's got Russell with him," I said, then added, "I'm going to make it fun for him."

287

She smiled at me, but there was something I couldn't read in the smile, as though she didn't believe that "fun" was a real possibility on this trip. She drew me into a hug. "I love you," she said. They were rare words from her, and all at once, I pictured her opening the door to a social worker and a beautiful young woman with honeysuckle-scented hair holding a little girl covered with a rash. Her husband's child. Her husband's former lover. Somehow, my mother'd found the strength not to slam the door in their faces.

I hugged her hard. "I love you, too," I said.

We drove out of Swannanoa and I felt a yearning as we passed the turn to Stacy's house, which had become all tangled up with Chris in my mind, as though if I showed up there, he'd be sitting on the sofa, smoking a joint, waiting for me. I'd found that picture of Genevieve and me and cut it in half so Chris would only have me to look at. I'd addressed it to him and left it in our mailbox. I wondered how long it would take to get to him, and if I'd have one of him when I got back from the trip.

"How about some music, Moll?" Daddy asked from his chair behind the driver's seat.

"Okay," I said. I picked up the black case

containing Daddy's cassette tapes from the floor between Russell's seat and my own. I turned to look at my father. "What do you want to hear?" I asked.

"You pick," he said.

"I'll pick one we can sing along to," I said, knowing how much he loved it when we sang. I looked at Russell as I unzipped the case. "You have to sing, too."

A faint smile came over Russell's lips. "Bossy," he said.

I looked through the tapes. Daddy's collection was bigger than mine and very different. He had a bunch of jazz, which was useless for singing along with. I knew I wouldn't find any New Kids on the Block, but I thought he might have some Bon Jovi, which would let me think about the next time I'd be with Chris. No luck, though. I put on one of his mix tapes and we sang along to the Temptations and the Beach Boys and the Beatles, who I'd just discovered and who I thought were very cool, and Eric Clapton and, of course, the Eagles. Russell actually knew a lot of the lyrics. He got into it, rocking in the driver's seat, turning even the Beach Boys into soul music with the way he moved his upper body. He was usually so serious. Seeing his playful side made me laugh, and when I turned to look at my father, his eyes were crinkly with humor. I had the best feeling about this trip. It was going to be better for my father than any of those drugs on that list in my backpack.

"How about a little classical now?" Daddy said after about an hour. "I'd like to rest for a while." We were approaching Hickory, and Russell was watching for the turn that would take us to Charlotte, which was the first stop on the tour.

"Okay," I said. He had Rachmaninoff's second concerto in the case, but I remembered what he'd said about "wrist-slitting music" and decided to stick with Beethoven. I put on his third symphony and leaned my head against the window, shutting my eyes. For some reason, I remembered Chris on the phone saying he'd never hurt me. They weren't his exact words. I wished I could *remember* what he'd said exactly. But that was what he'd meant: he'd never hurt me. Those words played tenderly through my mind as we drove.

"Graham?" Russell said after a while. I opened my eyes to see him looking in his rearview mirror.

"Mm?" Daddy sounded only half awake.

"We're a few miles from the hotel," Russell said, "and you wanted to stop at a mall,

290

right? I think there's one at the next turn."

I heard my father yawn. "Yeah," he said. "Let's stop. We can get something to eat."

"Why do we need a mall?" I turned to look at him.

He gave me a tired-looking wink. "You'll see," he said. "Just be patient."

We found a handicapped parking space and Russell got Daddy out of the van, then pushed the wheelchair into the mall while I walked alongside them. This mall was a lot bigger than the one I knew in Asheville, and even though it was a completely different place, all I could think about was where I would meet Chris if he asked to meet me at *this* mall. That bench? Or maybe in front of the music store? I knew I was being ridiculous, imagining something that could never happen, but I couldn't seem to help myself. I was obsessed.

We stopped to look at the map of the mall. "Are we looking for a restaurant?" I asked.

"I see it," Russell said to my father. Clearly, they knew where they wanted to go and saw no need to let me in on it, so as Russell turned the chair down one long branch of the mall, I tagged along, thinking, *Maybe we could meet over there, by the chocolate shop. Maybe he'd buy me one of those little boxes of chocolates.*

Russell stopped pushing the chair and I saw we were in front of a shoe store.

"What are we doing here?" I asked.

"Somebody I know wants purple Doc Martens," Daddy said. "Let's go get them."

I let out a scream. "You're kidding!" I said. "But I haven't saved enough yet."

"This is an 'accompanying me on the book tour' gift," Daddy said.

I bent over to hug him. "Thank you!" I said, and I ran ahead of them into the store.

I wore the purple Doc Martens out of the store, my sandals tucked inside the shoebox. I felt like everyone in the mall was looking at me, the cool girl, in her pink T-shirt, white shorts, and purple Doc Martens.

We found a restaurant and Russell re-arranged the chairs at our table so Daddy's chair would fit. They both ordered burgers, but I had a chicken salad sandwich on a croissant that was delicious but a mess to eat, the salad falling out of the bread and onto my plate.

"Bet you five bucks you can't eat that sandwich without licking your lips at least once," Daddy said. He could be such a dork, but I would humor him.

"You might as well hand the money over

to me now." I grinned.

"You gotta earn it," Daddy said.

Russell rolled his eyes. "You two," he said. He fed Daddy, who was keeping an eagle eye on me while I carefully worked my way through my messy sandwich.

Daddy swallowed a bite of his burger. "You nervous about tonight?" he asked me.

I shook my head. "Nope," I said around a mouthful of chicken salad. I was concentrating hard on not licking my lips, so after every bite of the sloppy sandwich I had to wipe my mouth with my napkin. "Are you?"

"Well," he said, "I'm not nervous about speaking, but I *am* a little nervous no one will show up."

"They'll show up," Russell said, like he had some insider knowledge.

"You almost blew it," Daddy said to me.

"What?"

"Your tongue. It was getting ready to lick."

"Was not," I said, though he was right. I was too old for his lame bets, but I would play along if that's what he wanted. Anything to make him happy. I finished the sandwich and Russell handed me a five-dollar bill from his wallet.

We were headed back to the mall exit when my father suddenly asked Russell to stop pushing the chair. "Buy that for Molly," he said, looking in the window of a cosmetics shop.

"Buy what?" Russell and I asked at the same time. Daddy once told me he missed being able to point to things more than anything else.

"That glittery blue nail polish."

I saw the bottle he was talking about. The polish was the color of a night sky filled with stars. "Yes!" I said.

Russell pulled another five-dollar bill from his wallet and handed it to me. I ran inside the store, bought the polish, and came out again.

"Tonight," Daddy said, as we started toward the exit again, "you are going to sparkle."

Russell found the radio station where Daddy was supposed to be interviewed and we parked in a handicapped spot outside. We were early, but only by fifteen minutes. Inside, I sat in a small waiting area while Russell wheeled Daddy down the hall to the room where they'd do the interview. I felt nervous for my father. I pulled my palm stone from my backpack and held it in my hand. It soothed me, that old stone. I rubbed my thumb over the smooth indentation in its surface.

The waiting area consisted of six green upholstered chairs with wooden arms, a small table with a coffeemaker and a pitcher of water, and a large speaker hanging near the ceiling in one corner of the room. Classical music played from the speaker, but after a moment a woman announced that "Dr. Graham Arnette, the pretend therapist, will be joining us after this newsbreak." I rubbed my stone harder but I was smiling. How could anyone turn off their radio after an introduction like that? Wouldn't they want to know what on earth a pretend therapist was?

Russell returned to the waiting area and poured himself a cup of coffee.

"Too cramped in there for me," he said, sitting down next to the table.

"He can manage alone?" I asked, worried.

"I put the headphones on him and the microphone is in the right place, so he's all set."

"Is he nervous?" I asked. "I'd be nervous."

"He's pretending not to be." Russell smiled, and I had the strongest desire to give him a hug and thank him for everything he did for us — and especially for never again mentioning anything about what happened at Stacy's house — but I stayed in my seat and let the gratitude quietly fill me up.

We didn't speak as the woman interviewed my father. He talked about his Pretend Therapy book for kids and how parents could help their children use it to cope with their fears or their various misbehaviors. Daddy's voice was strong, and I heard his smile even though I couldn't see it. You would never guess he was sitting immobilized in a wheelchair.

"You'd never know he's helpless," I said.

Russell raised his eyebrows at me. "Your father is anything but helpless, Molly," he said, lifting his coffee cup toward his mouth. "You can trust me on that."

We had a handicapped-accessible room at the hotel for Daddy and Russell to share and it was connected by a door to a room for me. They had two double beds and I had a giant king-sized bed all to myself. I flopped spread-eagled onto the bed the moment I got into the room, enjoying the space that was mine-all-mine. I stared at the ceiling, trying to remember the last time I'd stayed in a hotel. It was before Russell came to live with us, so it must have been three years ago when we drove to Pennsylvania to visit my mother's mother. I'd had a connecting room then as well. I remembered Daddy using a mobility scooter in the hotel, so he must have still had some use of his hands. I distinctly remembered getting in the elevator with him, just the two of us. He'd tried to push the button for the lobby, but his hand wouldn't cooperate. I'd felt his frustration as I reached in front of him to push it myself.

"Will you ever get better, Daddy?" I'd asked, once the elevator started its descent.

He didn't answer right away. He was staring at the buttons as though he wished he could push them with his eyes instead of his uncooperative fingers. "I'm afraid not, darling," he'd said finally, turning his head to look at me. "I will only get worse, so I have to make the most of the time I have now."

I remembered crying myself to sleep that night. I couldn't imagine him getting any worse than he already was. But, of course, he did.

The three of us rested before the event at the bookstore, which was scheduled for seven o'clock. I stared at the phone on the nightstand next to my bed. I had Chris's number written down in the little notepad in my backpack and I wanted to call him so much, but there would be a bill, wouldn't there? I read the instructions written on the phone. Local calls were free, but long distance calls would be charged to the room. I didn't dare, yet my fingers itched to dial his number.

I painted my nails with the night-sky polish, then lay down on the bed to let the polish dry. Staring at the ceiling, I slowly became aware of an ache low in my belly. It took me a few minutes to place the feeling. Was I getting my period? I'd only had four of them, the first coming a year ago when I was thirteen. I'd been the last of my friends and had begun to think I'd be the one girl in the world who never got her period. It "sputtered" — that was the word Mom used to describe its irregularity. "It will get regular eventually," she'd assured me, and I wished she'd thought to tell me to be ready for it on this trip. It had been so long since the last time, though — three months at least — that she and I had sort of forgotten all about it.

I jumped off the bed and raced into the bathroom, and sure enough, there was a spot of red on my underpants. I tucked folded sheets of toilet paper into my underpants and tried to figure out what to do. This hotel was in the middle of nowhere. I didn't remember seeing anyplace nearby where I could get supplies.

I knocked on the door between our rooms, hoping they weren't both asleep.

"Come in," Daddy said.

I found him propped up in bed, a book on the automatic page turner in his lap, while Russell was ironing a blue shirt on the ironing board next to the window.

"I need to talk to Daddy alone for a minute," I said to Russell.

Russell looked only mildly surprised. "No problem." He turned off the iron. "I need to make a quick call from the lobby, anyhow," he said.

I climbed onto Daddy's bed, waiting for the door to close behind Russell. Daddy looked at me with an expectant frown on his face.

"What's up?" he asked.

"This is embarrassing," I said.

"You don't have to say anything tonight if you don't want to."

"What?" I was momentarily confused. "Oh no. That's not it." My cheeks felt hot. "I got my period and don't have any . . . I didn't bring anything to use because I didn't expect it."

"Ah," he said. "Well, Russell can take you to the store."

I scrunched up my face. "It's so embarrassing."

"Nah." Daddy shook his head like I was making a big deal out of nothing. "We'll just tell him you need to pick up some personal items."

"That's so obvious."

"All right." Daddy chuckled. "A few things then. You need to pick up a few things." His gaze fell to my nails. "Hey! I love it," he said.

I held up my right hand to admire the sparkly dark polish. "Thanks," I said. "Me, too." I wished Russell would get back, but he was probably giving us lots of time to talk. Daddy told me about the book he was reading, while I felt that miserable ache get a grip on my stomach and worried the blood would seep through the toilet paper.

I finally heard Russell's key in the lock and he poked his head into the room. "Can I get back to ironing?" he asked.

"Molly needs to make a run to the store," Daddy said. "A convenience store will be fine. She just needs to pick up a few things."

I couldn't look directly at Russell. My gaze was somewhere off to his left.

"Sure," he said. "Now?"

I nodded and he walked across the room and picked up his keys from the dresser. "Are you okay, Graham?" he asked my father. "Do you need anything yourself?"

"Not a thing," Daddy said. I felt bad leaving him with his finicky page turner. If it got stuck as it usually did, he would have absolutely nothing to do except sit and think until we returned.

Russell and I didn't speak as we rode the elevator to the lobby, then walked out to the van. He turned the key in the ignition. "Let's see if we can find a store for you," he said. We drove a short distance and I spotted a gas station with a little store attached to it. He pulled up in front of it, then took his wallet from his pocket and handed me a ten.

"That enough?" he asked.

I nodded. My cheeks were burning again, and he gave me a sympathetic smile.

"I came up in a house full of women, Molly," he said. "No daddy. One mama. One auntie. And five sisters. This ain't no big thing." I'd never heard him use the word *ain't* before. Except for his colloquialisms, Russell spoke the same language I did. But the way he said it — lightly, kindly — eased the color from my cheeks and I gave him a grateful smile. "I'll be right back," I said.

I bought a package of sanitary napkins, eyeing the boxes of tampons wistfully. I'd tried to use one of my mother's when I got my first period, but there was no way that thing was going in.

Back in the van, I tried to hold the thin plastic bag so Russell couldn't see the box inside it. I didn't know why I still felt so embarrassed.

"All set?" he asked.

"Uh-huh."

We were halfway back to the hotel when he spoke again. "I've been thinking," he said. "Tuesday — the day we're heading home — my family's having a pig pickin' at our homeplace outside Hendersonville. Think it'd be fun to stop there for a couple hours?"

I thought I'd rather get home so I could talk to Chris, but a pig pickin' sounded like the kind of thing Daddy would love. He was crazy about barbecue. "Would it be okay for Daddy?" I asked. "I mean, would everything be accessible for him?"

"Well, it'll all be outside, unless it's pouring rain, so shouldn't be a problem."

"I think it's a good idea then," I said. "He'd like it." I felt proud of myself for putting my father's wants ahead of my own, even though my heart sank a little as the words left my mouth.

"Let's see how he's feeling," Russell said. "He might be too worn out by then." He shook his head with a grin. "We might *all* be too worn out by then."

We showed up at the bookstore a few hours later to find it packed with people. I could practically hear our collective sigh of relief at the sight of a crowd. A bunch of chairs had been set up in the middle of the giant store, and they were full of mothers — and some fathers — and lots of squirmy children. The staff was setting up more chairs for the people who were standing.

"We don't usually get this big a turnout," the store manager, a dark-haired man with wire-rimmed glasses, said to us as he reached out to shake my father's hand. He awkwardly put his hand behind his back when he realized Daddy could not lift his own. "It was your radio interview," the manager said. "We started getting phone calls to reserve your book as soon as the interview was over."

I stood there talking to the manager, feeling somewhere between cute and cool in my short pink skirt and my purple Doc Martens. I'd taken a couple of Daddy's Advils for the cramps and I felt really good. I wished Chris was there to see me right then.

Daddy wore tan pants and the blue shirt Russell had been ironing, along with a smile nothing would ever be able to erase from his face as he took his place in front of the audience. *This is exactly what he needs,* I thought.

The manager introduced him as "pretend therapist Dr. Graham Arnette," and everybody applauded. Russell and I sat in the front row and neither of us seemed able to stop grinning as Daddy spoke. He briefly explained why he was in the wheelchair, because it was obvious that the people who'd heard him on the radio had had no idea. Then he launched into a description of Pretend Therapy, saying that while it could work for anyone, children were particularly receptive to the techniques he talked about in his book.

"Pretend Therapy means having control over your life," Daddy said. "The tools you need to 'fix' yourself already exist inside you. Pretend Therapy simply helps you track down those tools to make them work for you." I'd heard him say those few sentences a hundred times before, but I heard them differently on this night, when the parents sitting around me seemed to hang on his words with interest and hope.

"There's someone here tonight who's been my guinea pig over the years as I've developed Pretend Therapy techniques,"

Daddy said after he'd talked for a while and was ready to take questions from the audience. He smiled at me and my heart started pounding, surprising me. I suddenly wished I hadn't left my palm stone in my backpack at the hotel. "I'd like her to join me up here," Daddy said. "This is my daughter, Molly."

I got to my feet and everyone clapped as I sat down next to him in a chair. There were so many people in front of us! I smiled, pretending I did this sort of thing all the time, and I felt my heartbeat begin to steady itself.

People began asking Daddy specific questions about their children, and he offered suggestions. The hands flew up faster and faster, and he answered question after question, often brilliantly suggesting they could find more answers in his book. He was a natural at this.

Finally there was a question for me.

"What's it like, growing up with a father who has such a fascination with pretending?" a man asked from the back row. The little girl he held on his lap was nearly asleep, her head on his shoulder.

"It's normal, I guess," I said with a shrug. "I mean, for *me* it's normal, anyway. I don't know anything different. Doesn't every father tell his kids to pretend to love doing their homework or washing the dishes or eating broccoli?"

The audience laughed, and I glanced at my father. There was pride in his eyes. We answered a few more questions together, and I felt as though we were a team. I realized, with a sense of joy and wonder, we always had been.

Daddy was happy but exhausted by the time we returned to the hotel. I took a bath while Russell got him into bed, and then I sat and stared at the phone for a while, wishing I could call Chris. I suddenly remembered Russell saying he was going to make a phone call from the lobby earlier that day. There had to be a pay phone down there.

I pulled my wallet from my backpack and counted out my change. A dollar fifty-five in quarters, dimes, and nickels. Would that be enough?

I changed into my shorts and stuck Chris's number, my room key, and the change into my pocket. Leaving my room, I shut the door as quietly as I could in case Daddy and Russell could hear it in their room. I rode the elevator to the lobby, growing excited over the thought of hearing Chris's voice. I'd tell him about my Doc Martens and how cool the bookstore event had been tonight. As I searched the lobby for the phone booth, I tried to think of questions I could ask him about his day.

I had to ask someone at the front desk where the phone was. There were three booths tucked into an alcove near the bank of elevators, but only one of them was free. I tried to make the call, but the operator asked for more money than I had. I'd have to get more change tomorrow. I sat staring unhappily at the phone for a moment, and that's when I became aware of the voice coming from the booth behind me. It was muffled, the words hard to make out, but it was definitely Russell's voice, and I was relieved then that I hadn't been able to reach Chris. If I could recognize Russell's voice, he would have been able to recognize mine. If I left now, I'd have to walk right past him, so I burrowed deeper inside my booth to wait out his call. I tried to listen in, feeling nosy, wondering who he might be talking to.

I heard him laugh. Maybe he was talking to someone in his family to say we might come to the pig pickin'? That was probably it. I couldn't make out more than a couple of words, but I didn't care. All I wanted was for him to get off the phone and go back upstairs so I could get out of this booth. Finally, he said, "love you, too," clear as day. I heard the door to his booth open and burrowed my head between the phone and the wall, hoping he wouldn't see me as he left. I heard him walk away from the bank of phone booths and breathed a sigh of relief, but then I thought of those words *love you, too.* They made my heart freeze. Would he say them to someone in his family? Or did he have a girlfriend we knew nothing about? And if he had a girlfriend, would he leave us someday to be with her? That thought was unbearable — we'd be so lost without him — and I suddenly felt the burden of needing to keep not only my father happy, but Russell as well.

32

By the time we piled into the van three days later for our trip back home, Russell and I were pretty well worn out, though Daddy seemed almost perky. His publicist had called our hotel that morning to say how thrilled — that was the word she used — the publisher was with the response to the tour. She'd spoken with the six bookstores we visited and they were happy with their sales, even though a couple of stores had only a few people in the audience. In those stores, I'd done my best to fill the seats, walking through the aisles in my Doc Martens, encouraging people to come listen to my dad talk about the "importance of pretending." I thought that sounded better than "pretend therapy." Still, while I got a few people to come listen to him, I discovered I couldn't make people do what they didn't want to do. I couldn't make them buy his book. But the publisher was happy and he was happy. That was all that mattered.

Charlotte and Raleigh — the two towns where he'd had radio interviews — had the best turnouts by far.

"So, we have to remember that for the next time," I'd said the night before, as we drove to the hotel from the book signing in Raleigh. "More radio interviews!" Neither of them responded, and I figured they were tired out and ready to crash at our latest in a string of hotels.

In general, though, the four days on the road seemed to have energized my father rather than tired him. Every time I spoke to my mother, she sounded worried and I had to constantly reassure her he was fine. In our phone call that morning, I told her he had more energy than me. That wasn't quite true, of course, but something was definitely going on with my father. There was a lightness in him that was new. He wanted to go to Russell's family's pig pickin' on the way home, too. "We have to eat somewhere," he'd said the night before as we planned our itinerary. He'd nodded toward Russell. "I'd rather eat with your family than at another McDonald's any day." Although I was anxious to get home so I could talk to Chris and Stacy, if the pig pickin' would

310

make Daddy and Russell happy, I was all for it.

"How about some music?" Daddy said to me now, as we pulled out of the parking lot of our Raleigh hotel.

I groaned. I was really tired of his music collection and the thought of four more hours of it was almost too much for me.

"Maybe we could just listen to the radio for a while," I suggested.

"Nah," Russell said, "I personally haven't gotten my fill of Willie Nelson yet."

I laughed. Russell really had issues with some of Daddy's taste in music and I knew he'd gotten his fill of "On the Road Again" a long time ago.

"Oh well," Daddy said from his chair behind Russell. "If she doesn't want to hear the new music we bought her, it's her loss."

I turned to look at him. "When did you have a chance to buy some new music?" I asked, lifting the case onto my lap, curious. I'd complained that he had no New Kids on the Block tapes and wondered if he'd sent Russell out to find one for me for this long trip home.

I unzipped the lid, and there, on top of the cassettes, were two tickets to the August 8 New Kids on the Block Magic Summer Tour concert in Atlanta. I grabbed the

311

tickets and held them close to my face in disbelief.

"Omigod omigod omigod!" I shouted. "Are these real?"

Daddy laughed. "They'd better be, for what they cost," he said. "I've had them a while, but I wasn't sure how we'd get you there. Now that I see how I've managed on this trip, I think Russell and I will have no problem carting you down to Atlanta for a couple of days."

"Oh my God, I can't believe it!" I was still staring at the tickets, reading every word on them. "There's only two tickets, though."

"Well, Russell and I will pass, thank you."

"Thank you, Jesus," Russell said, and I punched his arm. I knew he thought the New Kids on the Block were pretty bad.

I unbuckled my seat belt and jumped between the bucket seats to hug my father. He laughed. "Get back in your seat," he said. "You're scaring me."

"So, I can bring a friend?" I asked him as I buckled up again.

"Whoever you'd like."

I thought momentarily of Chris, but knew that was impossible for about a hundred reasons. Besides, Chris's opinion of the New Kids was only slightly higher than Russell's.

"Can I bring Stacy?" I glanced at Russell, knowing how he felt about her. His face was impassive. If he still thought Stacy was "trouble," though, he didn't say a word about it.

"Of course," Daddy said.

I couldn't wait to get home to call her.

We were getting close to the turnoff for Hendersonville, and I had a sudden terrible thought. What if the woman Russell had told he loved on the phone was at his family's get-together? In my imagination, she had quickly become a seductress who could pull him away from my family and I didn't like her.

When we stopped for gas and Russell got out of the van, I turned to my father.

"I think we should fix Russell up with Janet," I said.

Daddy looked surprised. Then he laughed. "The only two black adults you know, so you think they belong together?" he asked.

"Don't you think they'd like each other?" I asked.

"I think Russell has his personal life all figured out," Daddy said.

I thought of telling him I'd overheard Russell on the phone, but then he'd know I'd been in a phone booth myself. "I was just worried he'd find a girlfriend who lived far away from us and leave us," I said.

"Since when did you get to be such a worrier?" Daddy asked. "Trust me, darling," he said. "You don't need to worry about Russell."

A short time later, Russell switched off the Beatles tape we'd been listening to for the last half hour. Then he turned onto a winding country road for a few miles, and then onto a hilly gravel lane that reminded me a little of Morrison Ridge, the way it was cradled by acres of thick green trees on either side. The silence in the van felt good after hours of music, and it gave the road an almost sacred feeling. I remembered Russell telling me about his great-great-great-grandfather getting this land from his master. I looked at Russell and thought I'd never seen his face so peaceful. This was his home place. His Morrison Ridge.

"That's your sister's house back there on the left, isn't it?" Daddy asked Russell.

"Right," Russell said. "Wanda's place."

I looked into the woods to our left and could make out the corner of a house behind the trees.

"You've been here before, Daddy?" I asked, surprised, as the lane twisted and turned through the woods and the gravel crunched beneath the van's tires.

"A couple of times, right, Russell?" Daddy asked. "Last year for your niece's baptism and . . ."

"The year before for my birthday," Russell said.

The road curved sharply through the trees and I thought I could already smell the barbecue through the closed windows of the van.

"Only seventy-five degrees out today, Graham," Russell said into his rearview mirror. "But if it gets too hot for you, there's an air conditioner in Mama's bedroom and I know she'd let you take a break in there."

"I'm sure I'll be fine," Daddy said.

Russell drove into a huge clearing and the woods gave way to a different scene entirely. A large log house sat in the middle of the clearing. The brown logs and white mortar formed thick irregularly shaped bands, and the house looked ancient but solid. A half-dozen picnic tables covered with white paper tablecloths had been set up near the side of the house. Cars and trucks dotted the lawn, and I could see the pig cooker attached to the rear of one of the trucks, smoke and shimmery heat rising off it.

"The house has been added onto about

315

half a dozen times," Russell said to me as he parked the van next to a small red car and pressed the button to lower the ramp. He pointed toward the house. "That was my room, up in that corner," he said. His voice was nostalgic. I heard tenderness in it, and pride, the same sort of pride I heard in Nanny's voice when she talked about Morrison Ridge. "That part of the house is the original," he said.

A few men surrounded the cooker, bottles of beer in their hands, and one of them raised his bottle in our direction as Russell and I got out of the van. A bunch of little kids ran around like a swarm of bees, and music — Marvin Gaye singing "Sexual Healing" — poured from a boom box on the top of one of the cars. Russell climbed the ramp into the van, unlocked Daddy's chair, and wheeled it to the ground.

"That's my favorite sister, Wanda." Russell pointed toward a woman who set a big blue bowl on one of the tables, then started walking toward us.

"Rusty!" she called. "You made it!"

Russell took a few steps toward her, wrapping her in a hug.

"Smell that 'cue." Daddy looked up at me. "We're going to eat well today, Molly."

Wanda leaned over to buss my father's

cheek. "Good to see you again, Graham," she said. She was light-skinned, much lighter than Russell, and her eyes were a mesmerizing greenish-gold shade I'd never seen before. She looked at me. "Is this Molly?" she asked.

"Yes, ma'am," I said.

She held my hand and looked at Russell. "Amalia's girl?" she asked, and Russell nodded.

I was shocked. Not very many people knew I was Amalia's daughter. "You know Amalia?" I asked.

"Wanda met her one time when she came out to Morrison Ridge to visit Russell," Daddy said. "Right, Wanda?"

Wanda looked briefly confused, then seemed to remember the meeting. "Right!" she said. Then she suddenly tugged on my hand. "So, come on," she said, heading across the lawn toward the pig cooker. "Let's meet everybody."

We moved around the yard for a while, Russell introducing us to everyone. I met so many people that their names and faces quickly got tangled up in my head. Uncle So and So. A bunch of aunts, all of whom Russell called "auntie." Loads of cousins, many of them men Russell's age who were hanging around the pig cooker, stealing

317

crispy bits of pork. Daddy and I were the only white people I could see, and I thought I was having a tiny taste of how the two black kids in my school must have felt every day.

Wanda took me into the house, where the doorway into the kitchen was so low I had to duck to keep from hitting my head. "People were shorter back when this house was built," she said. The kitchen was hot, filled with steam and women and the pungent, unmistakable smell of collard greens cooking. Wanda introduced me to her four sisters. "This is Carla. She's a nurse. And Ree-Ree, she's a teacher. And Tula, nurse. And Janice, nurse." The names and faces ran together, but I counted three nurses and two teachers. "And this is Mama, who's making her world-famous deviled eggs." Wanda led me to the head of a long table, where Russell's mother sat expertly squeezing the yolk mixture into the whites from a canvas pastry bag.

"You sit here, sugar." Russell's mother pointed to the bench on one side of the table. "You can chop the pickles for the potato salad."

I was glad to have a task. I needed something to take my mind off how much I was dying to call Chris and Stacy. I still wasn't sure which one I'd call first. I started chopping the pickles on a little wooden cutting board Wanda handed me, and I was instantly sweating, as though chopping was hard physical labor. The kitchen was full of people and chatter and steam and the sounds of chopping and mixing along with the muted sound of music coming from that boom box outside.

I felt a chill from a couple of the sisters. A "what's that white girl doing in our kitchen?" sort of chill, but maybe I was mistaken. Maybe they just had chillier personalities, but when you were the outsider, it was easy to misinterpret. The others were really nice to me, one of them handing me a sharper knife as I moved from chopping pickles to slicing tomatoes, and another told me I had the prettiest blue eyes. "They're just like your daddy's, aren't they," she said.

"Rusty loves working for your family," Russell's mother said as she sprinkled paprika on the tops of the deviled eggs. Her graying hair was pulled back in a bun, and her face, unlike mine, was dry, as though her body had long ago gotten used to the heat of her kitchen. "He says you're real nice folks."

A bunch of responses went through my

head. How we really couldn't get by without him. How he seemed to figure out what Daddy needed before Daddy even knew it himself. How he could do the most horrible tasks without complaint. "He's more like family to us than just somebody working for us," I said, the words surprising me. They sounded adult and I'd never verbalized them before, but they were the truth. I felt a couple of the sisters turn their heads toward me when I said it. One of them, Ree-Ree, laughed and said something I couldn't hear under her breath.

"Shut up, Ree," Wanda said. I felt my cheeks color, wondering if Ree-Ree had been mocking what I'd said.

"Everybody Rusty ever worked for says that," his mother said proudly, ignoring whatever was going on between her daughters.

It was the first time I thought of Russell working for someone else. I knew he'd had other aide jobs before he came to us, but now I felt jealous of those people. I wanted him to be ours forever.

"But I never heard him like a job as much as this one," Wanda said. I could tell she had a way of smoothing things over. The peacemaker in the family, I thought, like Aunt Claudia, and I looked at her with gratitude.

When all the food was ready and had been carried outside, Daddy and I sat at the table closest to the house. The Temptations were singing "Treat Her Like a Lady" from the boom box. I offered to feed Daddy so Russell could hang out with his family. Russell had a foot in two worlds, I realized, watching him joke around with his cousins and sisters. As comfortable and content as he seemed in our world, here he moved with a different sort of ease, his body relaxed, a perpetual smile on his face. I watched how he related to the women who were there, keeping my eye out for the one he told he loved on the phone, but he seemed to be related in some way to every single person he talked to. Maybe it had been Wanda or his mother on the phone, I thought, relieved. Seeing how close he was to his family, it would make perfect sense that he told one of them, "Love you, too."

"Now *this* is the way barbecue should taste," Daddy said after swallowing a bite of the pork. He then got into a heated debate with Wanda's husband, who sat across from us and who was from the eastern part of the state, where the barbecue sauce was vinegar based instead of tomato based, and if Daddy could have used his fists, I think they would have ended up duking it out. He was happy, though, and he didn't seem to care a bit about the calories he was consuming. I must have fed him a dozen hush puppies along with the pork and all the sides that came with it, followed by a big bowl of to-die-for banana pudding. Once I'd given in to the fact that we were going to be hours later getting home than I'd hoped, I felt a sense of contentment come over me. Daddy was happy. Russell was practically glowing with the joy of seeing his family. I had New Kids concert tickets, sparkly fingernails, and purple Doc Martens, and with any luck, in a couple of hours I'd be on the phone with the boy who had captured my heart.

33

I thought something had changed at home while we were away. It was more of a *feeling* than something I could see or hear, and I knew it the moment we pulled up in front of our house and Mom came running down the porch steps to greet us in her white pharmacist coat. I'd gotten out of the van and she ran right past me and up the ramp to get to my father. I saw her crouch down next to his chair, one of her hands wrapping around his wrist, her other reaching up to touch his face. I turned away, jarred by the sheer intensity of her emotions. I caught Russell's eye as he waited to unlock Daddy's chair, and he quickly looked away from me. I felt alone, standing there. Alone and left out. And I remembered something Dani had said: *She had to take you in to hold on to Uncle Graham.* For the first time, I wondered if that was the truth.

There was an envelope addressed to me on the table in the hallway. No return address, but I knew who it was from and I stared at the way he'd written my name and address. I loved his handwriting. It was more like printing, actually, boxy and with a backward slant. It was very masculine, I thought. I carried my suitcase and the envelope upstairs, where I sat on my bed and tore it open. A note fell out along with a photograph. On the phone, he'd told me the picture was lame, but I thought it was beautiful. His hair was shorter than it was now and his blue-gray eyes were heavy-lidded and definitely sexy. His smile was cockeyed, and I couldn't remember if it really looked like that or if it was just that way in this picture. He had a dimple in his left cheek. I didn't remember that at all. It made sense that there were so many details I couldn't remember, though; I'd seen him exactly once. And I desperately needed to see him again.

As soon as I unpacked, I called Stacy from my bedroom phone to tell her about the concert tickets. I'd been worried that she wouldn't be all that excited about the concert — she was far more into Bryan these days than the New Kids — but she screamed so loudly into the phone that I

324

had to hold it away from my ear, and I grinned, relieved.

"That is so cool!" she said. "And we'll stay overnight in Atlanta? I'll ask my mom, but I know she'll say yes. Have you called Chris yet?"

"As soon as I get off the phone with you."

"He is really into you, Molly," she said. "I know he can't wait to see you again."

"Me, either," I said, and I got off the phone as quickly as I could, anxious to call him.

"So, who did you cut out of that picture you sent me?" Chris asked, right after we'd said hello. I heard the smile in his voice. I could picture his eyes and his long eyelashes. I could imagine that dimple flashing in his left cheek.

"Just a friend," I said.

"Well, I'm glad you cut her — or him — out so I could just focus on you."

He was so sweet! "It was a her," I said. "And thanks for your picture, too. It's so good."

I told him about the tickets to the New Kids concert and was relieved when he said he thought it was cool Stacy and I would get to go.

"This'll be your first concert?" he asked.

"Yes."

"Awesome," he said. "Me and Bryan saw Aerosmith in Charlotte a few months ago. It's such a different experience, hearing a band live."

"Was that *your* first concert?" I asked.

"Hell no!" He laughed. "That was Van Halen, 1984. So awesome. You never forget your first concert."

"I can't wait," I said.

He was quiet a moment. "You never forget your first *time,* either." He spoke slowly, as though he wanted me to get his meaning. It took me a minute, and when I caught on, my stomach knotted up and I didn't know what to say. He kept on talking. "I want to be your first time, Molly," he said.

Oh my God. I couldn't believe he'd come right out and say that to me. I was both happy and flustered. "I . . . um," I stammered. "I'd like that, too," I said, "but not for a while. Okay? I'm really . . . I just don't want to . . ."

He laughed. "Relax," he said. "We have all the time in the world."

"Right," I said, relieved.

"But seriously, now, Molly." His voice sounded so grown-up all of a sudden. He sounded like a man. "When do I get to see you again?"

■ ■ ■ ■

At dinner that night — just salads for Daddy and me, since we were still stuffed from the pig pickin' — Mom told us that Uncle Trevor had brought a survey team out to look at Morrison Ridge while we were away. Her voice was tight as she talked.

Maybe this is why everything feels different, I thought. Mom was upset over whatever Uncle Trevor was up to.

"I told him to stay off our acreage," Mom said, as she held a forkful of lettuce in front of Daddy's mouth, "but I doubt he listened. He was already three sheets to the wind when I talked to him and it was only two in the afternoon."

My father shook his head, frowning. "His drinking has gotten way out of hand," he said.

"I'm almost certain Jim and Claudia let him on their land," Mom said. "I don't think they see the harm in it, and Trevor can walk all over Claudia."

Daddy ignored the lettuce. "Does my mother know he had a surveyor out here?" he asked.

Mom shook her head as she lowered the fork back to my father's salad bowl. "He's keeping her in the dark," she said.

"Son of a bitch." There was an uncharacteristic growl in Daddy's voice. "He can be a selfish bastard when he wants to be."

"What does it all mean?" I asked, shaken by Daddy's rare anger. We'd had such a good time on the tour and he'd been so upbeat. Now his good mood was disintegrating before my eyes, and I was angry with Uncle Trevor for being the cause.

"He's gathering more ammunition to try to persuade us to sell some of our land," Daddy explained. "It's nothing for you to worry about. He's wasting his time and riling everyone up, that's all."

I had a feeling it was worse than that, but Daddy abruptly changed the subject, asking my mother how the plans were going for the midsummer party. Clearly, he didn't want to talk about Trevor and the land anymore.

"We met to assign tasks while you were away," Mom said. "You and Molly are supposed to select the music. Bess says we need something for all ages, so you'll have to keep that in mind."

"Nanny likes big band music and Frank Sinatra stuff," I said, happy to get my father's mind on something other than

Uncle Trevor. I didn't like Nanny's taste in music myself, but I guessed she was right: we should have something for everyone.

"Jim is planning to have a beer tasting," Mom continued. "Claudia and I have been baking up a storm and freezing everything, and we're hiring a couple of college kids to walk around with hors d'oeuvres and glasses of wine."

"Fancy," Daddy said. He sipped water through the straw my mother held to his lips.

"We'll check the weather a couple of days before to make sure we don't need to set up the tent over the pavilion," Mom said.

Daddy groaned. "I hope not. Major production, during which I can only help by shouting directions that are never appreciated." He smiled at me, but it looked like it took some effort. I remembered someone's birthday party a couple of years ago when we had to set up the tent. Uncle Trevor ended up cussing Daddy out, shouting something like, "If you don't like the way we're doing it, you can come up here and do it yourself!"

"What about chairs?" Daddy asked.

"Trevor and Jim already carted them to the pavilion. They're under tarps for now. They set up the lights, too. And the trash cans. And the volleyball net in case anyone feels like breaking an ankle in that rutted field in the dark."

Daddy sighed. "I'm exhausted just thinking about all the work they've done." He sounded sad and I wished I had a magic wand to lift his spirits again. He shook his head at the cherry tomato Mom held on the fork in front of him.

"Well," I said brightly, "we're taking care of the music, which is actually way more challenging than carting chairs across the field."

My parents looked at me with blank expressions on their faces. Then Daddy gave me a tired smile. "Nice try, Moll," he said.

"Well, it *is* challenging," I insisted. "Putting together mix tapes and everything. We have to use our brains. Anyone can cart a bunch of chairs across a field."

"If you say so," Daddy said. He really was tired.

Mom looked at me. "You've invited Stacy, right?" she asked.

"Right." I was so tempted to ask if I could invite Chris and Bryan, too, but I didn't dare. Daddy had never said another word about that crazy day at Stacy's, and I didn't want to remind him of it.

■ ■ ■ ■

After dinner, Mom and I cleaned the kitchen while Russell got Daddy ready for bed. The trip had finally caught up with my father and he wanted to turn in early. I worried that all the talk about Uncle Trevor and the land had gotten him down and I was so angry at my uncle. Why did he have to stir things up? Did he realize how he was hurting my father? Did he realize how he was hurting *everybody*?

I was loading the dishwasher, dancing a little to the music in my head, when I noticed my mother reach into the pocket of her white pharmacy coat where she'd hung it over the back of one of the kitchen chairs. Then she opened the cabinet near the stove and I could see one end of Daddy's white-and-blue stained-glass pencil case sticking out from behind a bowl on the middle shelf. So that's where the case was. Weird. I started to ask her what it was doing there, but something stopped me. I watched as she opened the case and dropped whatever had been in her hand inside it.

Closing the cabinet door, she picked up a dirty glass from the counter and handed it to me. "He had a good time on the tour, didn't he?" she asked. Her voice was soft and pensive.

"He really did," I said, drying my hands on a dish towel. "I think he loved every minute."

She reached out to touch my hair. "How was it for *you,* Molly?" she asked. Her voice was as tender as I'd ever heard it. "I worried it was too much responsibility for you, keeping those two men in line." She smiled.

"Oh yeah," I said. "They're wild and crazy, all right." I stuck out my foot. "See what Daddy bought me?"

"Your Doc Martens!" she said. "I didn't notice them till now."

Of course she didn't, since she'd barely looked at me since we got home. But I felt her attention on me now that my father was no longer in the room to absorb it.

"I love them," I said. "And he bought me this cool nail polish, too." I held out my hand and she took it in hers and studied my nails. I felt the warmth of her fingers and was surprised that I didn't want her to let go of me. I thought of how Daddy was always after me to have deep conversations with her, and for a fleeting moment, I wondered if that might be possible.

"It's so you," she said, freeing my hand, and I was slow to lower it to my side. Then she picked up the sponge from the rim of the sink and began wiping down the counter. "By the way, honey," she said, "there's another family meeting next Tuesday night. Nanny will be at this one, so do you want to ask Stacy if you could sleep over — as long as her mother will be home?"

Perfect, I thought. "Sure," I said. "I'll ask her." Maybe Chris and Bryan could come over, and maybe Stacy's mom would go upstairs and we'd have the living room to ourselves.

I could dream, couldn't I?

34
SAN DIEGO

"Molly?"

I sit at attention at my desk, my phone to my ear. By now, I recognize Zoe's voice. I'm between client appointments at work. Every once in a while, I imagine Zoe will call to tell me Perky Patti needs to talk to me again. *Since your home study, we've had some reports of your instability and Patti just wants to have a little chat with you.*

"Zoe?" I say into the phone.

"Yes, it's me. With some very good news!"

I stand up from my desk and shut my office door.

"Tell me," I say. I sound like I'm pleading. I long for good news.

"Sienna has changed her mind again," Zoe says. "She's been meeting with Kate, one of our counselors, and has decided she'd like to place her baby. She really would like to talk to you and Aidan, but she's a bit embarrassed by how she handled things before.

Are you two still willing to meet with her?"

"Yes!" I say. Maybe this was why I've been unable to stop thinking about Sienna despite our one brief contact. Have I been on her mind the way she's been on mine? In the last week, though, I've tried hard to take Aidan's advice and relax. He's made it easy for me. We've taken walks through Kensington after dinner each evening and gone to the movies twice and out to dinner with friends once and we've made love. A lot. I took sleeping pills all week to try to keep Amalia out of my dreams and it's worked. Aidan had been right. I needed to chill. And here, finally, is the payoff.

"We'd *love* to meet with her," I say.

"She said she could meet you for lunch this Saturday if that works for you, but she'd rather not meet in Leucadia. She doesn't want to bump into any of the girls she goes to school with. They're still giving her a hard time."

Poor kid, I think. "We can meet in San Diego then," I say, and I tell Zoe the name of a restaurant in Old Town. We set up a time, and when I hang up the phone, I sit still, eyes closed, trying to breathe. I'm so afraid to get my hopes up and don't want to be alone with the anxiety for another mo-

335

ment. I reach for the phone again and dial Aidan's number.

35
MORRISON RIDGE

The afternoon before the party, Mom, Aunt Claudia, and Aunt Toni bustled around our kitchen, thawing all the food they'd been making over the last week and putting together a bunch of appetizers and desserts. The flurry of activity reminded me of the kitchen at Russell's family's pig pickin', only our kitchen was bigger and brighter and quieter and you didn't have to duck your head when you walked through the doorway of the room. The sense of anticipation was the same, though. Everyone was working hard and looking forward to tonight.

While the food was being prepared, I sat on the floor in a corner of the kitchen, decorating my father's wheelchair. He was napping, so I had the chair to myself for an hour or so. I unspooled Amalia's long rolls of red, white, and blue crepe paper, weaving the streamers through the spokes of his big back wheels. I used to really get into decorating his chair for special events, but now it seemed sort of lame. I had the feeling this would be the last time I did it. I doubted he would mind.

I saw my mother take a bowl from the cabinet next to the stove and could see the stained-glass pencil case still tucked away on the middle shelf. I'd looked inside that case when I was alone in the kitchen the night before, curious to know what she'd dropped inside it from the pocket of her pharmacy coat. White pills. There were tons of them in there. For some reason, those pills were being kept separate from Daddy's other medications. I wondered if they were for a study. Maybe she was getting him into a study on the sly? I wouldn't blame her. Whatever she was doing, I hoped it worked.

Mom and my aunts had been talking about all sorts of things while they worked — recipes, the perfect weather predicted for this evening, Uncle Jim's beer tasting, who was coming to the party tonight — and I wasn't paying much attention to them until I became aware that they were whispering. I stopped threading the crepe paper through the spokes, keeping my hands still as I tried to listen. They huddled together at the counter near the sink, their backs to me, their hands busy, and I caught only a few words.

"Will the doctor be there?" Aunt Claudia asked.

My mother said something I couldn't hear, then added, ". . . a friend of Amalia's."

"Oh Lord," Aunt Claudia said. "No doubt a quack, then."

"Doesn't really matter, does it?" My mother sounded tired all of a sudden. She glanced over her shoulder at me, and I quickly busied myself with the crepe paper. When she started talking again, her voice was a whisper and I couldn't understand a word. I probably wouldn't have cared if they hadn't been so secretive about their conversation. So, some doctor was coming to the party tonight? Amalia's friend? Maybe Amalia finally had a boyfriend. So what if she brought someone? Why were they being so hush-hush about it? I supposed this was the way they usually gossiped about Amalia, and it was not meant for my ears.

I ran the red streamer up the back of the wheelchair and wrapped it around the support for the headrest, then glanced at the clock on the microwave. It was a little after four and Stacy's mom would be dropping her off any minute. I couldn't wait to see her — it had been ages. We had to make our plans for Tuesday night. Mom had verified that Stacy's mother would be home and Bryan and Chris were definitely coming over. Stacy was annoyed that her mother had to be there, but maybe it was a good thing as long as she gave us some privacy. I didn't trust myself to be able to stop Chris when he started kissing me the way he had that day we got together. His kisses were too amazing. Katherine and Michael went all the way in *Forever,* but they were three years older than me. Plus, Katherine had birth control pills. If I got pregnant . . . Oh my God. I didn't even want to think about it!

Uncle Trevor came into the kitchen through the back door and he instantly seemed to take up all the air in the room. He didn't seem to notice me as he walked over to the counter where Mom and Aunt Toni were now frosting a big tray of cupcakes. He stood between them, a beefy arm around each of their waists, a beer in his right hand. "Look at these two lovelies," he said. His empty hand slid from my mother's waist to the seat of her jeans, and I watched her calmly reach behind her to brush his arm away.

"Trevor," she said without looking at him, "do we have enough charcoal? Have you checked?"

"Plenty of charcoal, Nora," he said, taking a step away to lean against the counter. "Everything's ready at the pavilion. Jim and I are setting up the fireworks. Going to be the best show ever." I could see the definition of every muscle in his bulging thighs and calves. The mounds of his biceps. I thought of Daddy's body, wasting away, and felt angry over the unfairness of it all.

"How many beers have you had already?" Aunt Toni turned to him, the spatula in her hand slathered with chocolate frosting. He didn't answer her but I knew he was pretty well loaded. I didn't think he'd touch my mother the way he had unless he was well on his way to getting drunk.

"Molly" — Mom turned to look at me — "Stacy will be here soon. Why don't you take the wheelchair onto the porch? It's already crowded enough in here."

She was right. I piled the tape and scissors and the rest of the crepe paper onto the seat of the chair and pushed it out of the kitchen, through the living room and onto the porch just as Stacy was getting out of her mother's van in our driveway. Stacy slung her backpack over her shoulder and waved to me.

"Hi, Molly!" she called as she ran up our

341

driveway. Her mother drove off, tooting her horn, and the van had disappeared behind the trees by the time Stacy reached the porch. She ran up the steps and gave me a hug. "I've missed you so much!" she said. "And where's your dad? I need to give him a hug, too. I can't believe he got us those tickets!"

"He's lying down," I said. "He wants to have some energy for the party tonight."

"This is going to be so amazing!" She lowered her voice to a whisper. "I brought a little bag of you-know-what," she said.

It took me a moment to understand. I was so dense. "Cool," I said, though I wasn't sure where we could smoke it. I'd have to figure it out. I wanted to feel that buzz again. "I'm not sure where we can do it, though."

"Maybe in the woods?" she suggested, then seemed to notice the wheelchair for the first time even though it was sitting right there between us. "What are you doing?" she asked.

"Decorating it. What do you think?"

"Cute!" she said. "It looks like the Fourth of July."

That worried me. "It does," I said, realizing she was right. "I should add some green or something."

"No, it looks great." She leaned over to straighten a strand of crepe paper where it sagged on one of the wheels.

"Hi, Stacy." My mother appeared in the doorway, drying her hands with a dish towel. "Nice to see you again."

"Hi, Mrs. . . . Nora." Stacy smiled at her, and I noticed the total innocence in her face. She could be an actress. I still didn't know if my father or Russell ever told my mother exactly what happened at Stacy's house. She'd never said a word to me about it, but since she was so adamant that Stacy's mom be home when I went over there on Tuesday, I figured she and my father must have talked. How much detail he went into — how much *he* knew, for that matter, since it was Russell who had been inside to get a whiff of the weed — I had no idea.

"Why don't you girls get ready for the party and then you can help us load all the food into Trevor's truck to take to the pavilion?" Mom asked.

"Okay." I looked at Stacy. "I'll take the chair to my father and meet you in my bedroom."

In my room, we helped each other with our makeup, which felt kind of stupid since there'd be nobody at the party for us to

343

impress, plus the sun would soon be going down and it would be dark, but it was still fun. I showed her Chris's picture, which I'd started carrying around with me in my pocket, and she told me she was seriously considering going all the way with Bryan. I was torn between excitement and flat out fear when she talked like that.

"What about . . . you know, getting pregnant?" I asked.

"He'll use a condom." She shrugged. "No big deal."

"Katherine took birth control pills." We talked about Katherine from *Forever* as though she truly existed.

"Like I could tell my mother I wanted the pill!" Stacy said.

We changed into our short skirts and tank tops and she squealed with envy when I put on my Doc Martens. "You are so lucky," she said, and I realized this was not the first time she'd said those words to me. She might have been beautiful, but I had the parents with a happy marriage and a nice house and the hundred acres that would always be in my family. I looked down at my beautiful purple boots with their bright yellow stitching. "Do you want to wear them tonight?" I offered.

Her dark eyes widened. "Are you kidding?" she asked. "I'd love to! I'm size six and a half, though. What are they?"

"Nine," I said. "Do you want to try?"

She shook her head sadly. "I'd swim in them," she said, looking down at her sandals. "I don't know how I got such puny feet. It's amazing I don't fall over. Thank you, though." She hugged me again. Her hair smelled like peaches. "They look awesome on you."

Stacy pulled a joint and a book of matches from a plastic bag in her purse and tucked them inside her tank top, working them into the side of her bra.

"Can you tell?" she asked me. Her tank top was skintight — same as mine — but as long as her arm was down, the bumps beneath the fabric were undetectable.

"No problem," I said. Then I reached for the bottle of insect repellent I kept on my dresser. "One more thing we need to do before we go downstairs," I said, holding up the bottle.

"Ugh, you're kidding."

"I wish," I said, spraying my legs. I handed the bottle to her and she gave her own legs a spritz.

"Oh my God, we stink!" She laughed.

We did, but I imagined nearly everyone on the pavilion would be wearing the same scent tonight.

Downstairs, Mom and my aunts were loading trays of food and ice chests into the bed of Uncle Trevor's truck and we got to work helping them. We rode to the pavilion in my mother's car with her, following behind the truck. Mom talked about the college students she'd hired to help pass trays of food tonight and I told Stacy about the mix tapes Daddy and I had put together. Stacy kept touching the side of her breast where she'd hidden the joint. *Not too obvious,* I thought. When we got out of the car, I'd have to tell her to leave it alone. I still wasn't sure we should try to smoke that joint here tonight.

When we arrived at the pavilion, we helped my mother and aunts spread the trays out on the tables that were scattered around the perimeter. Uncle Jim was setting up a portable bar with his varieties of beer. Someone had placed a bunch of chairs on both the pavilion and the lawn and someone else had raised the giant floodlights. I loved seeing those lights. It always felt magical to me, late at night, when all the people were illuminated. One of my favorite things to do was to walk out on the lawn during a party and look back at the pavilion. The chatter of the crowd would be a little muffled, the music hard to make out, and the whole party would be a small luminous rectangle of joy. I couldn't wait for tonight.

It was amazing how quickly the pavilion and the scruffy lawn around it filled with people that evening. The Morrison Ridge families were there, of course, and each family had invited their friends, so that by the time daylight had faded and the floodlights came on, there had to be over a hundred people milling around the food tables and drinking bottles of beer and plastic glasses of wine. Uncle Trevor had a beer in his hand every time I saw him, and he was spending a lot of time at Uncle Jim's bar. I overheard Aunt Claudia tell him to slow down and knew he was already loaded.

Dani and a friend — a guy with a white Mohawk — sat on the edge of the pavilion smoking cigarettes. I pointed her out to Stacy from where we stood by one of the appetizer tables. "There's my cousin Dani," I said.

Stacy nodded. "Who's the guy she's with?" She reached for another tortilla chip. We'd been gorging on them for the last ten minutes.

"No clue," I said.

"Bryan remembers her from when she was in public school," Stacy said, dipping the chip into a bowl of salsa. "He says she's really weird."

"She is," I said, but I remembered that she'd defended me to Chris and I didn't feel all that good about dissing her just then.

Someone suddenly turned the music up loud and the party kicked into high gear as people started dancing to the mix tapes Daddy and I'd put together. We'd created a mishmash — Sinatra followed by Michael Jackson followed by the Electric Slide followed by Eric Clapton followed by Patsy Cline followed by some big band music for Nanny and on and on like that. It was my idea to throw all that different music together so no one would have any idea what was coming up next. Daddy said the mixture was "nauseating," but he went along with it anyway.

Stacy and I danced like crazy, teaching some of the adults the electric slide and a few other dances we knew. I watched for Amalia, thinking it would be fun to dance with her, but I didn't see her. Everyone seemed to like being surprised by the music, waiting after each song to hear what would come next, sometimes laughing when the music started, sometimes groaning, but nearly everyone was on their feet.

After a while, Stacy and I piled little plates with cheese and crackers and sat scrunched together on one of the big speakers in the corner of the pavilion to people-watch while we ate. Most people danced on the wooden floor, but some of them spilled onto the lawn, which was only one big step down from the platform. Many of the women danced in their bare feet. I watched them move around on the rough grass and leaned over to shout in Stacy's ear, "They'll have chigger bites in the morning!"

"Along with their hangovers!" Stacy laughed.

There were so many people, a lot of them strangers to me, that Nanny's initial refusal to invite Amalia seemed particularly mean and ridiculous. Amalia and my mother could both be here and not even see each other, not that I thought either one of them would care one little bit.

Janet and Peter and Peter's wife, Helen, had all arrived together, and Janet had a man with her, so there went my idea of fixing her up with Russell. The man she was with was tall and blond and I thought he looked like a Viking. She had on her Whitney Houston wig and she and the Viking looked amazing together, especially when they danced. By comparison, Peter and Helen seemed subdued, keeping to themselves in one little spot on the pavilion. They nibbled things from a shared plate and talked to each other as if they were socially inept, which I knew they were not. At one point Russell pushed Daddy over to them and left him there for a while. The three of them talked, but there were no smiles or party faces, although my father had his back to me so I couldn't see his expression. It made me wonder about Peter's so-called professional jealousy and if that was what was behind his serious look tonight. When Russell came back to wheel Daddy away, Helen bent over and hugged my father, holding on to him for a long time, her cleavage practically in his face. It was sort of bizarre.

Stacy leaned over to speak in my ear. "No one would miss us if we went into the woods and smoked a J," she said, nodding toward the woods at the side of the pavilion. I still hadn't decided if we should try to sneak away or not. I saw Nanny walking toward us at that moment and knew that we wouldn't be sneaking anywhere quite yet.

"Hi, Nanny!" I shouted over the music.

"Hi, dear!" she shouted back. She wore a loose red blouse over a long white skirt and lots of gold jewelry, and her hair was in some sort of updo. I wasn't used to seeing her dressed up. "Didn't we pick a perfect night for this?" she asked.

"Yes," I agreed, as though we had something to do with the weather.

Nanny leaned over to get a good look at Stacy. "The girl on the bike, right?" she asked.

"Right." Stacy smiled her beauty queen smile. "I'm Stacy."

"Welcome, dear," Nanny said. Then she frowned as a new song poured out of the speakers. "What the heck kind of music is this?" she asked.

I laughed. "Michael Jackson, Nanny," I said. "It's called 'Thriller.'"

Just then, Janet and her Viking lookalike boyfriend danced past us on the pavilion floor, the Viking doing a decent moonwalk. Stacy and I laughed, but Nanny shook her head.

"It's called moonwalking, Nanny," I said, though I wasn't sure if she was reacting to the dance or to seeing a black woman and white man dancing together. I thought Russell was the first black person Nanny'd ever really gotten to know.

I saw Russell now as he pushed Daddy toward us across the pavilion.

351

"Hey, girls. Hey, Mom," Daddy said, when Russell parked him between us and Nanny. He was facing the dance floor. "Great shindig, don't you think?" I couldn't tell if he was talking to Nanny or to Stacy and me.

"It's wonderful," Nanny said, her voice suddenly thick. She reached down and lifted my father's hand into both of hers. Gently, she kneaded his useless fingers and I felt my eyes burn. What was it like, watching your grown child being taken inch by inch by such a cruel disease? I wished Stacy wasn't sitting between me and my father and Nanny right then. I wanted to be a part of them at that moment.

Russell sat down in the white plastic chair next to me. "Feels good to sit," he said. His voice was loud above the music. "Crazy mix tape you came up with," he added, and I laughed.

Next to me, Stacy suddenly caught her breath. She tipped her head toward mine and whispered in my ear, "Isn't that woman your . . ." She nodded toward the dancers and I spotted the woman she was looking at: Amalia. The music had changed to Eric Clapton's "Layla," and Amalia was on the dance floor — where else would she be? — dressed in a gauzy turquoise skirt and a tank top the same color, her thick hair spilling over her shoulders.

I whispered back, "Yes," I said. "Amalia."

Amalia was dancing with an older man I didn't know, and I wondered if it was the doctor my mother had mentioned in the kitchen that afternoon. But she only danced with him a moment before moving on to another partner, and then on to the Viking, and the sea of dancers parted a little to let them have the floor. Maybe this was why Nanny hadn't wanted Amalia here. She was like a magnet, attracting everyone's attention. It was impossible for her to simply disappear into the crowd. My mother, wherever she was, could hardly avoid seeing her. Amalia spun around the floor with the Viking for a moment, then turned him loose and headed for Peter, who held up his hands to ward her off. Peter was smiling but immovable, and everyone laughed as she gave up, twirling in a circle as she looked for her next partner. I saw her zero in on Russell and knew she was about to be turned down again. But she grabbed Russell by the hand and pulled him out of his chair and onto the dance floor before he could protest. Next to Stacy, Daddy laughed.

"Come on, man!" Daddy shouted to him. "Show her what you've got!"

To my absolute shock, Russell turned into a dancing machine, rocking his hips, punching the air with his arms, bopping his head. I couldn't remember the last time I'd heard my father laugh so hard, while I gaped openmouthed at this new side of Russell.

"Woo-hoo!" Stacy cheered, fists in the air.

"Oh, good heavens," Nanny said, turning away from them as though the very sight of Amalia and Russell dancing together offended her, which I supposed it did.

"Mother." Daddy was still laughing. "Get a grip."

Amalia finished the dance with Russell and curtsied to him as he left the dance floor. He was grinning when he walked back to us, and Amalia moved away from our side of the pavilion, most likely looking for her next partner.

"High five!" Daddy said to Russell, who lifted my father's arm so he could high-five him. Russell laughed as he took his seat next to me again, beads of sweat on his forehead.

"That was awesome!" Stacy leaned past me to say to him, and he smiled at her. I had the feeling that, with those three words, she might have changed Russell's negative feelings about her. I hoped so, anyway.

After a while, Nanny disappeared into the

crowd of people and Russell and Daddy went to check out Uncle Jim's beer tasting. I looked at Stacy. "Finally!" I said. "Let's go."

We quickly left the pavilion, keeping the giant lights and speaker between us and the crowd as we jumped to the ground and made our way quickly to the woods. The music grew muffled behind us as we slipped between the trees. I led the way, grateful for the nearly full moon.

"This is far enough, isn't it?" Stacy asked after we'd gone a short distance. I remembered how nervous she'd been when we'd had to walk through the woods near the springhouse that night we slept out there.

"A little farther," I said. She would probably not be happy to discover where I was taking us.

Soon, the woods opened up to a small rectangular clearing.

"We're here," I said. "This is perfect."

"Where are we?" she asked. Then she seemed to catch on as the moonlight cast boxy shadows on the ground. "Oh no!" She took a step backward. "Is this the graveyard?"

I laughed. "It's a good place to sit," I said, climbing over the low iron fence, which was nearly invisible in the darkness. I sat down on the ground, leaning against one of the three big double headstones. I wasn't sure whose it was and didn't really want to know. My grandpa Arnette was buried beneath one of them. His name was on one half of the headstone, while the other half remained blank, waiting for Nanny. That was a little creepy, and I hoped I wasn't resting against their stone. I was acting much braver than I felt.

Stacy reluctantly climbed over the fence and sat down next to me. "You know," she said, "I really like your house and even your springhouse and your family and Russell and everything, but there's still something spooky about Morrison Ridge."

"Well, let's smoke your joint and then we won't care," I said.

She reached into the side of her tank top and brought out the joint and the matches. She lit the joint and we both took a hit from it. I leaned my head back against the cool headstone and closed my eyes, waiting to feel something. I could hear the music from the party. I loved how it sounded from this distance, dampened by the woods. I loved how the rise and fall of the music played against the steady hum of voices and the occasional peal of laughter that bounced off the trees around us.

Stacy suddenly let out a yelp and I opened my eyes to see her jump to her feet. Two figures had risen up from one of the other double headstones and were moving toward us. I tried to jump to my own feet, but I was so shocked I couldn't move. Then I saw the white Mohawk catch the moonlight and let out my breath. Dani and her friend.

"It's only my cousin," I said to Stacy, tugging the hem of her skirt as Dani's pale face came into view.

"Boo!" her weird friend said as they walked closer to us. In the darkness, they seemed to float.

"You two going to share that joint with us?" Dani asked.

"You scared the shit out of me!" Stacy said. She sat down next to me again and I felt the tremor in her body. I was shaking myself. I didn't know if Dani would narc on us, but the fact that she wanted to share the joint seemed like a good sign.

I took the joint from Stacy's hand and held it out to my cousin. Dani took it from me, and then she and the boy with the Mohawk sat down across from us, their backs against another of the headstones.

Dani took a long hit on the joint. "This is my cousin Molly and her friend," she said to the boy, her voice straining as she tried to hold in the smoke. She looked at Stacy. "I don't remember your name," she said.

"Stacy," Stacy said.

"And this is Ralph." Dani nodded to the boy, who now had possession of the joint.

Ralph? The name of Michael's penis in *Forever*? I didn't dare look at Stacy. I was sure we were both cracking up inside.

"Hi," I managed to say. Ralph said nothing, but he leaned forward to hand the joint to me and I took another hit and passed it to Stacy. I was beginning to feel it now. My arm seemed to belong to someone else when Stacy took the joint from me.

"You two shouldn't be doing this." Dani motioned to the joint. "You're only what? Twelve now?"

"Fourteen," I said. She knew perfectly well how old I was. She was just trying to put me down in front of her boyfriend or whatever he was. *She acted like your personal bodyguard,* Chris had said about Dani. Why was she such a bitch to me, then? She was probably still angry with me for hitting her. I thought I could still see the shadow of a bruise on her cheek, but it may have been the way the moonlight fell on her face.

"Do you go to Owen High?" Stacy asked Ralph.

His slit-eyed nod was barely perceptible and I had the feeling our joint was not the first he'd smoked that night.

"Do you know Bryan Watkins?" Stacy asked.

Ralph nodded. "Asshole," he said, and Stacy wrinkled her nose at him.

"Like you would have a clue," she said.

"He probably has more of a clue than you ever will," Dani said snottily.

I wanted to put an end to this stupid conversation, afraid it was about to escalate, but before I could think of something to say, the steady hum of sound coming from the party suddenly ceased as though someone had flipped a switch. We all turned our heads in the direction of the pavilion. We couldn't hear a thing.

"What's going on?" Stacy asked.

"I don't know," I said. "Maybe someone's going to make a speech or something?"

We heard a sudden shout. I couldn't tell if it had come from a man or a woman, but I was certain there was alarm in the sound.

"Something weird is happening," I said, getting to my feet. I stepped over the fence and headed through the woods in the direction of the pavilion. I could hear a couple of male voices now, loud and angry. I picked up my speed and heard Stacy close behind

359

me, probably not wanting to lose sight of me in the dark woods. I thought Dani was behind me as well, though I didn't turn to see.

When I broke free of the woods, I saw the pavilion illuminated by the four floodlights, the partygoers frozen in a sea of color. There was no music. No dancing. Just those angry voices. Most of the people stood clotted together on one side of the platform and soon I was close enough to see what they were looking at: my father and Uncle Trevor in the middle of an argument at one side of the platform.

". . . sick of talking about this!" my father shouted when I reached the corner of the pavilion. "Leave it alone, will you? No one's selling any land to you, and if you —"

"So now you speak for everybody?" Uncle Trevor towered over my father. His face was bright red, and in the overhead lights I saw spit fly from his mouth when he shouted. "No one else gets an opinion? You always have to have your own fucking way!"

I stood there frozen. One of the big speakers and the base of a floodlight were between my father and me, but I could see him perfectly. He sat immobilized while Uncle Trevor bobbed and weaved around him like a boxer, moving in and out of my

360

vision. My heart ached at how skinny and frail Daddy looked in his chair.

"You think I give a shit about the god-damned 'family land'?" Uncle Trevor made quote marks with his fingers around the words. "This so-called family's dwindling to nothing, anyhow. There's nobody left to carry on with the Ridge, anyway."

I hoped Nanny wasn't close enough to hear him talk about Morrison Ridge that way. I searched the people circled around Uncle Trevor and Daddy, but didn't see her.

Aunt Toni suddenly shot out of the crowd, trying to grab Uncle Trevor's shoulder. She said something I couldn't hear, and I gasped when he pushed her roughly away, nearly knocking her over. She let out a yelp and someone yanked her back into the press of people.

"Damn it, Trevor!" my father was shouting. It was his furious voice, the voice I so rarely heard, and yet it was no match for Uncle Trevor's threatening physical presence. I gripped the corner of the pavilion, frightened. "Go home and sober up!" Daddy shouted.

Stacy was suddenly next to me, her hands circling my arm so hard they hurt. "He's totally drunk," she said, and I felt her shudder. "God," she added, "he reminds me of my fa—"

"I'm developing my land no matter what the rest of you assholes choose to do!" Trevor barked at my father.

"Only if you're a selfish son of a bitch," Daddy shouted. "Don't you care that you'll break your mother's —"

"You call *me* selfish?" Trevor took a step toward him and I could swear I felt the whole pavilion tremble beneath my fingers where they rested on the wood. "I've never known anyone as selfish as —"

"Shut up!" Daddy yelled. "Just cool it, will you? You're too drunk to talk rationally. And you're wrecking the —"

"And you're always the rational one, right?" Spit flew out of Uncle Trevor's mouth. "The fucking golden boy. Off to college while I bust my back helping Daddy and you get your string of degrees. You were so special, weren't you?"

Daddy went quiet, but only for a few seconds. When he spoke again, his voice was very calm. "There's still a hurt little kid inside you, Trev," he said.

"Shut the fuck up!" Uncle Trevor took another menacing step toward my father and my whole body tensed. The older man Amalia had been dancing with — the doctor? — suddenly grabbed my uncle's arm, holding him back. "I don't need you psychoanalyzing me!" Uncle Trevor shouted at Daddy.

"You're forty-six years old," my father said. "It's time you let go of your adolescent grudges and grew up."

Uncle Trevor seemed to run out of words. He pulled out of the man's grasp, his eyes wide with fury, and I could tell he was about to explode.

"Uncle Trevor!" I called, hoping to get his attention on me and off my father, but I didn't think he even heard me. He grabbed the armrests of Daddy's wheelchair and gave it a forceful shove, all of his weight and bulk behind it. In the darkness, maybe he couldn't tell how close the chair was to the edge of the pavilion, but from my vantage point, I saw the catastrophe about to unfold in front of me.

"Stop!" I shouted, waving my arms helplessly in the air. *"No!"*

"Uncle Graham!" Dani screamed as she ran past me, reaching her arms out in front of her as though she could somehow prevent the chair from tumbling off the pavilion, but Uncle Trevor had pushed it with so much force that the chair shot off the platform like a bullet. It seemed to be suspended in midair for a split second before tipping backward and landing on the ground with a terrible thud.

I screamed, standing there in horror, unable to make my legs move until Stacy grabbed my arm and propelled me forward.

Dani reached my father first. "Uncle Graham!" she cried, dropping to the ground next to him. "Oh my God!"

I reached the chair and saw that Daddy had spilled out of it and lay a couple of feet away on the ground. Horrified, I knelt down on the opposite side of him from Dani.

It was too dark to clearly see his face, but I thought he was looking up at me. "I think I'm all right," he said, his voice a whisper. Hearing him speak reassured me. Someone on the pavilion yelled to call an ambulance and I looked up to see Uncle Trevor backing away from the edge of the platform, hands over his face, as if afraid to see any damage he'd caused. "I'm sorry!" he shouted. "*Fuck.* I'm sorry!"

Aunt Toni suddenly appeared in front of him and she smacked him across the face like she was trying to snap him back to reality. "Go home, you big bully!" she shouted, but he stood there crying into his hands like an overgrown little boy. I turned away from him, my attention back on my father — and on Dani, who had gently lifted his head to her lap. Someone had turned one of the floodlights so it illuminated Daddy and the rest of us on the ground. I saw Stacy sitting with her back against the pavilion, her hands at the sides of her head as though she couldn't believe what she was seeing. And I saw that Dani's thick black eyeliner and mascara was smeared, the skin wet around her eyes. Ralph had disappeared, but Dani didn't seem to care. *This is my real cousin,* I thought. *Beneath the hard edges, beneath the bitchiness, she's a good person.*

I was aware of the hushed crowd above us on the pavilion, but not who was in it. All I knew was that there were women with hands to their mouths and men unsure what to do to help. My mother pushed through the clot of people and jumped to the ground next to me, dropping quickly to her knees at my father's side. His head still rested in Dani's lap.

"Oh, Graham," my mother said, almost in a whisper. She smoothed a hand over his hair and leaned over to press her lips to his forehead. "Where are you hurt?" I knew she had to see what I was seeing: tears welling up in Daddy's eyes. I'd never seen him cry.

"I don't want that ambulance," Daddy said quietly to her. "Just get me up."

"All right." She turned to look above us at the crowd. "Where's Russell?" she called to no one in particular.

"I'll look for him!" Stacy got to her feet and climbed onto the pavilion, disappearing into the crowd.

"I can help get him up," Dani said.

"Me, too," I said, though I knew how hard it was to move my father's body even an inch, much less back into his chair.

Amalia suddenly appeared next to me, as if she'd materialized out of thin air. She bent down to touch Daddy's shoulder, her hair brushing my cheek as it fell forward, and my mother suddenly snapped at her.

"I've *got* him, Amalia!" she said.

Amalia's eyes widened in surprise, but then she nodded. "I'll help find Russell," she said, backing away, and I watched her disappear into the darkness as quickly as she'd appeared.

Peter walked around the corner of the pavilion. "How can I help?" he asked my mother.

She looked behind me, and I knew she was searching for Russell. "We can't do it without —"

"I'm here!" Russell appeared on the pavilion above us.

"Thank God," Mom said under her breath.

In a moment, Russell was on the ground with us. He knelt next to Dani, attempting to check the back of Daddy's head with a small flashlight. "Good thing we changed out that head support on your chair," he said quietly to my father. "The old one could have snapped your neck."

No one said anything and I guessed we were all thinking the same thing: Daddy was already essentially paralyzed from the neck down. How could it have been any worse?

"Any pain, Graham?" Russell asked him.

"I'm *fine,*" Daddy insisted. "Just get me up, Russ, all right?"

Russell looked at my mother. "I'll move him back into the chair," he said. "Then I'll need some help to lift the chair upright."

"No ambulance." Daddy said again. "The last thing I want is a damn hospital."

Russell looked at someone above us on the pavilion — I couldn't see who. "Stop the ambulance!" he shouted.

"Are you sure?" my mother asked Daddy, worry in her voice.

"*Yes,* I'm sure." He sounded impatient and I knew he wanted this whole ordeal over with.

We all drew back a little, letting Russell

and Peter move Daddy's legs and arms and body into the toppled chair, while Dani still cradled his head carefully — almost expertly, as though she worked every day with disabled people.

"Molly and Nora," Russell said, "stand up and stay right in front of him so he doesn't fall out of the chair when Peter and I set it upright."

I stood up and was instantly hit by that spacey feeling from the marijuana. I wished I hadn't smoked it now. I braced myself, my feet wide apart, hands forward, ready to help. I watched Russell and Peter lift the chair and my father into an upright position. They seemed to be moving in slow motion. Mom leaned forward to hold on to Daddy's shoulders, and I placed my hands against his chest in case he slid forward. His ribs felt like twigs beneath my palms. His head was close to mine and only then did I realize I was sobbing.

"I'm fine, Moll," he said, his voice almost a whisper. "Utterly humiliated, but that's the worst of it."

I couldn't speak. I wished I could hug him right then. What must it have felt like to fall backward off the pavilion? My stomach lurched thinking about it. I could imagine the fear. I thought of how I'd been trying to make him happy these past few weeks. I'd tried to make his life fun and worth living. I felt as though all that effort had been snuffed out in one single second.

Russell bent over to speak in my father's ear. "Carry you home?" he asked.

"And miss the fireworks?" Daddy asked. "No way."

But he did go home. My mother insisted and he didn't put up much of a fight. Some other people left as well — Uncle Trevor and Aunt Toni among them — and I couldn't find my grandmother anywhere. I didn't know if she was even aware of what had happened. I hoped not.

Stacy and I sat side by side on one of the speakers again to watch the fireworks and she kept saying she was worried about me and asking if I was all right and I felt touched by how protective and caring she was. The fireworks were lost on me, though. Lost on most of us, I thought. Our oohs and ahhs sounded forced, and I knew that something precious had been stolen from the night.

36

Stacy and I walked the zigzagging eastern half of the loop road home from the pavilion, dodging the cars that were leaving the party. I knew I should have stayed to help clean up, but I would come back in the morning. Right now, I wanted to see my father. I needed to know he was all right.

As we walked, Stacy talked nonstop about how crazy the night had been. "Your family might be as screwed up as mine after all," she said. "Alcohol makes people do insane things. My father drank like a fish. He punched my brother so hard one time he had to go to the hospital. Child Protective Services came to the house and everything. I'm going to stick with weed myself."

I couldn't think of anything to say back to her. I kept walking, shining my flashlight ahead of us on the dirt road, too overwhelmed with my own family's problems to think about hers.

Once we reached the house, Stacy went upstairs while I walked down the hall to Daddy's room. The door was open and Russell was arranging the pillows behind his head, though Daddy appeared to be asleep. The light in the room was dim, most of the illumination coming from the open bathroom door.

I walked into the room and stood at the end of the bed. "Hi," I said to Russell.

Russell straightened up from arranging the pillows. "Did you see the fireworks?" he asked.

I nodded. "They were okay, but I was worried about Daddy." I looked at my father, who appeared to be sleeping peacefully. There was a definite bruise forming on his temple. Possibly another on his chin. "Are you sure he doesn't have a concussion, Russell?" I asked. I knew you weren't supposed to sleep if you had a concussion.

"No concussion," Russell said. "He's very lucky. I don't think he's going to feel that great tomorrow, but I've checked him out from stem to stern and there's no broken bones. So he's okay. Physically, at least."

"What do you mean, he's okay physically?"

Russell shrugged. "I think it shook him up," he said. "It would shake anybody up, don't you think?"

I nodded. "It was terrible."

Russell stepped closer to me, turning my head toward the bathroom light with two fingers on my chin. "Those big blue eyes of yours have some mighty dilated pupils," he said.

"What do you mean?" I asked.

He took his fingers from my chin. "You're a great girl, Molly, but you're just fourteen. Don't mess yourself up, all right? You need to stay strong and healthy."

I turned my head away from the light. "I don't know what you're talking about," I said, "and I'm going to bed." I left the room and headed for the stairs, trembling a little at being caught. What right did he have, judging me that way? I should have resented that parental tone he took with me, but I was having trouble working up a righteous indignation. Just then, I didn't feel as though I *had* a parent, and I couldn't help it: I felt glad that someone cared.

Upstairs, Stacy and I washed the makeup from our faces and climbed into the double bed in my room. I stared at the ceiling.

"Do you get dilated pupils from weed?" I asked.

"Oh yeah," she said. "And the munchies. I'm starving, aren't you? But I think I'm too tired to eat."

"I'm not very hungry," I said. The events of the night had killed my appetite.

Stacy didn't say anything, and after a few minutes, I heard her even breathing. I knew it would be a long time before I fell asleep myself, though. I kept picturing the scene on the ground, illuminated under the floodlights. It wasn't so much my father's face I remembered, but my cousin's. I'd been strangely touched by that smudged eyeliner. The way it trailed down her cheeks like the makeup on one of those sad clowns. I'd felt a taste of her life tonight. I could imagine how she didn't fit in well anywhere, and how she must have been mocked at school just for being who she was. Her hostility toward me — toward the world — was a defensive shell, I thought. I'd be kinder to her from now on. I wouldn't let her nastiness bring out my nastiness.

I heard voices through my open bedroom window and lay still to listen. My mother? Quietly, I got out of bed and walked over to the window. Kneeling on the floor, I pressed my face close to the screen in the darkness.

Our front steps were only a few yards below me, and my mother sat on the top step, Amalia next to her. They both clasped mugs of something balanced on their knees, and my mother held a cigarette between her fingers. I'd never seen her smoke before. I was stunned. It was as though my whole family was changing before my eyes.

I watched her lift the cigarette to her mouth and the tip glowed orange as she inhaled. She blew out the smoke, then shook her head. "I feel as though I'm losing my mind, Amalia," she said. She sounded as worn out as I'd ever heard her.

Amalia didn't say anything right away. Watching them from above, I thought she looked much younger than my mother, her hair falling in waves over her shoulders. Finally, she spoke. "Tonight felt like the last straw," she said.

My mother nodded. "Trevor could ruin everything," she said as she lifted the cigarette to her mouth again.

"I know," Amalia said. I wished I knew what they were talking about. It felt like a code to me, one only the two of them understood.

"Do you think of him as weak?" Mom asked after a moment. Her voice was so quiet I had to hold my breath to hear her.

"No," Amalia said, "but he's tired. He's so tired, Nora."

My mother seemed to catch her breath. She set her mug on the step next to her, then lowered her head to her knees, her shoulders shaking. Amalia put an arm around her, and there they sat — my two mothers, so close to me I felt as though I could raise the screen and reach out to touch them.

I wished I could.

37

I started carrying my palm stone around with me the day after the party. I didn't give the decision much thought. I simply pulled the stone from my dresser drawer and stuck it in my pocket. Every once in a while, I'd wrap my hand around it and feel an instant sense of comfort wash over me. I needed that comfort in a way I didn't understand.

Chris and I talked on the phone for a long time that day and I told him everything that happened the night before. Each time I shut my eyes, I saw Daddy and his chair sailing off the pavilion and my stomach dropped down to my toes. It was the only thing on my mind and it all came spilling out while I talked to Chris. He turned out to be a good listener, although after a while he said he had something to tell me and I realized I'd made the phone call all about me, me, me.

"Sorry," I said. "I didn't mean to dump everything on you like that."

"No problem," he said, "but I think you're going to like what I have to say. It's about Tuesday night."

"Oh my God!" I said. "Are you coming to Stacy's?"

"You've got it," Chris said. "We'll show up around midnight, once Stacy's mother's asleep. She'll never know."

"Awesome!" I said. Finally, I was going to get to see him again. I only hoped Stacy's mother was a sound sleeper. The last thing I needed was for my parents to find out I was sneaking around with Chris again.

On Monday afternoon, I was back in Daddy's office with him, typing chapter 12 of his book. I'd barely seen him the day before. He'd slept a lot, worn out from everything that had happened at the party, I guessed. Mom had stayed with him in their bedroom much of the day, and even this morning at breakfast, she was still hovering over him, brushing Russell aside so she could feed my father herself. Now, though, except for the bruises on his temple and chin and an ugly scrape on his right arm, he seemed like himself.

I looked down at the keyboard and noticed that my starry blue nail polish was chipped and ragged looking. I'd take it off later today, I thought, and give my nails a fresh coat for tomorrow night when I would finally see Chris again.

"Start a new paragraph," Daddy said.

I hit the return key, then turned to look at him. "I just realized you haven't asked me to type any case notes lately," I said. "Are all your patients on vacation or what?"

"Well," he said, "you've probably noticed over the last few months there've been fewer and fewer case notes to type."

"I figured Mom did most of it for you in the spring while I was in school because of my homework and everything."

"No," he said, "there were actually fewer." He was looking past me to the computer screen. I could see the screen reflected in the blue of his eyes, the image so perfect, I could nearly see the individual words. "I stopped taking new cases in late April and I've gradually been winding down the ones I have," he said, looking directly at me then. "I'm actually ready to terminate my practice."

"Terminate?" I was shocked. "You mean . . . *end*?"

He nodded. "Exactly."

"Why would you do that?" I asked. "You always say how much you love helping people and everything. It keeps you in touch with what's happening in the world. It gives your life purpose." The words raced out of my mouth in a panic. "That's what you always say."

He smiled at me. "You actually do listen to the things I say, don't you?" he said. He tilted his head to one side. "I'm a bit worn out, Molly," he admitted. "It's getting harder to make the trek into the office, and —"

"People could come to you!" I swiveled in the desk chair to face him. "They would! You told me about therapists who see their patients in their houses. And we need the money, don't we?"

He laughed. "No, we don't need the money," he said. "We're fine."

"Well, you could still see people here and rest in between appointments," I said. "I could help you fix up the office for them. It'd be fun and —"

"Molly," he said calmly, "I *want* this. I want to terminate. You won't change my mind. It's time and it's nothing to get so alarmed about."

"I'm not alarmed," I said. "I'm just trying to understand." I *was* alarmed. He loved his work. It gave him joy, he told me once. I felt overwhelmed at the thought of him not working. How could I find enough for him to do to keep him from getting depressed? "Will you still work on the book?" I pointed to the computer screen.

"Sure," he said. "We're nearly done with this draft, though. This is the last chapter. And then I'll turn it over to Mom and she'll whip it into shape. She's so good at —"

"You'll write another one then, though, right?" I interrupted.

"Well . . . let's see." He leaned his head against his headrest and studied the ceiling. "I've written one for kids, one for adults, and one for therapists." He looked at me with a smile. "I'm not sure who's left."

"Teenagers," I suggested.

"I think I covered teens in the one for kids, wouldn't you say?"

"You'll be bored!" I said.

"I can read. You know how much I love reading."

"That won't be enough for you," I argued. "I know what your mind is like. You'll need more to —"

"It's an early retirement, Moll," he said, his voice calm. "Lots of people take early retirements. People lucky enough to be able to afford to do it, anyway."

I turned at a knock on the doorjamb and saw Uncle Trevor standing there. The last person in the world I felt like seeing. "Hey," he said softly, and his smile was uncertain, as though he wasn't sure he'd be welcome in the room. My father's chair faced away from the door, but Daddy knew who it was without being able to see him.

"Hey, Trev," he said, as though he wasn't talking to someone who had nearly killed him two days earlier. "What's up?"

"Can I come in?" Uncle Trevor asked.

"Of course," Daddy said. I wished he'd told him "No, we're busy," but that obviously wasn't the way he planned to handle the situation. I would rather not have to see my uncle at all, ever again.

Uncle Trevor crossed the room and sat in the only spare chair, which was against the wall behind me. Daddy could easily see him in that chair, and I swiveled around to face him so the three of us formed a triangle. I could tell right away that Uncle Trevor was a different man than the sloppy drunk who'd pushed Daddy off the pavilion. He looked like he'd just gotten out of the shower, his salt-and-pepper hair damp. He was neatly dressed in khaki pants and a green Hawaiian print shirt, and his expression was sheepish.

"Just here to apologize," he said, then closed his eyes for a moment. When he opened them again, he leaned his burly forearms on his thighs, pressing his hands together. "Actually," he said, "I'm mortified." He looked like he might cry. I hoped not. I didn't want to feel sympathy for him, and that would do it. "I hardly remember what happened," he said. "What I said. What you said. What I *did.*" His chin trembled and I looked down at my hands, embarrassed for him. "*Shit,* Graham," he said, "I can't believe I did something like that."

"Apology accepted," Daddy said simply, and I could tell he meant it. He really did forgive him. I wasn't ready to.

"I'm not going to drink anymore," Uncle Trevor said. "I get stupid when I drink . . . not that that's any excuse for what I did. I didn't mean to push your chair clean off the damn pavilion. I just . . ." His voice faded and he looked down at the floor, rubbing his hands together again. "I don't think I'm an alcoholic or anything like that, but —"

"No?" Daddy asked.

Uncle Trevor looked surprised. "You think I am?"

"You have a problem with alcohol, Trevor," Daddy said. "You always have. Your personality changes when you drink . . . and quite honestly, you don't have the best personality to start with."

I stiffened, afraid of how Uncle Trevor would react to that, but he laughed. "I know," he said. "I'm a lot like Daddy." It took me a minute to realize he was talking about my grandfather. Nanny's husband. I'd never known him, but suddenly I felt as though I did.

"Right," Daddy agreed. "And he never got it under control. You can."

I was beginning to feel as though I didn't belong in the room. This was a conversation between brothers with a shared history.

"Toni says I have a way of hurting the people I love," Uncle Trevor said.

"Only when you're toasted, Trev," Daddy said.

Uncle Trevor sat back and ran his hands through his hair. "I talked to Toni for a long time last night." He glanced at me, then back to my father.

"Let's save this conversation for another time," my father said. "Molly and I need to get back to work here."

"Just . . ." Uncle Trevor began again. "I want you to know I've decided to come to the meeting on Tuesday." He stood up and took two steps to reach my father's chair. Putting his big hand around the back of Daddy's neck, he bent over to kiss the top of his head. "I love you, man," he said. "I'll be there and I'll be stone-cold sober, too. Okay?" He stood up straight again.

Daddy smiled up at him. "I appreciate that, Trev," he said. "More than I can say."

Uncle Trevor left without saying good-bye, and I looked at my father who stared out the window in a sort of trance. We were both quiet as we watched Uncle Trevor cross the yard to his truck.

"That was intense," I said, when I heard the door of the truck slam shut.

"He can be an intense guy." Daddy seemed to pull himself out of the trance, nodding toward the keyboard. "You ready to get back to work?" he asked.

I didn't lift my hands to the keys. "I'm never going to forgive him," I said, shaking my head. "He could have *killed* you, Daddy."

"You'll feel better if you do," he said.

"Maybe someday," I said, "but I'm still too mad at him right now."

"It's hard to move on if you don't forgive," he said. "It's like trying to dance with a lead weight on your shoulders. The anger can weigh you down forever."

He was talking to me in his shrink voice and it was all I could do not to roll my eyes. Instead, I swiveled to face the keyboard, lifting my fingers with their chipped starry blue nail polish to the keys. "So," I said, "where were we?"

38

SAN DIEGO

I check the screen on my cell phone for the fifth time. It's nearly twelve-thirty. Sienna had told us she'd meet us at noon. We're not off to a good start with this girl.

I dip a tortilla chip into the bowl of guacamole next to my iced tea. From across the table, Aidan gives me a weak grin. "I thought you were going to wait till she got here?" he says.

"I need something to do with my hands," I say, then I add what we're both thinking. "Has she chickened out again?" I'm insanely nervous.

Aidan looks through the restaurant window, where the view of the street is blocked by massive flowering shrubs and birds of paradise. He sighs. "God, I hope not."

Our hearts sink as the minutes tick by. I'm afraid to call Zoe. Afraid to be disappointed one more time.

"Look," Aidan says, and I follow his gaze to the door of the restaurant where a teen-aged girl stands looking a little lost, her gaze scanning the diners. Her blue knit shirt stretches over her belly.

"Oh my God, it's her," I say, getting to my feet. I walk toward her, holding out my hand. "Sienna?" I ask.

Her smile has a visible shiver to it, her lower lip quivering. Instantly, I ache for her and feel the urge to pull her into my arms, but I shake her hand instead. I'm not sure if the dampness I feel between our palms is from her hand or mine.

"I'm sorry I'm so late," she says. "I got totally turned around somehow. I've never driven in San Diego by myself before."

"No problem," I say, taking her arm, turn-ing her toward our table. Aidan stands as we near him. His smile doesn't betray his nerves, not one bit.

"Sienna," he says warmly, taking her hand in both of his. "It's wonderful to meet you." He pulls out a chair for her.

"I'm so sorry about before," she says as she awkwardly lowers herself into the chair. Her stomach brushes the table. She is hugely pregnant and I have to force my eyes away from that beautiful round belly.

"No problem," Aidan says.

"You've had a very tough decision to make," I add.

She nods with a small roll of her eyes. "It's been so hard," she agrees. "I don't have a single friend who thinks I'm doing the right thing."

"You must be a really strong person to be able to stand up to them," I say.

"I don't know how strong I am," she says with a rueful smile. "I let them talk me out of adoption once already. I'd still be planning to keep the baby if I didn't have Kate at the agency to talk to."

Thank you, Kate, I think.

Aidan and I had talked about how to structure our conversation with Sienna. We'd start out light, we'd decided. Learn about her and let her learn about us before getting into the nuts and bolts of the adoption.

"Tell us about your friends," I say. "Do you still see your old friends from before you moved into that classroom?"

"No," she says, "and I miss them a lot. That's part of why I'm choosing adoption." Her words come out quickly, a little breathlessly, her anxiety showing. I study her face as she speaks. She looks nothing like Julia Stiles. She's quite pretty, her cheeks round, her shoulder-length hair a rich brown. The overhead light picks up strands of red in her hair, and she wears glasses the same red color. Behind them her eyes are as deep and chocolaty as Aidan's and I think, *Is this what our daughter will look like?* She grows more beautiful to me by the second.

"I miss my friends and my old life," she says. "Does that sound really selfish?"

Aidan and I shake our heads in unison. "It makes sense," Aidan says.

I'm relieved when the waiter arrives and we give him our orders. I think all three of us need to take a few deep breaths.

We ask her about her family and she tells us that her father has "moved on" and has a new family. "My mom is great, though. She's totally behind the adoption."

I know a little about Sienna's mother. Zoe told me she'd wanted to join us at lunch today, but that Sienna pleaded to let her have this first meeting with us on her own.

"She doesn't want me to mess up my education and everything," she says. "My little brother's excited about being an uncle, though. He can't wait to see the baby."

I know Aidan is watching my face to see how I react to the news that Sienna's little brother apparently plans to be in our baby's life. I keep my expression impassive.

"I had kind of a lame childhood," she says.

"No father around, so I really wanted a couple that had a good marriage and yours seemed really good."

"It is," Aidan reassures her.

"It's solid," I say, smiling at my husband.

"We never did *anything* fun growing up," Sienna continues. "My mom works all the time — she works at this car place — and we never go anywhere fun. So when I saw all the pictures of the things you do, I could imagine my baby growing up getting to do things and be active and everything. It was a no-brainer."

I am dying to ask her how we beat out the couple with the little girl and the dog, but don't want to bring that family up if she's forgotten about them. The waiter delivers our food. Sienna ordered vegetarian quesadillas and I wonder briefly if she gets enough protein in her diet. I will not ask. For now, her baby is her baby. I have to remember that.

"Are you into music?" she asks as she cuts a small bite of quesadilla on her plate. "Because I really am and I hope my baby will be, too."

"We love music," I say honestly, although I'm thinking, *Doesn't everybody?*

"Do you play an instrument?" Aidan asks.

"Guitar, a little. Though it's gotten hard

to do with this." She pats her stomach.

Aidan asks her about her favorite musical artists and then he begins talking about the musicians he loved when he was her age and I cringe inside. He sounds like an old man she'll never be able to relate to. She's never heard of Depeche Mode or the Smiths or Morrissey, but Aidan sings a little as he tries to convince her how awesome they are, and soon she's laughing, and then she sings something by Lady Gaga until she realizes that other diners are turning to look in our direction. She stops singing abruptly and the three of us crack up and I can hardly believe how comfortable this is becoming. I like her so much.

Our conversation stays light until we're nearly finished with our meals. As we watch Sienna take the last bite of her quesadilla, Aidan and I exchange a look: *Time to get serious.*

I take in a breath. "You're about seven months now, right?" I ask her.

"Thirty weeks, almost exactly," she says, putting down her fork. "I'm getting nervous," she admits.

"What can you tell us about the baby's father?" Aidan asks. "Dillon, is it?" I've never heard him speak so gently.

Sienna drops her gaze to the table. "I . . ."

she begins. "He . . ." She lets out a sigh. Lifts her eyes to mine, then Aidan's. "He wasn't who I thought he was," she says.

"How long were you going out with him?" I ask.

"Just a month," she says. "But I've been in love with him since, like, freshman year. And things were really good, but then he broke up with me. But he came over to talk and I thought maybe if we had sex . . ." She realizes her voice has gotten loud and lowers it. "I thought maybe I could get him back. Which I know is stupid. I knew it even then. And the other stupid thing is that I didn't think you could get pregnant the first time. But you can."

The first time. Poor kid.

"We understand that Dillon's okay with relinquishing his parental rights?" Aidan asks.

"More than okay," she says. "He wants nothing to do with her. When I told him I was pregnant, he said he'd give me money for an abortion. I almost did it — I made the appointment and everything, but then I realized I was doing it to please him. As usual. But I was afraid if I went through with it, it would upset me for the rest of my life. So I canceled the appointment and then I had to tell my mother and Dillon got really mad at me because my parents told his parents and . . . it was just a giant mess."

"I'm sorry you had to go through all of that," I say. I truly am sorry. *There but for the grace of God . . .* I think. We will need to meet Dillon at some point, I know. If we're going to have an open adoption, whatever form that takes, it will have to be open to our baby's father as well as her mother. But I'm afraid to say that now. I don't want to say anything that might scare Sienna off.

"Anyhow," Sienna says, "Dillon would have been as crappy a father as my own father. I hate both of them. I want my baby to have a father she can love." She looks at Aidan and I am certain she sees in my husband's face the same thing I see — a man who knows how to love.

Aidan gives a nod and clears his throat, and I know he's a little choked up. His cheeks are pink.

"Let's talk about our expectations — yours and ours — for your involvement after the baby is adopted," Aidan says once he's recovered his composure. "I think it's important that we work out an agreement we're all comfortable with. It might change over time, but —"

He stops speaking as he feels my foot against his shin beneath the table. He looks

393

at me and I nod in Sienna's direction, and only then does he realize her eyes have filled with tears.

"Sienna" — I lean toward her — "where are those tears coming from?"

She takes off her glasses and sets them on the table, then presses her fingertips to her eyes. Aidan and I look at each other and I bite my lip as we wait. Finally she lowers her hands. Her eyes are red.

"This is the part I'm afraid of," she says in a near whisper.

"What are you afraid of?" I match the tone of my voice to hers.

"My mother's best friend. This woman, Joan. She keeps calling and e-mailing me, telling me how she gave up her baby eighteen years ago and she never knew what happened to him. She's tried to find him and can't and she worries about him every single day of her life and wishes she hadn't given him up." She pauses to pull in a breath. "So she keeps trying to talk me out of adoption," she says. "My mom tells her it would be an open adoption, but Joan says you can make all these promises to me now and then once you have my baby, forget about them. And I can't stand the thought of not knowing how my baby is or ever getting to see her or anything."

Aidan and I exchange a glance. I nod for him to speak. "This is why we'd make a very clear agreement, Sienna," he says. "So all of us would know exactly what our open adoption would look like."

"I hope as you get to know us better, you'll know we won't break a promise to you," I say.

She looks down at her empty plate. One fat teardrop falls from her eyelashes to the table.

"In a perfect world," I say, "what sort of contact would you like to have with your daughter?" I can't believe I've asked such an open-ended question about a topic that's giving me at least as much angst as it appears to be giving her.

Sienna licks her lips thoughtfully, then looks at me. "Could you send me pictures of her every month? And could I see her a couple of times a year?"

That's all she wants?

"Absolutely," I say.

"And she'll know I'm her mother? I mean, her birth mother?"

"Of course," Aidan says. "And you know what would be cool?" he adds. "You could make her a scrapbook about you and your family, if you like. Something she could always have and treasure."

"She'll know her roots," I add. "We *want* her to know her roots, Sienna."

Sienna smiles. "Cool," she says.

"You think about this," I say. I feel enormous relief that she's not asking us for more than I'm prepared to give. "Talk it over with Kate and your mom. Then sometime before the baby is born, we'll draw up an agreement so all three of us are very clear what 'open adoption' means in our case."

She nods. "Okay."

"Excellent." Aidan takes a final swallow of his water. "So, is there anything else we need to discuss today?" He looks from me to Sienna.

"Well, Kate said we have to talk about the hospital," Sienna says shyly. "The, you know, the delivery and everything."

Zoe had told us to wait for her to bring this up and I feel proud of Sienna for addressing it so soon. I hold my breath. I have terribly mixed feelings about this. I want more than anything to see our daughter come into the world, and yet, it feels wrong somehow. The baby will be Sienna's at that moment. She should have that private, sacred time with her without us hovering nearby, hungry to hold our daughter in our arms.

"How do you feel about it?" I ask.

"I just don't think . . ." She wrinkles her nose. "I just want my mom in there with me," she says.

I nod, disappointed in spite of myself. "That's your choice and of course we'll respect it," I say. Once the baby is ours, Sienna's choices will be so few. I would never argue with her over this one.

I look at her again and I'm struck by her strength, the thought she's put into the decision to place her baby for adoption, the way she's bucked her friends, the hurt she's endured from her baby's father. I put my hand on hers.

"We're here for you, Sienna," I say. "Even if you change your mind again. Even if you decide to keep your baby. We'll be here for you."

I know Aidan is watching me. Later, he'll probably tell me I've gone too far, but I don't care. This girl needs our support.

"We'll help you in any way we can," I continue. I'm speaking clearly, as though I'm talking to someone much younger or much less bright than Sienna. I hear the lawyer in my voice. "We'll help you emotionally and we'll help you financially. I know money is tight for you and your mom." Zoe told us their medical insurance isn't the best. "We'll pay what your insurance won't cover. But . . . here's the thing. No matter how much we contribute to you financially or emotionally or in any other way at all, you do not owe us your baby." I look hard into her eyes. "I want to be sure you understand that."

Her brown eyes are glossy again behind her glasses. She nods. "I know all that," she says, "but I'm not going to change my mind. You don't have to worry."

In front of the restaurant, Sienna hugs each of us. I feel the bulge of her belly against my body.

"You two are the first people I've met who are actually *happy* that I'm pregnant." She laughs.

We give her directions to get out of Old Town and watch as she heads for her car. Aidan and I are quiet as we walk hand in hand in the opposite direction to our own car. We don't speak until we're seated inside, seat belts fastened. He looks at me.

"Wow." He smiles.

"I know." I smile back.

"I do worry," he says gently, "that in your effort to be sure that she's sure, you're going to scare her away."

"How would I do that?" I ask.

"Just . . . your intensity." He smiles again, letting me know that, in general, he likes my intensity. It's only in this situation that it worries him.

"I want to be sure she knows her rights," I say. "If she places her baby with us, I want to be sure it's with her whole heart and —"

"It will never be with her whole heart," he says. "You could feel her pain. There's always going to be pain."

"Nine tenths of her heart then."

He reaches across the gearshift to take my hand.

"I think you missed your calling, babe," he says.

"What do you mean?"

"The way you talked to her." He runs his thumb over the back of my hand. "The way you drew her out. Supported her. I've really never seen that side of you before. You should have been a counselor," he says. "You could have been a therapist like your father."

The smile I give him is weak, but he doesn't seem to notice. He lets go of my hand and turns the key in the ignition, and by the time he pulls the car into the street, my eyes are burning.

He can't know how much his words disturb me.

39
SWANNANOA

In my world, grown-ups were honest, and — except for the occasional drunken pushing of my father off a pavilion — good. So I was totally shocked when I got to Stacy's house and discovered that her mother planned to spend the night at the apartment of the man she was seeing. Stacy and I would have her house to ourselves for the entire night.

"Don't tell your mom," Stacy's mother said with a wink as she got ready to leave. She combed her black hair, which was only slightly less shiny than Stacy's, in the hallway mirror and applied her ruby-colored lipstick. I was standing next to Stacy inside the front door, my backpack over my shoulder, still in shock at the realization that she was leaving us alone for the night.

"What your mom doesn't know won't hurt her," Stacy's mother added. "She sounds like one of those mothers who hovers, is she?"

"Yes," I said. Did she hover? I didn't think I'd really describe her that way.

"I believe in trusting my kids," Stacy's mother continued as she picked up her purse from the table by the front door. "It helps them grow up, having to make choices for themselves instead of me making them for them," she said. "That's the way I've always done it and they're all still alive, right?" She smiled at me, and I could see where Stacy got her prettiness from. "None of them has ever been arrested or flunked out of school, so I think I'm doing a fine job."

Stacy rolled her eyes at me.

"Bye, now," her mother said with a wave. She pecked Stacy on the cheek. "Be good!"

We watched her walk out the front door, and neither of us said a word until we heard her car door slam. Then Stacy let out a whoop. She spread her arms wide, and tipped her head back to look at the ceiling. "Freedom!" she shouted. "Woo-hoo!"

I smiled. "This is going to be so amazing!" I said, but my hand slipped into my shorts pocket and circled my palm stone before I even realized what I was doing.

We sat in Stacy's room listening to *Step by*

Step as we put on our makeup. "I talked to Bryan once I realized we'd have the house to ourselves," Stacy said. "They're bringing pizza over. He said they can stay all night if we want them to." She gave me a knowing look in the mirror. "Like we wouldn't want them to." She laughed.

Oh my God, I thought, as I applied mascara to my lashes with a trembling hand. What was wrong with me? I wished I could have been as calm as Stacy. I was a nervous wreck.

We had the music pumped up in the living room when Chris and Bryan showed up around nine-thirty. I'd taken my glasses off but even blurry Chris looked hotter than I remembered. His blond hair had grown a little and it curled over the tops of his ears and at the nape of his neck, and his dimples — there were actually two of them — were so deep and sexy, I didn't know how I'd missed them the first time I met him. Bryan pulled Stacy into a long, deep kiss, but the kiss Chris gave me was sweet and tender and I liked that. I liked that he seemed to know me that well already.

They'd brought two pizzas with them and a six-pack of beer they'd somehow been able to get and we sat in the kitchen eating and talking. I remembered Stacy saying she'd never drink because of her father being an alcoholic, but she was first to pull a bottle from the six-pack. I sipped the beer. I didn't like the taste at all but I was determined to get it down.

"So when's this New Kids concert you two are going to?" Chris asked.

"August eighth," I said. "In Atlanta."

"Only a bunch of teenyboppers'll be there," Bryan said.

"Yeah," Stacy agreed, "but it'll be cool anyhow."

I felt betrayed by her for dissing the New Kids, but I knew she was under Bryan's spell and couldn't really help herself.

The guys ate a whole pizza between them and Stacy had two slices, but I couldn't even make it through one. I watched Chris's hands as he ate. He had the most beautiful hands in the world and I wanted him to hold my hand like he had that first day when we'd sat together on the couch. I felt his gaze on me no matter what I was doing in the kitchen. When I stood up to get him another beer from the refrigerator or carry my plate to the sink, he was watching me. I could tell he liked looking at me, and for the first time ever, I felt truly pretty. I smiled a lot, trying to imagine what he was seeing when he looked at me.

"We're going upstairs." Stacy said suddenly. She and Bryan stood up, holding hands. "We'll be in my mom's room," she said to me. "You guys can use the guest room if you want."

They went upstairs and my heart pounded against my rib cage. I thought of suggesting that Chris and I go into the living room and listen to more music. I wasn't at all ready for a bedroom.

"Check this out." Chris reached into his back pocket and brought out his wallet. From inside, he handed me the half photograph I'd sent him of myself and I saw that he'd actually *laminated* it. I laughed. Dani was so wrong about him. He wasn't a player.

"I need to do this with yours, too," I said, touching a corner of the photograph.

He put the picture back in his wallet, then stood up and held his hand out to me. "Let's go find that guest room," he said.

I couldn't say no. I was so afraid of sounding fourteen. I took his hand and we climbed the stairs. In the upstairs hallway, we heard giggling coming from behind the closed door of Stacy's mom's room. Chris pushed open another door and turned on the overhead light, and I saw a big bed, neatly made. "This must be it," he said.

He turned the light off and I followed him into the room. He sat down on the side of the bed and drew me down next to him. He smelled of beer and cigarettes and I wanted to sink into the scent of him. He kissed me softly, his arms around me. "I won't ask you to do anything you don't want to do," he said.

I tried to say *thank you,* but the words didn't come out. I nodded instead, though I knew he couldn't see me in the dark. He stretched out on the bed, drawing me down next to him. He leaned over to kiss me and I tasted pizza and beer. His promise of not doing anything I didn't want gave me courage and I parted my lips as he slipped his tongue inside my mouth.

"You can put your tongue in my mouth, too," he said after a while.

"I didn't know the girl could do that," I said.

He laughed. "There are no rules," he said. "The girl can do whatever she likes."

I put my tongue in his mouth and felt his teeth, and his warm tongue touched mine. He put his hand on my breast through my T-shirt. I was on my back and knew my breast was almost completely flat in that position. When I imagined being with Johnny Depp, I was always on my side exactly for that reason, but Chris didn't seem to care. He reached under my shirt and around my back. "Sit up a little so I can . . ." I turned so he could unhook my bra, and when he covered my breast with his warm bare hand, a moan came out of my throat, unexpected.

"Can we take your shirt off?" he asked.

"Yes," I said, sitting up. I slipped my T-shirt and bra off, glad of the darkness. He took off his T-shirt, and when we lay down again, I felt his chest against mine. *Amazing.* "You're so beautiful," he said. He lay on his back and lifted me on top of him until I was straddling him. I was stunned by how easily he could move my body, as though I was made of cotton instead of flesh and bone. His strength both excited and scared me.

"You okay?" he asked, his hands on my ribs.

I felt his hard penis pressing against me through his jeans and my shorts. "Yes," I whispered. We kissed and began to rock together, the pressure of his penis electrifying against my body. I felt an alien sensation in my groin, something building, something that seemed utterly out of my control, and I stopped the rocking motion, afraid of what was happening to me.

"What's wrong?" he asked.

"I don't know," I said. "I just felt . . . strange."

"Define *strange.*"

"Like I was going to explode or something."

He laughed. "You were going to come," he said. "You shouldn't have stopped, you crazy girl."

Oh my God. That was what coming felt like?

"You don't know what that means, do you?" he asked. "I keep forgetting how young you are."

"Yes, I do too know," I said. I didn't want him to think about my age. "I know what it is. I've just never felt it before." The phone rang from the hallway. It rang and rang and rang while we talked over the sound.

"It feels good," he said. "You'll like it." He slipped his fingers under the waistband of my shorts. "Take these off and I'll show you what coming's all about."

I held on to his hand to stop him. "I don't want to have sex yet," I said.

"It's okay," he said. "I'll just touch you. I promise. I'm not going to hurt you or do anything you don't want, remember? Do you trust me?"

"Yes," I said. I *did* trust him. I let go of

407

his hand and he gently lifted me from his body to the bed. He pulled my shorts off, then my underpants, and I swallowed hard against how vulnerable I felt, lying there naked. He kissed me, then slid his hand down my belly, over my pubic hair. I clamped my legs closed. "What are you doing?" I asked.

"I'm going to make you come. I promise you'll like it. But you have to let me in."

I opened my legs about an inch and nearly died when he touched me.

He groaned. "You feel so good," he said. "It makes me want to fuck you so bad."

His fingers were moving. He slipped one inside me and I gasped. My legs had moved apart on their own and my breathing was coming in short, sharp bursts. His hand seemed to be touching me everywhere down there at once, and I felt that going-to-explode feeling I'd had moments earlier when we were rocking together. He kissed me, but I could hardly concentrate on his lips, I was so breathless.

"How's that feel?" he asked.

There was no way I could possibly answer. My body was on fire and I nearly yelped when he suddenly took his hand away.

I opened my eyes to see him standing at the side of the bed, unzipping his jeans. He started to pull them down.

"No!" I said, sitting up, grabbing his hands. "Please, no."

"I have a Trojan," he said. "It'll be all right. I won't hurt you."

"No, Chris. I don't want to. *Please.*"

He stopped tugging at his jeans. Then wordlessly, abruptly, he walked out of the room. I felt like crying. He was angry. I'd totally ruined the moment. I groped around on the bed for my underpants and my bra, fighting tears as I put them on. I was trembling all over. I felt the beer at the back of my throat.

By the time he came back in the room a few minutes later, I'd found my bra and had it halfway on. "You're getting dressed?" he asked. It was too dark to make out the expression on his face.

"I didn't think you were coming back," I said.

"I just had to go . . . take care of something." He laughed. "You got me so heated up, I was going to end up with blue balls if I didn't jerk off."

I knew what *jerk off* meant. I wasn't sure about *blue balls.*

He sat down next to me and kissed me softly. "I told you I wouldn't do anything you didn't want," he said, and I felt terrible for doubting him.

The phone rang again as he helped me hook my bra. We cuddled together on the bed and I was relieved to be in his arms again.

"Have you done it with a lot of girls?" I asked, remembering what Dani had said about him hooking up with "everybody." Suddenly, I wondered if she might have been one of them.

He didn't answer right away. "A few. Remember, I have a bunch of years on you."

"Did you ever do it with my cousin Danielle?"

"That skank? No!"

I remembered Dani at the party, sitting on the ground next to my father, crying as she tried to comfort him. I didn't want anyone calling her a skank.

"She's not so bad," I said.

"Whatever."

He rolled onto his side so he could reach into his jeans pocket, and he pulled out a crushed joint and a lighter. Lighting the joint, he inhaled, then passed it to me. I took a hit, held it in. He put his arm around me. I wanted to tell him I loved him, but I was nervous about saying those words. I didn't think I could handle it if he didn't say them back.

We smoked the entire joint, lying there. I heard music coming from somewhere in the house. Aerosmith. I felt deliciously spacy and calm. Chris's arms around me felt delicious, too. The darkness felt delicious. I must have drifted off because the next thing I knew, someone was ringing the doorbell. Pounding on the door. And after a moment, Stacy burst into our room.

"I think your mother's at the door!" she shouted. "Her car is in the driveway!"

40

"Oh my God!" I scrambled to find my shorts and top in the light spilling through the open door. The room spun and for a moment, I thought I was going to get sick, but fear seemed to sweep the nausea away.

"I'll answer the door," Stacy said. "Bryan's in my room. Chris, you better stay in here." She sounded calmer now as she planned how to deal with the mess we were in. I had the feeling Stacy had a lot of experience getting out of scrapes.

I was dressed except for my Doc Martens. I had no idea where they were. My body trembled as I started down the stairs in my bare feet, and I heard Stacy open the door.

"Nora!" she said, like she was totally surprised to see her there. "Hi!"

"Where is your mother?" my mother asked. I knew that voice — tight with anger.

"Mom?" I said as I walked into the room. She was inside the door, looking around the living room with her eagle eyes, her blond hair out of her ponytail and hanging loose around her face. "What are you doing here?" I asked, trying to sound casual, like it was any other night, but I felt as though what I'd been doing was written on my face and body. She could tell just by looking at me that I'd been touched all over by a boy.

"Where is your mother?" she repeated to Stacy. "And whose truck is that in the driveway?"

"It's my uncle's truck," Stacy lied. "He stopped by and him and Mom just went out for a few minutes. She should be back any second. You want to wait for her?"

"A few minutes?" Mom said. "I don't think so! I've been calling and calling and no one's picked up. What's going on?"

I finally noticed that her eyes were red, and I suddenly got scared. Why had she been trying so hard to reach me? "Is something wrong?" I asked.

"*Yes*, something's wrong!" she shouted. "Two fourteen-year-old girls have been left home alone for . . . what? All night? And your mother lied to me about being here. I can't believe it!" She slammed her purse down on the table by the door.

"I told you, she just went out for a little bit," Stacy said, cool as ice.

413

"Why were you calling?" I asked, still worried about her red-rimmed eyes.

"Just to say good night," she said, "but when there was no answer, I got worried. Looks like I had a right to be."

An unmistakable thud came from upstairs. The three of us stared at each other. Stacy and I acted like we'd heard nothing.

"Who else is here?" my mother asked.

"Just my uncle," Stacy said.

"You just said he went out with your mother." My mother stared her down.

Neither of us said a word and after a moment's loaded silence, my mother marched past us, heading for the stairs. Stacy and I looked at each other in a panic, and Stacy darted after her.

"Nora!" she shouted. "Mrs. Arnette! What are you doing? That's so rude! You can't just barge into someone's house like that and go up their stairs!"

"Oh no?" my mother said without turning around. "Watch me!" This was a part of my mother I'd never seen before and it was terrifying. Stacy stopped following her midway up the stairs, while I couldn't seem to move from my spot near the front door. I had a crazy thought of running through that open door, escaping from the disaster I knew was ahead of me, but my body stood there frozen in place. I could hear my mother yanking doors open, slamming them against the wall.

"Which one of you is Chris!" I heard her shout. I guessed the boys were together in one room now, and she'd found them.

I heard a mumbled answer.

"She's fourteen!" my mother yelled. "Would you want your fourteen-year-old sister hanging out with someone like you? Get out!"

"This isn't your house!" I heard Bryan say, and I cringed. He would make things worse. "You can't order us around!" he added.

"Let's go," Chris said in a quieter, saner voice. In a moment, I saw them walking down the stairs, my mother close behind them. They looked like they were heading to a firing squad and Bryan didn't even glance at Stacy as he passed her at the bottom of the stairs. I was shocked to see that Stacy was crying. For the first time since I'd known her, she looked like a little girl.

The boys headed straight for the front door. They wore smiles my mother couldn't see, and I had the feeling they'd be laughing at her once they were outside and away from the house. I stepped aside to let them pass. Chris looked directly at me as he walked past me and he mouthed the words *I love you.* Unmistakable. *I love you.* Even after the two of them had walked onto the porch and I'd shut the door behind them, and even as my mother rushed down the stairs toward me, I could see his face, his mouth forming those words.

"You should have called me!" my mother snapped at me. "As soon as you realized Stacy's mother wasn't here, you should have called. Get your things." She turned to Stacy, who now sat pale and wide-eyed on the bottom step. "Stacy," Mom said, "where *is* your mother? I need to talk to her. I can't leave you here alone."

"At her boyfriend's," Stacy said.

"Give me his number."

"She'll be mad."

"I don't care." My mother marched through the living room and into the kitchen. I followed her into the room, hoping against hope that she didn't notice the beer bottles on the counter. I couldn't make eye contact with her, but she didn't seem to want to look at me, either.

She reached for the wall phone. "His number," she said again to Stacy, who had walked slowly into the room as if she could somehow put off the inevitable.

"She's going to be so pissed," she said, as

she pointed to a list of phone numbers taped to the wall next to the phone. She read off one of the numbers and my mother dialed.

"May I speak to Mrs. Bateman?" my mother said into the phone. "This is Nora Arnette."

Behind my mother's back, Stacy gave me a pleading look as though I could do something to change what was happening.

"I'm at your house where your daughter and my daughter were alone with two much older boys," Mom said. "I don't appreciate being lied to about you being here." She said nothing for a moment, listening. "Well, I don't believe that," she said. "Not for a minute! I'm taking Molly home, but you need to come home now to be with Stacy. She can't stay here alone."

"Oh God," Stacy muttered as she dropped into one of the kitchen chairs. "She's going to kill me."

"Mom," I pleaded. "You're getting her in trouble."

My mother covered the receiver with her hand. "You'd better worry about your own skin," she said, looking directly at me for the first time since she'd come downstairs, and I had to look away.

After another few minutes of conversation, she hung up the phone and turned to Stacy. "She says she's coming home," she said. "I don't believe her, though. I'm sorry you can't trust your own mother."

"I *do* trust her," Stacy snapped. "She lied to *you*. She didn't lie to me."

My mother stared at her, the skin on her pale cheeks blotched with red. "Get your things, Molly," she said to me again.

I ran upstairs and shoved my makeup in my backpack. I found my Doc Martens and sat on Stacy's bed to put them on. I grabbed my glasses from the dresser and carried them downstairs with me, moving as quickly as I could, not wanting to leave Stacy stranded alone with my mother any longer than I had to.

"Lock this door behind us, all right?" my mother said to Stacy when I'd come downstairs again and was ready to go. "And make sure your back door is locked, too."

"Yes, ma'am," Stacy said.

"Let's go," Mom said to me, opening the front door.

I looked at Stacy and mouthed the words *I'm sorry.* Yet I wasn't sure what I was sorry for. That my mother had totally blown our night with Chris and Bryan, or that Stacy had a mother who simply didn't care what she did.

41

We were both quiet in the car until we pulled onto the main road. When we drove under streetlights, I could see how tightly she held the steering wheel, her knuckles white.

"No more Chris," she said. "We should have put an end to that before it even began, but your father didn't think it would go anywhere. And no more Stacy."

"Mom!"

"She's not the sort of girl you should be spending your time with."

"Well, first of all," I argued, "she's the *only* girl around this summer, and second of all, I really like her. It's not her fault if her mother is . . . irresponsible." I was talking about Stacy, but my mind was back on Chris. I would see him somehow. I was sure of that.

For a moment, she was quiet and I thought I'd won her over with that argument. Really, it wasn't Stacy's fault if her mother left her alone, was it? "What was she supposed to do?" I added. "Beg her mother to stay home with us?"

"I'm sure it wasn't your idea to invite those older boys over," my mother said. "She's playing with fire and I'm worried you're the one who'll get burned."

"That's, like, so overly dramatic!"

My mother groaned. "You're even starting to talk like her," she said.

"Why don't you trust me?" I asked, but knew right away that was the wrong direction to take my argument. I'd proven myself completely untrustworthy in the last few hours.

"I'm not even going to honor that question with an answer," she said, and I fell quiet.

She was crying, softly, maybe trying to keep me from noticing. I couldn't see her well and might have missed it in the darkness, but I could tell by her sniffling, by the liquid look of her eyes when we passed beneath a streetlight. My mother had been acting down and just plain weird since Daddy's fall from the pavilion, and I knew I'd made things a whole lot worse tonight.

I reached over to touch her hand on the steering wheel. "I'm sorry," I said.

She turned her head away from me, wiping her eyes with the back of her hand.

"I don't want to argue with you, Molly," she said. "I only want you to be safe and healthy. You understand that, don't you?"

"Yes."

"You may not realize that you're too young to make wise decisions, but you are. Daddy and I still have to make them for you."

No you don't, I thought, but I kept my mouth shut.

She let out a long sigh. "It's just been a difficult night," she said, and I suddenly remembered the family meeting had been tonight.

"What did Uncle Trevor say about the land and the surveyors and everything?" I asked. He'd been so kind and apologetic when he talked to my father in his office the other day, I had the feeling he was ready to back down.

Mom waved a hand through the air. "Oh, who knows what's going to happen," she said.

She was so upset, I decided it was best if I asked no more questions. For a few minutes, I wondered what my father would have to say to me in the morning after Mom told him what happened tonight, but my mind soon wandered back to Chris and how extraordinary it had felt to be with him. I wouldn't let my parents keep me from seeing him, but I had the feeling they might never let me out of the house again. I wondered if, somehow, some way, Chris could meet me at Morrison Ridge.

42
SAN DIEGO

"What a beautiful neighborhood!" Sienna's mother says when I open our front door. She and Sienna stand on our porch and Sienna holds a mixed bouquet of flowers in a vase. The sun is still blazing above the houses across the street and it lights her face with a peachy glow. She is beautiful.

"Thank you," I say, stepping aside to let them into the house. "Please come in." I reach for Sienna's mother's hand. She's my age at the very most, and I'm surprised. I'd expected her to be much older. "I'm Molly," I say.

Sienna introduces her mother. "This is Ginger. And these are for you." She hands me the vase.

"Thank you," I say, setting the vase on the coffee table. "That's so sweet of you." It feels strange to take anything from someone who will, if all goes according to plan, be giving us the greatest gift I can imagine.

Less than a week has passed since our lunch with Sienna, and I've spoken with her a couple of times on the phone since then. The first time was to invite her and her mother for dinner tonight. The second call was Sienna's doing, though, and she just wanted to talk. "The girls at school are giving me a hard time again," she said. "I thought it would help if I could just hear your voice." Her call both touched and unsettled me. She is counting on us as much as we're counting on her, I thought. I don't know if that is good or bad, but it is what it is.

"I love these older homes." Ginger looks admiringly around our freshly vacuumed and dusted living room. The smell of lemony furniture polish is strong in this room and I wonder how obvious it is that Aidan and I spent the day scrubbing and polishing. The house hasn't had such an extreme cleaning since the day Perky Patti visited us for our home study. I've been cooking as well and the scent of eggplant parmesan mixes with the lemon. I wasn't sure if Sienna was a vegetarian after the quesadilla she'd ordered in Old Town, so I'd decided not to take any chances.

"The house was built in nineteen-thirty," I say, walking with them into the heart of the living room.

"Beautiful!" Ginger says. "Except, I worry about lead paint?" She looks at me questioningly, and I'm so taken aback by the question — practically the first thing out of her mouth — that for a moment I don't respond and Sienna looks embarrassed.

"Mom," she says. "They're not going to let the baby eat lead."

"We actually had the house tested for lead paint when we first moved in," I reassure them. It's the truth. We had such hopes of filling the house with children back then. We hadn't realized the wait would be this long.

"Sorry," Ginger says. "I'm a worrier." She peers behind me. "This must be Aidan, right?"

I turn to see Aidan walking toward us.

"Right," he says as he shakes Ginger's hand. He smiles at Sienna. "Good to see you again, Sienna."

"We're so happy you could both come," I say. I'm very aware that Sienna is examining the room, taking everything in. The tiled fireplace. The arched doorways. It's not a big house but it's cozy and warm and aching to be filled. I hope she can see that.

We give them a tour of the house, and it's clear that Sienna's favorite room is the nursery, even though it has a long way to go before it's ready for a baby. Aidan and I have talked about our reluctance to fix it up. It boils down to fear. We're afraid to buy more furniture. Afraid to buy baby clothes or bottles or diapers. We'd bought things far too early for Sara and the pain of giving everything away is still fresh in our minds. Waiting for a baby — any baby — feels like walking through land mines to us, and what happens with Sienna's baby is so out of our control that we don't dare to buy a thing for her yet. We can hope, but we can't plan.

Still, I feel as though I need to tell Sienna and Ginger how I want this room to look by the time the baby arrives. I want them to know we've at least thought about it.

"We're thinking of painting it yellow," I say. "And I've seen some bedding I love. I can send you a picture of it, Sienna." That slips out of my mouth so naturally that I hadn't stopped to think it might be hard for her to see anything we buy for the baby. "Would you like that or would you rather I didn't?"

She smiles. "I'd like it," she says. She's discovered the small white bookcase and bends over to check out some of the titles.

"I love that you have all these books," she says.

"Sienna could read a whole book by the time she was four," Ginger says, nodding toward her daughter.

Sienna turns from the bookcase to look at me. "Will you read to her every night?" she asks.

"Yes," I say. *Oh yes.*

"Mom read to us every night, didn't you, Mom?" Sienna asks her mother. "It's so important."

We walk back to the living room, where Aidan is fiddling with the CD player. The flowers have overpowered the lemon scent in the room and the air now smells fresh and sweet.

"Hey, Sienna." Aidan looks up from the controls of the CD player. He's holding a CD in his hand. "I made a compilation disc for you," he says. He loves that Sienna's into music.

"Cool," Sienna says. She is nothing if not polite. She walks over to take the disc from his hand.

"Want to help me with the salad?" I ask Ginger, and we head for the kitchen. Behind us, I hear Sienna add, "If I listen to *your* favorites, though, you'll have to listen to mine one of these days."

427

"Deal," Aidan says, and I smile to myself. I'd groaned when he told me he was making the CD. I'd wanted to say, "Aidan, sweetie, how would you have felt if some much older guy, like your father for instance, tried ramming his favorite music down your throat when you were seventeen?" And this from the guy who told me not to mention that I liked *Mad Men.* I said nothing to stop him, though. This is who Aidan is. Sienna already chose us. If she changes her mind because of Aidan's musical taste as a teenager, there is little I can do about it.

I hear Morrissey singing from the living room as Ginger and I chop vegetables for the salad. "You and your husband are just as sweet as Sienna said," she says, tossing a handful of celery slices into the salad bowl.

"We feel the same way about her," I say. I'm making salad dressing and I measure the olive oil into the carafe.

Ginger quietly slices a cucumber. "I'm so worried about everything, though," she admits after a moment.

I nod. "It's uncharted territory for all of us, I guess."

"My first grandchild." Ginger stops slicing to look pensively toward the ceiling. "I won't be able to see her and hold her and

428

tell her stories and . . ." She turns to me as though I can say something to ease her distress. "Our dreams don't work out as planned sometimes, do they," she says.

Aidan and I haven't talked about how an open adoption incorporates grandparents. We'll have to figure that out. "We'll be sharing pictures and information with Sienna," I say. "You won't be left behind."

She smiles. "Thank you," she says, and she returns to her slicing.

Over dinner, we talk about the open adoption and Sienna's request for pictures and the occasional visit. Aidan says he'll put together a private Facebook page where we can share photographs, and Sienna and Ginger seem to love the idea. Sienna tells us that she's already started working on the scrapbook about her family. I'm so touched by this girl.

"Who gets to name the baby?" Ginger asks as she spears a piece of lettuce with her fork. Ginger, I'm discovering, gets right to the point.

"We haven't really thought about it," I say, although that's not quite the truth. Aidan and I have certainly pondered the question. Is it fair of us to name the baby without consulting Sienna? Should she have any say at all?

"She'll be your daughter," Sienna says. "So I guess you should name her." Her sadness is palpable.

"Maybe we can come up with a name we all like," Aidan suggests.

"Or," I say, "Aidan and I can give her a first name and Sienna can give her a middle name."

The four of us begin throwing names around and soon we're making lists on sheets of paper and laughing, mostly at Sienna's suggestions. She likes Ocean and Star and Echo and Tulip. She's perfectly serious and I'm glad we haven't given her carte blanche when it comes to naming the baby.

"How about Natalie?" Aidan suggests. I look at him across the table. Natalie had been our second-choice name when Sara was born. I don't think I want a name that reminds me of our lost child, but he raises his eyebrows at me. *What do you think?* he's asking.

"Natalie Echo!" Sienna says.

Natalie Echo James. There is something so wonderful about that name that I can't help but laugh. Is it just the heady feeling of this evening that makes me love it? I don't dare agree to it tonight, when I feel drunk on the reality that Aidan and I are — almost certainly — going to be parents.

"Let's put it on the list," I say.

"At the top of the list," Aidan adds. And I have the feeling we have just named our daughter.

It's still light after dinner and Aidan shows Sienna around the backyard while Ginger and I clean up. We have the table cleared, the dishwasher turned on, and coffee brewing by the time Aidan walks into the kitchen a while later. He's alone.

"Where's Sienna?" I ask.

"I left her in the nursery," he says. "She wanted to look through the books you bought."

I take the half-and-half from the refrigerator and set it on the counter. "How about you two slice the peach pie and I'll let her know it's time for dessert," I say, heading for the hallway.

I hear Sienna sniffling even before I reach the nursery. I walk into the room to find her sitting cross-legged on the floor, an open book in her lap. Tears stream down her cheeks and I feel a moment of panic. Her tears frighten me.

"Sienna?" I sit down next to her on the

431

floor, my hand light on her back.

She makes a valiant effort to smile at me as she holds the book so I can see the cover. *Love You Forever.* Oh yes. It's hard to read that book without a lump in your throat.

"I had this book when I was a kid," she says. "But honestly? I don't think I understood it until right now."

I think about the story. It's about a mother who holds her child every night, promising to love him through all stages of his life. She holds him as an infant and a mischievous toddler and a rebellious teenager and on into adulthood. That's when the tables turn and it's the adult who holds his frail mother in his arms, promising to love her forever.

Sienna looks at me, her eyes big and round behind her red glasses. "Which one of us is our baby going to hold when she grows up?" she asks in a whisper, her eyes full of tears, and before I know what's happening, I have my arms around her, hot tears running down my own cheeks. When I finally pull away from her, we both smile sheepishly, and I know right then that, scared as I am, I want Sienna to have a solid place in my child's life. We will all be richer for it.

43
MORRISON RIDGE

I got up at six the morning after the whole big mess at Stacy's, long before anyone else in the house was up. Before I even brushed my teeth, I climbed the Hill from Hell to the springhouse, my hand wrapped around Chris's picture in my shorts pocket. I was afraid to keep the picture in the house any longer, worried that if my mother found it, that would be the end of it. I'd stared at his picture half the night, remembering how he'd touched me, how he'd made my body go crazy, how he'd mouthed those words *I love you* to me as he headed out the door. It took me forever to fall asleep.

In the springhouse, I stood on my bed and pulled the fake stone loose. Inside were the treasures that suddenly seemed silly. The shells and shark teeth. The glass bird and old corsage. The damp pack of cigarettes. So stupid. I put Chris's picture inside, then fit the fake stone back in place and climbed down off my bed, barely glancing at the posters of the dark-haired boys who no longer meant that much to me.

Back in the house, I brushed my teeth and washed my face, then started toward the stairs. I dreaded seeing either of my parents at the breakfast table. I was on the top step when I heard my mother's voice coming from the living room. I sat down on the step, listening, trying to gauge how angry she was. I hoped her anger from the night before had been tempered by a good night's sleep. It didn't sound like it.

"It's like you're *rewarding* them for terrible behavior," she said.

"I already have the tickets," Daddy said.

The concert. I'd nearly forgotten about it.

"What kind of lesson does that teach her?" Mom argued. "She disobeys us and you take her to a concert? Besides, I told her she can't see Stacy anymore. That girl has no supervision."

"It's not Stacy's fault she has no supervision." Daddy sounded like his usual calm self.

"You sound just like Molly!" my mother said. "Stacy's a terrible influence."

"Hon," Daddy said, "Molly *needs* Stacy. She needs a good girlfriend right now."

"A *good* girlfriend would be one thing," my mother said. "Stacy Bateman is another thing entirely." Her voice was tired, and I knew she was winding down. Daddy was going to win this round.

"Stacy needs some guidance," Daddy said. "Maybe we can be that for her."

"Don't you think we have enough on our plate right now?" Mom asked. "We can't fix what's wrong with that girl. She's had a lifetime of shitty parenting. And I have to go to work," she added. "I'm late already."

"Let's table this," Daddy said. "Let's sing an opera before you go instead, okay?"

"Oh, Graham." I could actually hear her sigh from where I sat. "Sometimes I can't believe you're a shrink. You can be so simple. I don't *want* to sing a damn opera. I don't think we've resolved anything. I still think the concert is a terrible idea."

Neither of them spoke for several seconds and I held my breath, waiting. "Nora . . ." Daddy said finally. "Molly's always going to remember this as the worst summer of her life. Let's let there be something good in it."

44

Sitting at the top of the stairs, I waited to hear my mother's car pull out of the driveway, wondering how much she and Daddy knew about what had actually happened the night before. They couldn't possibly know how far I'd gone with Chris, although Mom had no doubt found him in the bedroom and might have guessed. My cheeks grew hot at the memory. I would act as though nothing at all happened. She was overreacting, pure and simple.

I wished today was an Amalia day. She'd know nothing about what happened last night and we could put on music and dance and I could feel free and happy. But tomorrow was my day with Amalia this week. Today was a long nothing day, and there was no way I could think of to avoid my father. I was grateful at least that my mother had to work.

I heard her car leave the driveway and pull

onto the dirt lane. I waited another minute, then went downstairs to the kitchen, where Russell sat at the table feeding Daddy a piece of blueberry pie.

"Morning, Molly," Russell said.

"Hey, girl," Daddy said once he'd swallowed a mouthful of pie.

"Hey," I replied. I thought of skipping my own breakfast and going for a bike ride to avoid conversation, but I was hungry. There was a plate of scrambled eggs and grits on the counter next to the stove. "Is this yours?" I asked Daddy.

"It was," he said, "but I decided to have pie instead, so that's yours if you want it."

I stuck the plate in the microwave. "Why are you eating pie?" I asked. Maybe he wasn't going to say anything about the night before with Russell there. That would be fine with me.

"Because it's here." Daddy smiled. "And life is short."

"It's not good for you to eat sweets for breakfast," I said, struggling to make conversation.

"Today might not be the best day for you to lecture me, darling daughter," he said.

Ouch. His voice, though teasing, had a serious undertone. The corner of Russell's mouth twitched as he lifted the last forkful of pie, and I had the feeling he was trying not to smile.

Daddy swallowed the last bite of pie as I put my plate of eggs and grits on the table.

"Need anything else right now?" Russell asked my father as he got to his feet, picking up the empty pie plate from the table.

"No, thanks, Russ," Daddy said. "Give us a few minutes, all right?"

Oh no. I dragged my fork through the grits, my appetite waning as Russell left the room. I felt my father's eyes boring into me.

"So tell me what happened last night," he asked once we were alone.

"Mom probably told you all of it," I said.

"I assume Mom doesn't *know* all of it," he said. "She's pretty sure you were in a bedroom with Chris, though."

My face felt hot again and I knew my cheeks were red. "I don't want to talk about this," I said.

"Boys Chris's age have zero self-control," he said. "They —"

"That's not true!" Chris hadn't forced me to do anything I didn't want to do.

"It's not?" He wore an annoying look of fake surprise. "Well, I'm glad to hear it. But I was young once and I know for a fact that it's tough for a guy to stop, Molly. And he isn't the one who'll pay the consequences if something happens. You need to dial it back, all right? Don't ever go into a bedroom with a boy. Please."

I was squirming with the memory of the night before, afraid my father could read my mind.

"Stacy has so much freedom." I pouted as I changed the subject. "Her mother isn't always on her case about everything."

"She's not as lucky as you are," Daddy said.

I resisted the urge to roll my eyes.

"I agree with Mom," he said. "You can't see Chris anymore. He's too old for you — he expects things from a girl, and you're not old enough to decide whether that's a good thing for you or not."

"It's not like he raped me or anything."

"Good to hear."

I shivered, remembering lying totally naked with Chris the night before. The way he touched me. I dropped my gaze to my plate. I couldn't look my father in the eye with that memory running through my head.

"It's important you feel able to talk to Mom about stuff like this," he said.

"Never," I said. "I could never talk to her about stuff like this. She gets too angry."

"Why do you think that is?"

I shrugged. "Because she has a short temper?"

"Cop-out answer," he said. "Why do you think she got angry with you last night?"

"It's not like I lied to her or anything," I argued. "I honestly didn't know Stacy's mother wasn't going to be there. It's not like we planned it or —"

"Why do you think she got angry?" he asked again. "Close your eyes and put yourself in her place for a minute."

I stared at him, feeling obstinate.

"Do it, Moll," he said. "Close your eyes."

There was no way out of this. I shut my eyes.

"Now you're Mom, showing up at Stacy's last night."

I resisted putting myself in my mother's shoes, but I felt myself slip inside her anyway. I showed up at Stacy's house to find my daughter there with two boys, probably in a bedroom, with no parent around for an entire night. My stomach clenched at the thought. *What had happened? What had they done? Was my daughter now pregnant?*

"How do you feel?" Daddy asked.

"Worried?" I asked, opening my eyes. "Scared?"

"Bingo," he said.

"Then why did she act so angry?"

"Because fear often comes out as anger. Look at Trevor. He's afraid he's going to lose this big opportunity to make a fortune on the land, so he's mad at me for not selling him our share. And your mom is . . . she's terrified, Molly, that something bad might happen to you. I am, too, frankly. So I know when you hear us telling you that you can't do this and you can't do that, it pisses you off because it sounds like we're being unfair, but it's just that we're scared for you. We know a little more than you do about how the world operates out there and it's frightening sometimes. All we're trying to do is keep you safe."

"Could I see Chris here?" I asked. "Like, with you and Mom around?" Would Chris want that? If he loved me, would he do that for me? I was having trouble picturing it.

But Daddy shook his head. "No, sweetheart," he said. "Chris has burned his bridges. I'm sorry."

"It wasn't his fault nobody was home at —"

"No," he said, and this time he said it with such uncharacteristic force that I clamped my mouth shut.

"You *may* still see Stacy," he said, "but it has to be here, not at her house."

"All right," I said, as if I was giving in, but

I knew I wasn't. I would see Chris again. Somehow. Some way. I would see him.

45

When I showed up at Amalia's for my dance lesson the following day, I was surprised to find Daddy in her living room.

"Hi, Moll," he said when I walked in. He sat in his wheelchair by the glass wall, the sunlight catching the blue of his eyes. Amalia sat on one of the Papasan chairs in her long purple dance skirt, her legs tucked beneath her, her hair curling softly over her left breast. Through the open doorway of the kitchen, I saw Russell pour himself a cup of coffee.

"Hi," I said to my father from inside the front door. "What are you doing here?"

"Just chatting," he said.

"Stay for our lesson?" Amalia asked him.

I sat down on the edge of the second Papasan chair to take off my shoes, hoping he would say no. I wouldn't feel as free with him and Russell there.

"We've got to get back," he said. "Some

paperwork to tidy up."

Russell leaned against the doorjamb between the living room and the kitchen and raised his cup to his lips. He looked relaxed and at ease, in no hurry to take my father home. The colors from the stained glass in the windows lit up his pale blue shirt.

Amalia turned her attention to me. "That New Kids concert is next Wednesday night, isn't it?" she asked. "You must be excited."

"I can't wait," I said. I looked at Amalia's stereo system instead of at anyone in the room, hoping they didn't hear the flatness in my voice. I felt all their eyes on me. The New Kids on the Block simply weren't on my mind, and the thought of a long car trip with Daddy and Russell, when Stacy and I would be together but unable to talk openly with each other, was unbearable. Chris was all I could think about. My whole body shivered every time I remembered the way he'd touched me. I was pretty sure he'd tried calling a couple of times the night before, but each time my mother beat me to the phone. When she answered, no one was there.

"Amalia and Mom are going to Atlanta with us," Daddy said now, and I turned my gaze back to him in surprise.

"Really?" I said. "Cool." I had to process this. I had the feeling Mom was going with us to keep her eagle eye on Stacy and me, but I had no idea why Amalia would be going as well. Really weird. Our van would be packed, which meant Stacy and I would be crammed into the seats in the rear for the nearly four-hour trip. There was a benefit to that, though, I thought. We could talk back there without being easily overheard.

"What will you all do while we're at the concert?" I asked.

"We'll just chill," Amalia said. "Have dinner out someplace. Check into the hotel."

"Mom booked four rooms for us," Daddy said. "We're taking over the Hyatt."

"Stacy and I get our own room?"

"Of course," he said. "No one would want to share with you two, anyway. You'll be up all night talking about Joey and Jordan and . . . whatever the rest of their names are."

"Donnie and Jonathan and Danny." I smiled. I knew right then that he missed the girl I'd been a few weeks ago. The girl who lived in a teenybopper fantasy bubble. I suddenly missed her myself. Her life had been a whole lot simpler.

"Right," Daddy said. He glanced at Amalia, then looked at me. "Listen, darling," he said, "the Saturday after we get back from the concert, we're going to have another family meeting, and —"

"Another?" I asked. I'd thought Uncle Trevor had backed down and everything was settled.

He smiled. "This will be the last one," he said. "Promise. Anyway, Nanny's sitting this one out, too, so she said you should stay overnight with her. How's that sound?"

"Fine," I said with a shrug.

Daddy looked as though he wanted to say something else, then changed his mind. He turned toward Russell instead. "You ready?" he asked.

Russell nodded, then took another sip of his coffee and walked back into the kitchen, where I saw him wash out his cup and set it on the wooden rack to dry. Daddy and Amalia and I talked about the music we'd dance to today while we waited. Back in the living room, Russell took the handles of my father's chair and pushed him toward the door.

"See you later," Daddy said to me.

Amalia stood up and stretched, her hands high over her head. "Find some Ennio Morricone, Molly," she said to me, gesturing toward the CD shelves. "That will be an interesting change." Then she followed them outside, shutting the door behind her.

I stood up to walk to the CD shelves, but through the open window I saw the three of them on the dirt road in front of the house. I could hear their voices, and I held still, listening.

Amalia touched her eye as she looked down at my father. "How bad is it now, really?" she asked.

"Just about gone in the right," Daddy said, so quietly I could barely hear him. "And going in the left."

I caught my breath. His vision? He'd never said anything to me about losing his vision.

My father said something else that Amalia needed to lean close to hear. She nodded, then kissed him on the temple. "I know, baby," she said. "I understand." Then she looked at Russell, reaching up to touch his shoulder, and some wordless communication seemed to pass between them that I wasn't close enough to understand.

Amalia turned to walk back to the house and I moved quickly to her CDs, hunting for the Morricone music.

Amalia was not herself. She suggested the same exercise to me moments after I'd already done it, and she didn't watch me while I danced. Instead, she kept looking

447

toward the window as though she could still see my father and Russell out there. I followed her gaze to the dirt road but saw nothing other than the forest and my bike, where it leaned against the tree stump that had been carved into a chair.

I knew I wasn't acting like myself, either. My mind was too full to let my body feel the music, and I finally stopped dancing and stood still in the middle of the room, ignoring the music pouring from the stereo. It took Amalia a few seconds to realize I wasn't moving. She looked at me quizzically.

"I heard you ask Daddy about his eyes," I said. "What's wrong?"

She stared at me, her mouth open a little in surprise, and I thought she was trying to decide whether to answer me or not. She walked over to the stereo and turned the music down low. "Do you want some iced tea?" she asked. "It's peach. So good."

I hated when she did this and she did it a lot. She gave me whiplash sometimes, the way she'd veer away from my questions. It was like a game we had to play for me to be able to get the information I needed.

"Okay," I said, and I followed her into the kitchen.

"It happens with MS sometimes," she

said, reaching into the refrigerator for the jug of tea. I took two glasses out of the cabinet near the sink and dropped a couple of ice cubes into each of them. I was operating on autopilot. My chest felt tight as I waited for her to tell me more. "It's an off and on thing, and it's been going on quite a while now," she said, as she started to pour.

"Why didn't he *tell* me?" How could this ever be a good summer for him if he was going blind?

"Oh, you know your father." She leaned against the counter and took a sip from her glass. "He doesn't like to worry anyone."

"Does Mom know?" I asked. It seemed I was asking that question all the time lately.

She nodded. "Yes," she said.

I'd often tried to imagine how it felt for my father to be unable to move his body. Not to be able to scratch his cheek or roll over in bed or eat or even pee on his own. But the thought of being locked in darkness was worse. I held the glass to my lips but knew I'd never get the tea past the lump in my throat. I set it down again.

"Why can't they do something to *help* him?" I asked angrily.

She set down her own glass and reached for me with both arms, pulling me into a hug. "It's a terrible feeling, isn't it," she said, holding me close, stroking my hair. "So hard, knowing there's nothing we can do to change what's happening to him."

"I hate that stupid disease!" I said. My arms were wrapped around her waist and I hung on to her tightly, my eyes squeezed shut. "Is there anything else going wrong with him I don't know about?" I asked.

She didn't answer. Beneath my arms, I felt her body rise and fall with a sigh.

"Amalia?" I let go of her. "Is there something else?"

"Isn't that enough?" she asked, picking up the pitcher of iced tea from the counter and putting it back into the refrigerator. Then she turned to face me. "So, tell me, Molly," she said. "Are you excited about the concert?"

She was doing it again, diverting me from the subject I wanted — *needed* — to talk about, and I could tell by the look in her green eyes that we were finished discussing my father for the day.

"Yes," I answered, my voice flat and disappointed. "I can't wait."

That night, I gave Daddy the palm stone back.

I didn't tell him why. I knew he didn't want me to know about his eyes, and even

450

if I said something about them, he'd deny it was any big deal. But I could hardly think about anything else. That evening, he and Mom and I watched a movie on TV and he acted like he could see the whole thing, though a couple of times Mom quietly asked him *did you catch that?* when something important happened on the screen. Each time he nodded, so either he did see it or he was lying. I wouldn't put lying past him. I was sure he didn't want Mom to worry about him any more than she already was.

I had the stone in my pocket during the movie and after it was over and Mom left the room to find Russell, I got up and stood next to my father's recliner. I held out my hand, the purple stone resting on my palm.

"I want you to have this," I said.

He looked puzzled. "It's yours," he said. "I gave it to you."

"I know, but I think you need it right now."

His smile was both tender and suspicious, and I wondered if he thought someone had told me about his eyes. "That's sweet of you, Moll," he said slowly, "but I think a palm stone is a bit challenging for me to use."

I sat down on the sofa, still holding the

stone out in front of me. "I thought maybe if you kept it in the pocket of your jeans, you'd know it's there and it would work just as well," I said. "I mean, it's a psychological thing, anyhow, right? So it doesn't matter if it's in your hand or in your pocket."

"Or in your room or your secret rock, for that matter."

I wrinkled my nose. "You're missing my point," I said. "I want you to have it."

He studied my face for a long moment, then nodded. "You're worried about me," he said.

"Yes." I waited for him to say there was nothing to worry about, but he was quiet.

"I'll borrow it," he said finally. "How's that?"

"Good." I smiled, getting to my feet. "I'll give it to Russell and ask him to put it in your jeans pocket in the morning. Okay?"

"Deal," he said.

I headed down the hall to look for Russell, my emotions mixed. I hoped the stone would give my father courage and comfort, but I knew I was going to miss it, and later, as I climbed the stairs to my room, I was keenly aware of the empty place in my pocket.

46
SAN DIEGO

Life is amazing.

That's my new mantra and I've gotten to the point where I really believe it. Aidan and I cuddle in bed at night, giggling about the latest baby picture Sienna posted of herself on the private Facebook page we share or running through our list of names and somehow always ending up laughing over — and loving — Natalie Echo. Laurie and her husband, Tristan, gave us an early baby gift by painting the nursery the yellow I've been fantasizing about. I can walk in that room with courage now, though we still haven't bought things for the baby. There's still fear. We know how many things can go wrong in so many different ways. We know that Sienna might take one look at her baby and decide to keep her. I would never hold that decision against her, much as I pray she doesn't make it.

I've been to two of her obstetrician appointments with her now. She's doing well. Everything is progressing "perfectly," according to her doctor. After each appointment, Sienna and I have done something fun. The first time we went to the Wild Animal Park. The second time out to lunch. I've been reading up on the problems that can come with open adoptions. Adoptive mothers can form a strong bond with a birth mother before the baby's born, only to pull away from the birth mother once the baby's been adopted. It's not a malicious pulling away, the author stresses, but a natural progression in the relationship. Still, when that happens, the birth mother loses not only her baby but a meaningful friendship as well. It scares me that I might do that to Sienna. She becomes more precious to me every day. One thing I'm sure of: we are not Nora and Amalia. We are nothing like Nora and Amalia. We never will be like Nora and Amalia.

47
MORRISON RIDGE

I'd worried about how my parents would treat Stacy since I knew they — especially my mother — didn't think much of her, but they were really nice to her as we all got into the van in our driveway for the trip to Atlanta. Stacy's mother had dropped her off in front of our house, pulling out of our driveway so quickly that her silver van disappeared in a puff of dust from the road. I was sure she didn't want to speak to either of my "hovering" parents.

Stacy and I sat way in the back of our van, which made Stacy freak. "I'm so claustrophobic," she whispered to me, her face absolutely white. "We're, like, trapped back here."

"Not really," I said. "The back door is right behind us." I didn't point out that we'd have to somehow climb over our seats and scrunch into the little space behind us to be able to open that door. I wasn't even sure it was possible to open it from the inside. But she seemed reassured, and by the time we pulled onto the main road, the color was back in her cheeks.

Daddy sat in front of me, locked into place in his wheelchair, and Mom had the seat next to him, while Amalia and Russell rode up front.

Russell put a cassette in the van's tape player once we were rolling on the highway. Jazz — my least favorite — but I was glad of it because it meant Stacy and I could talk without being overheard. We hadn't had a chance to really talk since the week before, when my mother showed up at her house. We'd talked a few times on the phone, but I was paranoid that my parents were listening in and I didn't dare say anything that might come back to bite me.

"I saw Bryan last night," Stacy said quietly to me now.

"Where?" I asked. I was so jealous that she got to see him.

"At his house," she said. "His parents were out." She glanced at the seats in front of us, where my parents sat talking quietly with one another. "We did it," she whispered.

I was shocked. "All the way?" I whispered back.

She nodded. "Actually, the first time was

that night your mother showed up," she said. "I haven't been able to tell you because . . ." She nodded toward my parents. I'd told her talking on the phone wasn't safe. "We've done it twice since then," she said.

"Oh, my God." I felt so left behind. "What was it like?"

"It sucked the first time." She laughed quietly. "It hurt and just . . . well, it sucked, period. But then it got better."

"He used those . . . Trojan things?"

"Of course." She smiled this secret, knowing smile that made me feel like an ignorant little kid. "Guys hate them and I love that he wants to protect me that way," she said.

I was so agonizingly jealous! She got to be with Bryan and I couldn't even talk to Chris on the phone.

"I have to tell you something." She made a pained-looking face. "It's going to upset you."

I stared at her. "What?"

"I wasn't sure if I should tell you, but I'd want you to tell *me,* so —"

"What?"

"Last night at Bryan's? Chris was there. With another girl."

She may as well have punched me in the stomach. What did I expect, though? My parents wouldn't let me see him. He couldn't reach me on the phone, and there'd been no more of those hang-up phone calls in days. I guessed he'd given up. I couldn't expect him to sit home every night and wish I was with him.

"Who was it?" I asked.

"This girl . . ." She shrugged. "I never saw her before," she said. "She lives in Asheville. Julie somebody."

"What did she look like?" I braced myself, not really wanting to hear the answer.

"She's okay-looking," Stacy said.

I knew that meant she was pretty. Stacy didn't want to hurt my feelings any more than she already had.

"Is he really into her?" I asked. *Did he love her?*

"I don't know. They were kind of off on their own. I didn't talk to her much. I sort of gave her the cold shoulder out of respect for you."

"I have to see him again!" I said.

"Sh!" She pointed toward my parents.

"They can't hear us," I said, but I lowered my voice just in case. "I have to get him back, Stacy!" I knotted my hands in my lap. "How can I do it?"

"You have to sneak out or something," she said. "If you can figure out a time you can get together with him, I can get a message to him through Bryan. I'm sure he wants to see you. He really liked you."

I noticed the past tense. I had to see him somehow!

And then I thought about Saturday night. The upcoming family meeting. Me, sleeping over at Nanny's.

"I have an idea," I said quietly. I told her about Saturday night. "My grandmother always goes to bed early. Like at ten. I could sneak out then and she would never know. Maybe Chris could pick me up and we could go to your house if your mother —"

She shook her head. "Saturday is my sister's birthday. She's coming down for the weekend and we're having a party for her that night."

"Oh," I said.

"What about that creepy springhouse?" she asked. "You could meet him there. It would be perfect."

Oh my God, she was right! I smiled for the first time since we'd gotten in the van. It *was* perfect. "When we get to the hotel," I said quietly, "I'll make a map of Morrison Ridge for you to give him, all right? Will you see him before Saturday night?"

"I'll see Bryan Friday," she said. "He can tell Chris the plan and get the map to him."

Then she grabbed my hand, grinning. "This is so cool!" she said. "I'm so glad you'll get to see him!" Then she leaned over to whisper in my ear. "You and Chris really belong together, Molly," she said. "I know this is going to work out perfectly!"

48

The concert was held in a football stadium, the chairs set up in the field facing the stage. It took us forever to find our seats and we were amazed to discover we were only about thirty rows back.

"I can't believe your father was able to get these seats!" Stacy said, when we finally found our row. "Totally awesome."

The stadium was packed with people of all ages wearing New Kids T-shirts and New Kids buttons and New Kids jackets, even though the night was hot. We sat through some opening performers and a magic act, but I had trouble concentrating. All I could think about was Saturday night. What if Bryan couldn't get the map to Chris? What if Nanny decided that was the one night of the year she wanted to stay up late? So many things could go wrong, and while the crowd grew antsy and loud as we waited for the New Kids to take the stage, those possible

461

mishaps were all I could think about.

When the New Kids came on stage and everyone started screaming their heads off, I felt out of it. *I don't belong here any longer,* I thought. The girls around me jumped onto the seats of their chairs, waving their arms, begging for the guys to look in their direction. I stood on my chair, too — it was the only way to see — but I didn't scream. I watched the New Kids dance around on stage — five guys who had absorbed every spare moment of my life for the last couple of years and now seemed so silly and sort of plastic compared to Chris. I'd been wasting my time on a total fantasy.

But as the concert continued, I was drawn back in. They were so good. So exciting to watch. So passionate about what they were doing up there on the stage. I missed those guys and I was surprised when I felt tears burn my eyes. It was like watching old friends I'd lost and couldn't figure out how to get back. I missed the longing for them. The safety of them. With Chris, I felt as though I'd crossed some sort of invisible threshold into another life that was scarier, harder to manage, and way too real. I wanted my old life back. The one where I could happily stare at posters of the New Kids and Johnny Depp for hours upon hours upon hours, where my parents trusted me, where Daddy could see the world clearly and the hardest thing I ever had to do was walk my bike up the Hill from Hell. I stood on my chair, holding on to Stacy's arm as she screamed, and after a while, I screamed along with her.

49

I woke up the following morning with the sun pouring through the hotel room window. In the bed closest to the door, Stacy slept with the covers over her head, and I lay there for a few minutes, letting the memories of the night before wash over me before I realized I was starving. I got out of bed and dressed quietly so I didn't wake Stacy. I'd see if my parents were up. Maybe I could go down to the coffee stand in the lobby and get some muffins or something for everyone. I'd need to get some money from my mother first.

I took my room key and stepped out into the hallway. I was nearly to my parents' room when the door to Amalia's room opened and Russell emerged, buttoning the cuffs of his shirt. He stopped short when he saw me and we stared at each other. I wasn't sure which of us was more shocked.

"Morning, Molly," he said finally, and he

continued walking toward his door, which was right next to my parents'.

"Morning," I said, my cheeks warm. *Oh my God,* I thought. What would my parents say if they knew he'd been in Amalia's room, maybe all night long? I knocked on their door while Russell slipped his room key into his own door and stepped inside.

Mom opened the door, one of the hotel room's little black plastic coffee cups in her hand. "Oh good," she said. "You can help me sit Daddy up. I think Russell must still be sleeping."

"Hi, darling." Daddy smiled from his pillow. "Did you two get any sleep last night or were you too wired?"

"Not a lot," I admitted. Stacy had spent much of the night talking about how Joey looked like Bryan, and I'd felt my brain ping-ponging between the magic of the concert and the reality of Chris. Now I moved to the side of the bed next to my father, while Mom knelt opposite me on the mattress. We both got a grip on him beneath his shoulders. "One, two, three," Mom said, and together we propped his back up against the pillows. We had it down to a science.

"Much better," Daddy said. Mom had made him a cup of coffee and I held it to his lips. "Even better," he said after a sip.

"Russell's up," I said. "He's in his room."

"How do you know?" Mom asked.

"I saw him in the hallway," I said. "He was coming out of Amalia's room." I waited for their reaction.

They looked at each other, their faces too blank to read. Then my father let out a laugh. "So much for discretion," he said, and my mother smiled.

"I think you're old enough to know, Molly," she said.

"Know . . . what?" I asked.

"They're a couple," Daddy said. "We've kept it from you because they're not married, obviously, and we thought it could be confusing, but . . . you're not a kid anymore, are you?"

"No," I said. Still, I was shocked. Not because Amalia and Russell weren't married, and not because he was black and she was white. I was shocked this had been going on between two people I thought I knew so well and I'd never had a clue.

"How long have they been . . . a couple?" I asked.

"Year and a half?" Daddy looked at my mother.

"More like two years," she said.

"Two *years*?" I couldn't believe it. "Why don't they get married?"

"A little challenging for them right now, with Russell always at my beck and call," Daddy said.

I imagined what Russell's life was like. He was so thoroughly tethered to my father. How could he and Amalia ever have a normal relationship as long as he worked for us?

I thought about my dance lesson the other day, when Russell pushed Daddy's wheelchair out to the road. I remembered the way Amalia'd touched his arm and looked into his eyes. I thought she'd been communicating worry about my father to him, but maybe she'd been communicating something deeper than that. I felt afraid all of a sudden that they might get married and things would change. But Amalia loved my father. She and Russell both did. That was one thing I was sure of. They would both always want to do what was best for him.

I thought of how Nanny tried to keep Amalia away from Daddy and had to smile to myself. "Does Nanny know?" I asked.

"Good Lord, no," Daddy said. "She couldn't handle it."

Mom knocked on the door that connected their room to Russell's, and in a minute he was in the room.

"Ready to get out of bed, Graham?" he

asked, all business and avoiding my eyes.

"Molly's on to you," my father said.

Russell glanced at me. "Yes, I figured she might be," he said, and I thought he was fighting a smile.

"It's okay," I said, sort of shyly. It was too weird to imagine him and Amalia together, and I needed a change of subject. "Do you want me to get some muffins from that coffee shop in the lobby?" I asked my mother.

"Good idea," she said, and reached for her purse.

"Blueberry for me," Daddy said as Russell wheeled his chair to the side of the bed. "And get me two, please," he added. Clearly, Daddy was no longer counting his calories.

I left the room and turned in the direction of the elevator. I thought about Amalia and Russell and shook my head with a smile. I never would have guessed, and I wondered what other secrets I was missing at Morrison Ridge.

50
SAN DIEGO

Aidan and I work at our desks in our home office. He's checking e-mail. Across from him, I'm supposed to be working on a property settlement for a client. Instead, I'm looking at maternity clothes in an online catalog. Sienna is popping out of everything she owns and I want to buy her a few things. What I really would love to look at is baby clothes, but I won't let myself do that. Not yet.

Our landline rings. The phone is on Aidan's desk and he glances at the caller ID. I don't even bother to look away from my screen. We've been talking about ditching the landline altogether. The calls are always solicitations for one thing or another.

"It says 'unknown,' " Aidan says, and before I can tell him to ignore it, he picks up the receiver. "Hello?" he says, then he glances across our desks at me. "Yes, she's here."

I stand up to reach for the phone, then sit down again. "This is Molly," I say.

"Molly, it's Dani."

I can't remember Dani ever calling me. I didn't even know she had my number.

"Hi, Dani. What's up?" I ask, but I'm afraid I already know and the muscles in my chest tighten.

"I thought I should let you know that Amalia passed away," she says. "I didn't want to just write it in an e-mail."

"Oh." I hear the lack of emotion in my voice, but my insides are churning. "Was it that infection you told me about?"

"Yes. She just couldn't fight it. My mother heard about it at church."

"Oh," I say again. I feel as though I'm standing outside myself, trying to figure out how I'm supposed to react. I'm aware that Aidan's watching me from across our desks.

"Molly?" Dani prompts. "They had a service for her at some art studio in Asheville. I'm sorry I didn't know about it in time to tell you."

"I . . . It doesn't really matter," I say. Did she think I would have gone?

"I thought you might want Russell's number."

"Maybe you could just e-mail it to me." I feel as though I might get sick. "I have to

470

go, Dan—"

"Don't get off yet," she says quickly.

I wait, staring out the window. From where I sit, I can see the three white Spanish-style houses across the street. One of them is in desperate need of painting. I think about that instead of Amalia as I wait for Dani to continue.

"Aunt Nora called me last night," she says. "She really wants to talk to you. She asked me to plead with you to call her or let her call you. Can I give her your number?" she asks. "Or at least your e-mail?"

"I'm sorry. No."

Dani says nothing and an uncomfortable silence stretches between us. I'm ready to hang up when she speaks again.

"She's your mother, Molly," she says finally, as if I've forgotten.

"I know," I say. If Aidan wasn't sitting across from me, would I say more? I don't think so.

"She loves you," Dani says.

"I need to go. Thank you for letting me —"

"You know what, Molly?" Dani suddenly barks at me.

"What?"

"You're an unforgiving bitch," she says. "And I'm done with you! I've had it."

471

The line goes dead.

I think of saying good-bye, putting up the pretense that the call has ended normally for Aidan's sake, but I'm too numb to fake it. I set down the receiver on my desk and look over at him.

"Your cousin?" he asks.

I can't answer. I see Amalia in the slave quarters, dancing across the floor. *Dance what you feel, baby.* I lower my head to my hands, and before I know what's happening, I'm sobbing and Aidan is at my side, leaning over, his arms around my shoulders. I cling to him like he's a life preserver, and when he says, "Talk to me, Molly. Please," I know I'm going to tell him the truth.

At least, most of it.

51
MORRISON RIDGE

At breakfast Saturday morning, I stared at my pancakes and grapefruit, unable to eat. Tonight was the family meeting and I hadn't heard a word from Stacy about Chris getting together with me at the springhouse. She was supposed to talk to Bryan about it and he was supposed to talk to Chris and get the map of Morrison Ridge to him, but I didn't know if any of that had happened. I'd tried calling her a couple of times, but there was never any answer at her house. I worried she'd forgotten. Or worse, that Chris was seeing that other girl and no longer cared about me and Stacy was afraid to tell me.

Russell fed my father an entire stack of pancakes in the time it took me to eat two segments of my grapefruit.

"What's the matter, Molly?" Mom asked. She'd eaten two pancakes herself and was now sipping her coffee, one hand locked with my father's on the arm of his chair. She didn't usually sit right next to him at the table like that, especially not when Russell was feeding him.

"Nothing," I said. "Just not very hungry."

"I'd like some time with you today," Daddy said to me. Russell blotted a drop of syrup from my father's chin with a napkin.

"To type?" I asked.

"No, just to visit." Daddy smiled. "We could meet in the springhouse if you like."

That suggestion completely derailed me. The thought of spending time with my father in the springhouse hours before I'd — maybe, possibly — be there with Chris felt too weird.

"Maybe someplace else?" I said. I really didn't feel like a big talk with him today, either. Ordinarily, I loved time with my father, but right now I wanted to be by myself. I wasn't going to be able to concentrate on anybody or anything with all I had on my mind.

"Want to suggest a place?" he asked.

"Maybe the screened porch?" I said.

He nodded slowly, his gaze so intent on me that I looked down at my nearly intact grapefruit half again.

"All right," he said. "I want to spend some time with Nanny this afternoon, so how about this morning? Say an hour from now? Do you have anything else on your agenda today?"

I shook my head. "Just reading," I said.

"I'll take you over to your grandmother's a little before seven tonight," Russell said.

"Okay." I looked at my mother. "May I be excused?"

"You didn't eat a single pancake," Mom said.

"I'll eat hers," Daddy said with a smile. "Wouldn't want them to go to waste."

Stacy finally called later that morning as I was heading out to the porch to sit with Daddy. I answered the phone in the kitchen, and when I realized it was Stacy, I stretched the cord so that I could talk to her from the hallway, afraid my father might be able to hear me through the kitchen window.

"It took forever!" She sounded breathless. "But Bryan finally reached Chris last night, and he'll do it! He'll be there at ten tonight."

"Oh my God," I whispered.

"You'll be there, right?"

"Absolutely. Does he have the map?"

"Bryan's dropping it off at his house this afternoon," Stacy said. "What are you going to wear?" Then she laughed. "Not that it matters. You won't be wearing it long."

I didn't answer. I felt prickly all over, as though I might be breaking out with a rash.

"Is someone there?" Stacy asked. "You can't talk now?"

"Right," I said. "I'll call you tomorrow?"

"I can't wait to hear everything!" she said, and then she was gone. And for the first time since I'd given the palm stone to my father, I wished I had it back to hold in my pocket.

"Glad to see that smile," Daddy said, as I sat down on the old white rocker next to his chair. "What's up?"

"Oh, Stacy just called."

"You two still high from the concert?"

I nodded. "Yeah. It was awesome." The concert seemed like a lifetime ago.

He looked toward the mountains in the distance. "Nice out here," he said. "I'm glad you suggested the porch. I haven't simply sat and admired this view in a long time." He looked thoughtful. "I should have done more of that," he said.

I looked toward the mountains myself. I briefly wondered how much of the view he was able to see, but the truth was, all I could think about was me, tonight, opening the springhouse door and finding Chris inside. I didn't know how I was going to survive until then.

"What did you want to talk about?" I asked.

"Nothing special," he said. "Just wanted time with my daughter."

"Well, here I am." I felt awkward. I didn't usually feel that way with him, but I worried he would somehow know what I was up to, as though it might be written on my face.

He looked at me. "Ever since you and I talked about that day Amalia brought you to us, I've been thinking about it." He smiled. "Remembering it. It was such a shock. Can you imagine? Suddenly there's this fully formed little human being you created but who you never knew existed."

"Must have been weird," I said. I was over that whole topic and surprised he was still thinking about it.

"So, what do you think you'd like to be when you're older?" he asked. The question was so insanely out of the blue that I thought I'd misheard him.

"What?" I asked.

"What are you hoping to do with your life?"

I was exasperated by the question. I wanted to be upstairs in my room, looking through my closet as I figured out what to wear tonight. Maybe I should change the sheets on one of the beds in the spring-house, I thought. And I should probably take down the New Kids and Johnny Depp posters, too.

"Molly, are you in there?" Daddy asked, and I sighed.

"Why are we talking about this?" I asked.

"Just wondering," he said. "Humor me."

I sighed again. I'd give in. Get it over with. I hadn't thought about that question in a while, though. What did I want to do with my life? Last summer's plan to become an entomologist had lost its allure for me. I thought what my mother did was pretty cool, the way she understood how drugs worked, how they interacted with one another and I felt proud of her when I saw her in her white coat. But my father had the coolest job of all, helping people feel better about themselves. "Maybe a pretend therapist," I said.

"Really?"

I saw a spark of joy in his eyes.

"Maybe," I said.

"You'd be very good at it. Your sensitive nature would be an asset."

I tried to imagine myself in an office like his — the one he didn't go to any longer — helping a girl like that Dorianna from the

478

tape. I could picture it. I couldn't quite see myself counseling an adult, though.

"Maybe just with kids," I said.

"Do you want to have kids yourself?" he asked.

"You mean . . . when I get married?"

"Of course. Marriage first. Please."

"Sure," I said. "And definitely more than one."

He laughed. "Are you saying you haven't adored being an only child?"

"That's what I'm saying," I said dryly.

"I imagine it's been rough at times." He looked thoughtful, then smiled at me. "I like the idea that I'll get to live on through you and your children," he said.

Whatever, I thought. It seemed like a weird thing to say.

"Do you think you'll live here when you're an adult? At Morrison Ridge?"

I tried to read the time on his watch, but the angle was wrong. "I'll always live here," I said. Living any place else was unimaginable.

"Where will you build your house?"

"Maybe on the other side of Nanny's." I pictured the thick woods at the northern end of the Ridge.

Daddy smiled. "You mean as far from home as you could get and still technically be in Morrison Ridge."

I returned the smile. "Right."

I wanted to ask him if we were done talking for now. I thought again about the sheets in the springhouse. Mom would be suspicious if I changed them. It was better if I left them alone. Chris wouldn't care.

"I just wanted to tell you that I'm proud of you, Molly," Daddy said, pulling my mind back onto the porch. He'd told me he was proud of me any number of times, but the fact that I was planning something I should be ashamed of made me wonder what he was talking about.

"What for?" I asked.

"Well, I'm always proud of you just for being a great girl and for how well you do in school, and how uncomplainingly you've helped me with my writing and . . . everything. But I also know this has been a rough summer for you. All your friends have been away and then we cracked down on how much you could see Stacy. Plus we cut you off from Chris, and you had feelings for him and thought he was 'the one,' but there will be lots of other guys in the future. Guys who are better suited to you."

"You don't even know him," I said, "so how can you say he's not suited to me?" I didn't want to argue with him — I really didn't — but the words popped out before I could stop them.

"I know his age and that's all I need to know for now," Daddy said.

"That's so lame," I said. "You're three years older than Mom."

"And if I were seventeen and she was fourteen, we wouldn't be right for each other, either. Not until we were considerably older."

"You were nine years older than Amalia," I argued.

"We were both adults," he said.

"You should have given him a chance!" I said. "It's not his fault he's seventeen."

"We've already settled this, Molly," he said.

"No, *you* settled it," I snapped. "I didn't get to have anything to say about it. I just had to go along with what you say."

"In this case, yes. You did. You do."

I stood up. "I think you're being very unfair."

He looked up at me with those big eyes. They reflected the sky and were bluer than I'd ever seen them. "I know you think that," he said, "but —"

"You always say, 'Oh, Molly, tell me how you really feel about things' and you tell me how you admire me and you're proud of me and everything, but you don't *trust* me. If you admire me so much, why don't you trust me to know what's right for me?"

"Because you're fourteen."

"That's such a cop-out!" I took a step toward the house. "I'm done talking."

"Molly!" he said. "Stop."

I did. I stopped mid-step. Shut my eyes.

"I know you don't understand, darling," he said. "I wouldn't have understood it when I was your age, either. But you will. When you're older, you will." He paused for a moment. "That's the best I can do," he said.

I looked at him. "Can I go now?" I asked.

Time stretched between us as I stood there, staring at him, waiting to be released. Any other kid my age might have simply left, but I couldn't seem to take another step toward the door.

"Those kids you're going to have?" Daddy said finally.

"What about them?"

"Be sure to hug them a lot," he said, "in case someday you can't."

I knew he needed me to hug him right then. I knew it, but my anger was too raw. I walked past him to find Russell. I'd tell him our visit on the porch was over.

52

Mom stared at me across the dinner table that night and I was afraid she was going to tell me I was old enough to be at tonight's family meeting. I loved that I'd been left out of whatever boring talk was going on at those meetings and I was particularly glad to be left out tonight. I was ready to argue that Nanny needed my company, since she wasn't coming. I figured Nanny had had it with talk about the land. As long as she went to bed by ten, everything should work out fine, though I had to admit the thought of walking through the dark all the way from Nanny's house to the springhouse was freaking me out a little. It would be worth it, though, to be with Chris.

Mom had made Daddy's absolutely favorite food tonight: meat loaf with mashed potatoes and gravy. He was the only one of us who seemed interested in eating, though. Russell didn't even have a plate. The four of us were weirdly quiet, and I didn't know if Daddy was still upset with me for the way I'd acted on the porch or if I was still upset with him or what. I had this terrible fear Mom and Daddy and Russell were all on to me, though I didn't know how they could be. I thought I felt their eyes on me, but when I looked at each of them, they didn't appear to be interested in me at all. Mom was no longer looking in my direction. Instead, she stared at her plate, poking her fork slowly in and out of the meat loaf without lifting a bite of it to her mouth. Daddy's meat loaf was nearly gone and he asked Russell to put another spoonful of potatoes on his plate. Then he looked over at my mother.

"You're not eating," he said.

When she turned her face toward him, I could tell she was trying to smile, but her eyes were full of tears. What was going on? "I have no appetite," she said. She pushed her plate in his direction. "Want mine?"

Daddy shook his head. "No, darling," he said. "It was perfect, though. Russell, you have to have some."

"Later," Russell said.

"Do me a favor and put your hand on my miserable wife's hand for me," Daddy said to him.

Russell and my mother exchanged a look of surprise, but Russell leaned across the table and set his hand on my mother's.

Daddy looked at her intently. "You are stronger than you know," he said.

She turned her hand so that she and Russell were palm to palm and she smiled at my father, though the tears never disappeared. "I'll try to remember that," she said.

If it had been any other night, I would have asked, "What's going on?" Tonight's meeting marked some kind of change, I could tell. Were they going to give in to Uncle Trevor and sell our land after all? Was that why Nanny didn't want to be there? I didn't have the patience to invite that sort of conversation tonight. My mind was on one thing: Chris. That was why my own meat loaf was barely touched.

Russell let go of Mom's hand and got to his feet to clear my father's plate from the table. I stood up, too. "I'm going to get ready to go to Nanny's," I said. I felt like I'd been drinking coffee, something I'd only done once in my life and once had been enough. It had made me feel like squirrels were running around inside my body.

My father looked up at me. "Hug?" he asked.

I debated a moment before leaning over to give him a little hug. I was still angry.

"Longer," he said, and with a sigh, I gave in to him. I held my arms around his shoulders. Rested my cheek on his temple. "You're so beautiful," he said, and in spite of myself, my eyes stung.

When I stood up, I saw that my mother had turned away from us. She stared out the window with such concentration that I followed her gaze, but I saw only trees and, in the distance, the mountains.

"Bye," I said to all three of them as I headed for the door to the hallway.

No one said a word in reply.

53
SAN DIEGO

Aidan treats me as though I'm very ill, and that's the way I feel. He makes me tea and tucks an afghan around my shoulders and we sit together in the corner of our sectional. I rest my head on his shoulder and begin to tell him all the things I should have told him long ago.

"That family friend I told you about?" I say. "The one who broke her leg?"

He hesitates and I know he doesn't really remember the conversation. "Yes?" he prompts.

"She wasn't really a family friend," I say. "She was . . ." I lean my head back to look at him. At his pretty, loving brown eyes behind his glasses. "She was my birth mother."

I feel his body stiffen next to me. "What are you talking about?" The words come out slowly. I try to listen to discern if there is any anger behind them.

"I haven't told you the truth about my childhood," I say. "About Morrison Ridge. I've left things out because . . . I was afraid."

"Afraid of what?" No, there is no anger, I think. Not yet.

"You know I was engaged before we met, right?"

"I'd forgotten, actually," he says. "Jordan somebody?" He's frowning, and I turn my head so I don't have to see his face.

"I told Jordan everything about my family," I say. "It was two months before our wedding and he called it off, he was so . . . so disgusted by it all, and so I decided never to tell you. I didn't see any reason to." *I'm sorry, Molly,* Jordan had said. *This is too much.*

"He was disgusted by what?" Aidan asks.

"He said I was screwed up and he didn't want to raise a family with me," I say. "And maybe I *was* screwed up back then, but I'm not now. Or at least I thought I wasn't. But now —"

"Molly," he says, "would you start at the beginning, please? I can't follow you, and frankly, you're scaring me right now."

I take a deep breath.

"I told you my mother is dead," I say, "but she's not. Well, she's dead to me, but she's still alive."

"I thought your cousin just called to tell you she died?"

"That's my birth mother." I tell him about my father's relationship with Amalia and how she disappeared once she realized she was pregnant with me. How she showed up on our doorstep with the social worker. How Nora adopted me.

"My father set it up so that she could live on our land," I say, "so I would have her close by. I lived with my father and Nora — my adoptive mother. And Amalia lived nearby."

"Molly . . ." Aidan's voice is incredulous. "Why didn't you tell me this? With all we're going through right now with the adoption, and you've had this experience, I just don't get —"

"I know you don't," I say. "I know it's —"

"What was your relationship like with them? I mean, it sounds like you had the ultimate in open adoptions. Is that what's worried you about an open adoption with Sienna?"

"I think so, yes," I say. "I loved them both . . . although I don't love either of them any longer." When those words leave my mouth, I feel sick to my stomach again and I squeeze my eyes shut. I no longer know what I feel for anyone at Morrison

489

Ridge. "But," I say, "Amalia was warmer. She was easier to be around and I think I turned to her when I was annoyed with Nora. And you're right. I worried our child would bond more with her birth mother than with me. I don't think I was actually conscious of that fear. I just knew I didn't want to share our baby. Although now that I know Sienna, I'm not so worried about it."

"Why did you tell me your mother — this Nora woman — was dead?"

"Because it was the easiest way to explain why I'm not in touch with her."

"And why aren't you in touch with her?"

"Oh . . ." I hedge. "Just . . . her coldness." Nora had loved me; I was quite certain of that, but had she loved me for myself or had she loved me because I was Graham's daughter? That I didn't know. I'd never forget the day Daddy, Russell, and I returned home from the book tour. How she'd raced past me as if I were invisible to get to my father in the van. "Everything changed after Daddy died," I say. "To start with, my relatives all kicked Amalia off Morrison Ridge and Nora did nothing to stop them."

"Wow," he says. "They didn't have your best interest at heart, did they? Was Nora jealous of her?"

"Yes, I think so. I hated Nora by then, and —"

"Why did you hate her?"

I tried to think of a reason that wasn't the truth. "She was just so cold," I lie. "And I told her I wanted to live with Amalia, but Nora said she would fight it. That Amalia had been accused of neglecting me when I was two and there was no way a court would take me away from Nora and let me live with Amalia."

"Wow," Aidan says again. "I'm sorry this was so rough on you, babe. So you were cut off from Amalia?"

I'd cut *myself* off. How could I explain that to Aidan without telling him everything? I was starting to get tangled up in my story.

"I was mad at her, too," I say simply. "I was just in a bad place and angry with everyone and I wanted to get away from them." I hated to remember that time in my life. I'd been too young to run away for real after Daddy died — where could I go? — so I ran away inside my head, where I was alone with the extraordinary pain of my father's absence. He'd been my life. The person I could talk to about anything. The person I knew loved me no matter what.

491

For the rest of that horrible summer, I locked myself in my room, refusing to talk to anyone.

"So, my cousin Dani was going to this boarding school called Virginia Dare," I say, "and I told Nora I wanted to go there, too. I had to get away from the Ridge. And she agreed. She was probably glad to get rid of me once my father was gone." I wince. I'm not sure if that's the truth. "Dani went home from our boarding school on occasional weekends or holidays," I say, "but I almost never returned to Morrison Ridge once I left. I spent holidays and summer vacations with school friends and their families, and Nora never fought me on my plans to stay away, although Amalia would call me at school and plead with me to come see her. Daddy had left money that became mine when I turned eighteen, and as soon as I graduated, I moved here to San Diego with a girlfriend. And you know the rest of the story. I went to college. Met Jordan. Got engaged. Got unengaged. Met you, which is the best thing that ever happened to —"

"Molly," he says. "I still don't understand. So Nora was cold. Why didn't you try to work things out with her? And with your birth mother? This doesn't sound like you, babe. I don't get why you would just cut your family out of your life like that."

I start to cry. Of course he doesn't understand. I've given him the muddied abridged version of my childhood and it makes no sense.

"There's more to this, isn't there?" he says. "What is it you're not telling me? Were you abused there? Is that it?"

I shake my head. "I'm afraid of what you'll do if I tell you," I say.

"Molly . . . I love you. Do you think I'd leave you? I will never do anything to hurt you."

I move away from him on the sectional so I can see his face. Pulling the afghan more tightly over my shoulders, I fold my arms around my legs, scrunching myself into a protective ball. He watches me and I know I have to trust him. If I don't tell him the truth now, the past will always be between us, a wall of lies that will ruin us.

I pull one of my arms from beneath the afghan and reach for his hand. He holds it on his knee. Studies my face. And I look into his warm eyes and gather my courage.

"Nora killed my father," I say simply, and it's the last simple thing I will say for a while.

54
MORRISON RIDGE

On the night I was to meet Chris at the springhouse, Russell drove me to Nanny's shortly before seven. I was glad that we left the house before anyone had arrived for the family meeting. I didn't want to have to make small talk with my relatives tonight. Russell and I were both really quiet in the van, and I worried that he knew I was up to something. I was seriously paranoid tonight. There was no way he could know, yet I kept waiting for a lecture that never came, and I was relieved when he turned into Nanny's circular driveway. "I'll pick you up in the morning," he said, as I opened the van door.

"I can walk, thanks." I grabbed my backpack from the floor of the van. Shutting the door, I headed up the walkway to the house.

"Nanny?" I called, once I'd let myself in through the unlocked front door. The house was so quiet and still, I could hear the tick-ing of the clock on the mantel beneath the head of the buck. I headed up the hallway toward the back door, thinking my grandmother must be outside. But when I passed the library, I saw her. She sat in a wingback chair by the library window, a book open on her lap.

"Nanny?" I said.

She was slow to turn her head toward me as I walked into the room.

"Hi, dear," she said.

I leaned over to kiss her cheek. Her hair smelled as though she hadn't washed it in a few days. It hung limply against her cheeks instead of in her usual bouncy bob. "Are you feeling okay?" I asked.

"Tired," she said, tipping her head back so that her blue eyes met mine. "I'm just very tired lately."

I barely heard her response to my question. My mind was not in this room. "Want to watch a movie?" I asked. It was a few minutes before seven. If we watched a two-hour movie, I could pretend to go to bed about nine-thirty and maybe that would inspire her to go to bed, too. Then I could be out the door by ten. It would be perfect.

"Did anyone arrive at your house yet?" Nanny asked, as though I hadn't said a word about a movie.

"Not yet." I sat down in the only other comfortable chair in the library and hugged my backpack to my chest, where the squirrels continued to run around inside my rib cage. "Did you hear what I said about a movie?" I asked. "Do you want to watch one?"

She looked down at the book in her lap again as though she hadn't heard me.

"Or would you rather just read?" I asked, growing frustrated.

"I suppose a movie," she said finally. "You can pick one out. I don't care what we watch."

Neither did I, really. But I was glad she'd finally made a decision, and I got up to find a movie that ran two hours or less.

Sitting on the sofa, we watched *Dial M for Murder,* or rather, the movie played on the TV while I kept an eye on the clock on the mantel, imagining my escape from Nanny's house. I was so wrapped up in my own thoughts that it took me a while to realize Nanny was staring into space rather than at the TV screen. She was obviously troubled tonight, most likely about Uncle Trevor and the family meeting, and I knew I should ask her what she was thinking. "Draw her out," Daddy would say. But I didn't have the energy tonight for anyone but myself.

The movie had a half hour to go when Nanny turned to look at me. "I'm so tired tonight, Molly," she said. "Do you mind if I go to bed? I hate to leave you alone but —"

"No, that's okay," I said quickly, wondering how I got so lucky. "I'm fine. I'll just watch the end of this and then read in bed for a while."

"Thank you, dear." She held on to the arm of the sofa as she stood up and her first couple of steps seemed tentative. She seemed a thousand years old tonight.

Once I heard her bedroom door squeak shut, I sat nervously on the sofa, waiting for the movie to be over. The last half hour seemed to stretch into eternity. Once it ended, I turned the TV off, then walked down the hall and pressed my ear against Nanny's door, hoping to hear her gentle snoring. Instead, I heard the unmistakable sound of weeping. I stood still, unsure what to do. I should knock on her door. I should sit on her bed and comfort her. But she'd gone to bed, so she obviously wanted to be alone. I convinced myself of that as I walked down the hall to the guest room.

I stayed in the guest room until quarter to ten, sitting rigidly in the dark, my backpack over my shoulder, wishing I had my palm stone in my pocket. Then I got up and went into the hall and put my ear against Nanny's door again. All was quiet inside.

I left the house by the back door since I was less likely to wake her that way. I waited until I reached the road before turning on my flashlight and then I walked as fast as I could toward the springhouse. I passed the lane that led to Amalia's house. The forest was full of unearthly animal sounds that rose above the buzz of the cicadas. Something was definitely being killed out there tonight. I shuddered.

I finally reached the turnoff to the springhouse. The path was completely covered by a tangle of ivy and weeds now that we were deep into summer, but I was still able to separate it from the rest of the forest floor as I walked, and soon I saw lights burning in the windows of the springhouse. *Oh my God.* He was there! This was really happening!

I took off my glasses, dropping them into the outside pocket of my backpack. Then I forced open the door and there he was, standing in the middle of the room, grinning at me. "You made it," he said. "I was getting worried."

I felt suddenly shy — just a little — but he walked toward me, slid my backpack from my shoulders and set it gently on the floor. Then he put his arms around me and simply hugged me. It was so nice. Nicer than if he'd grabbed me and kissed me, which is what I'd been expecting in my fantasy of this moment. But this was better. So much better. He cared about *me*, not just about having sex with me.

"You definitely have a thing for the New Kids and Johnny Depp, I see," he said, and I buried my head against his shoulder, embarrassed. I knew I should have taken the posters down before he got here.

"They're from last year," I said. A white lie. They *were* from last year, but I'd only moved them from my bedroom to the springhouse this past June.

"Not a big deal," he said, running his hands down my sides. "We all still have stuff from our childhoods."

"What do you have?" I asked, while he nuzzled my neck. "From your childhood, I mean?" I needed to talk a while. I wasn't ready for him to touch me all over again.

He leaned away from me, grinning, his dimples flashing. "Are you nervous?" he asked.

"No." I wished I had my stone! I tried to grin back. "I'm really curious about what you have from your childhood."

"Mostly *Star Wars* stuff." He held me close, his hands pressed flat against my back. He kissed me lightly. So lightly, I shivered. I wanted more. "Action figures," he said. "That sort of thing."

"Mm," I said to let him know I'd heard him. I was done talking about our childhoods. He kissed me again, more seriously this time. It was as good as the last time when we were at Stacy's house. He was such an amazing kisser. Not that I had anyone else to compare him to.

After a minute, he started lifting my shirt over my head, but I caught his hands.

"We have to turn out the light," I said, pulling away from him to switch off the floor lamp. "Anyone outside can see in."

"Who'd be way out here?" He led me over to the bed in the darkness. We lay down together on top of the thin brown bedspread and he kissed me some more. He started to pull off my shirt again, and this time I let him, laughing when the collar got stuck on my ear. He unhooked my bra, but he barely touched my breasts before reaching down to slide off my shorts. When I was down to my bikini underpants, he took my hand and put it on the snap of his jeans. I unsnapped them, but I couldn't get the zipper down, my hands were shaking so hard, and he had to help me. Then he pulled off his jeans and his shorts — oh my God, I couldn't believe how quickly this was happening! Suddenly he was naked next to me. He took my hand and wrapped it around his penis. It was bigger than I'd expected. A hundred times bigger than a tampon. It would never fit inside me. I wasn't sure what I was supposed to do with my hand around him, but he showed me and his penis only seemed to grow bigger and harder beneath my fingers.

"You're making me crazy," he whispered in my ear. His hand had slipped inside my underpants, and he was touching me, but I couldn't concentrate on the feeling, I was so nervous.

"Chris?" I whispered back.

"What?" It sounded like it was hard for him to get the word out.

"I don't think . . . I think I'm too small and you're too big." I felt unbelievably embarrassed and was glad the light was off.

He laughed, and I felt him slide a finger inside me. "You're not too small," he said. "There's no such thing as too small. It might hurt this time because it's the first time, but it'll be better the next time. And you are so ready." He knelt next to me and slipped off my underpants, then moved on top of me, spreading my legs apart with his own. "I'll go as slow as I can, okay?" he said.

"The Trojan thing!" I said.

"Oh yeah. Shit. Sorry." He leaned down from the bed and found his jeans in the darkness. I heard him tear open the package. Then he was back on me and I felt him pushing into me and it *did* hurt. I let out a yelp and dug my nails into his shoulders, and then it was over. Three seconds. Just like that. His body fell against mine and I remembered Stacy telling me, *It sucked the first time.* But even with that warning, I'd expected something more. He hadn't even said he loved me. This hardly felt worth all the deception.

He rolled off me and leaned over the side of the bed and I heard him rummaging around in his clothes. Then he lit a match, the flame catching the blue-gray of his eyes as he held it to a joint. "The postcoital smoke," he said, handing the joint to me.

"What's that mean?" I asked. "Post . . . what you said."

"It means 'after sex.' " He took the joint back from me. "It's so cool that you have this place," he said, his voice tight with smoke. "We could have parties here."

"Well . . . that's probably not a great idea." I pictured his friends parking down at the entrance to the Ridge. Walking up the loop road. My relatives might drive by and see them and know something was up.

"We'd be careful," he said, holding the joint to my lips while I inhaled. "You wouldn't even have to be here if you didn't want to be. That way you couldn't get in trouble."

What was he talking about? I let out the smoke. "What do you mean, I wouldn't have to be here?"

"Like, if I had a party and you didn't want to risk getting caught."

I had to be misunderstanding him. "This is *my* springhouse," I said. "If there's a party, I should be here."

He took a long hit on the joint, then sighed. "Look, Molly," he said. "You know it's okay when it's just me and you together. Or when we're with Stacy and Bryan. But you and Stacy don't fit in with our other friends. I mean, I like you and think you're cool and everything, but most people I hang out with are a lot older."

Panic filled my chest. I knew I was losing something. Something I'd never had to begin with. "I thought . . ." I pressed my lips together hard. I didn't want to cry. "You told me you loved me," I said.

He laughed. "Well, yeah," he said. "I love you as a friend."

I sat up, hugging my arms protectively over my breasts although I knew it was too dark for him to see me. "You just had *sex* with me," I said. "Doesn't that mean anything to you? Do you always have sex with your friends?"

"Oh great," he said sarcastically. "Are you going to turn into a whiner?" He sat up, his back to me and his feet on the floor. He pinched out the joint with his fingers. "Don't go getting all emotional on me, all right?" I heard him reach for his jeans. "That's what I mean about hanging out with older people. Older girls. They don't freak out about hooking up."

"I'm not freaking out!" I said, though I knew my voice made a liar out of me.

"What do you call it?" He pulled on his jeans and stood to zip them up. "I've got to go," he said, and I heard him hunting on the floor for his shirt. It was too dark to clearly see his face and I felt as though he'd turned into another person in the last few minutes.

I felt desperate to keep him there. I wanted to wind back our conversation to whatever I'd said that had so thoroughly and suddenly turned him off.

"Please," I said. "What did I say that's so terrible? I don't —"

"Bryan told me you were a mistake," he said as he pulled on his shirt. "I can see now he was right."

I hugged my arms more tightly across my chest. *Don't leave!* I wanted to shout. *I'm not a mistake. I can be what you want me to be! You can have parties in the springhouse. Anything you want. Please don't go!*

But he did go. He blew out of the springhouse without another word.

I sat alone in the dark, my body trembling convulsively. I felt nauseous, as though if I tried to get up off the bed, I'd get sick. My body was sore and my heart ached. I'd been used. I felt stupid and dirty and ashamed.

Worst of all, I felt alone, like a tiny little speck of a girl in a cold stone springhouse. I was fourteen but felt four. I didn't want to go back to Nanny's. I wanted to be with my parents, the people who I knew loved me. Would always love me, no matter what. I needed them at that moment worse than I'd ever needed anyone in my life.

I dressed in the darkness, slowly, crying quietly. My soft sobs seemed to bounce off the fieldstone walls. I sounded pathetic. I *was* pathetic. I stumbled out of the springhouse and felt my way down the path to the loop road, the beam of my flashlight flickering against the trunks of the trees.

I was still crying by the time I turned onto our road. The meeting would long be over by now, I thought, and my parents would be in bed. That was all right. That was good. I didn't want to see them; if they saw my face, I'd have too much explaining to do. I only wanted to be close to them, that was all. I wanted to feel the security in that house. I wanted to feel the love.

55

It was eleven-thirty by the time I climbed the steps to the front porch. I slipped quietly into the living room, which was eerily still and deserted, lit only by a table lamp in the corner. Someone must have left that light on after the meeting broke up. I didn't take the time to turn it off, but headed for the stairs, trying to prevent my Doc Martens from squeaking on the hardwood floor.

"Molly?" Russell's voice came from the hallway behind me.

I'd reached the stairs and I froze on the bottom step, my hand on the railing. I had to offer some explanation for being there. I turned around slowly to face him.

"Why aren't you at your grandmother's?" he asked.

"I couldn't get to sleep," I said. "I wanted to come home to my own bed."

He took a step closer to me and I was afraid he could see my horrible night written on my face, but it was *his* face that told me something was terribly wrong. Despite the dim light in the room, I could see that his eyes were red, his cheeks drawn.

"What's the matter?" I asked.

He hesitated, looking uncertain. I'd never seen him so unsure of himself. So *sad*.

"It's your father," he said finally. "He's very ill, Molly."

I sucked in my breath, looking past him down the hall. I started walking in the direction of my parents' room, but he caught my arm.

"You can't go in there," he said.

"I need to *see* him." I tried to wrench my arm free but he held it fast.

"Molly . . . it's better if you don't." His fingers bit into the flesh of my arm.

"Why?" I tried to stare him down.

He hesitated again, studying my face as if he could see through my eyes to my soul, and I saw the exact moment he gave in. He let go of my arm. "Come with me," he said, and with a hand on my back, he started walking me down the hall toward my parents' bedroom.

My heart pounded as we neared the bedroom. The way Russell was acting, I was afraid of what I would find inside. I pushed open the door and stood there paralyzed as

I took in the scene. In the dim lighting, I saw Daddy lying on the bed. He was propped up slightly on some pillows, his eyes shut. My mother lay next to him, her cheek against his shoulder, an arm across his chest. She lifted her head when I opened the door, her eyes wide. I thought she looked terrified. "Molly!" she said, jerking me out of my paralysis. I ran toward the bed.

"What's wrong with him?" I said, reaching for my father's arm. He was very still. Too still. I needed to shake him awake. "Is he breathing?" I asked.

"I explained that he wasn't feeling well," Russell said to my mother.

I saw Daddy's chest rise and fall. He was alive! "Did you call the ambulance?" I asked.

My mother looked up at Russell. "Please take her to her room, Russ," she said. She sounded exhausted.

"Is the ambulance on its way?" I shook off Russell's hand as he tried to take my arm again.

"I didn't call an ambulance," my mother said.

"Why not? Are you crazy?" I reached for the phone on the night table, but Russell leaned past me, his hand holding down the receiver.

"He wouldn't want that," he said.

"But he's really sick!" I didn't understand them. What was going on?

"Honey, listen to me." My mother lightly rubbed Daddy's shoulder with her hand as she spoke to me. Her voice was soft and controlled. "Listen, please," she said. "He knew he was getting very sick over the last few weeks and months. He knew he would die soon and he didn't want to go to the hospital when the time came. He didn't want . . . heroic measures to save his life. He wanted to be allowed to die peacefully. And that's what's happening, honey. He's —"

"He's dying?" I stared at her, incredulous.

"Yes," she said.

I started to cry. I reached across her to grab my father's hand and shake his arm. "Daddy! Please!" I begged. "Don't die! I need you!"

I felt Russell's hands on my shoulders and my mother held on to my wrist. "Sweetheart, stop," she said, her voice firm.

"But we can't just let him die!" I sobbed.

"Sh, Molly. You have to stop." She let go of my wrist, cautiously, as though she didn't trust what I might do. "Let him have these last moments in peace," she said.

I pressed my hands to my face. I couldn't believe what was happening. "Please," I begged her from behind my fingers. "Please." I wasn't even sure what I was pleading for any longer.

"Molly." Russell's voice was unbearably calm. His hands were still on my shoulders. "There's nothing to do," he said. "It's all good. He's right where he wanted to be."

I felt beaten down. I lowered my hands from my face and looked at my father and knew that Russell was right. Daddy looked peaceful. There was nothing to do.

My mother lightly touched my hand with her fingertips. "If you're okay . . . if you can sit quietly . . . you can stay here with him and me. You can help me let him go."

I hesitated. "Okay," I said, so quietly I barely heard myself.

She wrapped her hand around mine, squeezing gently. "Come around the other side of the bed, honey." Her voice was gentle. "It's okay." I saw her look up at Russell. "We're all right," she said to him.

"Okay." Russell sounded uncertain. "Call if you need me."

I didn't hear him leave the room as I walked around to the other side of the bed. I climbed onto the bed and sat next to my father, my back against the headboard. I was still crying quietly, my throat tight with tears. Daddy's breathing was irregular. It seemed to stop, then suddenly start again, but his face was almost serene. He looked like he was simply asleep. Was this really, truly what he wanted? I remembered the night of the party, when he didn't want the ambulance to come. *Yes,* I thought, my heart full of sorrow. He probably would want us to simply let him go.

"Do you want to hold his hand?" Mom asked.

I looked down to where Daddy's hand rested on the bed. I nodded, lifting his still warm hand into mine. I remembered the last time I'd lain with him on this bed. We sang "Lyin' Eyes" together. He'd been so alive that night. So happy.

"He was fine at dinner tonight," I looked across his chest at my mother. "He ate all that meat loaf, remember? He was fine."

"I know he seemed fine," she said. "But he's been up and down for a while."

"Did it start during the meeting?"

She hesitated. "We cut the meeting short because he wasn't feeling well," she said. "He was exhausted." She looked past me, toward the dark windows. "Let's not talk about it, Molly," she said. "Let's just be with him right now. It's his time. He knew it was coming and I promised I'd be here for him."

She rested her head on Daddy's shoulder again and closed her eyes. *She's so brave,* I thought. I'd try to be brave myself. I rested my cheek against his other shoulder and shut my own eyes. Immediately, though, I was back in the springhouse. I remembered the stupid, reckless thing I'd done with a boy who didn't care about me at all. Daddy would have been so ashamed of me. *This is the worst night of my life,* I thought. *The worst night ever.*

I wasn't sure exactly when he died.

I woke up in Russell's arms as he carried me up the stairs to my bedroom. I felt tired and confused and let him put me on my bed without a fight. I was still in my clothes and he covered me with a blanket.

I jerked awake as the sun began streaming into my room. *Daddy.* Instantly, I was on my feet and racing down the stairs. I ran into my parents' room to find it empty and felt an insane sliver of hope that Daddy had recovered. I would find him in the kitchen, wolfing down his pancakes. I started to turn toward the door, but something on the night table caught my eye. I took a step closer to see the stained-glass pencil case, partially hidden by the phone. Next to it was my father's water bottle, an inch of water in the bottom.

I sat down on the bed and reached for the pencil case, holding my breath. I lifted it to my lap and raised the lid, but I already knew what I would find inside. Nothing.

I remembered seeing my mother reach into the pocket of her pharmacy coat the night after the book tour. I remembered watching her as she slipped pills into the case, hidden away in the kitchen cabinet.

Jumping to my feet, I threw the case to the floor with such force that I heard it crack. I stomped on it, flattening the glass to the floor beneath my Doc Martens. I ran out of the room and down the hall to the kitchen, where Russell was folding up Daddy's wheelchair near the back door, and my mother was taking a bowl of something from the microwave. They both looked up when I burst into the room.

"You killed him!" I shouted at my mother as I rushed toward her, my arms outstretched, and she dropped the bowl to the floor, a look of alarm on her face. I wanted to push her into the wall, but Russell grabbed me from behind.

"Hey, hey," he said. "Cool it, Molly."

My mother stared at me. "Why on earth would you say that?" she asked. Her eyes were bloodshot. Her hair was a mess and she was still in the same khaki pants and shirt she'd had on the night before when she'd sat next to Daddy on the bed.

"I found the pencil case on the night table!" I said, struggling to free my arms from Russell's grasp. "You gave him all those pills. How could you do that?"

"Honey!" She frowned at me, then stepped over the broken bowl on the floor to reach the counter near the phone. She picked up a sheet of paper and held it out to me. Russell let go of me so I could take the paper from her. "We called the doctor right after Daddy died," she said. "He came over and this is the death certificate. See?" She pointed to the line that read *cause of death* and I saw that the doctor had written *natural causes* and signed his name.

I looked up at her. "Where did all those pills go?" I asked.

"I flushed them this morning," she said. She was crying, trying to wipe the tears away with her fingertips, but they kept on coming. "They were for his pain and he wasn't going to need them any longer," she said.

"I don't believe you," I said.

"Why on earth would I *kill* him?" There was anguish in her eyes.

"I don't know!" I said. "Maybe he was too much trouble. Maybe you wanted to get him out of the way."

She slapped me. I gasped, my face stinging and my eyes instantly full of tears. I watched her turn away from me and head for the hallway. I heard her footsteps on the hardwood and the slamming of the bedroom door. I looked at Russell.

"I think she's been taking pills from the pharmacy," I said. "Saving them up to kill him."

"Molly," he said patiently, "the doctor examined him and determined he had complications from the MS. I don't know why you'd think anything else. Why would you want to hurt your mother like that?"

I hated him at that moment. I hated both of them. I stormed out of the house and climbed onto my bike, heading for Amalia's. I found her sitting on the carved chair in her front yard. She stood up when I turned into her driveway and she stretched her arms out at her sides. I jumped off my bike and ran into her embrace. She clung to me and I knew she was crying as hard as I was.

"How did you know?" I finally managed to whisper.

"Russell called me this morning," she said.

I pulled away from her, looking into her

516

tear-streaked face. "Amalia," I said, trying to make my voice very calm. I needed her to take me seriously. "Mom did it," I said. "She was keeping these pills in that stained-glass pencil case you gave Daddy. And I found it by their bed this morning. Empty. She killed him."

Amalia stared at me with such a stunned look on her face that I thought she actually believed me. "Oh baby," she said after a moment, "that's nonsense."

"It's not!" I said. "I think we should call the police."

"No, we should not." She ran her hands over my hair. "You're grieving, baby. Grief can make you crazy. You aren't thinking straight."

"I'm the only person who *is* thinking straight!" I said.

She put her arm around my shoulders. "Come with me," she said, and she led me inside her house. From the living room, I could see the phone in her kitchen and I thought of running to it. Dialing the police before she had a chance to stop me. But almost as if she knew my plan, she turned me firmly in the direction of the floor pillows in front of the windows. "Let's sit here," she said, tugging me down to the pillows next to her.

"I want you to listen to me," she said, holding my hand firmly in her lap. "First, you need to get it out of your head that Nora had anything to do with Graham's death. That's crazy talk, all right? She loved him. You know that."

"But those pills!" I said.

"I don't know anything about 'those pills.' " She sighed. "He took so many pills, they're probably lying all over the house," she said. "You're reading too much into them. But there's something you need to understand."

She looked through the window into her yard, and I could see dozens of crisscrossed fine red lines in the whites of her eyes.

"What?" I asked.

"He wanted to die, baby," she said. "I know that's hard to hear, but if he could talk to you right now, he'd say how relieved he is that it finally happened."

"But *why*?" I was almost shouting.

"Sh," she said.

"His life was *fine*," I argued. "He had us. He had his . . . ramps and special bathroom and everything." Even as the words left my mouth, I knew they were simple and weak. "He had *us*," I repeated. "Why wasn't that enough for him?"

"You weren't inside his skin," she said.

"He hid it well from you. The bit-by-bit losses. The indignities. He was afraid of how bad it would get. He was afraid of being a burden. He wanted to be released from it."

"He wasn't afraid of anything!" I argued.

"Of course he was," she said. "He was human. But you know the one thing he wasn't afraid of, not even a little bit?"

"What?"

"Dying."

"I would have taken care of him forever," I said.

"He didn't want that. He didn't want anyone to have to take care of him forever."

"So she helped him die," I said, my anger at Nora boiling up again. "It doesn't matter if he wanted to die or not. She shouldn't have —"

"Molly!" Amalia said sharply, and she squeezed my hand hard enough to hurt. "She would *never* do that. It's cruel of you to think that of her."

I jerked my hand away from hers. "Why won't you believe me?" I asked. "Those pills were —"

"The pills don't matter!" She got to her feet and looked down at me, and for the first time in my entire life, I felt as though she was fed up with me. I felt as though she was *sick* of me. "I don't understand why you're fixated on this," she said.

"You just don't want to believe it," I argued.

"Because it's not believable. How could you think Nora would do something like that?"

"She's happy he's dead. She went on and on about letting him die in peace. She was glad —"

"Stop it!" She began to cry again, raising her hand to her eyes. "She can be relieved he's finally at peace, Molly," she said through her tears. "That doesn't mean she had anything to do with helping him get there."

I didn't know what to say. She was never going to believe me.

"I don't want to hear you say another word about this," she said. "It's ugly, what you're saying. How do you think your father would feel, hearing you accuse Nora of something like that?"

I stared at her. Who was this woman? This was the day no one seemed like themselves. Nora. Russell. Amalia. Maybe I didn't seem like myself, either. *Grief can make you crazy.*

"I need to lie down for a while," Amalia said suddenly, wiping the tears from her cheeks. "You can stay here if you want or . . ." She didn't finish her sentence, but she waved a hand through the air as if she didn't care what I did.

At the entrance to the hallway, she turned to look at me. "You want him back," she said, more calmly now. "I understand that. And I understand that being angry at Nora is a way to keep from feeling the loss. But you need to feel it, Molly," she said. "Just feel it."

She walked down the hall, but I stayed on the floor pillows, my back against the glass wall. I hated the way she'd talked to me just now. I could always count on her to listen to me, to love me no matter what. Today, she shut me out.

I closed my eyes and tried to do what she said. *Feel the loss.* But my emotions were jumbled together with the crushed pencil case on the bedroom floor and my mother reaching into her pharmacy coat pocket and the way she told me to stay with Daddy the night before: *You can help me let him go.*

And sitting there, I began to wonder. If I hadn't gone to the springhouse, if I'd been home where I belonged, could I have saved him? Could I have called the ambulance in time?

Could I have stopped my mother from taking my father's life?

56

For the most part, everyone left me alone over the next few days, although. Nora came up to my room at least twice a day. She brought me food I barely touched and I froze her out, ignoring anything she said to me. I stopped calling her "Mom" during those few days. She would forever after be "Nora" to me and I'd say her name in a cold voice designed to distance myself from her. It was my way of hurting her, the only weapon I had.

On the third day after Daddy's death, she told me his ashes were now buried in our family graveyard, and it was all I could do to wait until she left the room before I broke down. I wanted to open my window and scream, *"No!"* at the top of my lungs. He was nothing but ashes now. I couldn't imagine it. I couldn't bear it.

I tried to wrap my mind around the reality that he was gone. If I went downstairs, he wouldn't be there. I would never hear him call me "darling" again. I walked aimlessly around my room whispering to myself, "I want my daddy back," the words coming out in a child's voice, because I suddenly felt very much like a child. I didn't know who that girl was who snuck out of her grandmother's house to have sex with a boy. I didn't know how she could have been so reckless. So selfish. *So wrong.* The two things — sneaking out to be with Chris and Daddy's death — were twisted together so firmly in my mind now that I would never be able to untwist them. If I hadn't been with Chris, I could have saved my father. Logically, I knew it didn't make sense, but logic was no longer my friend.

Amalia came to see me, but she said she wouldn't talk to me if I insisted on believing that Nora had anything to do with Daddy's death. I felt as though I'd lost her, too.

On the fourth day, Nora set a grilled-cheese sandwich on my desk, then sat down on the edge of my bed where I had burrowed myself beneath the covers.

"There's going to be a memorial service for Daddy tomorrow night at the pavilion," she said. "I'd like you to come."

"No." I kept my eyes closed, the covers up

to my nose. I wasn't sure what a memorial service was, exactly, but I didn't want to be there and see her fake her grief in public.

"It's a way to remember him, honey," she said. When I didn't respond, she sighed. "I'm so afraid you'll regret it later if you don't come." She rubbed my shoulder through the quilt and I yanked the covers over my head and stayed that way until she gave up and left my room.

I waited until the very last second before deciding to go to the memorial service, which was why I was still dressed in the shorts and T-shirt I'd been sleeping in for days. I'd looked at myself in the mirror that afternoon for the first time since it happened. My hair was dirty and my eyes were so swollen, the lids looked like little pink sausages, but I needed to go to the service. I kept thinking that Daddy's spirit might be there, and if he was there, I wanted to be there, too.

Nora drove the two of us to the pavilion. I smelled disgustingly sweaty to myself and wondered if she'd say anything about it, but she just gave me a sad smile and said she was glad I'd decided to go. I said nothing in response. I was done talking to her.

Once we got to the pavilion, I wished I

hadn't come. The platform was crowded with our family and Daddy's friends. Chairs had been set up facing a microphone at one end of the pavilion, and about half the people were seated. They balanced little plates of food on their laps as they smiled and talked to one another, and I thought, *How can they smile?* Someone had set up a stereo and music rang out from the speakers near the back of the pavilion. I felt sick when I recognized the music as one of the mix tapes Daddy and I had put together for the midsummer party. It was wrong, playing that music now. Elvis followed by the Beatles followed by the Four Tops followed by Bing Crosby. It was all wrong. I picked up one of the chairs and moved it to a corner of the pavilion as far from the speakers as I could get and I sat there alone, out of the way, away from the crowd, trying to feel my father in the air around me.

Dani was sitting on the other side of the pavilion, and when she spotted me, she got up and started walking toward me. I didn't want to talk to her. I didn't want to talk to anyone, but soon she was standing next to me.

"Why don't you come sit with me and my parents?" she asked.

I didn't look at her. "I just want to sit

alone," I said.

She was quiet for a moment. "Mom told me you think Aunt Nora had something to do with Uncle Graham dying," she said.

"She killed him."

"Molly . . ." I could see her shaking her head from the corner of my eye. "That's so crazy. Are you cracking up?"

"Fuck you," I said.

"You know," she said, her voice breaking, "I loved him, too."

I looked up at her. She wore no makeup today. No lip ring. I remembered her at my father's side the night he fell from the pavilion. *She's not your enemy,* I thought. "I know," I said, contrite.

"Come sit with us?" she tried again, but I shook my head.

"No, thanks."

She walked away and I went back to sitting alone and cursing the music. After a while, I noticed that Peter and Helen were sitting at the edge of the crowd, not far from me. They sat next to Janet and her Viking boyfriend. Peter spotted me and I groaned as I saw him leave his seat and walk toward mine. I lowered my gaze to my lap as he crouched down next to me. "I'm so sorry for your loss, Molly," he said.

"Thank you," I muttered.

"He was an inspirational man," he said and I felt my lower lip begin to tremble.

"Let me know if I can help you in any way, all right?" Peter stood up again, resting his hand on my shoulder. "If you need to talk, I'm there for you."

With your stupid Freudian therapy? I thought. *No, thank you.* I wondered if he was the slightest bit happy now that his professional rival was gone.

"Okay," I said. I was relieved when he walked back to his seat.

Soon, everyone was sitting down and someone turned off the music. Then people took turns at the microphone. Uncle Trevor and Aunt Claudia. Russell. Peter. They all talked about how wonderful my father was, but I hardly heard them. My arms were folded across my chest like armor.

Finally, Nora went up to the microphone, but instead of talking about Daddy, she lifted an envelope into the air. "Graham left this behind to be opened after his death." She smiled. Her ever-present pallor had lifted; there was color in her cheeks and the faint purple-smudged skin beneath her eyes was gone. *Your mom looks like Grace Kelly, don't you think?* My eyes filled at the memory. "Graham didn't want us to spend a lot of time grieving," Nora said, "so on the outside of this envelope, it says we should play that Kenny Loggins song 'Footloose.' " She pulled a sheet of paper from the envelope. "And on the piece of paper inside, he says 'pretend to dance.' "

I caught my breath. Everyone laughed. Everyone except me. I saw Janet shake her head, smiling, and heard her say to the Viking, "Typical Graham."

I gripped the seat of my chair with both hands. He'd known what he was doing when he told me to type those words weeks ago. I'd unwittingly had a part in this horrible charade. Had he *asked* Nora to give him those pills? I felt duped, suddenly angry with both Nora and my father.

"So, my dear friends and family," Nora said, waving the envelope in the air, "let's do him proud."

Someone turned the stereo on again, and "Footloose" came over the loudspeakers. People obediently stood up, pushing their chairs to the sides of the pavilion as they began to dance. They looked awkward at first and I knew none of them felt like dancing. But as my father had most likely predicted, pretending made it so, and soon they were dancing with abandon, arms in the air, laughter rising into the sky above the pavilion. Maybe there were tears behind

528

the laughter; I didn't know. I didn't stay long enough to find out. I stood up from my chair, jumped from the pavilion, and ran across the lawn, headed for home, my hands flattened over my ears. I ran past Nanny's house, across her circular drive and out to the loop road, and I kept running, running, running, putting distance between me and everyone I knew — everyone I'd loved — until I felt certain we'd be separated forever.

57
SAN DIEGO

"Do you still believe your father asked Nora to . . . help him end his life?" Aidan asks me. He's being careful with the euphemism. We'd been in the living room on the sectional when I started telling him about Morrison Ridge. Sometime during the telling, though, when I needed him to hold me, we'd moved to our bed.

"Yes," I say. "At least I think so. I think he and Nora had probably already planned it out when he had me type 'pretend to dance' on that sheet of paper. But it's still murder that she would be charged with if I'd ever turned her in. If I could have gotten anyone to believe me, of course."

"Would you actually have done that?"

"Well, I didn't. I . . ." My eyes burn. "When I'd bring it up to anyone — Amalia or Russell or my aunt Claudia — they'd get angry with me. They felt sorry for Nora and thought I was making things harder for her.

I knew if I turned her in, everyone would hate me. And also . . ."

"Also?"

"Deep down, I guess I still loved her."

"Of course you did," he says. "She raised you."

I press my forehead against his shoulder. Tighten my arm across his waist.

"Here's what I don't get." He rubs my neck as he speaks, and his voice is soft and a bit hesitant. "I know you believe people have a right to die. I mean, we've talked about it and we agree about it, don't we?"

"Yes," I say, "but we don't have the right to kill someone."

"Well, it sounds to me like your father had no alternative but to get someone else to help him."

I sigh. "I know, but . . . Maybe if she'd told me the truth, I could have dealt with it better," I say.

"From what you've told me, I don't think so," Aidan says. "You loved your father and you had mixed feelings about Nora. And you were only fourteen. I'm not sure what she could have said or done to make things right for you."

"I know," I say again.

"Do you think Amalia knew the truth? Or the aide? Russell?"

"I think they wanted to believe he died of natural causes so badly that when I told them about the pencil case with the pills, they just shut me out," I say. "I tried to talk to Dani about it once. She was a senior when I started at the boarding school and she took me under her wing. I brought it up early on; I was desperate to talk to someone about it. But she refused. She said it made me sound crazy and she wouldn't hang around me if I was going to talk that way."

"So you were really alone with it." He hugs me to him and my eyes fill again.

I was. I feel so sad for the fourteen-year-old girl I used to be.

"You have to go back there," Aidan says. "You can see that, can't you?"

I shake my head. "Amalia's gone," I say. "I feel guilty that I never got in touch with her. That I cut her out along with everyone else. But I don't see the point in going back now." I don't want to go back, ever. What I would really like is to erase my past. I've been trying to do that for most of my life.

"You have to see Nora," he says.

"I don't want to see her."

"Yes," he says. "You have to go."

"Why are you pushing me?" I'm annoyed by his persistence.

"Because it's in the way, babe," he says.

He strokes my cheek. "You can't run away from your past any more than I can run away from mine. Yours has been chasing you for a long time and now it's finally caught up to you."

"The timing's terrible," I say. "Sienna —"

"She's not due for another month," he interrupts me. Then he kisses me, and though the room has grown dark, I can see his eyes as he pulls away. "We're going to have a baby." I hear the smile in his voice. "A *family*. And there's going to be a birth mother and you're going to be an adoptive mother. You've got to go to lay those demons to rest, Molly. You can't let your past get in the way of your future any longer."

I sigh. He's right.

"All right," I say, my head on his shoulder again. "I'll go."

Still, I think, Aidan doesn't really understand what he's asking. I'm not sure I understand it myself.

58
ASHEVILLE, NORTH CAROLINA

I try to read on the long red-eye flight between Los Angeles and Charlotte, but I can't concentrate. The night is crystal clear and I have an awe-inspiring view of the illuminated earth during the entire trip. I search in vain for landmarks in the dark. Are we over Texas now? Arkansas? Tennessee? The closer we fly to North Carolina the harder my heart pounds. I feel overcome with a crushing sense of nostalgia. I've fought that nostalgia for two decades, but suddenly I can hear the cicadas and smell the summer scent of the mountains. I feel the wind on my face as I ride the zip line.

I have so many memories of Morrison Ridge, but the one that plays over and over in my mind as we near our destination is that last talk with Daddy on our screened porch. He'd needed a hug from me that day and I'd been too angry to give it to him as I plotted my time with Chris Turner in the springhouse. *I get it, Daddy,* I think now. *I understand now.* But I am way too late. I wish I had that day to do over. I would do it so differently. I'd give him that hug he'd needed.

I remember how happy he'd looked when I told him I might want to be a pretend therapist when I grew up. There had been such joy in his eyes when he heard that — on what he most likely knew was the last day of his life — his daughter wanted to follow in his footsteps. After everything that happened, though, a pretend therapist had been the last profession I'd aspired to. I picked law because it seemed as far from pretending as I could get. Law was all about harsh reality, I thought. All about facts and truth and justice. I was wrong. Practicing law lifts pretense to an art form. I pretend every day that my clients are in the right, that I am not twisting the truth to win their cases. I've loved the challenge and I love when I can help good people triumph, but I know the truth about myself and my work: I am a pretender of the first order. And I'm a little tired of it.

We arrive on time in Charlotte. After that long flight, I'd like to change out of my jeans and the red shirt I've been wearing all night, but I'm anxious to get to Asheville. I brush my teeth in the restroom of the rental car agency, then pick up my car and a map and head west.

A couple of hours later, I drive into Asheville for the first time since my teens. I've heard that the city has changed dramatically in the twenty years I've been away, and I quickly see that rumor is correct. The sleepy town is alive and vibrant now and I absorb it all, driving slowly, putting off my arrival at Amalia and Russell's house for as long as I can. I have her address, but I'd visited her only once before leaving Morrison Ridge and all I recall from that visit is my anger. Amalia had never bought into my contention that Nora had killed my father. Even though Nora did nothing to stop the family from kicking Amalia out of Morrison Ridge, Amalia defended her. I didn't understand her. I still don't.

The little Craftsman cottage is on a tree-lined street close to downtown Asheville, and it's unfamiliar to me after so long. I stay in my car as I check the address in my phone. Yes, this is it. So different from the contemporary glass house that had once been her home. I wonder if she was happy here.

536

I walk up the round pavers to the front porch. The doorbell consists of bells hanging on a cord. So like Amalia, I think. I give the cord a shake, wincing at the playful sound that rings through the air. I'm not in a playful mood. Not at all.

Although I can't hear footsteps or feel their vibration beneath my feet, I have a sense that someone is walking through the house. In a moment, the door opens and Russell stands in front of me. His hair is cropped short, the black dulled by a spattering of gray, but the cocker spaniel eyes haven't lost their warmth and the years have done little to change his tight, athletic physique. He's wearing jeans and a long-sleeved blue jersey, and he still looks like he could lift my father from his wheelchair with ease.

His face registers surprise. *"Molly,"* he says.

My throat locks up so tightly I can't speak. I read so many things into his expression. Gratitude that I have come at all. Sadness that I've come way too late. And something else: I don't know if it's blame or forgiveness or simply a deep sorrow. I don't know if they're his emotions I'm seeing or my own.

He opens his arms wide and I surprise myself by stepping into them. "I'm so sorry,

Russell," I say.

"Come in." He lets go of me, standing back to usher me inside.

I walk into a small Arts and Crafts–style living room. It seems the antithesis of Amalia's sunny, glass-walled living room at Morrison Ridge. Yet, the rich, dark wood molding and cabinetry and the numerous paintings on the walls give the room an inviting warmth. I can imagine Amalia in this room.

"Sit." Russell motions toward a heavy blue sofa on one side of the room and I sink into the deep, fluffy cushions. "Can I get you something to drink?" he asks.

"Water?" I ask. I need something to hold on to.

He disappears from the room and returns a moment later to hand me a cold bottle of water. I watch as he sits down in an upholstered chair across the room from me. I take a sip of water, then wrap my hands around the bottle while I search for something to say. My mind goes to the weather. To Asheville's rebirth. To the charm of the house. I open my mouth, but Russell holds up his hand as though he knows I'm about to say something banal and he plans to save me from it.

"She talked about you nearly every day," he says.

Oh God.

"I'm sorry," I say again. "I was too angry to —"

"She didn't deserve that anger."

I look toward the stone fireplace. I still feel it, the anger. It's bubbling up inside me at that moment. "You know Nora killed him, Russell," I say. "Even if it was out of kindness, she did it. But you and Amalia and everyone made me feel crazy for even thinking it. How was I not supposed to be angry?"

He opens his mouth to speak, but I rush on.

"Please don't give me that line about 'natural causes,' " I say. "I know she stole drugs from where she worked. Maybe you all wanted to believe he died of natural causes, but you were in denial. You just didn't want to believe she could do it. Or you didn't care. Or you thought that he wanted to die and the end justified the means. I don't know *what* you all thought. I only know that what happened was wrong."

Russell lowers his gaze to the hardwood floor and neither of us speaks. After a moment, though, he raises his eyes to look at me again. "Have you been in touch with

539

Nora at all?" he asks.

I shake my head. "Not since I left the Ridge."

"Will you see her while you're here? Morrison Ridge is so close."

"I flew all this way to see her," I say. I set the water bottle on the table next to me and rub my damp palms together. "I wanted to try to get some . . . I don't know. Some closure or something. I'm not sure closure's possible, though. I don't even know what to say to her at this point."

He lets out a long sigh. He lowers his hands from the arms of the chair to his knees and leans forward.

"We all killed him, Molly," he says.

I assume he's speaking metaphorically and it annoys me. "Because everyone ultimately came out in favor of selling the land?" I ask. "I don't see —"

"No, that's not what I mean." He stands up and walks toward the fireplace. He faces the window above the built-in cabinetry and I have the feeling he doesn't want to look at me as he speaks. "I mean," he says, "we *all* killed him." He turns then to meet my gaze.

A chill runs up my spine. "I don't understand," I say. "What are you talking about?"

He slips his hands into the pockets of his

jeans and faces me. "He wanted to die, but of course he had no way to make that happen by himself," he says. "He asked us . . ." He shuts his eyes for a moment, and I have the feeling he's lost in a memory. I wait and in a moment he opens his eyes again, looking directly at me. "Do you remember all those so-called family meetings that summer?" he asks.

I nod. How could I forget? Those family meetings gave me the time and freedom to rebel.

"I know you thought we were talking about Trevor's development ideas for Morrison Ridge, but we were actually talking about Graham at those meetings." Russell walks toward me and sits at the other end of the couch. "He asked us to help him die," he says. "At first we tried to dissuade him, of course, but once he convinced us that he was very serious, that he would find a way with us or without us, we tried to figure out how to help him. He didn't want any one person to be responsible. Not Nora. Not anyone."

I feel the blood leave my face. "How . . . I don't understand," I say again.

"You're right that Nora got the pills," he says, "and she knew what he should take and how much to give him. The idea was that none of us would give him enough to kill him, but altogether it would be plenty."

"Oh my God," I say, my hand to my mouth as I try to take this in. I frown at him. "You . . . helped?"

He nods. "And Amalia," he says. "Everyone but your grandmother, although she knew what was happening, and she understood, though it . . ." He runs a hand over his graying hair. "Well, I believe it sped up her own death," he says. "You remember how she went downhill after he died."

I do. She died within months of my father. Two devastating losses for me, back to back. I remember Nanny's weepiness when I was at her house the night my father died. I hadn't understood it then and had been too wrapped up in my own plans for that night to pay attention to her sadness. Suddenly it makes sense.

"Was it just the family?" I ask. "I saw Janet and Peter at one of those meetings."

"Janet and Peter and Peter's wife, Helen, helped." Russell leans forward, his hands resting on his thighs. His gaze is riveted on me. "And a few of his other close friends as well," he says. "Trevor balked at first. He really struggled with it because, with your daddy out of the way, he could plow ahead with his plans for the land, and I guess that

542

gave him some guilt. Ultimately, he came around, though. And your aunt Claudia wasn't on board until the last minute. When we were all there in the bedroom with Graham and she could see how grateful he was, she decided to —"

"Stop this!" I put my hands over my ears. "I can't believe that everyone . . . you all just agreed to do it? To kill him?"

Russell shakes his head. "We all agreed to help someone we loved escape from a life he could no longer bear."

I don't want to cry, but those words hurt and I feel my eyes fill. I lower my hands to my thighs again, my fingers curled into fists. *I'd* been a part of his life. Why couldn't he bear it for me? My chest aches with sorrow. I don't think I'll ever recover from hearing all of this. Suddenly, I remember the day I saw Dani in our kitchen waiting for one of the meetings to begin, and my eyes widen as I look at Russell.

"Dani?" I ask.

He hesitates, then nods. "They figured she was old enough to understand."

"I'm in touch with her," I say. "She's never said a word about it."

"Of course not," he says. "None of us has ever said a word to anyone. And I shouldn't be saying anything now, but —"

"Why didn't Nora just tell me that everyone was involved instead of taking all my anger herself?"

"How could she tell you?" Russell asks. "She wouldn't dare take the risk of telling *anyone,* least of all you. She took the anger from you instead of turning us all in. It cost her, though. She knew she was losing you because of it, and it was terrible for her, but she couldn't see any way to fix it." He tilts his head to the side as if trying to get a better look at me. "It took a toll on *all* of us, Molly," he says. "That's something your daddy never considered. Even though every one of us thought we were doing the right thing — the compassionate thing — there was still guilt. I didn't expect to feel it, to be honest. More than anyone except maybe Nora, I saw how your father suffered. He hid it from you and most other people, but I saw it, day in and day out. I knew he'd thought through what he was asking. I knew he wanted to die more than anything. And yet, when it was done, I felt guilty. I was angry that he'd had no other way out. I was angry that we were all put in the position of —"

"Of murdering him," I finish his sentence. He hesitates. "Yes." He sounds defeated.

"There's no statute of limitations on

murder in North Carolina," I say. I use my lawyer voice and feel on solid ground for the first time since walking into this house. "Weren't you afraid someone would break down and tell? Aren't you afraid about telling me now?"

"Should I be?" He raises his eyebrows.

I hesitate only a second before shaking my head. I'll never tell what I'm hearing here today. I'm not sure I'll even tell Aidan. It would mean another secret between us, but there is too much at stake. Too many people could be hurt.

"Of course we were all afraid one of us would tell," Russell says, "but that person would be incriminating themselves as well as the rest of us. We counted on silence."

"How did you ever get a doctor to say he died of natural causes on the death certificate?" I ask.

Russell's smile is a little sad. "He was a friend of Amalia's," he says. "He would have done anything for her."

I remember Nora and my aunts in our kitchen getting ready for the midsummer party. They'd been talking about a doctor. A friend of Amalia's. *No doubt a quack*, Aunt Claudia had said.

I rest my head against the back of the couch and rub my temples with my fingertips. "I think I'm in shock," I say.

He leans toward me, his brown eyes glistening. "It was an act of love, Molly," he says. "I hope you can see that. I only told you about it now because, while it's too late for you to make things right with Amalia, it's not too late with Nora." He touches the back of my hand. "Go to her, Molly," he says. "Go see your mother."

59
MORRISON RIDGE

After leaving Russell, I drive out of the city toward Swannanoa and Morrison Ridge, taking the mountain roads more slowly than necessary, overwhelmed by all I've learned. I will see Nora, but I'm in no rush. A lifetime of hurt and anger doesn't go away in a few minutes. I'm angry over her role in Daddy's death and over the lies I'd been told. I'm angry over being the only person on Morrison Ridge left out of what was happening, and I'm angry at losing my father with no chance to say good-bye. Everyone else had that chance.

The trees close around my car as the road narrows and they steal my breath away. I've grown accustomed to California's wide-open vistas. To suddenly be surrounded by tall trees, the leafy branches forming a suffocating tunnel around my car, is unnerving.

I slow down on the winding road, watching for the small white sign with black lettering that marks the entrance to the Ridge. I drive around the last curve and see that a sign, supported by two pillars and nearly half the size of a billboard, stands in the old sign's place. Made of routed wood, the sign has a rustic look to it but that is clearly just for show. The background is a dark brown, the lettering gold. MORRISON RIDGE, it reads, and in a smaller sign attached below, the word ESTATES.

Dani had told me about the changes to the Ridge, so I don't know why I'm so shocked, but I am. I stop my car in the road, staring. So ostentatious. The sign is so utterly intimidating, I'm afraid to make the turn, but I can see a car coming up behind me in my rearview mirror and know I have to move. I turn right and in a moment I'm on the road I'd once loved — the loop road that used to feel like home to me. It feels that way no longer. For one thing, it's paved. And it's certainly wider. I feel disoriented as I pass the left-hand turn that would take me to my childhood home. *Not yet,* I think. *Not quite yet.*

I drive straight, toward the Hill from Hell. Paved, it doesn't seem nearly as steep and the rental car takes it easily. When I reach the crest, I see that there is a walking path carved through the trees along the road. I see a few people on bicycles. A man walking a dog. A woman pushing a stroller. Morrison Ridge is booming. Roads that never existed before veer off to my left leading into new, densely wooded neighborhoods. The neighborhoods are new to *me,* at any rate. I guess that some of them have been here for nearly twenty years by now.

I continue up the loop road, past huge houses spread out on large landscaped lots. They depress me. A man washing his car in his driveway waves to a bicyclist as she rides by. I remember what Nanny said when she complained about Trevor's plans to develop the land: the neighborhoods would be filled with strangers who knew nothing about the Ridge and could care less. I feel like opening my car window and shouting at the guy in his driveway, *You don't really belong here!,* but instead I keep driving along the loop road, knowing it's me who no longer has any place on Morrison Ridge.

I slow down as I pass one of my grandfather's benches, the one where my father had sat with Amalia on that night so long ago. It's been rebuilt, I think. Maybe entirely replaced, with its perfect woodwork and rich mahogany stain. I'd been with Stacy Bateman that night. I never spoke to Stacy again after Daddy's death. I didn't call her and she didn't call me, and that was fine. In my memory, she is a big part of that whole nightmare summer. Even her name bothers me. Aidan works with a woman named Stacy, and every time he mentions her, my skin crawls. It's the same with the name Chris. When I was pregnant, Aidan suggested that if we had a boy, we name him Christopher. There was no way.

As I ride past the bench, I know I must be near the path to the springhouse and my heart begins to race. I have no desire to see that little building ever again. Besides, with all the changes on Morrison Ridge, I doubt it's still there.

I drive past the turnoff to the old slave quarters, wondering who lives there now but not really wanting to know. Soon, Nanny's house comes into view. I stop my car in front of it, staring in shock. On the left side of the house, the woods have been entirely cleared and in their place is a parking lot, half filled with cars — most of them, it seems, minivans. In front of the brick house is another brown routed wooden sign. CLUBHOUSE, it reads in gold letters. From somewhere behind the house, I hear the squeals of children despite my closed windows. There must be a pool back there now, I think, or some sort of playground.

Poor Nanny. I start driving again. Maybe it was a blessing that she died when she did. The changes to Morrison Ridge would have broken her heart.

I decide that I've seen enough. I turn around in a driveway and head back down the loop road toward my old home. And toward Nora.

I almost miss the turn that will take me to the house I grew up in. I make a left onto the road and see that, while our road is also paved, it's still narrow and tightly tucked into the trees. When the house pops up on my left, though, I barely recognize it. Sometime in the last twenty years, Nora has changed the color from that beautiful sky blue I'd loved to a buttery yellow. The house looks pretty, but it doesn't look like home.

I park in the driveway and slowly get out of my car. I can't see if Nora's car is in the garage and I don't know whether to hope she's home or not. Climbing the front porch steps, I see four brown wooden rocking chairs in the place of our glider and white rockers. I'm glad. I don't want that familiarity or the memories that would come along with it.

Nora pushes the front door open before

I've even reached the top step. She rushes onto the porch and, without a word, pulls me into her arms and I know that Russell must have called her and she's been waiting for me. I can tell by the intensity of her embrace that she's been waiting for me for more than twenty years. I can't believe I'm here, in her arms, when this time yesterday the thought of her still filled me with venom.

"Oh, Molly," she whispers into my hair. "You've come home."

My emotions are so mixed up. For two thirds of my life, I blamed her for my father's death. Now I don't know who to blame. Maybe no one. Maybe blame has no role here at all.

I'm first to pull away. "Russell called you?"

She nods. Takes my hand. "Come in, honey," she says. Her voice is thick, as though it takes all her effort to get the words out.

When I follow her into the living room, I see the familiar view of the mountains through the broad windows at the rear of the dining room. The peaks are crisp against the bright blue sky. So beautiful and so familiar. I walk toward the windows, glad to be away from Nora's gaze for a moment, but as I get closer to the view, I see a landscape of rooftops in the valley below our house. They're tucked among the trees and someone unfamiliar with our old view would barely notice them. To me, though, they're an eyesore. I know that Nora has only three acres left of our original twenty-five. She'd been the last holdout, but I imagine that at some point, with me gone and the rest of the Ridge developing, there'd been little reason for her to hang on to the land any longer.

I turn to look at her. "Everything's changed," I say.

She smiles from where she stands in the middle of the living room, her hands on her hips. "You've been gone a very long time," she says, tapping into my guilt. She's studying me. I'm studying her as well and I'm surprised at what I see. She wears black yoga pants, tennis shoes, and a blue top beneath a gray hoodie. Her fair skin is smooth, barely lined, and she has lively blue eyes. She still wears her hair in the short, low ponytail, and it's the same pale blond it has always been. I remember her as old and a bit stodgy, but she looks younger and more vibrant to me now than she did when I was a teenager. If Grace Kelly had lived to be sixty-five, this is what she would have looked like.

"You look beautiful, Molly," she says, "but

I bet you're tired from the flight. Do you want some iced tea? Or maybe some coffee? I still have a pot going."

"Coffee, please," I say. "I barely slept on the plane."

I follow her into the kitchen. The room has been remodeled and I would never have recognized it as the kitchen of my childhood. That frankly relieves me. I don't want to think about all those meals at the big table, Daddy in his wheelchair, someone feeding him. The cabinetry is now white, the countertops quartz, the appliances stainless steel. Even the layout is different.

"Are you still a pharmacist?" I ask as I watch her pour coffee into mugs.

She shakes her head. "I retired last year," she says, taking a small bottle of milk from the refrigerator and setting it on the table. "I thought I'd miss it, but I've gotten involved in so many things. Tennis. Yoga. Book clubs. Zumba." She smiles at me. "There's so much to do here now, Molly, you wouldn't believe it." She motions for me to sit.

She's so different from the way I remember. I can't picture her on a tennis court or in a yoga studio. And Zumba? There's an undeniable lightness about her.

"I hate seeing how Morrison Ridge has

changed," I say as I sit down. The square table is much smaller than our old table, but I've chosen the chair nearest the living room, the place where I always sat when I lived here.

"It must be a shock to see the changes all at once," Nora says. "Watching it happen gradually, it wasn't so bad." She hands me the mug. "It's not an evil place, Molly," she says as she takes a seat kitty-corner from me. "It's actually a beautiful neighborhood full of lovely people who only want the best for their families."

We talk about some of the changes and I ask her about Aunt Toni and Uncle Trevor, Aunt Claudia and Uncle Jim. I'm making polite conversation but after a few minutes she reaches over. Sets her hand on mine.

"We need to really talk, Molly," she says. Her eyes burn into mine. "We need to talk about far more than how Morrison Ridge has changed. I'm terribly upset that Russell told you what really happened."

"I'm not," I say, involuntarily pulling my hand away from hers. "Nora, he *had* to. I was still so furious with you. I'm still . . . I'm having trouble letting go of the . . . the shock of it all. And the anger," I add.

She nods. "Of course you are."

"I wish I'd known the truth."

"You couldn't have handled it, honey," she says. "It wouldn't have been fair for us to lay it on you. To expect you to keep it to yourself. You were very young, even for fourteen. Very . . . overprotected." She stares at me intently. "I'm not even sure you can handle it now," she says. "Can you?"

I look into the mug I'm clutching between my hands on the table. "Yes," I say. "At least I'm trying to."

"You were never to know," she says. "You were . . . perhaps you still are" — she waits for me to look at her and when I do she finishes her sentence — "a loose cannon."

I shake my head. "I considered turning you in," I say. "Just you. I didn't know about the others. So many times when I was a teenager, I'd sit in my room at Virginia Dare and I missed Daddy so much and I blamed you and . . ." I shake my head. "Oh, how I blamed you!" I say. "But I couldn't do it. I couldn't pick up the phone and call the police. Because even though I hated you, I guess in some way I still loved you."

She nods. "I knew how torn you were," she says. "How torn you had to be." She takes a sip of her coffee, then lets out a long sigh. "It was so hard for us, Molly." Her expression is a plea for me to understand. "He begged. He never asked for much, but he needed our help. He said he would stop eating and drinking if we didn't help him. He was completely serious, and that sort of death . . . starving to death, no hydration at all . . ." She shook her head. "It can be agonizing and takes so long. It's cruel. I knew I wouldn't have been able to watch him go through that. He was suffering in a way you and I can't even imagine. How could we turn our backs on him?"

"The thing I don't get," I say slowly, "is why he felt so desperate to die. He never seemed to be in terrible pain. That wasn't part of the MS."

"Oh, yes he *was* in pain, honey," Nora says. "He just never let you see it. But it wasn't the physical pain that was unbearable to him. That he could tolerate. The pain that tortured him most went far beyond the physical."

"What do you mean?"

She rubs her arms through the sleeves of her hoodie as if she feels a chill. "He felt trapped inside his body," she says. "He kept a lot of it from you. He was already having serious vision problems and he woke up a couple of mornings unable to speak. He'd have episodes where he was so short of breath, he'd panic. On a couple of occasions, he choked while he was eating and he was terrified of dying that way. Of choking to death. He was so afraid of what he would lose next. Would it be the ability to swallow? To communicate? The unknown terrified him. He felt as though the essence of who he was was slipping away and all he'd be left with would be his suffering. He didn't want to waste away like that. He wanted to die on his own terms."

I hate thinking about the anguish my father must have been in. I'd been blind to it. I imagine what it would have been like, watching him fade away. Unable to see, perhaps, or speak, or control any part of his body. How afraid he must have been to want to end his life. It was a fear that no amount of "pretending to be brave" could counter. A fear so strong that death seemed like a welcome release. My heart cracks in two at the thought of him being that frightened.

I look at Nora and realize she's not the person I thought she was when I was growing up. I remember her as harried. Worried. But this Nora is a vibrant woman with a full life. This Nora is unencumbered.

"Sometimes," I say slowly, "I thought you killed him so you could be free. It had to be hard on you, taking care of him the way you did. You were so tied down."

She doesn't seem shocked by my words. Instead, she nods in understanding. "Do you still think that?" she asks.

I shake my head. "No."

She leans back in her chair. "Graham and I talked about that a lot," she says. "I wanted to be absolutely certain that setting me free wasn't part of his motivation." She looks toward the window, and for the first time since my arrival, I see tears in her eyes. "I loved him so much, Molly," she says, looking at me again. "I didn't want to lose him, no matter how difficult the disease became to manage. He convinced me that giving me my freedom wasn't what he was after." She swirls her coffee gently in her cup.

I think back to that summer. "I was trying to make Daddy happy that summer," I say. "I thought it worked, too. He seemed really content most of the time."

"You always made him happy, Molly." Nora smiles. "You were the best thing that ever happened to him and he adored you. But honestly?" she adds. "The joy you saw in him that summer was primarily because people told him they would help him. He was happy because he finally had a way out."

"Oh God," I say. "Really?"

She nods. "Really." She stands up and

reaches for the coffeepot on the counter, then pours more into my cup. "So," she says with a complete change of tone. "I know nothing about your life. Almost nothing, at any rate. I know you're occasionally in touch with Dani, but I guess you told her not to tell us anything and she's guarded your privacy completely. But I want to know everything." She sits down again. "What sort of work do you do? Are you married? Do you have children?"

I tell her I live in San Diego. I tell her about Aidan and about my work. And then I tell her something I believe she'll be able to understand in a way no one else in my life can.

"I had a hysterectomy and can't have children," I say.

Her expression is full of sympathy. "Oh honey," she says.

"So we're in the process of adopting and I'm frankly terrified."

She studies my face, taking that in. "What's terrifying you?" she asks.

"Everything," I say. "The baby's due in about a month. The girl — her name's Sienna and she's very sweet, but she could change her mind at any time before the adoption's final. So I'm afraid of that. And I'm afraid . . . it'll be an open adoption, so

Sienna will still have a role in our child's life, and I . . ." My voice trails off and I look up to see Nora smiling at me.

"Well," she says, "I have a little experience with this."

"I know." I smile back.

"I assume, though, that your husband . . . Aidan, right?"

I nod.

"I assume Aidan is not the baby's father and Sienna is not his former lover."

I wince. "That must have been so hard for you."

"It wasn't easy," she admits.

"No," I say, "Aidan is not the baby's father." I lean forward and it's my turn to rest my hand on hers. "How did you do it, Nora? How did you stand it? How were you able to share me the way you did, especially with a woman your husband had once loved?"

She covers my hand with hers and it's warm from being wrapped around her mug. "Oh, Molly," she says, and for the first time I see lines in her face. In her forehead. Between her eyebrows. "It was the hardest thing I've ever had to do."

"What was it like?" I ask.

She sits back, looking at me as though truly seeing me for the first time since I ar-

561

rived in the house. She smiles. "I loved you," she says. "I adored you. But I was your mother. My role in your life was very clear to me. I had to be the one to discipline you and lay down the law. Amalia didn't have to worry about any of that. She didn't have to worry about keeping you clothed and making you three meals a day. She didn't have to worry about keeping you safe or teaching you to make good choices or help you grow into a responsible, capable adult."

"She was very . . . mellow," I say, not sure that's the right word.

"I was jealous of her," Nora says. "I admit it. I knew your father loved me and was faithful to me, but I also knew that Amalia would always have a place in his heart. And then as you grew up, it was clear she had a place in your heart as well."

I hear the crack in her voice. I feel her hurt.

"I even wondered," she continues, "once you cut me out of your life, if you were still in touch with her. If she'd become your —"

"No," I say. "No. Not at all."

"I know that now," she says. "Dani told me you'd cut ties with everyone."

I nod.

"I knew Amalia was a lot more fun than

me," she says with a half smile, "but Graham would say 'it's not a popularity contest, Nora,' and eventually I accepted that. I knew that I had to be your mother, not your friend. If that cost me some of your affection, so be it."

"I sometimes felt as though you didn't love me very much." I feel awkward saying that to her, but it's clear we are finally baring our souls to one another. Finally telling the truth. I remember all the times my father said that I needed to learn to talk to Nora. He wanted me to have deep, meaningful conversations with her. *It's happening now, Daddy,* I think. *At last.* "I worried it was because I wasn't yours — biologically —" I say, "and that I might feel the same way about the baby we're —"

"Really?" She looks wounded. "Oh, Molly. I'm sorry if I ever made you feel that way. I know I don't have the warmest personality." Her smile is rueful. "But in my own defense, I was under a lot of stress, working full-time and taking care of you and your father."

I nod. I can see that now, how much she'd had on her plate. I can imagine how hard it had been to keep our household running smoothly back then.

"I'll tell you how it's going to be." She wears a genuine smile now. "You are going to hold that baby in your arms and fill up with more love than you ever thought was possible. You'll instantly be her protector and her nurturer. You'll instantly be her mother."

"Is that how you felt about me?" I ask.

"Yes, honey," she says. "And to be honest? I didn't want to feel that way. I was so shocked that you existed and so *mortified* by the way you came into our lives, that . . . well, I wasn't happy about it, as you can imagine." She shakes her head. "But I distinctly remember rocking you one summer night on the porch. I was holding you on my lap and trying to get you to fall asleep. And suddenly it happened. The love came over me. It felt like a wave. Like a tsunami. It absolutely took my breath away. And then you were mine, from that minute forward."

She stands up and leans over to hug me. "I'm so glad you're here," she says. "I love you so much, Molly. I always have and always will."

I hold on to her and feel something uncoil inside my chest. It's as though, for the first time in twenty-four years, I can take in a full breath. I'd hurt myself when I escaped from Morrison Ridge, I can see that now. By cutting myself off from everyone I'd ever cared about, I'd cut myself off from the love.

I cancel my hotel reservations and carry my suitcase from the rental car into the house. Nora tells me that she turned my upstairs bedroom into a sewing room many years ago, so I will stay in the guest room — Russell's old room.

We order Chinese food that's delivered to the front door and sit on the porch steps to eat it from the cartons as she tells me more about the changes on Morrison Ridge.

"There's one thing I still don't get about Daddy," I say, after we've been eating and chatting for a while.

"What's that?" she asks.

"I think that, no matter how bad things got for me, I'd want to stay alive for my child," I say. "I'd want to see her grow into a good person. Get married. Have a family of her own. I don't understand how . . . if he loved me, how he could leave me the way he did." I'm saddened by what I'm saying, yet I've moved past tears. Now I'm merely curious to understand. "Why didn't he stay alive for me?"

"He certainly wanted to, Molly," Nora says. "It tore him apart to think of missing out on your life, and that fact kept him hanging on longer than he would have

565

liked." She takes a bite of broccoli and I wait for her to swallow. "He was always thinking of you, though, you can trust me about that," she says. "Even at the end, he was thinking of you. Remember the letter? I don't recall exactly what he said in it, but it was so important to him that you'd have that to remember him by. Did you keep it?"

I frown. "What letter?" I don't remember ever getting a letter from my father.

"The letter in the springhouse," Nora says. "In your hiding place. Remember?"

I think back. "I don't know what you're talking about," I say.

"Oh, Molly." Her face grows pale and she sets the carton down on the step. "Please don't tell me you never got it! He was certain you would."

"I'd remember a letter from him," I say. "How would he have written it, anyway?"

"I typed it for him," she says. "The day he died, he had me type it and put it in your hiding place in the springhouse. That hole in the fieldstone, right? He knew you'd find it there. Are you sure you —"

"I never went back to the springhouse," I say, setting down my own carton. I can't tell her how the springhouse had gotten twisted up in my mind with Chris and sex and my rebellion and Daddy's death. In the years after Daddy died, the thought of the springhouse had literally sickened me.

Nora presses her hands to her cheeks. "Oh, I feel terrible!" she says. "He told me you were always putting things in that little hiding place. He was sure you'd get it." She catches her breath and leans toward me. "I wonder if it's still there," she says, almost in a whisper. "Could it possibly be?"

I barely hear her. A letter from my father! I want to read it. I want to *touch* it. "Is the springhouse still there?" I ask.

"I . . . well, to be honest, I don't know," she says. "But I think you need to go look."

"What did he say in it?"

She shakes her head. "It was so long ago. I don't really remember. I just remember that it was his way of saying good-bye to you."

"I have to see if it's still there." I close the top of the carton and get to my feet. Twenty-four years have passed since my father's death, but I can't wait another second to find out if the letter is there. Another second would be too long.

"Do you want me to go with you?" Nora asks.

I hesitate on the top step. There's no way I can go to the springhouse with her in tow. This is something I need to do alone.

I look down at her. "If you don't mind, I think I'd like to take this trip down memory lane on my own," I say apologetically.

"Of course." She smiles. "Take my bike. It's around back. There's no place to park a car along the road up there."

I find her bike where it leans against the back porch. Her helmet hangs from the handlebars and I slip it on and buckle the strap. When Aidan and I ride our bikes these days, I often think of how I rode all over Morrison Ridge without a helmet. I suppose I was lucky I survived. Our daughter will wear a helmet. I picture her with training wheels, excited to have her first bike. *I will love that little girl,* I think. *I will love her with the strength of a tsunami.*

The thought makes me smile as I pedal up our forested lane and turn onto the loop road. For a moment, I worry that I'll stand out on the bike. My relatives might spot me and then I'd have to talk to them. But I am just one of several bikers on the loop road. I'm not going to attract anyone's attention.

Even on the bike, the Hill from Hell is no longer intimidating, and although I'm breathing hard, I don't have to walk the bike up the incline. I pedal steadily, past all the new roads and the turnoff to Uncle Trevor

and Aunt Toni's, until I near my grandfather's bench. I get off the bike then and
walk it along the road, hunting for the opening in the woods that will take me to the
springhouse. It's clear to me that the path
no longer exists, but I wheel the bike over
the brush and into the woods where I think
the path used to be, and I lean it against a
tree. Then I set off on foot in what I hope is
the right direction.

After a few minutes, I'm sure I'm lost. Is
it gone? There's certainly a good chance of
that and I prepare myself for disappointment. I walk a little farther and the scent of
the forest is overwhelmingly familiar, touching a place deep inside my chest. Vines wrap
around my ankles and I begin to think I
should have marked a trail to help me get
back to the loop road. I stand still for a moment, listening. I hear the spring. It's invisible beneath the wild overgrowth, but it's
very close. I squint through the greenery,
hunting for the fieldstone walls. *It's gone,* I
tell myself. Then I realize it's right in front
of me, hidden beneath a riot of kudzu on
one side and choking vines of ivy on the
other. The kudzu tangles with the ivy at the
peak of the roof. It covers the windows and
obliterates the front door. No one has been
in this building for a very long time. My

chest aches. I'm not sure why I'm doing this to myself. *The letter,* I think. *Please still be there.*

I reach through a tangle of ivy to try the front door. The vines are like a shield I need to tear through. I'm finally able to grasp the doorknob, but the door won't budge. The hinges are rusted shut and I tug on the knob and pound the wood to try to free the door, my heartbeat quickening. Suddenly the door opens, smoothly, with barely a creak, as though it has finally decided to let me in. The dank air sweeps into the forest, filling my head and making me dizzy. I take a deep breath of it, fighting for courage, and step inside.

Someone gutted the springhouse in the last twenty-four years and it is a shell of the place I knew. The furniture is gone except for two old kitchen chairs parked neatly against one of the stone walls. The twin beds and small dresser are gone. The microwave and table, gone. The counter with the little sink is still there, but when I try the faucet, it's dry. The stone walls are bare and I wonder who took down my posters. Someone who knew me or a stranger? My gaze is drawn to the wall that would have been above one of the beds. The fake stone is still in place. My heart thuds as I drag one of the chairs over to the wall and test it to be sure it will hold me before I climb onto it. I reach for the plaster stone and it unsnaps easily from the wall.

The hiding place is nearly at eye level and in the light from the open door I see the small glass bird Nora gave me. The old pack of cigarettes. The photograph of a seventeen-year-old boy. I gasp when I pick up that picture and look at his face. He's so young. This boy who will forever be linked in my mind to the worst night of my life was just a kid. Boyish. Dimpled. All these years, I'd given him — and the springhouse itself — so much power over me. He was a child, and I had been even more of a child. A lump forms in my throat. I'd been so young. So innocent and naïve. So mixed up.

I slip the picture back into the hole and stand on my tiptoes, hoping to see an envelope. Instead, I see a small paper bag, and although it's been two and a half decades since I've seen one of those little white bags, I recognize it instantly as being from the pharmacy where Nora worked. I pull it out and peer inside to see a folded sheet of paper . . . and an amethyst palm stone.

60

Darling Molly,

By the time you find this letter, you'll know that I've died. I haven't been well for a long time and I've asked Mom to leave this letter for you after I've gone. I can't possibly leave this world without saying good-bye to my favorite person. That's you, sweet girl.

The day you arrived at Morrison Ridge was the day my life changed for the better. Having a child changes everything. You will find that out for yourself one of these days.

I know you've recently been distressed to realize that your arrival — and the relationship between your mother and Amalia — was not quite as idyllic as we've made it out to be. We are all human and, therefore, somewhat screwed up. The bottom line is that you are deeply loved by two mothers. You don't ever need to doubt that fact. Trust me, darling: neither one of them is pretending when it comes to loving you.

Since I'm no longer around to give you advice in person, I will have to give it to you here. I'm not going to tell you to obey your mother; you know that. She has your welfare at heart. You may not agree with her rules and regulations, but she is looking out for your safety and happiness. Please listen to her.

Lately you've been testing your wings. Someday they'll be strong enough to carry you away, but for now you need to cling to the nest a while longer. I want you to find someone who loves you as much as I do. Don't settle for less and don't rush it. The right guy will make you laugh, will value your opinions, will treat you as his equal, and will never ask for more than you want to give. He's out there, Molly, but you haven't met him yet. I'm certain of that fact.

You are a remarkable girl and I know you will become a remarkable woman. I think you will make a very fine therapist, if that's what you decide to do. I was touched when you told me that might be the path you will choose.

I know you'll grieve for me, darling, but don't grieve for long, okay? I'm not afraid and I welcome this new journey. I'm looking forward to being in a place where I have no need for this old body and I'm free of pain and fear. It's a place of total freedom in my imagination, sort of like a perpetual zip line. I like the idea that I'll be able to look down on you from high above.

Treasure your family, Molly. Yes, they are a complex mix of personalities but they all love you. Eventually you'll come to realize that everyone comes from a dysfunctional family. There is no other kind. Someday, you'll create one of your own and it will be messy and crazy and full of love. I will be watching for it with great anticipation.

All my love,
Daddy

61

I sit in the springhouse for a long time, the palm stone tight in my fist. I've read the letter a dozen times. Maybe more. It rests on my thigh and it's damp from my tears. I would give anything to be able to talk to my father. I'd tell him I became a lawyer and that I was beginning to think that had been a mistake. I'd tell him how, like Nora, I can have no children of my own and that a baby might soon be coming into my life. And I'd tell him how — like Nora — I will love that child with all my heart.

I've lost track of time, and as I make my way back through the woods, I hope Nora isn't worried about me. I have no idea how long I've been sitting in the springhouse. Long enough that jet lag is catching up to me. I find the bike and begin riding down the loop road. I pedal hard and fast, wanting to get back to Nora. I want to share the letter with someone who will understand exactly how I feel.

We cry, both of us, as we sit side by side on the sofa to read the letter. We're quiet when we finish, and I believe she's as emotionally drained as I am.

"You didn't stay for the whole memorial service, I remember," she says after a while.

I recall my desperate escape from the service on the pavilion. I remember trying to run away from the pain. "I was too upset," I say.

"I think that's an understatement," she says, and I nod.

She sighs, lightly touching the letter where it rests on her thigh. "It was cathartic for those of us who stayed," she says. "But you were in a very different place."

"It's over," I say with a dismissive shrug. "It was long ago."

Nora moves the letter to my lap and stands up. When she looks down at me, she's smiling despite the sheen of tears in her eyes.

"Do you still dance?" she asks. "I remember how you used to dance all over the place. You couldn't hold still."

"Not so much anymore," I say. My dancing stopped when Daddy died. Neither my body nor my spirit felt light enough to dance after that. "Aidan loves music, but he's not much of a dancer," I add.

"You wouldn't dance at the memorial service," she says. "I understood," she adds quickly. "I knew you weren't ready."

I shake my head. "I wasn't ready at all."

"How about now?" she asks.

"How about now what?"

"Are you ready now?" She stands up and walks over to the built-in bookcase near the CD player. I watch her run a fingertip along the spines of the CDs. "Here we go," she says, pulling one of them from the row. She opens it, removing a folded sheet of paper from the case. It takes me a moment to understand.

"Oh no." I stand up and take a step backward.

"Here." She holds the folded paper toward me and I reluctantly take it from her. I watch her remove the CD from the jewel case and insert it into the CD player. I hold the folded paper in trembling hands while she bends over to unlace her tennis shoes. She looks up at me. "Unfold it, honey," she says.

I unfold the paper, biting my lip, afraid to see the words I'd typed so long ago.

Pretend to dance.

"Footloose" suddenly explodes from the

speakers. Nora steps out of her tennis shoes, then takes the sheet of paper from me and sets it on an end table. She reaches for my hand, drawing me into the middle of the living room floor. When she smiles, I let myself smile back. But when she begins to dance, I can't. I just can't.

I remember my father telling me that if you don't forgive someone, it's like trying to dance with a lead weight on your shoulders. That's how I feel. The lead weight still holds me down. Had Daddy known I'd one day need those words to help me forgive *him*? Forgive so many people I loved? Had he known I'd need them to help me forgive myself? I know it's time to cast off that weight.

"All you have to do is pretend, Molly," Nora says. She's moving across the floor with a playful ease I hadn't known she possessed.

I begin to move in time to the music, my muscles remembering how I used to sway and swirl to this song at the end of my lessons with Amalia. I feel stiff, forcing the motions as I pretend to feel the beat. Still, I keep at it, my arms in the air, dancing, dancing, dancing, and I see Nora — *my mother* — twirling in a circle, her blond hair coming loose from her ponytail and the ties of her hoodie flying around her shoulders. I hear her voice in my head — *you've come home* — and somewhere in the middle of the song, when my feet feel as light as my heart, I know I am no longer pretending.

An hour later, I'm hanging my clothes in the closet of Russell's old room when I hear the high-pitched whistle that signals a text on my phone. I take the phone from my purse and touch the screen. It's from Aidan.

Sienna's in the hospital. They're trying to prevent labor. Can you come home?

62
SAN DIEGO

I sit next to Aidan in the waiting room of the maternity ward. He's been sitting in this large, relatively uncrowded room for a day and a half while I've only been here a few hours, but I don't think I've ever been so tired. Finding flights between Asheville and San Diego at the last minute involved four plane changes, twenty-two hours, and a good deal of money, but I am here and Sienna is in labor, nearly four weeks early.

Sienna is more tired than you are, I tell myself. I have nothing to complain about.

Since my arrival, Ginger has come to the waiting room twice to give us a status report. Each time, Aidan gripped my hand, and each time, Ginger looked completely frazzled. The last time, she was in tears.

"She's cussing at everyone and she nearly hit a nurse." She sat next to Aidan, wringing her hands in her lap. "She told me to get the hell out of the room." She pressed one tremulous hand to her temple. "She's never talked to me that way before."

The third time she comes into the room, she wears a huge smile and I immediately jump to my feet.

"The baby?" I ask.

Ginger shakes her head. "No," she says. "The *epidural.* She's like her sweet old self now." She stands next to my chair instead of taking a seat. "She's resting," she says. "I'm going to run to the cafeteria and get a snack. And she'd like you to come in." She looks from me to Aidan. "Both of you."

I wonder if she heard Sienna correctly.

"She said she'd rather we not be in the delivery room," I say. I'm so afraid of stepping on Sienna's toes.

"She wants you to come in," Ginger assures us. The smile is still on her face. "Don't worry," she adds. "She knows what she's saying."

We find Sienna calm and smiling, the head of her bed raised, an open *People* magazine resting against her belly. "It was so awful!" she says as Aidan and I stand awkwardly next to her bed. "I felt like *killing* people." She shudders. "It's good I didn't have a weapon." Then she laughs. She seems a little giddy from the miraculous relief of her pain.

"I'm going to have to write apology letters to everybody who came into this room."

"I'm sure they're used to it," I say.

"Look at my stomach," she says, moving the magazine so we can see the mound of her belly beneath the thin gown she's wearing. "You can watch the contractions."

I can. I can see them both on the monitor and in the tightening of her belly beneath the gown, and yet it is clear she feels none of them. "Wow," I say. I'd planned to skip the epidural when I gave birth to Sara, but I'm glad Sienna chose to have it. I don't want her to suffer any more than she has to.

"I can't feel it at all, now," she says. "Before, I was going crazy it was so bad."

"I'm glad you've got some relief," I say, touching her arm.

We sit with her for about an hour. Aidan goes to the gift shop in the hospital and buys her a couple more magazines. I fetch ice chips and feel helpless to do more. Ginger comes back and nervously paces the room.

"I had an epidural with Sienna," she tells us, "but it only numbed one side of my body. That was fun," she adds sarcastically.

After a while, a nurse comes in and examines Sienna, while Aidan steps out of the room.

"You're ready," the nurse says simply.

"Ready?" Sienna turns to me, as if I know about these things. "Ready for what?"

The nurse pokes her head out the door and I hear her tell someone to "get Dr. Singh." She returns to Sienna's bed. "Do you feel any pressure?" she asks.

"No," Sienna says. "I don't feel anything." The monitor is going crazy with her contractions. I hope she'll feel the urge to push. I know an epidural can slow things down.

Dr. Singh comes in. "I hear your baby wants out." She smiles at Sienna. "Are you ready to start pushing?"

We should leave, I think. Aidan has returned, but he's nearly backed himself into the corner of the delivery room. I don't know if it's to give Sienna privacy or if it's stark terror. Either way, I think it's time for us to go. I rest my hand on Sienna's shoulder. "Aidan and I will be in the waiting room," I say, but she grips my hand.

"No!" she says. "I want you guys to stay!"

I glance across her at Ginger, who smiles and shrugs her shoulders. "She's the boss," she says.

Sienna's numb legs are out of her control and there are no stirrups. Ginger holds one of her legs and a nurse holds the other and I feel extraordinarily honored to be the only person near Sienna's head. Dr. Singh asks her for three pushes with every contraction, and she grips my hand as she struggles to push. I can tell it's hard for her, almost perplexing without that natural urge to push, but she hangs in there. Ginger, the nurse, and I egg her on, and the room fills with the chant of *Push! Push! Push!* Aidan wisely continues to hold up the wall in the rear of the room. I glance at him every once in a while and he gives me a pale but encouraging smile.

"Great job. Great job," Dr. Singh coos, and then, finally, "You're crowning."

"Omigod, omigod!" Sienna says, then she looks directly into my eyes. "What's happening, Molly? Go look and tell me what's happening!"

Whether intentionally or not, she's inviting me to watch her baby — my baby? — come into the world. Ginger is right there, holding her leg, seeing everything. She could be the one to tell Sienna what's happening. But Sienna has asked for me to do it.

Ginger smiles at me, although she's starting to cry. "Come see," she says.

I move to the foot of the bed and stand near the doctor as she tells Sienna to push again. And although I knew what I would see, I still gasp at the miracle in front of me as the baby's head slips from Sienna's body. "Her head is out, Sienna!" I say. My voice can't contain my excitement. "She has tons of hair!"

Dr. Singh suctions the baby's nose and mouth. The baby turns and I can see her tiny features, her wrinkled forehead. Her shoulders appear and then, suddenly, she's wailing in Dr. Singh's hands.

"Good job," Dr. Singh says to Sienna. Then she lifts her head to look around the room. "Does someone here want to cut the cord?" she asks.

"Her daddy," Sienna says quickly. She's shivering violently, and for a moment, I worry that she's lost it, imagining that Dillon is in the room. Then I understand, and I look to where Aidan stands against the back wall. His expression is one of utter shock, but he seems to gather courage as he walks forward and I'm proud of him that he thinks to touch Sienna's shoulder as he passes the head of her bed. He walks to where the baby now squirms in Dr. Singh's grasp. Aidan's hands are steady as he takes the scissors from the nurse. He cuts the cord and a nurse gives the baby a quick wipe with a cloth, then rests her on Sienna's chest and I see something I know I will

585

never, ever forget: a look of pure love from Sienna to her child. I see a bond that can never be broken. Not by me. Not by anyone. I'm moved and frightened and sad all at once. Aidan looks at me and I think he must feel it, too. Ginger doesn't look at us at all. Her gaze is on her daughter and her granddaughter. She bends over to embrace them both. Aidan and I are not a part of this.

When Ginger straightens up, I rest my hand on Sienna's arm. "We're going to go to the waiting room," I say. I try not to look at the baby. I'm afraid I'll start sobbing. "You should have some private time with your baby."

Sienna looks up at me. She has aged in the last two days and suddenly she looks like a woman instead of a girl. Her face shows a maturity that finally fits her voice.

She clutches my hand. She's still shivering. "You need to hold her," she says. "As soon as they'll let you, hold her, all right? I want her to know who her mother is."

My eyes fill with tears. "You are remarkable," I say.

The nurse appears at Sienna's side. "We need to check the baby's vitals now and get her cleaned up," she says. "So we're taking her to the nursery, but if she checks out all right, you can have her back once you get to your room." The nurse places the baby in a bassinette, then smiles at Sienna. "She'll be just down the hall in the nursery," she says.

Sienna looks from my face to Aidan's. "Go with her, all right?" she says to us. "Please don't leave her alone. Don't ever leave her alone." And then she starts to cry.

EPILOGUE
ONE YEAR LATER

Sienna and I sit on my living room floor, surrounded by a sea of wrapping paper and ribbons and birthday cards and we begin folding the paper and stacking it in grocery bags. If it were up to me, I would be tossing the paper in the trash, but Sienna was appalled when she realized that was my plan. She is a recycling maniac. "Don't you want the planet to be in good shape for when Natalie grows up?" she asked me. So we started folding the paper and slipping it into the bags. It is going to take us forever, because Natalie Echo James is one spoiled little toddler and wrapping paper is everywhere.

Natalie sits on the floor nearby, playing with the ribbon. She doesn't have a clue this day was for her, although surely she must have sensed that she was the star of the show. In the last week, she's started walking without holding onto furniture or our hands. She walks mostly on her toes, clearly proud of her accomplishment, and everyone at the party loved watching her totter around the room. She also knows how to clap her hands and shout "Yay!" which she did constantly during that afternoon, and she was rewarded by all of us clapping our hands and shouting "Yay!" in return.

Everyone was here. Aidan's parents. Laurie and her husband, Tristan, and Kai and Oliver. Ginger and Sienna. And Nora, who has been visiting us for the last four days. I can hear Nora's voice now. She's in the kitchen with Aidan and Ginger. They are supposed to be cleaning up in there, but I catch bits and pieces of their conversation and it doesn't sound like much work is getting done. They seem to have connected on some television show they all like. I hear Nora laugh. She's laughed often during this visit. I don't recall her laughing much during my adolescence. Those years when my father was so ill, and the years after he died, when I was more of a thorn in her side than a daughter, must have been terribly hard for her.

Nora persuaded me to call Dani and I copped out and sent an e-mail instead. I thanked her for encouraging me to contact Nora and told her that we'd reconciled. I said nothing about Dani's role in my father's death, not wanting to alarm her with the fact that I knew what had truly happened. I said nothing about *anyone's* role. I'll never speak of it to a soul.

"I'm going to save this piece to use again," Sienna says, holding up some gold-and-white-striped wrapping paper. "It's so pretty."

"It is," I agree.

Sienna is a high school senior now. She's returned to a world of cute clothes and weekend parties and studying for exams, and she's waiting to hear where she'll be going to college next year. In the first few months after Natalie was born, we saw Sienna often, but our visits have become less frequent as she moves back into her life and we're letting her set the level of her involvement. She has her eye on a boy at school and when I talk to her now, he, rather than Natalie, is often the topic of our conversation. That's the way it should be, I think. It makes me happy to see her return to her former life, even though I know it's not always easy for her.

"I'm so different from my friends now," she lamented a couple of weeks ago when we went out to lunch together. "I've changed too much to really fit in. I'm having fun and everything, but my friends will never understand what I've been through." She looked wistful. "I have this deeper part of me they'll never really know," she said.

Sienna made a toast during the party. We were sitting around the living room eating birthday cake when she lifted her glass of Pepsi in the air.

"I want to say something," she said, and everyone quieted down to listen. Nora lifted Natalie onto her lap and even Kai and Oliver stopped playing with their toy cars and looked in Sienna's direction. "A year ago today, when Natalie was born," Sienna continued, "it was the best day of my life and the worst day of my life, all wrapped up in one." She looked at Natalie and smiled. "I finally got to see my amazing baby and cuddle her and love her," she said. "And then I had to lose her. But I didn't really lose her, did I?" She looked toward Aidan and me. "In some ways, I gained so much more than I lost."

Aidan put his arm around my shoulders as she spoke. Our very best day had been Sienna's very worst. I will never forget that. I know there is still grief inside her. There is grief, but not regret.

Sienna's birthday gift to Natalie was a little quilt made from her maternity clothes.

She'd sewn the squares together by machine, admitting that she'd never used a sewing machine before "and I hated every friggin' minute!" The squares are a bit off kilter and the fact that she'd never sewn before is evident, but I am touched by that quilt and the love that went into it. I hope Natalie will treasure it forever.

There is one more gift to be opened, but it's not for Natalie. Once we have all the wrapping paper put away and it's just Sienna, Natalie, and myself in the living room, I hand Sienna the small jewelry box and I watch her as she lifts the lid.

She looks up at me as she lifts the bracelet from the box. "A charm bracelet?" she asks, and I nod.

"Empty, except for one charm. See?" I reach over and lift the tiny silver baby shoe with the tips of my fingers.

"It's so cute," she says.

"We want to give you a new charm for each birthday," I say.

"I love it," she says, and I help her put it on.

Aidan and I just wrote a new "dear expecting mother" letter. We hope to find a sibling for Natalie. The group meeting at the agency is next week, and now we will be one of the couples the other waiting parents resent, since we already have a child and are taking up precious space as we hope to complete our family. I think, with a jolt, we could even be that family that sits in the center of the circle to illustrate open adoption. How amazing is that?

Sienna and I finish cleaning up the living room, and she and Ginger get ready to leave. At the front door, I hug them both. My arms remain around Sienna for a long time. I worry how she will feel leaving the house tonight on this, the anniversary of her best and worst day.

"I love you," she says as she pulls away.

"I love you, too," I say.

She smiles gamely, and I am glad that Ginger will be there to pick up the pieces if she falls apart in the car.

Aidan and Nora are still in the kitchen and now Natalie is fast asleep on the sectional. I lift her gently into my arms and stretch out on the sectional, my head on a throw pillow, Natalie sleeping on my chest. I'm tired but so happy.

"How did you like your first birthday party?" I whisper to my daughter, my lips against her silky dark hair. "Pretty cool, huh?"

She makes little smacking sounds with her

mouth and settles more deeply into my arms.

Maybe it's having Nora in the next room that makes me think of my father. Or maybe it's because I finished my application for graduate school this morning. I want to work on a counseling degree. It feels right to me. A relief, actually. I know it is what I am meant to do.

Either way, I sense that my father is with me right now. It's a warm and comforting feeling and I smile at the ceiling.

"Are you watching, Daddy?" I speak softly. "Is this family messy and crazy and full of love enough for you?"

I rub my hand lightly over Natalie's back and let out a contented sigh.

I don't believe in an afterlife.

I don't believe my father can see me.

I don't believe he can hear me, either.

But I'm more than willing to pretend.

ACKNOWLEDGMENTS

As always, I have many people to thank for helping me write *Pretending to Dance* and getting it into my readers' hands.

My good friend and fellow novelist Emilie Richards read an early draft of the story with insight as an author, a reader, and an adoptive mother. Her input proved invaluable and helped me move the story in the right direction.

My stepdaughter, Brittany Walls, and my sister Joann Scanlon read the penultimate draft and offered their thoughts and suggestions. Joann, who has the same form of multiple sclerosis as Graham, helped me understand not only his physical limitations, but his emotional challenges as well. Joann's aide, Nina Babukhadia, provided a loving role model for Russell.

Kathy Williamson helps me in too many ways to count. From maintaining my Web site and blog to finding resources that make my research easier, Kathy does whatever it takes to keep my professional life running smoothly.

I admit it: I set *Pretending to Dance* in Swannanoa not only because it was geographically a good location for the story, but also because it was so much fun to say its name. I loved getting to know Swannanoa resident Deborah Potter, who was generous with her time as she shared her firsthand knowledge of the area. Carla Hollar and Caryl Houghton, librarians at the Swannanoa Library, were also enthusiastic sources of information, as were the folks in the Swannanoa Valley Museum in Black Mountain. I'm grateful to all of you.

For their various contributions, thanks go to Susan Stripling, who was at the same New Kids concert that Molly and Stacy attended in Atlanta; George Felos, who helped me understand the legal implications of the events at Morrison Ridge; and Gwen Crews, whose story of her North Carolina ancestry inspired Russell's background. Thanks also to Barbara Fisher and Myrtle Hepler for their input and friendship.

Rabbi Marc Gellman wrote about "Pretend Dancing" in one of his syndicated 'God Squad' columns and I'm happy that I stumbled across the article. As soon as I read it, I knew how pretend dancing would fit into my story . . . and I had my title.

My agent, Susan Ginsburg, is sweet and compassionate at the same time that she's tough and courageous — a rare and perfect blend of traits for an agent. I'm grateful to her and to all the staff at Writers House who make the business end of my life go smoothly so I can focus on writing. Thanks also to Angharad Kowal, my agent in the United Kingdom, for the work she does on my behalf.

Jen Enderlin, my editor at St. Martin's Press, once again helped me see my story with wise new eyes. Thank you, Jen, for your encouragement and patience and for helping me shape *Pretending to Dance* into a novel I can be proud of.

Thanks, too, to everyone else at St. Martin's Press for your faith in me and for the extraordinary energy and skill you put into publishing. I'm grateful to you all, particularly Sally Richardson, Jeff Dodes, Lisa Senz, Nancy Trypuc, Kim Ludlam, Malati Chavali, Jonathan Hollingsworth, Anne Marie Tallberg, Tracey Guest, and Lisa Davis and the entire Broadway and Fifth Avenue sales departments. A special thank-you to my publicist, Katie Bassel, whose responsiveness and creativity make promotion fun, and to Olga Grlic for once again giving me a cover that is both beautiful and haunting.

The team at Pan Macmillan in the United Kingdom has done an amazing job of getting my books into the hands of my awesome UK readers. Thank you Wayne Brookes, Louise Buckley, and everyone else at Pan Macmillan who's made my publishing journey in the UK so rewarding and enjoyable.

I couldn't possibly complete a book without the brainstorming retreats, lunches, and e-mail exchanges with my Weymouth 7 writing buddies — Mary Kay Andrews, Margaret Maron, Katy Munger, Sarah Shaber, Alexandra Sokoloff, and Brenda Witchger aka Brynn Bonner. What I would do without the friendship and support of these amazing women, I don't know.

My Facebook readers are an incredible resource when it comes to both research and to naming characters and places. For *Pretending to Dance,* they helped me with everything from christening Morrison Ridge, to personal memories of New Kids on the Block, to "material things a fourteen-year-old girl would yearn for in 1990." My readers' enthusiasm and playful willingness to help makes interacting with them both fun and fruitful.

I've lost count of how many dinners I've spent discussing this story with John Pagliuca. As always, John has been patient and creative as I struggle with structure and plot, tolerant of my panic as deadline nears, and more than willing to help me celebrate when my story and characters finally fall into place. Thanks, John, for sharing the dog care, the housework, the meals out, and the brainstorming. You're one of a kind!

ABOUT THE AUTHOR

Diane Chamberlain is the international bestselling author of twenty-three novels. She lives in North Carolina with her partner, photographer John Pagliuca, and her shelties, Keeper and Cole. Visit her online at www.dianechamberlain.com.